The True Account

BOOKS BY
HOWARD FRANK MOSHER

Disappearances

Where the Rivers Flow North

Marie Blythe

A Stranger in the Kingdom

Northern Borders

North Country

The Fall of the Year

The True Account

The

True Account

CONCERNING A VERMONT
GENTLEMAN'S RACE TO THE PACIFIC
AGAINST AND EXPLORATION OF
THE WESTERN AMERICAN CONTINENT
COINCIDENT TO THE EXPEDITION
OF CAPTAINS MERIWETHER LEWIS
AND WILLIAM CLARK

Howard Frank Mosher

HOUGHTON MIFFLIN COMPANY
BOSTON • NEW YORK
2003

For information about permission to reproduce selections from
this book, write to Permissions, Houghton Mifflin Company,
215 Park Avenue South, New York, New York 10003.

Visit our Web site: www.houghtonmifflinbooks.com.

Library of Congress Cataloging-in-Publication Data
Mosher, Howard Frank.
The true account : concerning a Vermont gentleman's race to the
Pacific against and exploration of the western American continent
coincident to the expedition of Captains Meriwether Lewis and
William Clark / Howard Frank Mosher.
p.   cm.
ISBN 0-618-19721-4
1. Overland journeys to the Pacific—Fiction. 2. Explorers—
Fiction. 3. Vermont—Fiction. [1. West (U.S.)—Discovery
and exploration—Fiction.] I. Title.
PS3563.O8844 T78 2003
813´.54—dc21   2002032804

Printed in the United States of America

Book design by Robert Overholtzer
Map by Jacques Chazaud

QUM 10 9 8 7 6 5 4 3 2 1

To Phillis

aka Yellow Sage Flower Who Tells Wise Stories

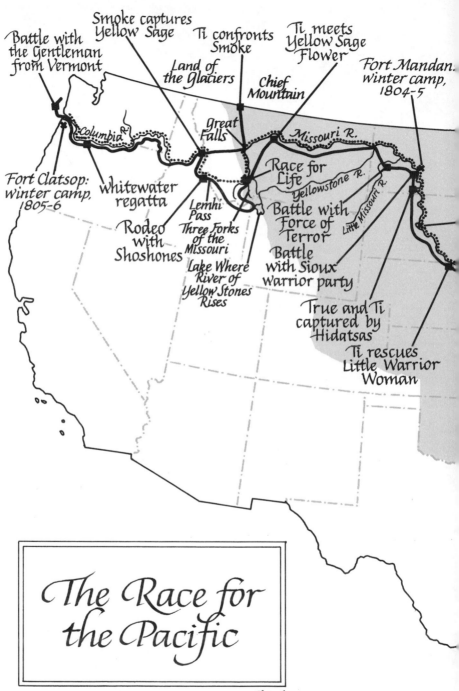

Battle with
the Gentleman
from Vermont

Smoke captures
Yellow Sage

Ti confronts
Smoke

Ti meets
Yellow Sage
Flower

Land of
the Glaciers

Chief
Mountain

Fort Mandan.
winter camp,
1804-5

Columbia R.

Great
Falls

Missouri R.

Fort Clatsop:
winter camp,
1805-6

whitewater
regatta

Race for
Life

Yellowstone R.

Little Missouri R.

Lemhi
Pass

Rodeo
with
Shoshones

Three Forks
of the
Missouri

Battle with
Force of
Terror

Lake Where
River of
Yellow Stones
Rises

Battle
with Sioux
warrior party

True and Ti
captured by
Hidatsas

Ti rescues
Little Warrior
Woman

The Race for the Pacific

Chazaud

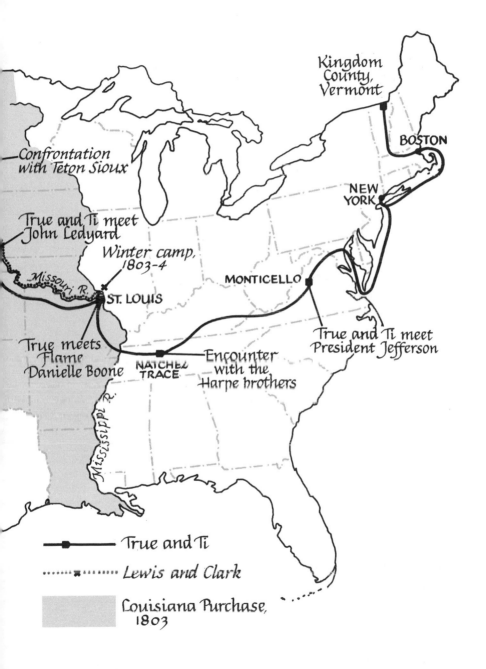

Kingdom
County,
Vermont

BOSTON

NEW
YORK

Confrontation
with Teton Sioux

True and Ti meet
John Ledyard

Winter camp,
1803-4

MONTICELLO

Missouri R.

ST. LOUIS

True and Ti meet
President Jefferson

True meets
Flame
Danielle Boone

NATCHEZ
TRACE

Encounter
with the
Harpe brothers

MISSISSIPPI R.

True and Ti
Lewis and Clark
Louisiana Purchase,
1803

Dr. Stephan T. Black Elk, Curator
Museum of the American Plains Indians
Browning
Blackfoot Nation, Montana Territory

Dear Dr. Black Elk:

Enclosed is the manuscript I wish to donate to your museum. As I explained to you during our conversation last week, the manuscript has been handed down in the Blackfoot branch of the Kinneson family from mother to daughter for five generations. My late husband, Professor J. D. Greenblatt, formerly chair of the American Studies Program at the University of Montana, was, of course, aware of the manuscript. Frankly, he did not put much credence in it. His skepticism brings a smile to my face even now because it was very nearly the single ongoing point of contention between us; finally we had to table all discussion on the topic in order to maintain matrimonial harmony. Perhaps it would have been different if I had shown him the contents of the crates that will arrive at the museum next week, after you have had an opportunity to review the manuscript. But I never felt comfortable showing those to anyone outside the tribe. And my husband the professor, for all his wonderful qualities, was not, as you might guess from his name, a member of the Blackfoot Nation.

At any rate, as the last living member of the Montana Kinnesons, I feel that, for better or for worse, the time has come for me to bring the manuscript and the contents of the crates before the public. And I can think of no more suitable occasion to do so than the upcoming bicentennial of the Lewis and Clark expedition.

As to being the guest speaker at your bicentennial ceremony next month, and formally presenting the manuscript and related materials to the museum — my word, what a very gracious offer! May I consider it for a few more days? It has been a long time since this retired schoolteacher and Blackfoot elder has done any speechifying. But I shall try to get up some brief notes to see how they sound, and will notify you soon.

Very truly yours,
Cora Soaring Eagle Kinneson

P.S. The crates will arrive by express truck next Tuesday. At the risk of sounding like the fussbudget old schoolmarm I am, please do use the very greatest care in unpacking them. Thank you again.

Vermont

1

We had set a very close watch over my uncle, Private True Teague Kinneson, since his triumphal return from the Pacific and the Columbia River. I say "we," but in fact, keeping track of the comings and goings of the renowned expeditionary, schoolmaster, inventor, and playwright had, since my early boyhood, devolved mainly to me. My father had his newspaper to print, the *Kingdom County Monitor*, in which he kept track of the events in our remote little Vermont village. My mother kept track of our family farm, a job that required her entire attention from before dawn until after dark each day. And ours being a very small, if very affectionate, family, this left me to keep track of my uncle. Who, as my father often said, clapping the heels of his hands to his temples and pressing as hard as he was able, as if to keep his brain from exploding, bore much watching.

From the time I was six or seven I was the private's constant companion, pupil, fishing partner, apprentice, and confidant, not to mention his co-expeditionary. Nor is it surprising that we were inseparable, when one stops to think that it was he who christened me Ticonderoga — Ti for short — after the principal matter of his play and the signal event of his life — the fall of the fortress of that name on the narrows of Lake Champlain to Ethan Allen and a handful of Vermont woodsmen and farmers in 1775.

Unfortunately, it was that same milestone in the history of our Republic that resulted in Private True Teague Kinneson's own fall and subsequent affliction — or, as my kindhearted mother called his strange disorder of the imagination, his "little ways and stays." As he was drinking rum flip with Ethan and celebrating their victory by singing a ballad, most of which has now been lost to posterity but whose refrain was "Tooleree, toolera, tooleroo," my uncle lost his footing and struck his head so sharp a blow on the gate of the fort that he never, I am grieved to report, quite regained his correct wits.

2

IT IS AN IMPORTANT POINT of information in the history of the Kinneson family that from the moment of his mishap at Fort Ti, my uncle supposed himself to be constantly engaged in the prosecution of many heroic enterprises. These adventures often involved travel to far-flung places, great raging battles, and encounters with all manner of plenipotentiaries and unusual personages. The hillock behind my mother's cow barn he called the Heights of Quebec; and many a summer afternoon we stormed it together, taking the Citadel on the Plains of Abraham — a large granite boulder atop the hill — as he believed he had done with General Wolfe in '59. In the winter, when a thick sheet of ice and snow covered the hill, he stationed me on this boulder in the role of the French commander, Montcalm, and had me repel his assaults by pushing him whirling back down the frozen slope on the seat of his woolen pantaloons — a terrifying spectacle to me and to my parents, calling up in our recollections his fateful accident of years before. There was no doubt, from my uncle's easy talk of embrasures, fortifications, enfilades, scaling-ladders, and cannonadings, that he fully *imagined* himself to have been present at the fall of Quebec. But when I drew my father aside and asked him privately whether True had been involved in that battle, his hands shot up to his head and he said that, while he ruled out no improbability when it came to his older brother, if he had been, he was the youngest foot-soldier in the history of the world — being, according to my father's calculations, but seven years of age at the time.

Sometimes my uncle and I journeyed to the rapids on the St. Lawrence just west of Montreal to reenact a historic meeting between the explorer Jacques Cartier and my great-great-great-great-great-grandfather, Chief Tumkin Tumkin of the Abenaki tribe. Hearing that Cartier was searching for China and the Great Khan, and learning something of the dress and customs of that distinguished emperor, Tumkin Tumkin had stationed himself just upriver from the rapids in a robe of muskrat pelts dyed bright vermilion, with an absurd little round yellow hat on his head; his design was to impersonate the Celestial Personage and receive whatever gifts the French explorer had laid aside for him. In the event, Cartier instantly saw through our ancestor's ruse, but was so amused that he gave Tumkin Tumkin his second-best chain-mail vest and named the region of the rapids Lachine — or China, as it is called to this day.

The cedar bog to the north of our farm my uncle designated variously as the Great Dismal Swamp, or Saratoga, or Yorktown. From it we routed many a vile Redcoat, every last one of whom we put to the sword. For Private True Teague Kinneson was a ruthless soldier and showed no mercy to his captives. In his capacity as an inventor, he attached a sail made from an old flannel sheet to my little fishing raft on the Kingdom River, where we played by the hour at Captain Cook and the South Sea Cannibals. And when the ice began to form on my mother's stock pond, we recreated the scene of Washington crossing the Delaware.

During the long Vermont winters, when the wind came howling down out of Canada and the drifts lay six feet deep between the house and the barn, my uncle taught me Latin and Greek and astronomy and mathematics and the physical sciences. He read to me by the hour from both the ancients and moderns, and in the evenings we frequently cleared away my mother's kitchen table and chairs and performed scenes from Homer or Virgil.

"*Arma virumque cano,*" he would roar out in his booming stage voice. And it was off to the races with the brave hero of the *Aeneid,* while my mother, baking the next day's bread or peeling apples or doing the farm accounts in her black daybook, smiled, and my father's ink-stained hands shot headward. When we undertook the *Iliad,* my mother sometimes agreed to play the part of Helen, and my uncle and I carried her in her rocker from the window by the door to the chimney corner we called Troy; and indeed, with her tall slender form and long golden hair and eyes as blue as the sky over the Green Mountains on the fairest day of summer, she fit the role of Helen as well as any woman could. But on another occasion my uncle mistook my father for a Cyclops and chased him round and round the kitchen with the fire poker.

"None of this is your fault, Ti," my terrified sire cried from the other side of the barricaded woodshed door. "Above all, remember that none of this is your fault."

Well. I had never supposed that my uncle's little ways and stays *were* my fault, or anyone else's, including his. Nor did I for a single moment believe that he meant the least harm to my father or any other creature in the universe. Though as my uncle's own history amply illustrated, accidents *would* happen; and perhaps it was as well for my father that he had the presence of mind to retreat until our version of the *Odyssey* had ended with the hero's return to Ithaca and his loving Penelope. Penelope was my mother's cat.

My uncle's favorite play, however, was his own. I shall come to that drama very soon. But first, a few words about the appearance of the playwright himself.

3

PRIVATE TRUE TEAGUE KINNESON — I refer to him by his full title because my uncle set great store by his military rank — was very tall and very lanky, with sloping, rugged shoulders, a trim, soldierly mustache, and keen yellow eyes that appeared to be as pitiless as a hawk's, though in fact he was the most sympathetic man I have ever known. He wore, over his scout's buckskins, Jacques Cartier's chain-mail vest, which had been handed down in our family from Tumkin Tumkin and which he believed had saved his life in battle a dozen times over; a copper dome, which had been screwed to the crown of his head by the regimental surgeon who operated on him after his fall at Fort Ti; a loose-fitting pair of galoshes, whose tops he rolled up to his bony knees for winter and down around his ankles for summer; a red sash about his middle somewhat resembling an Elizabethan codpiece; and, to cover the shining metal crown of his head, a red woolen night-stocking with a harness bell on the end, like the bell of a fool's cap, to remind himself where he was at all times, and also that "compared to the Almighty Jehovah, all men are fools."

My uncle was somewhat hard of hearing from being so much subjected to cannon fire over the course of his military expeditions, so he carried at all times a tin ear trumpet as long as my mother's yard measure. On those expeditions he went armed with a homemade wooden sword; an arquebus with a great bell-like mouth, of such incredible antiquity that even he was uncertain of its origin, though family tradition had it that this ancient firelock had been used by his Kinneson grandfather on the field of battle at Culloden just before the clan moved from Scotland to Vermont; and a large black umbrella to keep off the sun and rain, embellished on top with the family coat of arms — a crossed pen and sword, signifying that from time immemorial Kinnesons had "lived by the one and died by the other."

When not off adventuring, my uncle divided his time between his playwriting, his angling, his books, my education, his garden, and his inventions. To begin with the play. He had been working on his *Tragical History of Ethan Allen, or The Fall of Fort Ticonderoga* for twenty years and more. He styled it a tragedy because he believed Colonel Allen to have been much undervalued, and indeed thought that the old Vermonter should have been our first president. It was a long play, running well over three hours. And on the occasions when he had arranged for it to be performed, it had not met with a very kindly reception, even in our own state. From certain hints my uncle himself had let drop, I feared that it had been roundly hissed off the stage. But he had the greatest faith in the world in his *Tragical History*, and pegged away at it year after year, firmly believing it to be nothing short of a masterpiece-in-progress. What pleased him most about the play was that it violated none of Aristotle's dramatic unities. Aristotle the Greek philosopher, pupil of Plato, and chronicler of all branches of human knowledge known to his time? No, sir. Scholia Scholasticus Aristotle — my uncle's great tutor during his time at Oxford University — of whom you will soon hear more.

When it came to angling, my uncle loved to cast flies, like our Scottish ancestors. In fact, he and my father were both avid fly-casters and had taught me this noble art when I was very young. We three enjoyed many a fine May morning on our little river, enticing native brook trout to the lovely feathered creations that my uncle tied during winter evenings. He fashioned long, limber rods from elm and ash poles, wove fine horsehair leaders, and was the neatest hand in all Kingdom County at laying his high-floating colored artifices deftly over rising fish. There was just one difficulty. Private True Teague Kinneson was so tenderhearted that he could not bear to kill his catch, and so released every last trout he caught unharmed to the cold waters from which it had come. Yet no man ever enjoyed the art of fly fishing more or took more pains to match his flies to the natural insects emerging on the water; and the sight of my copper-crowned uncle, rod held high and bent, playing a fine splashing trout, and crying, for all the world to hear, "Hi, hi, fish on!" was a most splendid spectacle.

My uncle's books, of which he had many hundreds in several languages, he kept in his snug little schoolhouse-dwelling behind our farmhouse, which dwelling he called the Library at Alexandria. He spared no expense when it came to purchasing these volumes, and he supported his scholarly avocation with the proceeds from his garden in my mother's loamy water meadow near the river. There he tended half an acre of the tall, forest-green plants known as cannabis, whose fragrant leaves and flower buds he ground into a mildly euphoric smoking tobacco very popular in Vermont and of which he himself faithfully smoked half a pipeful each evening after supper.

Of all his books, my uncle loved best a hefty old tome bound in red buckram called *The Ingenious Gentleman Don Quixote de La Mancha* — of which he believed every last syllable to be the revealed gospel truth. In fact, it was partly in honor of this same ingenious gentleman that my uncle wore his chain mail and polished his copper crown until it shone like the top of a cathedral. For ever since his accident, he had fancied himself something of a modern-day knight-errant. Yet it was not giants disguised as windmills that he sought to fight but the Devil himself — until he cast that horned fellow out of the Green Mountains in a tow sack, in consequence of which expulsion he feared that "the Gentleman from Vermont," as he termed Old Scratch, might be doing great mischief elsewhere.

Being a kind of perpetual boy himself, though a big one, my uncle was a great favorite with all the boys and girls in the village, for whom he invented huge kites, spinning whirligigs, velocipedes with sails, magic lanterns, catapults, wheeled siege-towers, fire-ships, rockets, and I don't know what else — none of which ever, to the best of my knowledge, had the slightest practical application. Besides his vast fund of classical stories and poems, he knew a thousand tales of witches, ghouls, and ghosties, in the telling of which he terrified no one so much as himself. He was deathly afraid of large dogs, small serpents, lightning — he had been struck eight times since the installation of his copper crown, and it was said in the village that, like a tall ash tree in a Vermont hedgerow, he "drew electricity" — and of nearly all women, though he had the greatest respect for and confidence in my mother, as did my father and I.

One of my uncle's most curious inventions was a wooden, Dutch-style shelf clock, about a foot and a half tall, without any works or innards but with a very passable painting he had done on it of his hero Quixote, that Knight of the Woeful Countenance, doing combat with a windmill. The painted hands of this clock were set forever at twenty minutes past twelve, which hour had a triple significance to my uncle. First, he was utterly certain that this was perpetually the correct time at Greenwich, England, so that by knowing the hour where he was, and the altitude of the sun, he could always calculate his correct longitude and divine where he was in the universe. And it distressed him not in the least that no matter how many times he made these calculations, his position never came out the same twice but varied wildly, from the longitude of Calcutta to that of Venice.

The second point of significance concerned a saying in our family, which was that whenever a lull fell over the conversation, it must be twenty after the hour. Admittedly, between my uncle the ex-schoolmaster and my father the editor, one or both of whom seemed always to be discoursing from dawn straight through until midnight, there were not many such lapses of silence in our household. But when by chance no one happened to be talking, my uncle would leap up and dash out to his Library at Alexandria to check the time on the Dutch clock and confirm that it was indeed twenty past the hour, which was a great relief to him. And though the clock was less reliable as a timepiece than was entirely convenient to one wishing to know the *actual* hour, it was so reliable as a conversation piece that it never failed to set the talk in motion again.

Third, and finally, it was inside the hollow case of this remarkable clock that my uncle stored his hemp tobacco.

From what I have retailed to you thus far, you might well suppose that mine was a very odd and somber boyhood. Odd, I will grant you. But somber? Never in this world. For my uncle was ever a second father to me. In fact, it might be said that between my true father and my uncle True, the pair of brothers made one complete and perfect father. Or so I thought, at least. And no boy could *ever* have had a more complete education than I. When my interest first in sketching, then painting, birds and wildlife began to emerge, my uncle even took me on a tour of the great museums of England, France, Italy, and the Lowlands. By which I mean that we canoed across the "Atlantic Ocean" — our pond, that is — and on the far side he described the great paintings of the world so exactly that I all but saw them. Say what the village might, then, it was a splendid way to grow up. And to anyone who thought differently, Private True Teague Kinneson doffed his belled cap, bowed low, and said, "Why, bless you, too, sir. With a tooleree and a toolera and a tooleroo!"

4

OF ALL MY UNCLE's many schemes and projections, the one nearest his heart was no more and no less than to discover the Northwest Passage. From my earliest visits to the Library at Alexandria, I remember him poring over the old histories of his mostly ill-fated fellow expeditionaries and visionaries who for more than three centuries had sailed in quest of that elusive route to the riches of Cathay. On a wall map of North America behind his writing desk, the blank territory to the north and west of the Missouri River was labeled *terra incognita;* and when my uncle's saffron-colored eyes grew weary during our school lessons or his interminable revisions of his play, he liked to pause and gaze at those intriguing words and muse about the great foray that he and I would someday make into that unknown land.

In the spring of 1803, when I turned fifteen, my uncle received, from his Boston bookseller, Alexander Mackenzie's *Voyages from Montreal, on the River St. Lawrence, Through the Continent of North America, to the Frozen and Pacific Ocean.* The intrepid Mackenzie, it seemed, claimed to have done that which, above everything else in the world, my uncle himself had long wished to do — to have forged his way through the wilds of America to the Pacific. "'With a mixture of bear grease and red vermilion,'" my uncle read aloud to me in his harsh, nasal, schoolmasterly voice, "'I wrote on a rock above the western sea, Alexander Mackenzie, from Canada by land, the twenty-second of July, one thousand seven hundred and ninety-three.'

"Oh," he cried out, smiting his metal dome in a way that would have done credit to my father, "I am bested. It's already been done, Ti. And wouldn't you know, by a fellow Scotsman."

My uncle could scarcely have been more distressed had Mackenzie's words "from Canada by land," etc. been branded on his forehead with a sizzling hot iron. But then his eyes gleamed with a new light — for his spirits never flagged longer than a minute or two — and he said that to go overland in *Canada* was one thing; but to cross through the Territory of Louisiana, to Oregon and the River Columbia, was something else again. "*That* will be our route, Ti. Eureka! We leave tomorrow.

"What's more," he continued, "to make sure we get to the Columbia and not some puny, less illustrious *Canadian* river, we will *start* there. We will make the trip backward. From the Pacific."

"But, uncle," I protested, "how will we get *to* the Pacific? How can we *start* from there until we *get* there?"

Whereupon he smiled and said, "We will go round the Horn by ship, Ti. You might ask Helen of Troy to put us up a lunch."

Early the following morning we prepared to embark. We allotted an entire day for the journey, including our return trip overland. Besides his chain mail, the belled stocking cap over his copper crown, and his galoshes, my uncle carried a flagstaff and flag, his umbrella, his collapsible spyglass, his arquebus, and his homemade sextant and astrolabe for determining our latitude and longitude. Instead of sea biscuit and salt beef, we had laid in a stock of my mother's most delicious baked-bean sandwiches, a brown crock of her famous ginger cookies — which we called cartwheels because of their prodigious size — and a stone jug of switchel, the popular Vermont haymakers' drink distilled from pure mountain spring water slaked with a touch of molasses and a touch of vinegar; for we did not know where we would find our next supply of fresh drinking water.

We set sail at sunrise on my fishing raft, which my uncle had christened the *Samuel de Champlain*, he wiping his sleeve across his eyes at the thought of leaving his beloved Green Mountains for a whole day, my mother calling "Bon voyage, my brave expeditionaries" — and my father mouthing to me, "Not your fault, Ti. *Not your fault.*"

The first leg of our trip went capitally. We stopped to visit the Amazonian delta, where one Sucker Brook debouched into the Kingdom River. There my uncle, briefly disembarking from the *Samuel de Champlain* to perform a necessary office in the alders, was harried back onto the ship by a thirty-foot anaconda — which bore more than a passing resemblance to a spotted yellow newt sunning itself on a tamarack stump. Our vessel was three times beaten back around the tumultuous Cape Horn (the High Falls at Kingdom Common) by fierce headwinds laden with hail, sleet, and driving snow. At last, on the fourth attempt, we cleared the tip of the Cape with room to spare and sallied on up the west coast of South America past the Juan Fernandez Islands, as my uncle called the stone-filled timber cribs in the river designed to regulate log drives. Then on to the Galápagos, where he had arranged for us to be set upon by a party of three lads from the village, their faces all besmeared with blue river clay, in the guise of cannibals. After putting these savages to rout and beating up the coast of Spanish California past the mission of San Francisco — the little French Canadian chapel just outside town — we reached the mouth of the Columbia — Kingdom Brook — at noon. Out came my uncle's sextant and astrolabe, out came his book of navigational tables. After the most elaborate mathematical calculations, he estimated our latitude at about 60° north, from which he concluded that the Columbia entered the Pacific not far south of Alaska. To celebrate this surprising news he smoked half a pipe of hemp.

With the daunting overland portion of our trip through *terra incognita* now at hand, our explorations were about to begin in earnest. Reminding me that everything we saw next would be country viewed by Americans for the first time, and that we were about to venture where the foot of civilized man had never trod before, and, furthermore, that I should take particular notice of everything I saw so that, when home again, I could paint what had "ne'er been painted before," and commending us both to Providence and to our Maker, my uncle planted the flag on a little knoll overlooking the river and we started out again. Our struggles up the rapids of the Columbia, as represented by several old beaver dams, were Herculean — indeed, a hotter, wetter, more tedious and arduous four hours than we had getting to the Rockies, or Kingdom Mountain, can scarcely be imagined. But our travails were not yet over. In the thick hemlock woods on the mountainside we fought off a horde of black flies, which my uncle mistook for "the all-puissant Blackfeet"; and as evening drew near, and we waded back down the little foot-wide rill on the back side of the mountain — the "broad Missouri" — a swarm of mosquitoes descended on us with all the savagery of the "treacherous Sioux." Seth Hubbell's sheep pasturage my uncle denominated the great western prairie; Seth's dozen merino sheep, a thundering herd of bison.

As twilight settled over the mountain and we started down the last slope, my uncle said, "Ti, we've done it. We have discovered the Northwest Passage — backward. I only wish Colonel Allen could have been with us."

Exhausted, soaked through and through, bruised and bug-bitten, we arrived home at a little after eight o'clock, to a heroes' welcome from my father and Helen of Troy, who fixed us a late supper of ham and eggs and pancakes laced with maple syrup. I ate eleven pancakes, my uncle twenty-six, my mother four, and my father one and part of another, which I finished for him.

My uncle then fired up his long, curved hemp pipe and began to recount our adventures of the day. Stimulated by the mild cannabis fumes, he told how the *Samuel de Champlain* had been wrecked on the Columbia and how, having been cast away, we had made our way back afoot. My father's arms and elbows were now sticking directly out from his head in an attempt to exert more pressure upon that seat of reason. Warming to his subject, True fetched his map of North America, and, in the large blank section, began to trace our route very exactly, marking down the places where we had skirmished with the Blackfeet and Sioux and asking me to draw in a few bison. At this juncture my father rose from the table and declared that even if I should turn out to be a Vermont Michelangelo, he did not believe he could bear to have another artistical relative. My uncle, in the meantime, had neatly inscribed on the map, "Private True Teague Kinneson's Chart of the Interior of North America, Designating His Journey, by Land, from the Mouth of the Columbia to the United States. As attested to by True T. Kinneson, May 15, 1803."

5

SO MATTERS RAN ALONG in our home for the next several weeks. At fifteen, I was reading changeable old Ovid's lively Latin and, in the Greek, Thucydides, as well as my uncle's favorite historical chronicler of all time, Herodotus, who wrote of giant crocodilos and flying lizards and other marvels stranger still. When I came to Xenophon's *The March Upcountry,* we enacted his incredible trek through the land of the Persians and Medes by hiking up into Canada and back one sunny day. En route we encountered a great horned owl, which I later painted, life-size, presenting the picture to my mother.

By then it had become apparent — my father's concern

about another artistical Kinneson notwithstanding — that I had a real flair for drawing and painting, particularly birds. I loved best their colors. The reddish brown thrasher with its long narrow tail, the indigo backs of our little northern bunting, the bright lemon plumage of the winter grosbeak against the snow. Indeed, there was no bird or animal that I did not find beautiful in its own way. For several months my mother fed an orphaned fox at the back door, a slinking young vixen that tolerated only her. I sketched this she-fox and many other animals as well — deer, beaver, and a bear that raided my uncle's hemp garden and gourmandised on the ripening flower buds, then lolled on his back with his four black paws in the air like a big dog wishing to be scratched. But portraits of people were difficult. My best effort in this department was a group arrangement of my family seated in the farmhouse kitchen one winter evening. Here is my mother, Helen of Troy, baking her cartwheel cookies; my father slumps at the table with his hands pressed to his head, looking on as my yellow-eyed uncle, in full explorer's regalia and belled stocking cap, works on his "Chart of the Interior of North America." "And what, Mr. Mackenzie, say you to *this*?" he would say to himself as he inked in our route. What indeed!

There was, at about this time, some talk between my parents of sending me down to Boston to study with Copley or Stuart, or perhaps to the great artist-scientist Charles Willson Peale in Philadelphia. But they had meager funds to underwrite such a venture; and who would then keep track of my uncle? Whose little ways and stays, I must say, seemed to grow ever more extravagant.

Then came July 4 and the great news from Washington. "'President Jefferson, in a single bold stroke,'" my father read to us from the *Washington Intelligencer,* "'has more than doubled the land mass of our young nation by buying, from France, the territory called Louisiana, stretching from west of the Missouri River to the Rocky Mountains and north to Canada. Moreover,'" he continued, "'trusted sources report that the president will soon appoint an expedition to go overland to the mountains and beyond, to discover the most practicable watercourse to the Ocean Pacific.'"

My uncle, who, though listening to my father, had seen fit to thrust his ear trumpet close to the newspaper itself, was in a frenzy of anticipation. "Great Jehovah!" he cried. "Did you hear that, Ticonderoga? An overland expedition to the Ocean Pacific. I must lead that expedition. Having made the same tour backward, I can see no obstacle to completing it frontward."

He now put the trumpet to his mouth and, clapping the larger end to my father's ear, he roared into it, "I'm going back to the Pacific, Charles, or I shall know the reason why."

After recovering somewhat from this rather excruciating experience, my father started to say, "The reason why, dear brother, is that, not to put too fine a point on the matter, you have never been —"

"Ah, ah, Charles," said my mother, smiling and shaking her head, while my uncle now scanned the piece in the *Intelligencer* through the small end of his trumpet, alternately nodding his head in agreement or frowning and shaking it, so that the little bell on the end of his cap jingled like a whole carillon.

"The reason why, dear elder brother," my father tried again, "is that — is that — oh, to the devil with it — the reason is that you might as well undertake to guide Captain Lewis to the Great Khan of China, like our ancestor, Chief Tumkin Tumkin."

My uncle raised his thickety white eyebrows. "China," he said, casting a glance out the back window of the kitchen at the stone wall angling up the slope. "China —"

Hurriedly, to deflect this dangerous train of thought, my father read on. "'The expedition will travel up the Missouri, whose ultimate source is believed to rise near that of the Columbia, then proceed down that river to the Pacific, in what is projected to be one of the greatest journeys of discovery in history.'"

"Do you see, nephew?" cried my uncle, now gazing at me through the big end of his trumpet. "Exactly our route in reverse. They can't do it without us. Take a letter, lad."

The Honorable Thomas Jefferson,
President of the United States of America

Dear Mr. President,
Having just returned by land from the mouth of the River Columbia and the Oregon Territory, I will undertake, for two dollars a day and found, to lead an expedition safely across Louisiana to the Pacific Ocean, through the land of the all-puissant Blackfeet and the treacherous Sioux, whom I plan to pacify and win over by introducing them to the propagation, cultivation, and inhalation of that panacea for all the spiritual ills of mankind — hemp. Eagerly awaiting your confirmation of this assignment, I remain,

> *Your friend,*
> *Private True Teague Kinneson*
> *Green Mountain Regiment*
> *First Continental Army*

"And back?" my mother suggested.
"And back?" my uncle said.
"Yes. To the Pacific and back?"

"Oh, yes. Of course 'and back.' Write, 'Postscript — and back,' Ti."

I did so, and then, lest this matter of high state policy fall into the hands of spies, my uncle had me transcribe it into Greek. Not knowing the Hellenic for "Blackfeet" and "Sioux," I found myself at a standstill. But my unperplexed uncle, thumbing through Xenophon, found a phrase for "sooty-footed Persians," which took care of the Blackfeet; as for the Sioux, on reflection he thought it safe simply to write — Sioux.

He posted this proposal the next morning and followed it up with many more communications to the President, including a thirty-page treatise in Latin called *A Brief History of the Flora, Fauna and Native Peoples of the Oregon and Louisiana Territories.* Also, he sent Mr. Jefferson a copy of his revised "Chart of the Interior of North America."

The fact that we received not a single word in reply to these missives did not deter or discourage Private True Teague Kinneson in the least. Indeed, I must say that my uncle seemed impervious to discouragement. When he rose in the morning, he never once, so far as I knew, doubted that his commission and summons to Washington would be coming through that very day; throughout the summer and fall of 1803 we made trial runs with my raft on the Kingdom River and compiled lengthy lists of what we would need to take with us.

Vermont's red and yellow autumn gave way to winter. At Christmas, from his hemp income my uncle presented me with a new muzzle-loading flintlock rifle, my mother with a brindled cow for her dairy, and my father with a padded vise of his own invention, in which to clamp his head when the world was too much with him.

One day in March, when the sap had just started to flow in our maple-sugar orchard, my uncle strapped on his snowshoes and said he planned to go to the top of Kingdom Mountain and reconnoiter our route to the Pacific. It seemed safe enough to let him conduct this reconnaissance on his own, so I went to work with my father, the *Monitor* being due out the next day. That evening, however, we were met at the door by my most anxious mother, who had just discovered a note from the private informing us that he had left for Boston to raise money for our trip.

My father's hands were already fluttering upward, like two large moths toward a candle. Pressing his head down from the top, as if to prevent himself from taking flight, he said, "Fetch me my clamp, Ti."

I ran for the Christmas vise. After my mother and I had affixed this apparatus to his head, screwing it down very tightly, he seemed to experience some relief.

"What, sir," I inquired, "are we to do?"

"Why, Ti, I suppose that we must wait a day or two and see if your uncle comes back. If he does not, we will have to go after him and run him to ground. Else I fear greatly for his sake and, frankly, for the sake of Louisiana and the Republic."

In truth, my uncle had run off two or three times before, once to the neighboring village of Pond in the Sky, which he had mistaken for Dover, on the English Channel, to assist Lord Nelson against Napoleon; and again over the border into Canada, to escape the blandishments of a determined local widow-woman named Goody Kittredge, who had set her cap for him and his hemp income. In both instances he had been home by nightfall.

Now, as evening came and my uncle did not, my father had us ratchet the head vise ever tighter, until his kindly gray eyes began to start out of their sockets; my mother continued to go to the window and look out into the blue twilight creeping over our mountain; and I began to feel dreadfully remiss that I had not kept better track of my ward. The night wore on, and eventually my mother coaxed my father, still wearing the vise, to bed. But by then I was more alarmed than I could ever recall being.

The idea occurred to me sometime after midnight. I would, I resolved, run my uncle to ground myself, even if I had to follow him to the Pacific to do so. Before I could lose my nerve, I began to pack my watercolors, a cylindrical metal tube of blank canvases, my gun, and other possibles. Around two A.M., having stocked up with a good supply of my mother's cartwheel cookies, I stole out of our farmhouse and made my way down to the village, where I spent another two hours at my father's newspaper office, printing several dozen handbills that I believed would be useful in my search. Just as the sunrise struck the soaring peaks of the Green Mountains, turning them as pink as one of my mother's sugar-glazed apples, I boarded the southbound mail.

"Gone to find uncle. Much love, Ticonderoga," read the note I'd left on the kitchen table. Yet despite the confident tone of my message, I had the strongest feeling, as the stage jolted down the line toward Boston, that even if I were fortunate enough to locate Private True Teague Kinneson, persuading him to come home again might well prove impossible.

Boston

6

RUNAWAY UNCLE. Run off from Kingdom
Common, Vermont, an UNCLE, Private True
Teague Kinneson, about 50 years of age. His stature
is tall, his countenance fierce, his clothes and gear
those of a knight-errant, consisting of chain mail, a
belled night-stocking over a copper plate in his head,
a red sash, and galoshes worn high or low as the occasion requires. A former soldier with the Continental Army, a playwright, and a classical scholar,
this UNCLE imagines himself to have explored
from the Pacific up the Columbia River, across the
Rocky Mountains, and thence overland to St. Louis
and the United States. Whoever conveys him safely
home, or into the care of his nephew, Ticonderoga
Kinneson, shall have 5 dollars from

THE KINNESON FAMILY
KINGDOM COMMON, VERMONT

So READ the fifty handbills I had printed up the night before to distribute in the way stations between Vermont and
Boston and, should I not overtake my uncle sooner, in the principal places of that city.

As matters turned out, I had no trouble tracing my quarry

over the White Mountains into New Hampshire, and then on
to Boston, since he had made a highly favorable impression
in all the taverns, post offices, and inns where his coach had
stopped, because of his freehanded generosity and his general
good-humoredness. For as he had often told me, citing Homer,
a "cheerful man does best in every enterprise." And my uncle
maintained the most cheerful demeanor at all times.

By traveling day and night and sleeping in the coach, I arrived in Boston just three days after leaving Vermont. After
distributing a few of my remaining handbills around the harbor, which delighted me with its forest of ships' masts, pene-
trating odors of tar, salt, and fish, and sailors of every hue
speaking all kinds of lingos, I started up into the city proper.
On the way I came upon a general hubbub, in which I found
my uncle himself, in all his outlandish regalia, directing a gang
of street urchins in the defense of a knoll he imagined to be
Bunker Hill and pelting with snowballs anyone who attempted
to come up the street.

"Good morning, Ti!" said the private, tossing me two or
three snowballs as though we were at home in our dooryard
and he had never run away at all. "For the love of freedom and
your nation, take the east flank and don't fire until you see the
whites of their eyes."

Until now, I had supposed that my uncle might curb his little
ways and stays once he was away from Vermont. Indeed, the
opposite appeared to be true. "Attack, boys," he roared. "For
Vermont and Ethan Allen!" I attempted to hustle him away
into a tangle of steep little side streets, on the pretext of rein-
forcing a badly outmanned American garrison. But he instantly
smoked out my ruse and took to his heels, calling, "Hi! Hi!
Catch me if you can," with the tail of his jingling stocking
cap, like the belled tail of a kite, flying out of sight around cor-

ners. Suddenly I thought of my stash of cartwheel cookies. Rummaging in my bag, I held one up. "Private Kinneson," I shouted, "the British have been driven back into the sea. It's mess time."

He stopped and whirled around atop a snowy rise on the city common, above a frozen pond; and I sailed the big ginger cookie toward him like a twirling plate. To my amazement, he raised his arquebus and, training the muzzle on the flying confection as if it were a flushing partridge, blew it into a thousand pieces.

Immediately following this exhibition, my uncle and I had a long laugh that cleared the air between us. Then we sat on a bench near the pond, sharing my mother's cookies with some mangy-looking doves and some young skaters; and my uncle said that he was glad to see me, heartily glad, for he had missed me terribly over the past several days, adding that he had already hired the Beacon Street Lyceum for a lecture he would give that very night on our trip from the Pacific, as a means of raising a stake for our upcoming expedition.

He then rented a pair of wooden skates from a Dutchman in a little covered cart pulled by a blind pony and ventured out onto the ice to play at snap-the-whip with the children. It seemed to me that until I could contrive some stratagem to get him home, the better part of wisdom might be to join him in this exhilarating activity. So we spent the next two or three hours whooping and chasing each other across the ice and collapsing in gales of laughter. Then he and the skate man shared half a pipeful of hemp, a large supply of which my uncle had brought in his Dutch clock, along with a sack of the tiny hemp seeds to trade with the Indians of Louisiana. I sketched them puffing away together, as companionable as two old schoolfellows, and sold the drawing to the skate man for three shillings.

This was my first sale. Upon which my mellow uncle congratulated me on "turning professional," and repeatedly shook my hand, and laughed long and loud as if we had no cares in the world. Which, for his part at least, seemed to be the case.

7

"Fair ladies and fine gentlemen of Boston," my uncle announced from the stage of the Beacon Street Lyceum with the greatest assurance in the world. "It is my pleasure to make you acquainted with myself, the renowned explorer and playwright, Private True Teague Kinneson. I now present, for your entertainment and edification, a dramatized lecture on my recent journey overland to the United States from the River Columbia and the Ocean Pacific. Act I. The Shipwreck."

With his chain mail gleaming, he rushed offstage and, to a smattering of bewildered applause, returned in the skate man's cart, representing our ship the *Samuel de Champlain*, which he made go across the boards with his great galoshed feet like a child's scoot-toy. "Beware the perils of a lee shore," he shouted. "The breakers! The breakers! We are all lost."

With this alarming declaration, he deliberately tipped over the peddler's cart in simulation of a terrible shipwreck and, flailing his arms like a drowning man, sprawled his full six-and-a-half-foot length on the stage, where he continued to thrash and writhe.

"The explorer is washed ashore at the mouth of the noble Columbia," he at length explained. Getting to his feet, he rolled up his galoshes and made as if he were wading through crashing surf, swinging his elbows in time with his strides. Shading his brow with his hand, peering first in one direction, then another, rocking up on his toes, and dropping into a low crouch, he roared out through his tin ear trumpet, "Cast away on the far side of Continent North America, the undaunted explorer bethinks himself to journey overland, by canoe and on foot, to the United States."

The audience seemed puzzled. But as my uncle continued to charge about, now paddling the skate man's cart up the Columbia, now climbing a ladder propped against some flats at the rear of the stage to represent the Rockies, now harrying offstage several street urchins from the Battle of Bunker Hill, whom he had engaged to represent the "all-puissant Blackfeet" — the playgoers began to laugh.

A wag sitting beside me in the front row, wearing an academical cap and gown and no doubt from Harvard College, stood up. "I see Don Quixote," he called out. "But where's Sancho Panza?"

Another Harvardite inquired if we had met the Lost Tribe of Israel in our travels. A third augmented the attack of the Blackfeet with an egg rather past its prime, which splattered on the good ship *Samuel de Champlain*

The climax of the reenactment came when my uncle declared, "Hark, do I hear the thunder of ten thousand bison approaching?" At this cue, the skate man led his blind cartpony out onto the stage, caparisoned in a moth-eaten buffalo robe. Which sight produced, I am afraid, unrestrained peals of laughter.

Unabashed, the private stepped forward and made several flourishing bows, insisting that the urchins, the skate peddler, and the pony do the same. He then asked for subscriptions for his trip back to the Pacific. But so far from offering handsome investments in our project, the citizens of Boston, led by the Harvards, presented him with a barrage of spoiled oranges, eggs, cabbages, and dead rats, accompanied by jeers and cat-calls.

Astonished and enraged, my uncle whipped out his wooden sword. Turning to his cast, he shouted, "Beleaguered comrades, let us show these self-anointed cognoscenti of Boston what Green Mountain lads are made of!"

I truly believe he would have charged the audience had not five or six uniformed bailiffs just then burst into the hall, shouting, "There he is. The runaway uncle."

At this point, though frightened half out of my wits, I seized the academical cap of my seatmate and clapped it on my head as if I were one of their rank, then sprang to my feet and cried, "Fellow Harvards, six on one is foul play."

Pointing at the bailiffs, I shouted, "Down with the treacherous Sioux. Let us rally to the cause of the noble Vermont explorer and see him through!"

The laughing Harvardites and their confederates were more than willing to come to my uncle's rescue. On the pretext of assisting the bailiffs, they began to trip them up and block their way. In the excitement, my uncle touched off his arquebus. Out of its huge belled mouth came an orange tongue of fire a good two feet long, at which the startled pony bounded over the foot-candles, landing with its four legs splayed out in the midst of the affray and scattering bailiffs and Harvards and urchins alike galley-west.

"You have quite put the Sioux to rout, sir," I cried to my uncle. "My congratulations. President Jefferson awaits you in Washington with your commission. Shall we go?"

In the confusion I managed to hurry him out the stage door and down the slippery hill into the early spring night. But now, supposing himself back at Fort Ticonderoga and me to be Colonel Allen, he called, "I must take care, my commander, not to slip and strike my head again."

"There is no danger of that, private," I said, hustling him along lest the bailiffs spot us. "Quick. Jingle your bell."

He did so. But sometimes one jingle was not enough, and he now seemed to mistake *himself* for Colonel Allen, exclaiming, "But where is Private True, subaltern? We can't leave him in the hands of the British and their pitiless Iroquois allies." And stopping in his tracks and digging in his feet like a mule in galoshes, he declared, "We must go back."

"Private," I said, "your colonel *commands* you to ring your bell."

He did, then said, "Here comes True. I spy him. He's coming again."

"He is," I said, looking out around him and up the hill. "Here he is now. Here you are, uncle."

"Here I am, Ti," he said, taking my hand and dashing off again toward the harbor, "back in Boston. Did we put my detractors to rout or did we not?"

"We did. Ethan would have been very proud. He could not have done more himself. Boston will never forget your skit."

"We acquitted ourselves as well as any good soldiers could," my uncle said modestly, as we reached the wharves. Adding that he was astonished that the city fabled as the Athens of America should contribute so little to our project, and that he believed we would do better to seek assistance for our expedition from the good people and public-minded merchants of Manhattan and leave the blue-blooded patricians of Boston to their own devices. Despite all my protests, he immediately arranged for us to take passage on a packet just departing for Baltimore, with a stop on the way at New York.

"What could the treacherous Sioux have meant by 'runaway

uncle,' I wonder?" he mused half an hour later, as we glided out of the harbor with the ocean breeze in our faces.

Even if I had been disposed to answer him, I could not have. By then I was at the packet rail, overcome by seasickness, and sick at heart, too, that I had so miserably failed in my mission to bring the private safely home to Vermont, whose green mountains and comfortable little farms now seemed as far away as Louisiana and the Pacific.

New York

8

THE *LORD BALTIMORE* arrived in Manhatten early on the second morning of our voyage, with me much the worse for wear. My uncle, however, who had never been sick a day in his life, had sat up all night and all day and all night again, yarning with the captain and crew, lending a hand with a rope or a navigational measurement and even taking a turn at the wheel, where he demonstrated a very nice touch. He was so popular that the captain urged us to continue on to Baltimore with them the following morning. True allowed that we might avail ourselves of his offer, but first we would try once more to raise a stake for our expedition. Just how we would do this he did not say, and I could only hope that he did not have in mind another lecture. Also, he confided to me just before we docked that in New York he hoped to locate the "Gentleman from Vermont" "whose hash he would settle once and for all" by stuffing him into his carpetbag and heaving him into the ocean.

Once ashore, we had a breakfast of bacon and eggs, which was just the right tonic for me, at a little inn called the Sign of the Tipsy Argonaut, where we also secured a room for that night. Then we struck off up lower Broadway. It was a fine sunny morning, with a scattering of high white clouds and a touch of spring in the air. The street teemed with horses pulling beer wagons, lumber wagons, fruit wagons, vegetable wagons. On the corners evangelists preached, fishwives shrieked their briny wares, sailors lurched, boys hawked newspapers and blacked boots. My uncle was in his element, gleefully prying under flounders and cabbage leaves at an out-of-doors market and even popping into shops and offices and shouting "I spy!" — in an attempt to "flush out" or "start" the Gentleman. "Aye," he said, "I'm sure he's nearby, Ti, for I smell sulphur." As indeed he did, there being a little paper mill just across the street, where the newsprint for the *Times of New York* was manufactured. Which quite persuaded my uncle that somehow his friend was connected with the *Times* itself.

A lady approached my uncle, tweaked at his chain mail, and tickled his scarlet codpiece. "Anyone home?" she said.

"Nay, nay, madam," he cried, leaping back. "We shall have none of that."

At this he pulled me off down the crowded street — though not before he had pressed a shilling into the woman's hand. And though he continued to look for the sooty old lad he had expelled from Vermont, peering into every alleyway to see if he might catch a glimpse of him, he said that New York was "a *real metropolis*, not" — casting a scornful glance northward, in the direction of Boston — "a warren of tight-fisted, literal-minded, pedantical naysayers who wouldn't know a great adventure if it were to bite them in the hinderquarters."

In the meantime, the private was giving away our few remaining shillings to the beggars, orphans, and crippled people in the street at an alarming rate. Tears started to his eyes at the sight of these unfortunates, who were now flocking after us as if we were leading a ragamuffin crusade. One of their rank, a little chimney sweep of about ten, thrust into my uncle's hand a circular advertising the Circus of Grotesqueries, at the Orpheus Theater on Broadway and 35th Street.

There, for a penny apiece, we were treated to a peep-show featuring a giant named Joseph Hall from Auburn, New York, a sword-swallower, a fire-eater, and a genuine Seneca Indian princess. For another penny each we were permitted to interview the celebrated Mrs. Peg O'Shaye of Dublin, Ireland, who had enjoyed earlier existences as Mary Magdalene, Joan of Arc, and William Penn. I loved seeing these walking wonders, whom my uncle straightaway recruited for the cast of his *Tragical History of Ethan Allen,* which he then arranged to perform at the Orpheus that evening at ten o'clock, after the circus had closed.

During the luncheon hour, while he rehearsed with his recently acquired players, I wrote a letter to my parents, informing them of our whereabouts and bringing them up to date on my uncle's lecture in Boston and his plan to present his *Tragical History* in New York that evening. When I returned from posting the note, he said the rehearsal had gone exceedingly well. Indeed, he doubted whether such a varied company of players had ever been assembled under one roof before, an observation with which I could only agree.

That afternoon we went to a printer's and had five hundred handbills run off announcing the New York debut of the play. Afterward we repaired to the office of the *Times of New York* to visit Editor Tobias Flynt. When we arrived, Editor Flynt, a bespectacled man with a sharp nose, was composing one of his famous Federalist tracts — for he was a fierce supporter of Hamilton and adamantly opposed to President Jefferson. No sooner had my uncle announced that he was that very evening presenting a play to raise money to guide an expedition to the Pacific than he and Flynt fell into an argument. Flynt declared that the country would have absolutely no use for the great desert of Louisiana, which he repeatedly called "Jefferson's Folly" and which, in his estimation, was a pig in a poke. My uncle countered that Louisiana was no desert but a land of milk and honey, and the most important acquisition in our Republic's history. Flynt said that giving money, of which we had too little, for land, of which we already had too much, would bankrupt the government. Why, no one even knew the boundaries of the territory we had purchased. No American had ever been there.

"What, sir," demanded my uncle, "can you possibly mean? I, and my nephew, too, just last year came through Louisiana from the Pacific. We know every foot of the way as well as we know our dooryard in Vermont."

At this news Flynt seemed to change his tune. He inquired how long our trip had taken; and seemed most interested to learn that we had accomplished the odyssey in a single day. Flynt asked to see the manuscript of my uncle's play. I was afraid he might not find it up to the mark. But looking it over with a knowing eye, he praised the work for its originality, faithfulness to reality, vigorous language, and justness of character. My uncle replied that though he and Flynt might disagree on some few minor political matters, he was glad that those differences had not clouded the editor's artistic judgment; and he hoped Flynt would attend the performance that night and give it good play in the next morning's edition. Flynt assured him that he would be honored to do so and that he would mention our forthcoming journey to the Pacific as well.

Later we rejoined the grotesqueries at the Orpheus, where the play began at ten sharp to a rather sparse audience of about six, including the crew of the *Lord Baltimore* and Editor Flynt. The performance ran very long, with just the representation of

Colonel Allen's regiment rowing across the lake to Fort Ti taking more than an hour. When my uncle, in the role of Allen, demanded that the British general, as played by the giant, surrender the fort in the name of the Great Jehovah and the First Continental Congress, the three or four people remaining in the audience laughed heartily. All in all, he counted the night a huge success.

Afterward, Flynt went straight to his office to write his notice, which he assured us would be read by every literate resident of New York in the morning. My uncle, the cast, and I repaired to a nearby ale-house, where he treated the actors and himself to rum. Finally we made our way back down Broadway, which seemed as crowded at two in the morning as it had been at two that afternoon — my having first borrowed from the tavern owner a blue potato barrow in which to wheel the private back to our lodgings. "Hoist, hoist your flagons, roisterers all," he sang from the confines of the barrow. "For if summer be arrivèd, soon come the withering rimes of fall. Tooleree, toolera, tooleroo!"

9

THE NEXT MORNING the private awoke with a throbbing head and a tongue, as he put it, "as large as a full-grown buffalo's." But his expectations of being lionized in Flynt's *Times of New York* precipitated him from bed. He roused me out and inquired how, in my estimation, his presentation of *The Tragical History* had gone.

"Splendidly," I said. "No question, uncle. You put on an exhibition to be remembered."

He said he was certain of it, and that however unappreciative of his lecture the haughty academical intelligentsia of Boston town had been, and however undiscerning, good Editor Flynt and the *Times* would see him right and vindicate his reputation as an artist and a gentleman.

All this while he was shaving. But when he opened the door and stepped outside, all besoaped, to take in the morning air, he tripped over the potato barrow and was obliged to perform a very intricate fandango to keep from slitting his throat with his own razor.

"Why, Ticonderoga, is this plebeian conveyance blocking the way?"

"I brought your honor home from the play in it last evening — or rather this morning," I said.

"Well, for the love of Jehovah, Ti, trundle it down to the *Times* and bring back as many copies of today's paper as it will hold. I shall order us a celebratory breakfast."

When I arrived back at the Tipsy Argonaut with the papers, my uncle was dressed in his full knight's gear, and the captain of the *Lord Baltimore* was with him. I sat down at their table. My uncle clapped me on the back and cried up coffee with sweet cream, hot glazed rolls, and clay pipes all around for a smoke of hemp. Then, leaning back in his chair like a sultan, he bade me read his notice aloud to the assemblage, which, apart from myself and the ship's captain, consisted mainly of fishmongers, sailors, and ladies of the evening just arriving from their employment.

"Uncle, are you certain —?"

"Yes, yes, Ti, read on."

Clearing my throat several times, I began to read aloud from the *Times,* as follows. "'Last evening, our city was treated to an exhibition of sovereign entertainment, a play from the pen of one Private True T. Kinneson, recently arrived in New York from Vermont.'"

"'Sovereign entertainment,'" my uncle exclaimed. "Jesu, that's good. Did you hear that, my dear ladies and gentlemen? I must write a public apology in the *Times* to the excellent people of New York for ever supposing that the Dev — that the Gentleman from Vermont, ha ha — would be allowed to dwell for one hour in their fair city. Read on, Ticonderoga."

"Please, uncle, you must not break in on me," I said. "To continue. 'The play, which we shall come to presently, was performed at the stately old Orpheus Theater, a landmark of our noble city, though recently reduced to providing quarters for a circus of curiosities, with the design of raising funds for the author to lead an expedition to the Pacific Ocean.'"

"That's good," my uncle said. "That can only help our greater purpose. But come to the matter here, nephew. What says Mr. Flynt of my *Tragical History?*"

"Well, uncle, since you seem bent on hearing the rest, I won't try to dissuade you. 'The play itself, insofar as this commentator is fit to judge, is the greatest farce ever written. Juvenile in conception, violent in execution, puerile, nay, prurient, in its attempts at humor, and in the most vile taste, *Ethan Allen* violates all known principles of composition. Characters are thinly drawn, nor do their actions flow from human nature, but rather from the diseased imagination and self-conscious extravagancies of the author, who fancies himself a kind of American Quixote and has no more sense than his Andalusian prototype. And we add only, for the amusement of our readers, that in a wonderful epilogue to this hilarious masterpiece its bumpkin hero reportedly had to be trundled back to his lodg-

ing in a potato barrow after a drinking bout following the production.'"

The entire coffeehouse was now in a paroxysm of laughter.
But I feared the very worst as my uncle clapped his hand to his
wooden sword, leaped to his feet, and roared, "Where is this
man Flynt? He and I have a pressing appointment."

"Oh, uncle," I cried. "Aren't you delighted?"

"Delighted? This is an outrage to me and to all other play-
wrights in the universe. But vindication is near, Ti. Retribution
is at hand. Go out and cut me a stout cudgel about as thick as
my wrist —"

"Why, sir," I interrupted, pretending to be astonished.
"What can you possibly mean? Don't you see? 'Greatest farce.'
'Wonderful epilogue.' 'Hilarious masterpiece.' Critic Flynt is
praising you to all New York not for your supposed tragedy but
for your great *comedy*."

I quickly turned to the ship's captain. "Isn't that so, sir?"

"Why, I suppose it is, for I laughed all the way through it," he
said.

My uncle stared at the captain. He stared at me. Snatching
up the paper, he scanned the offending passage through his tin
ear trumpet and then stared at the trumpet. He took off his red
flannel night-stocking, folded it neatly in twain and in twain
again, and very vigorously began to polish his copper crown until his headpiece shone like the sun.

"Eureka!" he cried at last. "Gentlemen and ladies, my
nephew has set me right again. As Ti says, Critic Flynt, bless
his good heart, has seen through to the heart of my play. He —
ha ha — knows it better than I do. As of this moment I call it a
tragical history no more but *The Most Comical History of Ethan
Allen*."

And declaring that since he had taken the great literary bastion of New York by storm, as it were, with his new *commedia,* we would rejoin the crew of the *Lord Baltimore,* bound that morning for the city of its name, and from there flare out to Washington and plead our cause directly to the President. So although I had prevented my uncle from killing Flynt or being killed himself, in the end I had succeeded only in sweeping us farther along on a mad journey from which, I feared, there would be no turning back. And what might lie ahead was as blank and unknowable as the vast white space on my uncle's old "Chart of the Interior of North America."

Monticello

10

You would suppose we were waiting for an audience with an Oriental despot, Ti. I can't say I like this. I can't say that I quite approve of standing on all this formality, President or no. Particularly when the fate of America may well depend on our meeting."

Having found the President not in Washington but at his famous home in Virginia, after three hard days by coach and hired wagon we were at last standing in the great rotunda at Monticello. Finally, the inner door to the President's study opened, and there stood Thomas Jefferson himself, wearing his house slippers and a dressing gown, though it was late afternoon. With no hesitation my uncle said to the President, "I tell you, sir, the fate of the United States, and whether those states are to be one strong unbroken nation from coast to coast or a parcel of squabbling little hegemonies like rotten old Europe, may well depend on the next hour. And in particular, on whether you appoint as leader of your expedition to the Pacific Private True Teague Kinneson." He swept off his stocking cap and made a deep bow, in the process striking the bewildered President's outstretched hand with the metal plate in his head.

Then, with yet another flourish in my direction, "And my squire and nephew, Ticonderoga Kinneson."

Without further ceremony my uncle announced that though

he respected no living man more than Tom Jefferson, he would, by the Great Jehovah, pay fealty to no one; nor suppress his opinion in regard to what he believed right; nor dance attendance on any man in the world. The President seemed very surprised but also amused at the figure of my uncle, looming up in his knight-errant's habiliments as he pushed brusquely past into the study. Mr. Jefferson shook hands with me. "I like your name, sir," he said. "Ticonderoga. I imagine there's a story there."

"There is, Mr. President. My uncle named me. It's Ti for short."

"Well, Ti, come in and make yourself comfortable — as I see your excellent uncle has done. I admire a man who doesn't stand on ceremony."

I loved Monticello, with its beds of multicolored tulips and stately white columns and clocks and books and pictures — grand pictures such as I had never dreamed of painting, by all the leading artists of the day. My uncle immediately conferred upon himself the full freedom of the President's study, as if he were at home in his own Library at Alexandria. Unrolling his "Chart of the Interior," he began to point out to the President the sources of the Missouri and the Columbia and many other hitherto unknown features from our "trip" the previous summer, at the same time declaring that he stood ready to command the expedition being assembled to penetrate the wilds of Louisiana. And to show the President how well prepared he was to undertake this great journey of discovery, he got out his Dutch clock and astrolabe and, with the further aid of a sundial with the face of Jupiter inscribed upon it, which stood in the iris bed outside the study window, determined our longitude to be exactly that of — Bombay.

The President smiled. Assuring us that he was very impressed by the chart and by the drawings I had made on it of some bison and Indians, he asked if I would make a sketch of my uncle, which he would be honored to hang in his study next to Peale's portrait of himself. I was happy to oblige. As the private posed in his heroic gear, he reiterated his desire to lead the expedition to the Pacific. To which the President replied that, while deeply appreciative of such a kind offer, he had already appointed a young army captain named Meriwether Lewis, formerly his private secretary, to this commission, adding that Captain Lewis's official party would be leaving from St. Louis within a very few weeks.

Seeing my uncle's terribly disappointed expression, President Jefferson asked if he might have a word aside with me concerning my judgment of a little painting. My crestfallen uncle bowed his consent; whereupon Mr. Jefferson took me into an adjacent room and showed me a very pretty rendition of the Natural Bridge of Virginia. While I admired it, he said, "Ti, your uncle clearly has a superior imagination. Indeed, his faculties in that direction are those of a true genius. It appears to me that in his mind he really has traversed the continent, and back through time as well, and been in campaigns from Troy to Yorktown."

"He was in fact with Ethan Allen at Fort Ticonderoga," I said, unwilling to have the President suppose my uncle to be totally daft. "He was injured in the cranium there."

President Jefferson nodded. After a moment's reflection, he said, "Do you think that if I were to furnish you and your uncle with two mounts suitable for this great adventure that he believes lies ahead, and you gently trended north with him, persuading him at the same time that you were headed *west* — there is a somewhat similar ruse in his beloved *Don Quixote* — that you might get him safely home to Vermont?"

In fact, I did *not* think any such thing. But all I could say in response to this most handsome offer was, "It is possible."

"Well, let us try and see what happens," the President said.

He returned to my uncle and informed him that while the official expedition commanded by Captain Lewis would get under way very soon, he would *not stand in our way* if we wished to strike out on our own, and that he hoped the private would permit him to outfit us for our own epic journey, wherever it led. He then conducted us to some stone stables behind his house, where he presented me with a tall bay stallion named Bucephalus, after that fabled steed of Alexander's, and my uncle with a deaf white mule called Rosinante in honor of the Knight of La Mancha's mount. With which the private was much delighted, though he immediately rechristened the mule Ethan Allen. The President also provided us with saddles and two twenty-dollar gold pieces; and, shaking hands very warmly, wished us the best of luck in Louisiana.

Saluting our benefactor and thanking him profusely, but reminding him that he would pay no fealty to any man, or call any man liege, my uncle with all his fantastical appurtenances and I with my gun and paints and tube of canvases headed back down Mr. Jefferson's little mountain and due west toward the Blue Ridge. A few minutes later we stopped to watch the last rays of the sun sparkle on the dome of Monticello. My uncle said that though he disagreed with the appointment of a young upstart to lead the official expedition, he was much pleased with the President's promise *not to stand in our way*, which he saw as an endorsement of our own expedition. I then suggested that the route to St. Louis lay to the north, but he briskly told me that we must go due *west*, into the mountains, to elude any pursuers who might still be on the track of a "runaway uncle."

The Natchez Trace

11

Our passage over the mountains of western Virginia was very hard and very slow and most of all very wet. The road was little more than a wretched swamp, through which my uncle's mule and my horse picked their way, up to their fetlocks in mud. Usually they warned us well in advance of the approach of other travelers, tossing their heads and softly braying or nickering. At first when this happened, my uncle insisted that we rein our mounts off the track and wait out of sight until the wayfarers passed. It soon occurred to him, however, that if we were detected, this evasive conduct would seem suspicious; so, by the second or third day out of Monticello, he stopped avoiding the few people we encountered and merely kept his face turned aside and did not tarry to visit — though he and his costume drew many a long look. Fortunately, no one seemed much inclined to question us, perhaps because we were well armed — I with my flintlock rifle and the private with his arquebus.

I would not wish you to think that my uncle allowed my education to suffer merely because we were away from home. One morning the schoolmaster taught me the first thirty lines of the Prologue to Chaucer's *Canterbury Tales,* which he said was an appropriate poem for "two young blades" off on a springtide pilgrimage of their own. Another day he drilled me in the rudi-

ments of Italian and Russian; on another, the dynasties of ancient Cathay. Each day, too, he encouraged me to stop and
draw some of the many varieties of birds, both native and mi-
gratory, that were then in those mountains. Once we tarried for
more than an hour while I sketched a fierce battle between a
nesting pair of scarlet tanagers and a bold young blacksnake attacking their eggs; with some help from my uncle, who wished
to assist the birds without harming the snake (or getting too
close to it, if I did not miss my guess), the determined pair of
tanagers drove the scaly marauder away. On another occasion I
drew a rosy grosbeak that landed on my uncle's shoulder and
repeatedly attempted to pluck off a fringe of the buckskin shirt
he wore under his mail, to use in its spring house-raising.
Seeing that I was amused by this scene, and fearful of being
thought too tenderhearted, the private put on a blustering air
and cried, in his stage voice, "O for some William Tell to shoot
this feathered interloper from off my shoulder. See how even
the birds of this abandoned southland violate our persons, Ti.
Much more of this familiarity and I'll wring its neck like a
Sunday dinner cockerel."

Knowing that my uncle could never bring himself to harm
any wild creature, I could not help but laugh. At this he drew
his long-knife and made a vicious swipe — not at the bird but
at his shirt, cutting off half a dozen leather thongs, which he
left draped over a laurel branch for the grosbeak to appropriate
at its leisure, at the same time muttering that he wished it
would hang itself with them. Then he burst into such a hearty
laugh that I wondered if it would not do all the people in the
world the very greatest good to fall down and strike *their* heads,
and if the world would not be a much happier place for it.

One of my happiest early memories is of my uncle brewing
tea. He alone was the tea-maker in our household, and after

pouring himself a cup with great ceremony he would set me on his knee and slop half an inch of that delicious beverage sweetened with maple sugar out of his blue mug into the saucer and announce, "Now, Ticonderoga, you may *chisel*." Meaning sip tea from the saucer, which never failed to make me feel very grown-up.

Every day of our trip, rain or shine, we reenacted this pleasant ceremony. All morning and on into the afternoon my uncle would keep a sharp eye out for mint or wintergreen or pennyroyal or ginseng leaves or whatever local plant or herb came to hand for tea-making. He brewed the leaves in his all-purpose pannikin, then brought out the blue mug, and after pouring the tea he would announce, as if we were snug at home in our kitchen instead of in alien mountains a thousand miles to the south, "Now, Ticonderoga, you may chisel." And we would share the mug, as it was the only one we had, and instead of feeling grown-up I felt like a young boy again.

Sometimes a saucy chattering gray squirrel or a white-footed mouse or a chickadee with a neat black cap would venture near. As my uncle tossed it biscuit crumbs, he would say, "Oh, so you too wish to chisel. Is that it? Where is my arquebus, Ti? Well, well. Why waste good shot?" No wild creature that begged ever went hungry, and this was a very agreeable way to travel with a very agreeable man, and though I still missed home, teatime made me feel as if we were taking part of Vermont with us on our adventure.

My uncle cunningly resisted all further attempts on my part to nudge him gently northward. And though we passed several rude inns or, as they were called in that part of the country, "stands," he insisted that we stop only long enough to resupply ourselves with flour and cornmeal, otherwise steering clear of all vestiges of civilization in order to "harden ourselves off" for the western wilderness that lay ahead. But I was accustomed to hard lying and all kinds of weather from my hunting and fishing excursions in Vermont, and when we stopped in the woods for the night, while my uncle fashioned a snug little lean-to of woven pine boughs and kindled a cheery fire, I had no trouble acquiring our supper from the nearby forest. For while Private True Teague Kinneson could never bring himself to kill any living thing, and would gladly have subsisted on grass like an ox all the way to the Pacific if it had been left to him to get our meat, I did not share his scruples when it came to feeding ourselves. One evening I gobbled into range a fine bronze tomturkey, which made capital eating at supper and provided us with the next day's breakfast and luncheon as well. A few days later I shot a yearling buck a-watering at an icy little spring-fed creek. We were delighted to discover that the stream contained small speckled trout identical in every respect to ours in Vermont, down to the milk-white edging along their orange fins. And when no other game presented itself there were pigeons, always pigeons, it being their traveling time. About five o'clock each afternoon they roosted for the night in the forests we rode through, and all but invited me to knock them on the head with a club. How their fat, juicy breasts sizzled in our fry pan; we feasted on them all the way to Tennessee.

Sometimes it seemed as if my uncle and I were back in Vermont playing at being explorers. At other times I felt a million miles away from our beloved Green Mountains, as if in a dream from which I would never wake up. But whether it was a good dream or not, I could not yet tell.

Each noon, on days when the sun was out, my uncle religiously fixed our latitude with his homemade sextant and essayed to take our longitude with his Dutch clock. On starry nights he confirmed our location by training his spyglass on Jupiter and ascertaining the time at which the moon Io disappeared behind it — though I confess that I could never discern the presence of that satellite, nor the great abandoned pyramids, walls, and fortifications of the once-flourishing civilizations my uncle claimed to see on the surface of its controlling planet, either. But on overcast days and nights, when he could not take his celestial measurements, he was restless and said that even the clouds of the heavens conspired against him, and it was beyond him how a human man could be expected to know who and where he was in poor weather. Then he would bravely ring his bell and announce, "Regardless of where Jupiter may be, here I am, Ti."

To which I would reply, "Here you are, sir."

And in this manner we were three full weeks getting to Nashville.

Though we expected something of a metropolis, Nashville was little more than an ill-assorted clutch of cribs and hovels along a muddy track in a bend where the Cumberland River hooked north for the Ohio. The three-story Talbot House Hotel resembled nothing so much as a hulking wooden beehive. Even so, I hoped to put up there for the evening. But fearing he would be recognized by Federalist spies, my uncle insisted that we stop only long enough to have our mounts reshod by a local blacksmith. Then we would proceed by a very circuitous route, south through Tennessee on the notorious Natchez Trace, west to Chickasaw Bluffs on the Mississippi, and then up the big river to St. Louis, rather than taking passage from Nashville on a Cumberland flatboat and then down the Ohio.

The smith's name was Quick, but he took the better part of a whole afternoon at the job, interrupting his labors every three or four minutes to regale us with stories of the robbers and murderers we were likely to meet on the Natchez Trace. Quick ran the rope ferry across the Cumberland; and at last, about seven in the evening, he carried us and our freshly shod mounts over to the far side. My uncle was exceedingly displeased to discover that the boat was powered by six slaves winding a thick hawser around a turnstile. But when he asked the black-smith where he had procured those poor people, the man spat a dark jet of tobacco juice into the current and said only, "Harpes."

12

THE NEXT DAY was the first fiercely hot day of the year, and as we followed the Natchez Trace southwest from Nashville, we rode from spring into full summer. A dense ceiling of fo-liage reached out over the narrow trail from the trees on each side, in places roofing it entirely with a living green canopy. Nesting redbirds, mockingbirds, and warblers poured out their songs, and the orange trumpet-flowers were full of black and yellow swallowtails. Here in the Tennessee forest grew many tall trees unfamiliar to me. Some of these my uncle identified as chestnuts, live oaks, pecans, hickories, and tulip trees. But copperheads, cottonmouths, and rattlesnakes were everywhere, sunning themselves on logs, coiled on ledges beside the trail, and lying beside puddles and backwaters, and I was very glad, and my uncle as well, that we had no such long and deadly gen-tlemen as these at home in Vermont.

That evening we came to an inn known as Grinder's Stand, not far from the Buffalo River. As we rode into the dooryard, we were greeted by Mrs. Grinder herself, attired in a buckskin dress and a flop-brimmed slouch hat such as the backwoods-men in those parts favored. She showed us where to stable and bait our mounts, then conducted us into a log house consisting of a single large room with a packed dirt floor. On the hearth was a spitted joint of venison. The only other guest was a wooden dressmaker's dummy, seated at the head of a long tres-tle table, whom Mrs. Grinder introduced as George Wash-ington.

As our landlady laid plates and mugs on the table, a ruf-fianly-looking pair of mountain men arrived. Sitting directly across from us, they produced a stone jug from which they be-gan to swill, turn and turn about, laying the neck of the jug upon a massive shoulder and gurgling down prodigious quanti-ties of spirits. When these men tipped back to drink, their faces, behind thicketlike black beards, resembled those of boars. For apparel they wore stitched-together pelts of skunks, woodchucks, and possums, with bleached skulls of mice and moles dangling from the fringes of their blouses and trousers. Their sloping hats were fashioned from the skins of bitterns with the feathers still attached; the thumbs of both and the forehead of one were branded with the words HORSE THIEF.

Mother Grinder bustled about laying two new places in front of them and spitting another haunch of venison on the fire. The cooked meat she placed on a pewter charger, which she set before the larger of the two travelers, who was stuffing chunks of bread into his mouth with both hands. "Perhaps you'll do us the honor of carving, Bigger," she said. Bigger drew from his belt a glistening blade a foot and a half long; but in-stead of addressing the roast before him, he hurled this weapon backward over his shoulder without turning to look at his tar-get, burying the knife to its hilt in the bloody haunch of veni-son on the spit.

Bigger turned to the landlady. "Fotch us that un on the hearth. I and Big takes our meat *just singed*."

Mrs. Grinder instantly did as directed. Big and Bigger fell upon the oozing bloody joint, hacking off and carrying to their mouths on the points of their knives chunks of meat as large as the half-grown cat on the inglenook bench. They ate with such ravenous lust that the haunch was soon gone, after which they repaired again to the stone jug.

My uncle set about his meal with his usual good appetite, but my own hunger was now gone. Suddenly, the larger of our fellow travelers looked out from behind his vinelike hair and said, "Where did you Yankee-boys say you was a-going?"

"Why, friend," said my uncle with a pleasant smile, "we didn't."

Bigger said, "If you're going down the Trace, you'd best look sharp for robbers and killers. Particularly the Harpe brothers. Ain't that right now, Big?"

"It is," said the other. "They're a desperate pair. I heard they've murdered twenty men."

"Twenty-six," Bigger corrected him. "And afterwards drinked a toast to their wictims with mead distilled from their own bees' honey." He shoved the stone jug across the table and said, "Wet your whistle with our mead, Yankee. You can taste the wild honey in it and it goes down smooth."

My uncle shook his head and pushed back the jug. "We've heard of these Harpes, gentlemen. I wonder if you might be so good as to describe them for us? That way we'll know them if we encounter them out in the wilds. How many brothers are there? A gang of at least five or six, no doubt, from their desperate reputation."

"Only two," Bigger said. "But two such as unsuspecting travelers will remember for the rest of their lives."

"Which would be about three minutes," Big said, looking off at George Washington.

Bigger made a rumbling sound that seemed to begin and end far down in his massive chest. "What does these Harpe brothers look like, the Yankee wonders? Would you allow, brother, that one would be big?"

"I would. And the other bigger."

"Would you venture to say they wears clothing made from skunks and possums?"

"I would so venture."

"Would you further say that they wears hats of swamp-bird feathers, to shed the rain?"

"Yes, I would further say so. And has you heerd, brother mine, how they disposed of their twenty wictims?"

"Not twenty, brother. Twenty-*six*. Yes, I has. They gut them up the belly, like fishes, and fills up their insides with stones. Then they sinks them in the nearest river or stream. But don't worry, friends. We'll ride with you and protect you from the Harpes. For there is strength in numbers. And if we meet and overcome the Harpes, there is a reward of five hundred dollars apiece on their heads, which we shall split four ways."

By now, Big, Bigger, and the landlady were all holding their sides with laughter. I was stricken dumb with fright. But my uncle abruptly produced his arquebus from beneath the table. "Gentlemen, I am sure that we're much obliged to you for your good information about the Natchez villains we're apt to meet, particularly the feather-bedecked and skunk-clad Harpes. We appreciate, as well, your kind offer to accompany us. But as you can see from the good companion I hold here in my hands" — raising the arquebus so that it was now pointed straight at Bigger's head — "we already have protection enough."

With this he rose and rang a dollar down on the table.

"Ma'am" — without taking his eyes off the Harpes — "we thank you for the provender. Gentlemen, we thank you for the warning. Rest assured that if we encounter the Harpes, we will be ready."

Neither of the outlaws said a word as we backed out of the inn. A few minutes later we were riding south on the Trace in the red evening, my uncle cheerily whistling a Scottish ballad and I full of wonder at the scene I had witnessed at the inn. For the soldierly man who had coolly faced down the assassins as if they were schoolboys in his Vermont classroom was a man I had never seen before in the sixteen years that I had known Private True Teague Kinneson, of the First Continental Army of the United States of America, Green Mountain Regiment.

13

AROUND MIDNIGHT the moon went behind the clouds. Directly it began to rain, so we turned off the path and took shelter under my uncle's big umbrella beneath a spreading pine tree. Advising me to get some sleep, he got out his notebook — for with his large yellow owl-eyes he could see nearly as well in the dark as in daylight — and began jotting down ideas for his ever-evolving *Comical History of Ethan Allen*. Knowing that my uncle was watching over me, I slept as soundly as if I were home in my loft bedchamber above my mother's warm kitchen. The next morning I awoke much refreshed, with the sun already an hour high.

We made a hasty breakfast of several slices of bread we'd slipped into our pockets the night before at dinner, sharing them with Bucephalus and Ethan Allen. Upon returning to the Trace, the white mule paused and tossed his head; for, although he was deaf as a post, he had a very keen sense of scent. Bucephalus flared his nostrils to test the breeze sifting up from the southwest, struck the ground twice with his forehoof, and smelled the wind again.

Soon enough we came upon the faint, mostly washed-out tracks of two large dray horses such as those the Harpes had ridden in on the evening before at Grinder's Stand. To my alarm, they were headed in the same direction as we were. But my uncle assured me that by tarrying behind a bit, we would run no very great danger of stumbling upon them unawares before they passed the Buffalo River, where he intended to strike off on the Chickasaw Path to the Mississippi.

We reached the Buffalo about noon. As we approached the Metal Ford on that stream, so called from the ironlike rocks of the river bottom just below the horse ferry, we spotted a pillar of dark smoke rising from the trees across the water. It had a thick, sooty aspect and a most noxious odor. From the far bank of the river we could hear someone weeping.

We urged our animals across the hardpan ford and rode fast into a dooryard whose cabin and barn had both been burned to the ground within the past several hours. Low blue flames still licked over the charred logs. Wailing and rocking back and forth on a nearby stump was an ancient black woman with a bloody rag wrapped around her head. My uncle leaped off his mule and rushed to the woman's aid, unwinding her head-rag and dabbing at her wound with his nightcap. He told me to run to the river with the rag and soak it thoroughly. Then, with many soothing words, he bound her gashed head properly, at the same time urging her to tell what had happened.

At last she managed to convey that she was a free widow

who, first with her husband and, since his death, by herself, had operated the horse ferry. To her recently had come her grand-daughter, a girl named Cissie-Gal.

"Few hours ago, two men on plow horses come 'long from Nashville way, holla for the ferry," the old woman told us. "I bring them cross the water. They two giant white men. Soon's they set feet on dry land they say they going to ravishCiss 'less I tell them where I keep my moneybag. So I go fetch out my little pouch of silver. Then they drive the ferry horses in the barn and shut up the door and set the barn and house afire. I whisper to Cissie-Gal, 'Quick, run in the woods and hide.' Ciss run. She run like the wind. But they ride after and club she down and throw her over the horse. I grab the ax. They club me down, too. And ride off toward Nat-chez. Worst thing is, I can't do nothing to help my grandgal."

"How long ago did this terrible thing happen?" my uncle asked.

She stared at him without speaking, then let out another cry. He sat beside her on the stump and held her hand with the greatest distress on his face, as if wishing he could take some of her grief into himself. Finally, she caught her breath. "Old Sol, he just clear the tops of them 'simmon trees over yonder."

I gauged that to have been about eight o'clock, giving the Harpes — for I had no doubt that they were the kidnappers — a good four hours' start.

The main road to Natchez ran due south from the clearing. But a faint trail entered the forest to the west. "Where, my dear, does that old run through the woods lead?" my uncle asked.

"That the road through the wilds to Chicksaw Bluffs. Other road, he wind on down by Ten'see River, down old Mr. Colbert ferry, down Buzzard Roost and Nat-chez. That the way them men take Cissie-Gal. They say they carry she down Grace Plantation, sell to Kaintuck rivermen for slave-girl."

At this prospect the old woman wailed louder than ever.

My uncle looked long and hard at the faint gap through the trees that was the Chickasaw Trail. Then he looked at the road to Natchez.

"Ti," he said, rubbing the copper plate on his head with his stocking cap, "tell me. What must a man always do when he isn't certain what to do?"

I looked at him.

"Think, nephew. What did I teach you when you were a shaver? *What must a man always do — always — when he isn't certain what to do?*"

"Why — he must always do what's right, sir."

"There," cried my uncle, jingling his stocking-cap bell. "You have set me on course again, Ti. A man must always do what's right. And, by the Great Jehovah, we must do that now!"

14

BY MIDAFTERNOON we had passed three well-armed bands of Kaintuck flatboat men, wending their way afoot back from Natchez to the Cumberland and Ohio rivers. Of the first group we inquired about the Harpes and Cissie. They merely stared at us as if we spoke an entirely different tongue, so we judged it best not to query the next two parties.

Toward evening we had gained on our quarry so much that in wet places on the Trace water was still oozing into their horses' tracks. As the sun touched the rim of the low western hills, we emerged on an eminence all set about with tall pine trees. Riding ahead, my uncle held up his hand. In a narrow valley below, the Harpes, with Cissie tied up and thrown over Big's horse, were just turning off the Trace near a small brook.

They vanished into a thick canebrake alongside the stream. Training my spyglass up the defile, I could see water issuing from a dark opening in the hillside and falling in a white curtain down a rock face. On the hill above the mouth of the cave sat several thatch-roofed, cone-shaped huts, not greatly bigger than bushel baskets.

Motioning for me to follow, my uncle cut down through the pine trees at an angle to the stream. When he was abreast of the entrance to the cave, he halted behind a rock outcropping large enough to conceal our mounts. "Ti," he said in a hushed voice, "I cannot do better now than to follow old Caesar's advice and come at mine enemy from high ground. You wait here. When I give the signal, grab up Cissie and ride as if the Gentleman from Vermont himself were after you. Jehovah willing, I'll meet you back on the Trace."

With a smart salute, the private reined Ethan Allen around the outcropping and continued along the knoll and up through the woods toward the top of the cliff above the cave. I continued to study the conical huts through my glass, but it trembled so in my hand that I could not bring them into focus. My heart was drumming in my ears from fright, for I had no doubt at all that these Harpes would kill us if we did not kill them first.

Presently they emerged from the pines with Cissie onto a sandy clearing beside the pool below the waterfalls, no more than a stone's throw from the boulder behind which I was hiding. At the sight of the pelts they wore and their weird, sloped hats, my heart began to race even faster. With trembling hands I poured powder into my rifle. But which outlaw would I shoot at and when? Where would I aim? And how, with my hands shaking so, could I possibly hit what I aimed at?

The men dismounted, and Bigger dragged Cissie off his brother's horse. "I shall have her first," he muttered between pulls at his jug.

"You had the last one first," Big growled. "This un's mine."

As I trained the weaving barrel of my primed rifle first on one of these monsters, then the other, the clear tingling of a bell sounded from the hill above us. The quarreling Harpes whirled around and looked up. Pulling a pistol from his waistband, Bigger started up the path beside the waterfall. Big came along behind him, his own pistol at the ready. With surprising stealth, the huge men crept from tree to tree until they stood on a narrow shelf just before the mouth of the cave. Twenty feet above them, my uncle's stocking cap jutted over the lip of the cliff. The Harpes both fired at the same time, the report of their guns reverberating off the cliffsides like gunfire from a whole regiment.

Instantly a booming voice roared out, *"Veni, vidi, vici."* First one, then another, then yet another of the little thatch-roofed huts came tumbling down the cliff face, pouring out thousands and tens of thousands of angry bees, which swarmed over the Harpes from head to foot. The brothers whooped, danced, screamed, dropped their pistols, and, dripping broken slabs of honeycomb and straw and fist-sized clusters of bees, plunged into the deep pool. In a raging frenzy, the bees pursued them out of the stream and into the woods on the far bank. Big and Bigger crashed through the trees, while their horses, which had bolted at the pistol shots, galloped off in the opposite direction, hastened on their way by a blast from my uncle's arquebus.

"Now, Ti!" he shouted.

I rode out into the sandy clearing and called to Cissie to jump aboard behind me and hold on. Moments later we were racing north on the Trace, my uncle beside us on his white mule, and the screams of the Harpe brothers fading off in the distance.

"*Veni, vidi, vici,*" the private cried again. "Do you know your Caesar, Cissie? 'I came, I saw, I conquered.' We have conquered the Harpes. You'll be home with your grandmama by morning."

The terrified girl just held tighter to my waist, as though she never intended to let go, while my uncle congratulated me for doing yeoman's work, and said that his old colonel Ethan Allen would be proud. But for many days and nights after we had safely delivered Cissie to her overjoyed grandmother, I could not rid my mind or dreams of the feather-hatted, vermin-clad Harpes and their hillside den on the Natchez Trace.

St. Louis

15

Early one morning in mid-May we presented ourselves and our mounts at a quay just below the frontier city of St. Louis. I excitedly set up my easel and began to paint a picture of the waterfront, while my uncle made a short reconnaissance up into the town proper.

From the quay I could count the sign-boards of fifteen taverns. Besides these drinking establishments the street was lined with mercantiles, boarding inns, furriers, smithies, lumberyards, flatboat yards, and encampments of Indians, many of whom were strutting about in full ceremonial regalia. Every establishment flew the Stars and Stripes. For as the ferryman had told us, the citizens of St. Louis had chosen this very day to hold a jubilee in honor of the transfer of Louisiana to America, with a ball to follow that evening at the house of Auguste Chouteau, the town's principal merchant.

In my painting I depicted the muddy track called a street, the log houses, the men spewing tobacco, the ladies picking their way around milling hogs, and the effluvia of the riverside slaughterhouses, tanneries, and stables. Many of the celebrants were already drunk and had collapsed in the street, where they were constantly in danger of being run over by drovers and wagoneers near as drunk as themselves. For the entertainment of the more sober public, one man exhibited a live elk on a rope, and another showed a mangy buffalo in a pole pen. This was the first bison I had ever seen. Though it appeared to be rather sickly, I had no trouble imagining what a thousand such rugged giants trampling over the prairie in prime condition might look like, and it whetted my appetite to start up the Missouri and into the wilderness. Still, there was plenty to see and paint here in St. Louis. A fifteen-foot alligator named Monsieur Ponchartrain had been brought up from New Orleans for the celebration, a bear danced in a priest's frock and collar, whiskeymen clad in untanned buffalo hides dipped raw spirits out of barrels, hard-looking women sashayed past in ostrich boas, cardsharps gambled on planks thrown across trestles, and a doctor in a green velvet top hat hawked nostrums guaranteed to ward off malaria, smallpox, whooping cough, and cholera.

"You, boy. Be you fixing to paint the Battle Royale?" the quack asked me.

"I don't know," I said. "What is it?"

He gestured with his cane toward the buffalo's pen, where a throng of people was gathering. "It's a contest to see which wild beast will prevail when pitted against other savage beasts," he said. "In honor of the Louisiana Purchase they're a-going to enter Father Marquette — that's the bear — and the gator agin Old Teton, that big bull buff.

"It's to be the highlight of the jubilee," he continued. "I've put my money on the gator. Though I was sorely tempted to go with Father Marquette. A blow from a bear is a powerful blow, as any man who's ever watched a bearbaiting will attest."

The unfortunate animals were now being dragged and whipped toward the entry of the pole enclosure, roaring, growling, or hissing, as the case might be. What a cheer went up from the citizens of St. Louis when all three creatures were together inside the pen. But I had seen enough. I had hoped to paint the beasts of Louisiana in a natural state, not watch them tear one another to pieces for the fun of a drunken mob.

Before I could decide what to do, pell-mell down the street on his white mule, firing his arquebus into the air and scattering the crowd, came my uncle. Throwing a noose of a lariat over the flimsy corner post of the buffalo pen, he galloped off at an angle, yanking away the entire side of the cage and enabling Old Teton, Father Marquette, and Monsieur Ponchartrain to make their escape.

Now the creatures that had so lately been at one another's throats turned their full attention to their tormentors, who were fleeing down the hill in a panicked stampede. The buffalo, bear, and alligator were joined by the elk, which in the turmoil had broken its leash and was posting hard toward the Mississippi. There it leaped into the water, where it was soon joined by Old Teton and Monsieur Ponchartrain, all swimming hard for the Illinois side of the river and freedom.

The crowd now began to press around my uncle, shouting "Tar and feather him" and, more alarming still, "Lynch the old fool." My uncle objected to being called old, said he would not stand still for it, and began to cite instances from both the classics and the Bible in which men "well-stricken in years" had performed amazing feats of vigor. But before he knew what had happened, someone had thrown his own rope around his neck and yanked him off his mule.

I reached for my firelock as several men, led by the bear owner, hauled my struggling, protesting uncle through the mud toward a flagpole. I raised my rifle and, terrified though I was, felt fully prepared to shoot the ringleader, when another shot rang out over the streets and a deep, commanding voice shouted, "Unhand that man."

A tall rider dressed in buckskin, with long red hair flying out from under a black hat, galloped into the crowd on a big bay horse, striking right and left with the barrel of his gun. To the mob, some of whom demanded to know what authority the man had to curtail their sport, he shouted, "Unless you want my pappy and forty armed clansmen down on your town like the Furies of Hell, you'll restore law and order here yourselves and mind your manners. If you have any manners to mind."

With his stocking cap askew, one overshoe rolled up and the other down, and his crimson codpiece half undone, my uncle jumped to his feet and pulled the rope off his neck. "Private True Teague Kinneson, with eternal gratitude, sir," he said, saluting smartly.

"Flame Danielle Boone, scout and frontierswoman," cried his red-haired benefactor, grabbing his hand and pumping it up and down like a fellow soldier. "I'd be honored to invite you to escort me at the ball tonight, private, as my personal guest."

16

BY THAT AFTERNOON my uncle had begun to have second thoughts about attending the ball with Miss Flame Danielle Boone, who, according to St. Louis scuttlebutt, was desperate to procure a husband. But I was most eager to go myself and so came up with the following stratagem. By telling the knight-errant that, *having rescued a fair damsel in distress,* chivalry required that he escort her to that night's gala, I managed to persuade him to accept Flame's invitation. And I must attend, too, and sketch him "at the reel," where he would have an opportunity to show the people of St. Louis what dancing was all about.

We arrived about nine P.M. In attendance, besides the red-haired spinster, who at six feet and two inches tall cut a very striking figure in her lime-colored evening gown, were the governor-general of St. Louis; the mayor; an emissary from the Spanish seat of government at Santa Fe; Madame and Monsieur Chouteau; and Captain Meriwether Lewis and his friend and fellow officer Captain William Clark, who together would lead President Jefferson's official expedition to the Pacific.

Miss Boone introduced my uncle (dressed in his chain mail, galoshes, and codpiece, with his night-stocking set rakishly back on his head to reveal part of his copper crown) to the captains, who were both tall, fine-looking young men. Captain Lewis was very interested to learn that we planned to strike out for the Pacific ourselves, and more so yet that we had already, the previous summer, come overland from the western coast. But Captain Clark gave my uncle a skeptical look.

"You've been to the Pacific?" he said. "And come back through the Rockies?"

"Aye, of course," said my uncle, as if our great journey had been no more than a simple day's outing — which in fact was the case.

"And you, son?" said Clark with a broad smile.

"I was with my uncle," I said, feeling that to be the safest — and perhaps the *only* — thing I could honestly say.

"Well, what did you and your nephew see, Private Kinneson? It must have been a wonderful odyssey." This from Lewis, who was smiling himself now, though very good-naturedly.

"It was a great deal of hard walking. We went mainly by shank's mare, you know."

"Did you encounter hostile Indians?"

"Yes, sir, we did. It was touch and go with the Blackfeet all one afternoon."

"Your military background interests me, private," Lewis said. "You've been on many campaigns, no doubt?"

"Why, yes, sir, I believe I may say so without fear of contradiction. Besides my little jaunt across Lake Champlain with Ethan Allen, I was with young Alexander when he crossed the Hellespont; with Leonidas when he defended the pass at Thermopylae; and with Julius against the Visigoths. More recently, I stood beside Wolfe at Quebec and with Washington at Yorktown. I know how to besiege a city, defend a fort, joust in the lists, fight in single combat —"

"Well," Lewis interrupted, shaking his head and laughing, "those are mighty qualifications indeed, Private Kinneson. We have enjoyed meeting you, sir. We must get back to our men now, for we depart at dawn. Good luck on your expedition."

"And good luck to you, too," my uncle cried fervently, shaking hands with both captains in the most cordial way and giving his bell a jingle. "Good luck to you, too!"

Miss Boone escorted us to the dining room, at the same time engaging my uncle in a very lively conversation on the art of gigging catfish. We ate venison, bear meat both smoked and fresh, buffalo hump and tongue, jellied calves' brains, and Mississippi sturgeon. The damask cloth and the silver, the finewrought gravy chargers, the crystal and English bone china, the embroidered linen napkins — all were of the best quality. Flame Danielle gave a hilarious running account of a recent bear hunt with her famous father, which seemed quite to captivate my uncle. The wine flowed copiously, augmented by sparkling punch, rum, and whiskey from a gilded barrel.

The main topic of conversation was the Teton Sioux, who were said to dwell in a large village about a thousand miles, as the river wound, above St. Louis. For years, these "pirates of the Missouri," as they were called, had exacted heavy tribute from French and Spanish traders plying the river between St. Louis and the City of the Mandan Indians. The previous spring St. Louis's two rival fur companies had each sent traders — the Pariseau and Thibeau parties — upriver to buy furs from the Mandan Indians. Since then, no word had been received from either group, and there was now much anxiety over their fate. With the Thibeau party had gone a popular young priest, Father Gilles LaFontaine, who had lived for a season with the Teton Sioux and was determined to persuade them to adopt a more peaceable approach toward white traders. But no one seemed to hold out much hope that he would be successful in this endeavor. Flame Danielle was certain that the Sioux had annihilated them all, and urged my uncle to scalp every last redskin on the river, as her pappy would have done in his prime.

The music began after dinner. Monsieur and Madame Chouteau danced, their sons and daughters danced, the dignitaries danced, and my uncle danced — mainly with Miss Flame, who had conceived a rather terrifying affection for him and scarcely let him out of her sight. They made a wonderful pair, looming over everyone else in the room and stepping as gravely as two geese while gazing into each other's eyes with great fondness.

A mischievous idea occurred to me. At the time it seemed an inspired notion, but some evil genie must have planted it in my mind because soon enough I would have cause to regret its consequences. Drawing Miss Flame a little aside, as if to request the next dance, I hinted that my uncle would like to stroll over the darkened grounds with her, as he had a very important proposal to make, which would be much to her liking and contribute greatly to their future mutual happiness. I added that if she was willing to keep this assignation, she should invite the private to go bear-hunting with her — a suggestion that delighted Flame so much that before I anticipated what she was about she seized me up in a bear-hug herself, and gave me a joyful kiss right in the middle of my forehead.

Then to the attack.

"Would you like to *go a-bear-hunting* tonight, Private True?" the spinster inquired in a throaty whisper, holding my unsuspecting uncle in an iron grip on his arm and guiding him outside and down the lawn toward a thicket of mock-orange shrubbery. I slipped along behind in the shadows, holding my sides and pressing my hand over my mouth to keep from laughing.

The fair huntress then suggested that she show my uncle the arts of the chase in that region, proposing to enact the part of the "bear" and secrete herself in the fragrant shrubbery, where her "dear Private True" would duly "bring her to bay." He replied, with an uneasy chuckle, that he liked the sound of this game; and, pressing his hands to his eyes, began in his loud schoolmaster's voice to count to one hundred, as instructed. But the old bachelor had not reached twenty-five before he lost his nerve and ran inside, spoiling my entertainment and so enraging the lovely Miss Flame that she spent the rest of the evening darting looks in his direction as fierce as any her famous father ever shot at a ravening bruin. She declared that she was not used to being *jilted* and would soon find a way *to be made an honest woman of* — which frightened him a great deal. At the first opportunity, he whispered to me that we must strike out into Louisiana that very night, both to get a jump on the captains and to escape the furious blandishments of the spinster.

This alarmed me very much. I had harbored some hope that once we reached St. Louis and met Captain Lewis, my uncle would reflect upon what a vast and unlikely undertaking it was to penetrate Louisiana, and sensibly decide to return to Vermont. Now, however, I realized that he was entirely serious about kiting out into a wilderness two thousand miles wide and never before traversed by an American — or, so far as we knew, by any man at all. Though Flame Danielle's threats were the least of my concerns, nothing would do but we must instantly depart.

As we rode off into the night, the music and lights growing ever fainter behind us, I felt again that I must be dreaming, but do what I might, I could not find a way to shake myself awake. What had begun as an ill-advised practical joke had turned into a full-blown disaster.

A few hours later my uncle and I took breakfast on a knoll on the west bank of the Mississippi some miles north of St. Louis. Across the river was Captain Lewis's winter quarters, where, under his and Clark's direction, the official expedition was preparing to set out on its own great trek. Men were packing a long keelboat and two big flat-bottomed canoes, one red and one white, while the captains, dressed in their blue uniform coats, were superintending the last-minute arrivals of wagons full of whiskey, flour, meal, nails, bullets, and the thousand other items needed for such an ambitious excursion.

For some time, as we munched on bread and ham left over from last night's banquet, I had been aware of a steady, low, grumbling sound, resembling distant summer thunder, though the day was breaking fair. When I inquired what this noise might be, my uncle pointed up the river. There, in a gap in the bankside cottonwoods, I caught a glimpse of a huge, brimming tributary pouring in from the west. The growl was the boiling, swirling Missouri — bigger, faster, and more powerful than any river I had ever seen. Indeed, it seemed — and was — even larger than the Mississippi. This was a river of an entirely different order. Here came the snow-waters from the Rocky Mountains and the muddy scourings of the Great Plains. Rushing along in the dark current were partly submerged logs, entire trees pulled out by the roots, and chunks of sheared-off bank, some as large as houses. I felt a burst of excitement to think that I might one day allay my thirst from the headwaters of this river and paint the snowy mountains and all of the new animals and birds at its hidden icy source.

"Pardon me, sir? I was woolgathering."

"I was saying, Ti, that the race is about to begin."

"The race?"

"Why, yes," he said, "the race to the Ocean Pacific. It's our party against theirs, lad. And may the best men win!"

With that he sprang onto his mule and was off. For better or for worse, our great adventure was about to begin in earnest.

17

IT WAS A FINE SIGHT to see the Missouri unspooling from a vast and unknown region as we traced its course through the rolling hills west of St. Louis. Without pressing our mounts, we made twenty or thirty miles a day, camping where we pleased and supping when we wished. My uncle sometimes recited from his beloved old classics, sometimes exclaimed over a landmark familiar from our trip back from the Pacific the previous summer, and now and again trolled out some grim old Scottish ballad. He tendered fatherly advice on all kinds of important matters, from the origin of the universe in a great cloud of cosmic dust into which a Creator somewhat resembling his old tutor, Scholia Scholasticus Aristotle, had breathed form and life, to the proper way to fry up a whiskered catfish so that the meat fell off his bones in beautiful sweet snowy slabs. Soon I began to enjoy our vagabond life in Louisiana.

On our third morning out of St. Louis, we came to a knoll overlooking several cabins scattered about a good plank house hard by the river. This we presumed to be Boone's Settlement, where the great Kentuckian was then homesteading. The smoke from the breakfast fires of this outpost smelled delicious. Though my uncle was reluctant to risk another encounter with Flame Danielle, we had seen no other horses or riders since leaving St. Louis and were pretty sure that she could not have arrived here before us.

As we deliberated, up from the river came a redheaded boy of about twelve, dragging behind him a heavy string of popeyed catfish. He turned out to be Flame's nephew, Boone's grandson Danny, who told us gleefully that his grandpa was fixing to lay for True Kinneson, the ruffian who had "played his aunt false by deserting her at the altar" and was now said to be on his way upriver.

"Left her at the altar?" cried my astonished uncle. Then, with terror in his eyes, "Is your aunt Flame already here?"

"No, but my pa come up on horseback t'other side of the river yesterday and hollered for us to cross him over in the scow. He'd parlayed with Flame in St. Louie the morning afore and she was ripping and tearing and bound to catch up with True and marry him if she had to bring him to the church hogtied. She sent word through pa to hold him here if he showed up while she picked out her wedding dress and she'd be along directly. I can't imagine Flame in a wedding dress."

"What party is this dastard traveling with, did you say?" my uncle inquired, taking up the boy's string of fish.

"Captain Lewis and Captain Clark. Them are the soldier

boys going upriver to teach the red Sioux injuns a lesson they won't soon forget. Only grandpappy's going to teach True Kinneson a lesson first."

"What, pray, does this True look like?"

"Flame told pa he's a handsome young fellow, made for breaking a woman's heart."

"Handsome and young, you say?" said my uncle. "Did you hear that, Ticonderoga? Miss Flame sounds like a woman of considerable discernment. I'm of a mind to meet this charming Flame myself. Now that the dashing True Kinneson is out of the picture."

"I wouldn't care to be in that boy's shoes, that's the truth," Danny said. "Not for all the river-cats in the Missoura and Miss'ippi together, I wouldn't."

"Neither would I, Mr. Danny," my uncle said, shaking his head and winking at me. "Neither would I."

Boone's outpost had a willy-nilly frontier look about it, as if it had blown in on a cyclone and been left wherever the buildings happened to alight. With Danny trailing along behind, we rode up to the plank house, where we found the tall bear-killer out in his dooryard stirring a large kettle of pitch. As we drew near, I saw that he had scraggly, iron-colored hair and pale eyes. Nearby two redheaded girls, who looked as if they might be Danny's older sisters, were plucking a heap of dead chickens.

"Mr. Daniel?" my uncle said, lifting his stocking cap. "We're advance scouts with Captain Meriwether Lewis and Captain William Clark's expedition to the Pacific. Sent ahead to issue you an invitation to take dinner with the captains tomorrow noon. They said it would be a great honor to have the pleasure of your company."

"They shall have the pleasure of my company, all right," said Boone, who appeared to perceive nothing strange about my uncle or his mode of dress. "Tell me, friend. Is there a rascally young fellow named True Kinneson with them? Styles himself a regular tomcat with the gals?"

"Why, yes, sir, I'm afraid there is. Beau True is a bad one. He does like the girls, and he likes the redheaded ones best." At which the brace of carrot-topped feather-pluckers giggled.

Boone shot us a look. "I intend to make Beau True a bridegroom — that or tar and feather him for jilting my Flame Danielle," he said, stirring the bubbling pitch.

At this my uncle shuddered so hard his chain mail clinked and the bell on the end of his cap jingled.

"You boys want some breakfast?" Boone said.

"Why, yes," said my uncle, "we might at that."

We hitched Bucephalus and Ethan Allen to a tree on the edge of the clearing and joined Boone and Danny and the two redheads and some others at a long table. The table was downwind of the pitch fire, to keep off the bugs, so we ate coughing in the smoke. Over bacon and turkey and deer and fish and ham and bread and eggs and pie, washed down with whiskey straight from a brown jug, I said, "Excuse me, Mr. Boone. But are you the gentleman who blazed the first trail through the Kentucky wilderness?"

"I am," he said, with an eye on the scalding-hot pitch. "And afterward, when I commenced to see what riffraff and trash availed themselves of it to come through to the Ohio and St. Louie, I wished I'd let the wilderness well enough alone."

"Tell what you're going to blaze next, grandpappy," Danny said.

Boone got up and drew out of the fire a branding iron that had been heating in the coals under the pitch pot. "Do you see this implement, gentlemen? It has my initials on it. But I'm very much tempted to use it to blaze a great 'D' for 'devil' and a

'B' for 'bred' — 'Devil Bred' — in the middle of True Kinneson's forehead. That's if he don't yoke up with Flame."

To show how he intended to serve True Kinneson if he did not marry Flame Danielle, Boone thrust the business end of the iron into the top of the table directly under our noses. Seeing the great sizzling DB inscribed deep in the weathered plank, my uncle started up as if he had been branded himself. Collecting himself, he said, "This daughter of yours, sir. Miss Flame. She must be the apple of your eye."

"She is, and ever has been," Boone said. "But tell me now, boys. What manner of man is this True Kinneson? Speak freely. You're among friends here."

"Well, then," my uncle said, "as for young True. As reported, he is a fine, tall figure of a man, nigh as tall as you. And a famous scholar and playwright, not to mention a lexicographer of renown . . ."

But Boone's pale eyes were wandering, as if he had lost the thread of the conversation, though whether from the whiskey or some other addlepated condition, I couldn't tell.

"We aim to hold a turkey shoot," the woodsman said. "Foot races, wrastling catch-as-catch-can, horseracing. We aim," he said, fixing us with his milky stare, "to lift some of General Clark's money after we capture his boy True and marry him off to Flame."

At first we knew not what to make of Boone's "General Clark." But by degrees, as he rambled on, we realized that the aging bear-hunter had somehow gotten it into his head that Captain *William* Clark was General *George* Clark, under whom Boone had once served. Nothing we could say to the contrary shook his conviction, or his delight in the thought of "lifting some money" — a considerable amount of money — off his old crony and comrade-in-arms.

After breakfast, the men of the settlement practiced shooting. They tied a sick, half-featherless old tom-turkey to a post and took potshots at it in turn, missing entirely or only winging its tail. Old Boone decided to give the turkey some whiskey, claiming he couldn't shoot at a sitting bird, and the libation might enliven it to leap about and present a more suitable natural target. But the poor bird did not seem as fond of strong drink as the men were, and what the marksmen had been unable to accomplish, the liquor did; before they could take up their rifles again, the turkey fell over on its side, stone dead.

Next my uncle volunteered my services to draw Daniel's portrait, as a token of gratitude for our entertainment. After gruffly feigning much modesty, Boone got out a large bear rug, with the head still attached; throwing the skin over his head and shoulders, he told me to fetch my pencil and "do my worst."

While I set up my easel, Boone began to crack facetious about Thomas Jefferson, whose Republican principles he detested. He maligned the President as a whoremaster and the father of whores and whoremasters. Boone called him a traitor to his country for forbidding settlement west of the Missouri, and a pretender who had stolen the last presidential election through bribes and chicanery. This my uncle could not bear to hear; seizing my pencil, on the pretext of adding a few finishing touches to the sketch, he placed Boone, bearskin and all, cowering high in a tree, and a bear with a top hat and a rifle underneath, drawing a bead on him. This caricature he signed, boldly, "To Daniel Boone, with the compliments of TRUE TEAGUE KINNESON." My uncle then affected great diffidence about showing Boone the results of his pencil, at last consenting to let him see it only if we were first allowed to ride our mounts to a low hillock overlooking the settlement, lest he be entirely overcome by embarrassment at nearer proximity. Most of the company thought this stipulation curious, but Boone said we could ride clear back to St. Louis for all he cared, only be quick about it, for he longed to see his likeness. My uncle thrust the drawing into the crotch of the tree to which we had tied our mounts, and off we galloped to the hilltop, arriving just as Boone unfolded the sketch. There was a stunned pause. Then the enraged bear-killer roared, "To horse. And a double eagle to the man who brings the villain to me alive."

Up went a great bloodthirsty whoop. There was a wild, scattered flurry, and the chase was on. My uncle and I broke for the open grassland east of the settlement, then doubled back in the bed of a little stream that ran into the willow brakes along the river, counting on the whiskey that Boone and the others had drunk to assist us in this ruse. Our strategy seemed to work, as the cries of our pursuers faded off in the distance.

We had not proceeded far along the narrow trace through the willows, however, when a tanager-colored flash in the trees ahead caught my eye and I heard hoofbeats coming our way fast. And who should come galloping headlong out of the willows, straight at my uncle, but Flame Danielle herself, astride her big bay, with a pink cushion for a saddle and her long red locks flying. She leaped from her saddle and pulled him off Ethan Allen, quite knocking out his breath as he fell to the ground with her aboard him.

"Now, here are the rules, you absconding rounder," she cried, laughing. "There ain't no rules!"

In a trice they were in each other's arms, and I do not know what might have happened next had we not suddenly heard horses crashing through the underbrush. "Hold the ravisher off a minute longer, little darling," Boone roared out. "We be there instantly."

"I must flee for my life, my dear Dulcinea," cried my uncle.

"Then let us exchange tokens of our affection," Flame cried, "and meet again as soon as ever we can." She whipped off his codpiece, wrapped it around her head like a crimson turban, and threw him her little pink riding cushion to use in its stead. A moment later we were off toward the high ground to the north.

"He headed back toward the river slough, pappy," I heard Flame shriek. "We've got him cut off. He's ourn."

Leaving Flame to misdirect her relatives, we rode hard all the rest of that morning, pausing to breathe our animals just once. By noon we believed ourselves safe. Over cold venison from the night before, my uncle allowed that he owed his near-entrapment to the whiskey he had imbibed with his breakfast. Yet his smirking grin, along with a thoughtful gleam in his eyes whenever he spoke of Miss Flame afterward or hitched up his breeches and patted the pink cushion he now wore inside them in lieu of his codpiece, made me think that perhaps, if we survived our great odyssey, their little business in the willow brake might turn out not to be the end of their acquaintance.

Up the Broad Missouri

18

Now that we were completely beyond the reach of civilization, all nature seemed larger than in Vermont, Virginia, or Tennessee. The expansive sky, the wide river, the huge red morning and evening suns and palatial late afternoon thunderheads — this Louisiana was an altogether grander country than any I had ever dreamed of. Not an hour passed during the next week when I did not long to stop and paint the newest vista over a knoll or round a bend in the river. But I also had a strong urge to push on ahead, for I was terribly eager to meet and sketch a Missouri River Indian in his own surroundings.

"'Now mother, O mother, go dig my grave, go dig it deep and narrow,'" crooned my uncle. "'Sweet William died for me today, I will die for him tomorrow.'"

"Uncle, will not your singing frighten away every Indian within ten miles?"

"Hardly, Ti. The native peoples of Louisiana will soon be singing 'Barbrie Allen' with me. The dulcet strains of my ballads will call them nigh, as the Sirens did Greek sailors."

Sometimes my uncle was joined in his singing by field larks with flashy yellow and black cravats, or the softly melodious bluebird, or the twittering black-capped bobolink. Every copse on the great grassy terrace above the river held feeding deer, flocking turkeys, or black bears that sallied forth to graze on the first ripe strawberries, lifting their heads to watch us pass, then resuming their feeding unconcerned. The backwaters of the river were loud with ducks and teeming with fish. Tight-sitting snipe went up from under my horse's feet, hooting wildly as they traced out their intricate high dance against the dawn and twilight skies. The meadows were ablaze with many-colored wildflowers unknown to us New Englanders.

But on windless days the mosquitoes rose out of the tall grass by the millions; and though we besmeared ourselves with mud and tallow and bear grease, they assailed us all day and all night as well, insinuating themselves, along with their yet more numerous cousins, the stinging midges, into every opening in our clothing and every crease of our exposed skin — between our fingers, in the lines at the corners of our eyes and mouths, where the hair left off on our necks. My uncle did valiant battle with them, swatting right and left and crying, "Now the Sioux and Blackfeet show their true colors, Ti. Down with them. Crush them. We'll plow salt into their fields as the Romans did those of old Carthage." To no avail. All we could do was keep to the high ground, where the wind was most apt to blow. Evenings we built smudgy fires of sodden driftwood culled from the riverbank and crept as near to the smoke as we could get, coughing like a fine pair of consumptives. Soon our clothes and skin alike were cured like a Vermont ham.

Sometimes, when the endless rolling prairie grew tedious after we had been riding most of the day, we would pass the time by posing to each other the old riddles my uncle had taught me when I was small. "A stick in his hand, a stone in his throat, answer this riddle and I'll give you a groat," I'd call out.

Then my uncle would frown and ponder and knit his white brows until, abruptly, he would smite his copper crown with his hand and cry, "A cherry! Ha ha, Ti. You must get up early in the morning to get one past me."

After which he would think for a few moments, then smile slyly as though *this* time he would stump me once and for all, and say, "Little Nancy Ettycoat wears a white petticoat and has a red nose; the longer she stands, the shorter she grows."

"I can't imagine," I would say, after pretending to rack my brain. "You have me there, uncle. You have riddled me."

"A candle," he would cry, and then I would smite *my* head as though I should have known the answer all along — as indeed I had.

I was amazed by the flatness of the country. To a Vermont farm boy brought up in a land so tilted that it was said that the cows' legs were a foot shorter on one side from grazing steep hillsides all day, the endless prairie was dizzying; and sometimes we both felt lost under the ever-widening sky. "Here we are, Ti," my uncle would suddenly cry out, two or three times a day, with a jingle of his bell. To which I would always reply, "Here we are, sir."

When my head started to spin from the vastness of our surroundings, I found it best to fix my attention on some closer feature of the landscape or on my unchanging uncle, riding along with the sunshine flashing off his mail and trolling his old ballads. But exactly where we were, and exactly why, and exactly what sort of place this Louisiana might be, other than a very flat one, I could not say.

I missed my father and mother, especially at night. Then we would get out our spyglass and gaze upward into the heavens until we felt like the only human beings in the universe, and my uncle would jingle the bell on his cap all over again to convince himself of his own existence.

I don't know how a person knows when he's being watched. He does, though. Just as he knows when he comes to a bad place in the woods where a killing or some other terrible thing has taken place. About ten o'clock one morning, we both felt it and knew someone was watching us from nearby. "We're about to see your Indians, Ti," my uncle told me. "Limber up your paintbrush."

At the time we were riding through some tall cottonwoods close to the river. As we reemerged onto the open prairie, we sighted no one, and by noon we had decided that whoever it was had gone on about their business. But the next morning we spotted three young men on horses across the river on a bluff where no one at all had been a moment earlier. They were armed with bows and arrows, and their long hair was dyed bright carmine, with one side of their faces painted black, the other white.

Now, for reasons known only to himself, my uncle had long held the conviction that while our eastern Indians had probably originated from a band of nomadic hunters from the far north, western Indians might well have come from China. Therefore he called out loudly, in what he assured me was good Cantonese, "We greet your celestial personages with much respect and bring the felicitations of the Supreme Khan of America, Thomas Jefferson. We are travelers come to see your Great Wall from Vermont, where we have stone walls ourselves. And you must not think yours superior to ours, though I'm sure it's very sturdy."

This salutation, uttered in a high, fast singsong, seemed to have no effect upon the Indians other than, after a minute, to cause them to laugh. Whereupon my vexed uncle said he was surprised that so polite a people as the Orientals had not taught their youth better manners, and for all he cared the three newcomers could "go straight back to China in a handbasket."

As we rode on, my uncle muttered to himself about the sad state to which the young had sunk the world over, while the Indians kept pace with us along the opposite side of the river.

From their gaudy appearance, I believed they were out looking for enemies or for horses to steal, but I was not greatly alarmed so long as the Missouri lay between us. After a while they went away. But the following morning the trio appeared again, this time on our side of the river.

My uncle was now determined to force an audience with our admirers and put an end to this puss-and-mouse game. Accordingly, we stopped on the edge of the ever-present cottonwoods along the river, where he instructed me to paint his face black and white, which I must say gave him a very fearsome aspect. But though we remained there for above two hours, the Indians never came forward and after that we saw them no more.

Two days later we nooned it at the mouth of the Kansas River. As we ate our meat, we noticed many large white feathers drifting down the current. At first my uncle was greatly alarmed, supposing that some young Icarus of Louisiana, attempting flight with wings fashioned from feathers and wax, had flown too near the sun, which had melted the wax and precipitated him to his death somewhere up the river. I assured him that this could not be the case, since the river was choked with feathers, far too many to have come from one flying boy. Instantly he got out his "Chart of the Interior of North America" and boldly crossed out the word "Kansas," substituting *Fluvius Pennae,* or "River of Feathers." But where was all this plumage coming from? Determined to solve the puzzle, my uncle said that we would adventure up along the tributary for a certain distance and see what we could discover.

We had not gone far before we came to a large island covered with what I first mistook for snow. How this could possibly be I had no idea — my uncle feared it was a mirage thrown up by some giant or wizard to confuse us. But as we came closer we saw that the island, about half a mile long and a third wide, was covered with pelicans. The birds — so numerous that many had been crowded off into the water — were molting, and the white feathers choking the river were theirs.

More interesting still, just off the lower tip of the island, in a very primitive-appearing dugout canoe on a sandbar buried deep in feathers, sat a tiny, angry-looking man wearing nothing but a nightshirt. "Heyday, what have we here, Ti?" cried my uncle. Then, to the stranger, "Private True Teague Kinneson, at your service, sir."

"It's you, is it?" the nightshirted man called out in a querulous voice. "Throw me a rope and tow me off this accursed bar, and for God's sake be quick about it. I've been befeathered here for three days and two nights. The River Missouri, you said. Go west by the River Missouri, John Ledyard, if you wish to cross the continent. Well, gentlemen, thank you for the excellent advice. The River Missouri, I must inform you, is half a mile wide and an inch deep and too thick to drink and too thin to plow and I've gone so far wrong that I don't know if I'll ever go right again. What in the deuce held you up? Do you have any rum?"

"Jehovah forbid, no, John Ledyard," my uncle replied. "Rum has gotten me into trouble enough before now. We have no strong spirits, but something else that's far better for you. I mean, of course, hemp. Here" — throwing him a rope, which the angry little voyageur affixed to a spike in the bow of the canoe — "we'll pull you ashore."

"Uncle," I whispered. "Who does he think we are? And who is he?"

"I don't know who he thinks *we* are, Ti, but I know I've heard his name," my uncle said. "I just can't recollect where."

I had no notion what to make of this bad-tempered mannikin. Once we got him safely to shore and boiled up some tea and offered him half a pipeful of hemp, he asked in the same vexed voice if we would like to hear his story. We said yes, very much; so, crossing his legs like a tailor and puffing away like a miniature chimney, John Ledyard announced that he was a Connecticut man, born and bred, and the first American to set foot in the Oregon Country, when he was there in '76 with Captain Cook.

My uncle lifted his stocking cap and smote his copper crown. "I was certain that I knew your name, sir. You went round the world with James Cook on his first circumnavigation."

"I did," John Ledyard said, "stopping in Oregon en route."

Talking on at a great rate of speed, Ledyard explained that he had met with Thomas Jefferson when Jefferson was ambassador to France, and convinced him that he could travel *by foot* through Siberia, cross the Bering Sea on a Russian fur-trading vessel, then hike across North America west to east (much as my uncle believed we had done). "But I am nothing if not misfortune's stepchild," he went on, explaining that in Siberia he had been chased by a tiger, nearly trampled by a mammoth, impressed by a local warlord into a salt mine, taken into bondage by a fierce princess directly descended from Attila, and finally imprisoned by Queen Catherine the Great and then expelled from the country.

"But wait," cried my uncle. "Didn't you next undertake to journey to Africa, with the design of discovering the source of the Niger River?"

"Of course," Ledyard snapped. "Where else would I go?"

"But I thought you died along the way, in Cairo," my uncle exclaimed, and he began to tremble quite violently for fear that he was holding conversation with a ghost.

"No, no, that was a base, false rumor bruited about by my enemies, and mere wishful thinking. Though I *was* set upon by lions and hippopotami and a troop of pecking ibises, and finally I had to turn back in the face of an army of one hundred thousand Nigers armed to the teeth. But none of that was anything to what I've encountered here on this infernal Missouri River."

"This is the Kansas River, sir," I interjected. "It branched a short way back."

"Or the *Fluvius Pennae*," my uncle added. "I believe that is the name that will stick. It is the more poetic."

"Poetic?" cried Ledyard. "You call this waterway to Hell poetic? *Fluvius Hades* you might better call it. Let me tell you what's happened to me since I took the fork a month ago — evidently the wrong fork, if what you say is so. I have been robbed and stripped of all but my nightshirt by Missouri Indians, beaten with willow sticks by Kansas women, jeered at by the Omaha, stung in every pore of my body by each kind of vicious bug in Louisiana, bitten on the nose by a water viper, and pelted with Osage oranges by some boys belonging to that tribe — I mean the Osage. I was chased by the Yankton Sioux for twenty miles, and finally took refuge in a backwater inside a beaver lodge, and though I evaded the Sioux, a monstrous buck beaver flung mud at me and flailed me so brutally with his great tail that I still have the bruises to show for it. Finally, I found myself — I believe for the first time in the annals of exploration — *befeathered*. With Cook I was becalmed many a time; and often bemused by the marvels we saw; and once or twice nearly beheaded; but never befeathered. I am on my way back to St. Louis, gentlemen. Not to retreat. I never retreat. But to sail to New Orleans and thence Brazil and then round the Cape and up to the mouth of the Columbia on the first vessel going that way."

"Then for Jehovah's sake, allow us to help you," said my uncle. "We have extra clothing, and some cornmeal and meat, and a blanket — for the prairie nights are cold."

I voiced a wish to paint John Ledyard in his dugout, with the molting pelicans on the island in the background, and he consented. But in the late afternoon he set off down the river, with neither thanks for our assistance nor any farewell, paddling hard to get to New Orleans and Brazil.

I found Ledyard's story most foreboding and wished again that we, too, were posting back to St. Louis and safety. But as he passed out of sight, my uncle said, "I don't know, Ti, when I've met a fellow who pleased me more. John Ledyard is undaunted. Mark my words. That brave man will be heard from. For he has a vision and he cleaves to it. I should be proud to be beaten to the Pacific by an expeditionary of his mettle. God bless him. God bless all the John Ledyards in the world!"

"Amen," I said, thinking that they would need it, and we would, too. And for good measure I said again, "Amen."

19

THE FOLLOWING DAWN I awoke to discover Bucephalus gone. I whistled like a jaybird — his signal to come — to no avail. Though my uncle did not seem unsettled, my panic grew as the daylight strengthened. To be stranded horseless in this country would surely throw us upon the mercies of the local Indians, a prospect I found very alarming after hearing how John Ledyard had fared at their hands.

Nothing else was missing, only Bucephalus. But once more I felt that we were being watched closely. My uncle thought the same, and after a few moments of reflection, came up with an idea for recovering my mount and meeting our first Indians into the bargain. I thought his plan, as he explained it, improbable at best. But in the absence of any better strategy it seemed worth trying.

In what I hoped would appear to be an unhurried manner, I set up my easel on the prairie about one hundred paces from our camp and the same distance from the cottonwoods along the river. Then, while my uncle went a-fishing as if we had no concerns in the world, I began to paint. In the background I painted the river and the bluffs opposite, some trees, a pelican flying overhead, and our camp, leaving a large space in the center of the canvas blank. Presently an Indian rode out from the trees on a black and white pony. After watching me intently for a time, he began to dash back and forth along the edge of the cottonwoods, approaching a few feet closer with each sprint. I continued to fill in the background and foreground of the painting, which he could not yet discern from his angle.

As he drew closer, I was surprised to see that he was just a boy, one or two years younger than myself. He was dressed in buckskins much like my own, only with a fringe of yellow, white, and red quillwork on his leggings. His face was painted somewhat differently from those of the Indians who had followed us earlier, with red predominating on his forehead, upper cheeks, and nose, then black below to his chin. Perceiving that I was unperturbed by his darting feints, which were sometimes accompanied by a howl, he suddenly leaped off his running horse by bringing one leg and foot forward, vaulting over the animal's mane, and alighting perfectly balanced, strung bow in hand. As he sidled closer, nocking an arrow, I continued my work — though my heart was in my throat — now painting my young friend in the central space I'd reserved. He advanced one step at a time, edging around to come at me from downwind, as if stalking a deer or some other keen-nosed quarry. This very much amused me, though I was constantly aware of the arrow fitted to the string of his bow, which I painted at the ready in his hands, so that the boy appeared to be about to loose his barb directly at the viewer of the picture.

When I was done I casually boxed up my paints and returned to our camp, leaving the picture on the easel. As I walked away with my back to the Indian, the hair on my neck prickled; it would have been but a moment's work for him to send his long-shafted arrow straight through my heart. But when I reached the camp I could see him, from the tail of my eye, approaching not me but the easel, creeping closer and closer, and still taking great care to keep downwind of it.

I cut a willow sapling about eight feet long, attached a fish line and hook, and repaired to the nearby backwater where my uncle was angling. In the meantime, the Indian boy peeked around the corner of the easel and saw his portrait. Letting out a yelp, he jumped back. At this I laughed aloud, causing him to stamp his foot in anger. He then lifted his bow, pulled the nocked arrow to his shoulder, and approached the picture again, no doubt believing that he was taking his life in his hands. This time, after regarding his portrait for a few moments, he dropped his bow to the ground. Both his hands shot up to his mouth. Snatching up the bow again, he compared it to that in the painting. He appeared to count the colored hands of porcupine quills on the figure's leggings, then on his own, matching color to color. Again he was overcome by wonderment, covering his eyes with his hands and reeling. Finally he touched the canvas, smelled the wet paint on his fingertip, and brought it to his tongue.

This seemed the right time for me to withdraw altogether. I continued fishing down the slough behind my uncle, who soon hooked a fine catfish of two or three pounds, shouting "Fish on" as if we were home on our little Vermont river, seeing who could catch the most trout. As he played it he declared that he would fish his way across Louisiana, and he did not know but that the chance to do so was not half his reason for making such an odyssey in the first place. Which seemed to make as much sense as any other reason he had thus far advanced for our journey to the Pacific.

But when we returned to our camp half an hour later, the easel and portrait were gone. In their place, placidly cropping the wet morning grass as if he'd been there the entire while, stood Bucephalus.

20

Two DAYS LATER we came to a flourishing village on the riverbank. It was inhabited not by the Oto, Osage, or Sioux but by several hundred creatures much like our common groundhog in Vermont, yet more communal, each one living in a small hole by a mound of dirt close by its neighbors. But catching one for me to paint proved difficult.

At first we chased all round their village, stumbling over their dirt mounds and diving at these sleek little tricksters, which popped up out of one hole only to vanish immediately down another. Next we tried digging one out with a pointed stick. When I was down three or four feet, my uncle came up with a supple cottonwood pole longer than he was tall and thrust it all the way into the den without reaching the end. "We have discovered another Cretan labyrinth, Ti, with a thousand cunning small Minotaurs," he said. He next essayed to "whistle them up," a method he had used to converse with Vermont groundhogs, which would sometimes whistle back to him. But these western fellows were not so obliging and stubbornly remained out of sight, though my uncle tried several lively airs. Then he hit upon another idea. He filled with river water the pannikin in which we boiled our tea and poured it down a hole, expecting to flush out the animal. That wouldn't answer, either. It would have taken a barrel of water to drive them out, and we never did catch one. My uncle named them "Kinneson's hermit chucks" because of their extreme shyness.

There were many other new and quite wonderful animals to be met with on the prairie, and I loved making their acquaintance. One morning while the dew still lay thick on the grass we came onto four comical hopping deer with black tails, somewhat larger than our eastern white-tails and with ears half again as long, resembling the ears of jackasses; my uncle immediately denominated them "Kinneson's mule deer." Then he must dismount and imitate their method of locomotion, bouncing along on the prairie in his chain mail and galoshes, with his belled cap jingling, and encouraging me to do the same. I do not know what a party of traders or Indians might have thought had they come by just then and seen a man dressed as a knight-errant and his gangling young squire hopping hand in hand across the prairie like a pair of kangaroos.

A fortnight later we discovered a rabbit with long hind legs capable of leaping twenty feet at a bound, which we henceforward called "Kinneson's long-jumping hare." Near the mouth of the Platte River (which my uncle renamed the Helen of Troy on his "Chart of the Interior"), we encountered the slinking, doglike, smallish wolves that chorused at twilight in great numbers, causing the prairie to ring all round our campfires. My uncle said that when he marched with Cortez in the Southwest the Spanish called these fellows "coyotes," but he would call them *Canis kinnesonius.* One of these thievish rascals tried to run off with the tube in which I kept my finished paintings, but I scared him into dropping it by firing over his head. I would be many months learning how to capture their sidling, hip-shot gait on canvas.

A few days later, on a knoll at a distance of forty or fifty rods, we spied a horned creature resembling a cross between a large goat and a deer, blotched with white, tan, and black, with horns pronged like a two-tined fork. To my eye it was quite African-looking. My uncle had the same impression, which caused him to conjecture that at one time a great isthmus or land-bridge had stretched from Africa to the Americas, over which the ancestors of this gazelle-like citizen had migrated. For which reason he named it *Africanus kinnesonius.* But when we began to approach, it caught our scent, and ran much faster than even Bucephalus could gallop. This animal, I learned later, was the antelope.

Our idyll was marred by only one small contretemps, an argument over, of all things, a yellow-headed blackbird I'd spotted while off hunting alone on the prairie. When I painted this new bird perched on a tall shaft of grass, my uncle insisted quite vehemently that no self-respecting blackbird would ever sport a yellow head, even in Louisiana, and moreover that no single grass stem could possibly support the weight of a blackbird of any hue. I held my ground, and the conversation grew heated, until what should we see just ahead but exactly such a sight as I had painted, at which my uncle laughed heartily. And so we proceeded with all the good will in the world, two wide-eyed Vermonters at large in this wondrous Eden called Louisiana.

21

THE PRAIRIE GRASS was now beginning to turn yellow. The dawns and evenings were much brisker and a touch of fall was in the slanting afternoon sunlight and in the mist rising like smoke from the river each morning. Our idyll came to an abrupt end one morning when we were scouting along the Missouri for signs of the Teton Sioux, whom we did not wish to come upon by surprise. A dense fog lay over the entire river bottom, and we could see no more than ten or twenty feet ahead. The sopping grasses soaked us to our chests since we had left our mounts behind while we reconnoitered on foot. I hoped that the sun would break through soon and dry us out.

My uncle went ahead, using his wooden sword to push through a dense hedge of wild rose briars. For an hour or more we trudged along in unwonted silence, emerging at last onto a sandy bar piled high with driftwood, from cottonwood trunks to the smallest beaver cuttings. The sandbar extended into a quiet run of water below a bend in the river. Here we stopped to brew a midmorning cup of tea.

"Hark," my uncle said suddenly, looking upriver and pointing his hearing horn in exactly the opposite direction.

I cocked my head. At first I heard nothing. Then, from somewhere up the river, faint and faraway-sounding, came the tinkling sound of a bell, rather like the bell on my uncle's stocking cap.

I jumped up, thinking to shout or fire my piece; but my uncle shook his head, though I noted that he was pouring powder into his arquebus. Floating around the bend came a large timber raft with what appeared to be several makeshift masts. The bell continued to ring softly. Otherwise, all was as still as a Vermont churchyard at midnight.

By now my uncle had his pocket perspective out. The raft momentarily vanished in the fog. As it reappeared, drifting with the current, he said softly, "My Jehovah, Ticonderoga." He handed me the glass, through which I made out a horrifying sight. The masts were not masts at all, but crosses, to which the corpses of several men were nailed. Worse yet, I could see that these poor fellows had been skinned like beavers.

Around their flayed remains was a plague of flies, flies by the millions. Blackbirds and crows and ravens, and rats, too, were making a banquet upon the corpses, which had been lashed to the crosses in a hideous mockery of Our Savior's travail, and then filled with arrows. As this floating charnel house bore down on us, swinging willy-nilly in the current, I perceived, to my further horror, that the tolling bell was fastened on a cord around the neck of a crucified priest, still in his clerical collar. This then was the Thibeau trading party, about whom we had heard in St. Louis; and whether their rivals the Pariseaus had been served the same we could only guess.

In an urgent tone my uncle said, "Quick now, man. Do what I do."

As the raft came slip-sliding down the edge of the current, he plunged into the river up to his waist, directing me to follow. Laying hold of the planks, while the disturbed blackbirds and crows called angrily above our heads and the carrion flies settled all about on our faces, hands, and clothing, we hauled the raft into the slack water on the lee side of the sand spit and made it fast to an uprooted cottonwood at the bottom of the heap of driftwood. We then scrambled up onto the bar, where the dreadful stench caused us both to be violently sick to our stomachs.

My uncle recovered first. Scrambling to the top of the drift-wood, he began flinging branches and logs down onto the raft tethered below. Two of the jury-rigged crosses toppled over. The smell seemed likely to cause me to faint dead away, and the back of my neck prickled with apprehension that at any moment the Teton Sioux would descend on us from out of the fog and fill us full of arrows.

When the raft was entirely covered with driftwood, my uncle struck his flint and steel in some tinder at the foot of the pile. The flames tore up through the jumbled timber until the whole concern was an inferno, from which we retreated up the bank. Snapping tongues and jets of flame shot thirty feet high; and in a very short time, the raft, crosses, driftwood, and sad remains of the men were all gone, leaving only a few charred and smoking planks on the river.

My uncle's plan was to wait for the captains to come up to us — we estimated that they might be a week or two away — and then to report what we had witnessed to them privately in order not to alarm their men. But the next day something occurred to change our minds. After meeting no one except for a few shy river Indians and John Ledyard for three months, we encountered the Pariseau party — fifteen in all — so well loaded with furs that I wondered how they came by them. They were a hard-looking outfit who wanted only rum or whiskey, of which we had none. They claimed not to have encountered either the Thibeaus or the Tetons. But on one of Pariseau's pirogues we noticed a flour barrel stamped with the words "Consigned to R. Thibeau." And old Pariseau himself particularly asked us, with a snag-toothed grin, if we had not seen some sign of the Thibeaus coming down the river. For he had heard that they had been "skinned out of their furs" by the Sioux.

"A large American military party is coming up behind us," my uncle replied, "with the prerogative to exercise martial law over all crimes committed in Louisiana. Do you know of a crime that should be reported?"

"All I know is you'd best watch out for them thieving injuns upriver," the trader growled.

It immediately occurred to both of us that these ruffians might well have murdered the Thibeaus, priest and all, for their furs and made it out to look like the work of savages. Indeed, from the furtive looks of Pariseau's men, I thought this a very real likelihood. Without more proof than the flour barrel, we could do little. But my uncle, quite convinced that they, not the Tetons, were responsible for the massacre, now felt confident in proceeding on up the river. He assured me that we would make a full report of what we had witnessed when we returned to St. Louis.

Now, though, for a strange twist to a strange tale. We learned later that fall that the captains' party never saw a sign of the Pariseaus. The murderers had simply vanished in that vast and mysterious country, where, my uncle and I had no doubt, they had met their just deserts.

22

ONE CLEAR SEPTEMBER MORNING, Bucephalus and Ethan Allen showed signs of disquiet, sawing their bits and tossing their heads as we approached a low hillock, over which there drifted five or six ragged-winged turkey buzzards. Cresting the rise, I stiffened in my saddle. Not ten feet distant a figure lay face down on the prairie. It was an Indian boy, with hair cropped just below his ears, clad only in a buckskin shirt, clout, and moccasins. He had fallen across his lance, but since we saw no wounds or blood, my uncle believed that he had been struck by a rattlesnake, of which we had encountered a great many of late, taking advantage of the sunny autumn weather to wind their way through the grass to their winter dens in the stony bluffs above the river. "Be careful, Ti," he said with a shudder. "I have reason to believe that we are besieged by a squadron of dangerous vipers."

I judged the dead lad to be about my age or a year or so younger. I was trying to summon the courage to dismount for a closer look when out from behind a rock appeared another buzzard. Spotting me, the thing gave a great sideways hop, at which the boy raised his head and stared first at the vulture, then at me, then at my uncle. His eyes were nearly as large and dark as a deer's. And though I could see that he was in great pain, there was a look of defiance on his face that caused me to hesitate a moment longer before I jumped off my horse.

My uncle was at his side immediately. "What have we here, Ti? What strange new adventure awaits us? We must help this lad, even if the dreaded Lord Pluto himself is trying to drag him down into his fiery purlieus."

I now saw that the boy's left arm was trapped beneath him in a cairn of rocks. In the meantime the emboldened buzzard ventured closer, and with astonishing temerity drew back its naked red head as if to drive its beak into the boy while he was yet alive.

"See how the eagle torments poor Prometheus, lying chained to the rock," said my uncle, "whose only offense was to show mankind the use of fire."

"We'll see about that," I said, and reached for my rifle, poured powder into the pan, rammed in a ball, and took aim at the hideous creature. The boy began to chant in a dry voice, continuing as I blasted off the vulture's inflamed head. It struck me that he must have supposed that we had intended to dispatch not the bird — but him. But now my uncle, who still supposed the boy to be Prometheus, shook his fist angrily at the sky and loudly defied Zeus to manifest himself in his own shape, or as a white bull, or a ray of sunlight, or in whatever other guise he chose, and he would fight him to the death; for this was a mean, unworthy use of his omnipotence, and he should know better. "Smite me with your thunderbolts yet again, if you will!" the private shouted to the blue sky — not, perhaps, the wisest invitation, given his unfortunate history with electricity — "Jolt me again and again, but I shall never submit to your will."

"Sir," I cried, "you alarm the boy. Please."

"O Jesu," my uncle exclaimed, and instantly began trying, by many contorted gesticulations, to show the Indian that we meant him no harm. I knelt and helped him drink from my water-bag, which he greedily emptied in several gulps. His body was now turned in such a way that I could see that his left arm was imprisoned all the way up to his shoulder. It occurred to me that he had reached into this fissure, perhaps after a prairie groundhog or a burrowing owl, and by accident wedged his hand between two rocks. My uncle was still of the opinion that he was caught by the jaws of a great serpent sent by Zeus.

At that moment, from the hole in the ground we heard a low growl. Something very much alive had a death grip on the boy's arm. I tugged gently at his shoulder. The creature growled again, and the boy gave a yelp. Then he motioned with his free hand toward the lance lying beneath him. It was made of a dense, heavy wood, with the business end split to admit a flint point. At the other end were several crane feathers. Apparently our young friend had wounded the creature in its den and, supposing it dead, had reached in and been trapped in its jaws. With the aid of the lance tip I was soon able to widen the opening enough to peer by the boy's shoulder and see, deep in the earth, two fiery red eyes. Supposing this to be a bear — though the hole did not seem wide enough to accommodate a very big one — I unsheathed my rifle. But the boy shook his head and motioned again toward the lance.

"This Prometheus is a wise lad as well as a brave one," said my uncle. "He doesn't wish you to shoot his arm by accident, though no doubt" — with a fierce glance upward — "that would please the tyrant who torments him."

Maneuvering the lance gingerly in order not to further injure the arm, I lowered it into the hole, then drove it with all my strength between the glowering eyes. The boy screamed; but the denizen's skull was so adamant that the flint point glanced off it several times before I scored a clean hit and pierced the brain-pan. Even then, it was a great while dying, and the boy was in excruciating pain from the jarring.

When the beast finally expired, my uncle and I enlarged the aperture until I could reach in, disengage its long claws from the rock it had grasped hold of, and draw out the animal, its jaws still fastened to the boy's arm. What I had supposed to be a young bear was a badger. It weighed about twenty pounds and was striped gray and brown, with powerful mandibles and long feet. So strong were its jaws, even in death, that to free the boy I was obliged to wedge them apart with the spear point.

The lad's arm, just above the wrist, was bitten through to the sinews. Though no bones appeared to be broken, he had lost much blood. We cut away his shirt sleeve, and my uncle, who from his many campaigns knew as much medicine as many doctors, cleaned the wound and bandaged it with his spare neckerchief.

But imagine my surprise when, cleaning the blood away

from the Indian's neck and shoulder, I happened to glance down the front of his shirt and glimpse indisputable evidence that he was no boy at all. The young lady hunter, for her part, merely smiled and shrugged.

I helped Little Warrior Woman — for we later discovered that this was her name — onto Bucephalus behind me, and we set out for her village, which she indicated was about one and a half days' ride up the river. Each time I turned around to see if she was all right, she grinned. And though she must have been in great pain, she never uttered a sound. As for my uncle, though he was tremendously impressed by her bravery, he said that soon enough Zeus would try to punish us for interfering with his cruel plan. "When he does, Ti, he will find out that it is one thing to terrorize a defenseless Indian girl, and another matter altogether to fight a New Englander armed with an arquebus."

When we stopped to camp that night, Little Warrior Woman made us understand, through signs and pantomime, that she had come down the river by canoe to hunt alone, when some roving Omahas on horseback fired arrows at her. She escaped by crossing to the opposite side of the river and paddling down with the current for several hours, intending to come back upriver in the easy water under cover of darkness. But just before dusk she sank her canoe on a cottonwood sawyer — whose whipping motion beneath the surface she comically imitated with her good arm — and had to swim to shore with her spear and make her way back afoot. Her arm had been trapped in the badger hole for a day and a night when we'd come across her.

So far from repining over her mishap, Little Warrior Woman busied herself collecting seeds from the purple coneflower and some strips of the moist inner bark of the river willow. These she chewed up with her strong white teeth into a paste, which she applied to her hand and arm with such good effect that the relief seemed instantaneous. My uncle called her another Aesculapius; but thinking of that good healer reminded him of the serpent-headed staff, which he said made his flesh creep. Just at dusk Little Warrior Woman killed a rabbit with her lance, and cooked it for our supper. After which I drifted off to sleep, while my uncle swept his spyglass across the heavens from horizon to horizon, chuckling and exclaiming, and Little Warrior Woman sat nearby with her spear at the ready in case we should be attacked by the Omahas.

23

THE NEXT AFTERNOON, on the west bank of the Missouri, we came into a great village of soaring conical lodges painted red, blue, yellow, and green, covering the plains for a vast distance. Little Warrior Woman had led us straight into the metropolis of the Teton Sioux. Whether they were more astounded by her happy reappearance, having given her up as lost to the Omahas, or by my uncle the knight-errant was impossible to tell.

The men galloped their horses alongside him, yelling to prove their bravery. Women pointed. Boys dashed up and touched him with their riding crops. Several pretended to suppose him the long-awaited reincarnation of their chief's grandfather, a warrior named Black Wolf. The private was enormously gratified by this reception; he wondered if perhaps the noble Sioux might not have heard in advance of his great comedy and were showering laurels upon him, much as the foremost Greek poets were honored at the feast of the Dionysian Apollo.

Little Warrior Woman soon had enough of all this and began to lay about herself with a willow quirt, administering a good smarting cut to anyone who ventured near. At the same time, she directed us to the blue-painted lodge of the headman of the nation. His name was Black Buffalo, and he was Little Warrior's father. When we arrived he was speaking with a fur trader from the British North West Company named Tabor, who told us Little Warrior's name in English and said that from her earliest years she had been a great hunter, tomboy, and daredevil.

When Black Buffalo learned how we had rescued his daughter from a most horrible death on the prairie, he embraced us repeatedly. He carried at all times a war lance decorated with the scalps of forty enemies, but so great was his love for Little Warrior that he wept openly, and named me her elder brother and my uncle her godfather. His two wives, Pretty Elk and Bouncing Deer with a Black Tail, wept, too — Pretty Elk being Little Warrior's mother and Bouncing Deer her aunt. Though very fearsome-looking, these people seemed as affectionate among themselves as my family at home. It was hard for me to imagine them committing such an atrocity as we had witnessed on the death-raft. I was more certain than ever that that outrage was the work of the Pariseau party, causing me to wonder, though in St. Louis we had heard the Teton Sioux referred to as "savages," who the true savages were.

Black Buffalo ordered up a feast consisting of a ragout of venison, elk, antelope, wild goose, and dog. During the meal, Little Warrior refused to leave my side, which embarrassed me and amused my uncle. In token of his gratitude to Bucephalus for carrying his daughter safely back to the village, Black Buffalo brought him, too, into the lodge and gave him some cottonwood sticks, the bark of which was considered by the Sioux to be a great delicacy for horses.

As we ate, my uncle began his lexicon of the Tetons' language by pointing to items and asking their names and writing them down in his day-book, which impressed our hosts very much. Afterward came speeches by the three chiefs of the Tetons — Black Buffalo, the Partisan, and Buffalo Medicine.

Black Buffalo spoke first. With the trader Tabor translating for our benefit, he thanked us for saving his daughter's life, then politely inquired how we had come into their country. Did we fall out of a dark thunderhead? Or fly up out of the earth?

Just so, replied my uncle, and claimed that he had ebony wings, rather ragged at the outer edge like a turkey buzzard's, and had soared out of a gaping cleft (that we had earlier noticed) in the bluff above the mouth of the Teton River. A general clamor broke out among the Indians. Many seemed amazed, but others warned Black Buffalo to beware — that no man could fly, and my uncle must be the greatest impostor in the world.

The Partisan stepped into the firelight, looked all around, nodded sagely, and held up his jingling braceleted arms. Then he drove his lance into the ground and demanded to know where my uncle's wings were. With a very superior smile the private replied that they were folded up neatly beneath his buckskin shirt and chain mail, and that the purpose of the mail was to protect them.

Now Little Warrior Woman, presuming on her status as Black Buffalo's daughter and a warrior herself, sprang up and thrust her lance quivering into the earth next to the Partisan's, proclaiming that when she had first seen us, my uncle was in fact flying in over the prairie at about the height of a mature cottonwood. "And his white mule flew, too," she added with supreme haughtiness. "Though somewhat awkwardly."

I was touched by Little Warrior's loyalty to us. But the Partisan laughed so hard he doubled over.

Stepping into the firelight himself now, my uncle fired up his long clay hemp-pipe, took several puffs, passed it to each of the chiefs in turn, puffed again himself, and handed it round once more.

"What sovereign tobacco is this, brother?" Buffalo Medicine said with a very droll smile. "Where do you grow it and how can we get some?"

"Why, sir," said my uncle, with Tabor translating, "you can grow it along the river or wherever you please" — he refilled the pipe from his stock of crushed leaves and passed it again to the eager chiefs — "but it isn't tobacco. It's hemp. The same fibrous material my lariat is made of. As for procuring it, I'll supply you with one hundred seeds to plant in the spring like corn, each in a little hill with a quantity of horse manure; and if you water it faithfully, and keep away the weeds, it will grow taller than your tallest warrior. In the late summer, when the buffalo gather to migrate, you may harvest enough leaves from this stately vegetable to maintain a sanguine outlook for an entire year, not to mention all the seeds you could ever want and more left over for trading purposes."

"I'll tell you what, old friend," said the Partisan, who was becoming very mellow, "we won't trade the seeds, since once the other tribes have them, they won't need to rely on us. We'll trade the leaves, and hoard up the seeds for ourselves."

"That's a good idea," Black Buffalo said. "I'll volunteer my services to be keeper of the sacred hemp seeds."

"Oh, no you won't," Buffalo Medicine said. "Your two prying wives, Pretty Elk and Bouncing Deer, will get into the stockpile of seeds. We don't want our women using this great medicine. Heaven alone knows what notions it would put in their heads."

Then we repaired to the lodge of Black Buffalo, where Little

Warrior composed herself at the head of my robe. And, it being then very late, I fell asleep almost immediately.

The next morning we breakfasted on the same delicious stew we'd eaten for supper. Afterward my uncle assembled the whole tribe at the center of the village to watch me paint portraits of the chiefs. Out of deference to our host, Black Buffalo, who seemed to enjoy the largest following among the Tetons, I began with him.

I set up my canvas and easel, and although I was very nervous at first, I began by lightly outlining his dimensions with my pencil, then worked carefully on the planes and angles of his face. Soon I was entirely caught up in my work. Painting at my usual swift pace and using only nine colors (I had no more), I was able to catch Black Buffalo tolerably well. Over bare shoulders, he wore a painted robe depicting himself shooting, stabbing, or trampling beneath his horse many of the victims whose hair adorned his lance, which he held upright throughout the sitting, or rather, the standing, since that is how he wished to be painted. The feathers on his war bonnet pointed downward to indicate coups, and his leggings and moccasins were bright with vividly dyed porcupine quills.

The Sioux reacted to their chief's portrait in progress in a number of interesting ways. Some of the women, peeking at it through their fingers, declared that such sorcery made them feel faint. Some of the men glanced at it once, then turned their heads and stalked away, perhaps supposing that if they did not acknowledge the picture it would somehow cease to exist. Despite Black Buffalo's many censorious frowns, Pretty Elk and Bouncing Deer with a Black Tail kept up a running commentary, as they seemed to do on all that transpired in the village. Pretty Elk declared that the portrait was becoming a "fully living being," very probably a twin of their husband. Bouncing

Deer assured her sister that it was most certainly not a twin. Nor, in her estimation, was the portrait fully alive, though she allowed it to contain *some* life. Indeed, she believed that the picture might well outlive their husband, in which case he would never rest easy in his grave. At this notion, both of the good wives, and Little Warrior Woman as well, shrieked with delight.

Next came the sitting of Buffalo Medicine. He had clapped a great bison mask over his face for the occasion. The mouth and eyes were outlined in vermilion; its horns were painted the same color; and dangling from the neck-cape were coyote skins, a badger pelt, and the beaks and heads of various birds of prey. The Partisan, when his turn came, posed wearing only a clout and rabbit-skin leggings, his otherwise naked body painted in circles of yellow, blue, and crimson.

After finishing the headmen's portraits, I spent the remainder of the day with Little Warrior Woman. First we went fishing. Next we played a game whose objective was to throw a ball, using a sort of cradle, through a goal, and involving at least five hundred boys and young men, none of whom could keep pace with Little Warrior. Then she roped a buffalo calf for me to paint, ran down a young elk, and taught a prattling magpie she had tamed to say my name. Also she showed me, by many comical signs, how to get a buffalo's hump closer to right in my pictures by not making it so pronounced.

Little Warrior Woman and I were very happy together for the next several days. At the same time, she teased me mercilessly and constantly, as her mother and aunt did Black Buffalo, and asked me so many questions about Americans that we had to request trader Tabor's offices as a translator. How many wives did we take? What were their duties and prerogatives? She understood why our women were not allowed to participate publicly in the government of the nation; that would have humiliated our men, as the Teton men would certainly have been humiliated by their wives' superior sense had Sioux women been allowed to speak at councils. But surely our women, like theirs, privately told their husbands what to do and say in those meetings? She refused to believe that American women did not make constant fun of their husbands, both behind their backs and to their faces. What kept our men from becoming insufferably self-important?

After supper one evening I informed Little Warrior that it was our intention very soon to go to the great western ocean, a journey of a year or more, and I was quite certain that her doting father would not allow her to accompany us. Therefore, I proposed that she and I renew our acquaintance upon my return.

Renew our acquaintance, she angrily repeated and added that she was surprised I should imagine that she would ever consent to spend one day of her life apart from me; she would deal with her father and, if he proved unyielding, we would elope, since she, too, longed to see the ocean and all the country between here and there; and finally, if my uncle and I wished to have any hope of reaching our destination safely, we would need her to guide us, introduce us to the Indians we came upon, and provide food. In a word, she would be ready to leave when we were.

As Tabor translated, my uncle shot me many significant glances, mouthing the word "shrew" and muttering "Now you see why a certain playwright has eschewed the company of women." But before I could frame a reply to Little Warrior, she laughed, took me by the hand into her lodge, and proposed a flirtatious diversion similar to blindman's bluff, in which first I, then she, would play the blindman and conduct a most thorough search for the other. We had just commenced this entertainment when a tremendous hullabaloo broke out in the village, and my uncle, thrusting his stockinged head into our tepee, announced that Captains Lewis and Clark had arrived with the official expedition.

24

Now THE TETONS naturally supposed that the captains and their men must be traders. Still, many things about the American expedition they could not fathom, including the long keelboat and its cannon, the captains' uniforms, and the medals they passed out engraved with the President's visage. Finally, the Sioux concluded that the newcomers were not of this world but from a different realm altogether, in which conjecture my uncle encouraged them by suggesting that the Americans were from the *red planet Mars* and had come to earth by mistake in their keelboat and pirogues; but that they meant no harm, and he would help the Tetons deal with them. First, however, he was determined to tweak the captains' noses.

"Hear this, sirs," he announced to them, "and tell me what you think." Then, in his booming stage voice, he read the following letter.

The Editor
Washington Gazette

KINNESON PARTY TAKES HUGE EARLY LEAD IN RACE TO THE PACIFIC

Reliable reports from Louisiana and the West have placed the Vermont Kinneson expeditionaries well out in front of the Lewis and Clark party this fall in

*the Great Race to the Ocean Pacific. We have recently
learned that, in order to give their laggard opponents a
chance to catch up, and to help those same feckless
competitors pass safely through the land of the relentless
and treacherous Sioux, the Vermont party has stopped
at the Teton village to wait for the official government
party. It is widely agreed by those who have reason
to know that sporting gentlemen who wagered on
the Lewis party had best be prepared to <u>meet their
obligations</u>. Thus far, the Kinneson expedition has
shown all the advantage of superior speed, experience,
and <u>élan</u>. Further reports may be expected from the
Mandan City, Rocky Mountains, etc.*

After listening to this report with increasing astonishment, the captains looked speechlessly at each other, then at my uncle, who was even now handing the letter to Tabor to be delivered to St. Louis, and from there to be posted to Washington. "What can be the meaning of this strange epistle, sir?" Lewis demanded. "We are engaged in no race, but the most serious of enterprises in the interest of our country."

"Uncle," I said when the captains were out of earshot, "how is it that you dare to make so free with the officers?"

"Why, Ti," he said, "as for that, we would all do better to take ourselves less seriously by one half."

I expressed my concern that it would go hard with the Corps of Discovery, as the captains called their expedition, before they got past the Sioux. For though the Tetons loved to laugh among themselves, and greatly valued my uncle and me for having saved Little Warrior Woman, I was certain they would not let the expedition pass without exacting very heavy tribute.

My uncle rebuked me for needlessly worrying about the future, which, he reminded me, no man could control or predict. "Come, Ti," he said, "let us sing our tooleree, toolera, and not freight our minds with fears of many things that will never be. Life is short, and our way to the Pacific long, and both are fraught with all too many real difficulties for us to manufacture more this morning."

But though my uncle sang (through his nose, most horribly, so that his tooleree sounded more like one of his old Scottish dirges), I did not believe that my anxieties concerning the Sioux were needless fears. And what the captains could do, if the Tetons wished to stop them, I had no idea.

Captain Lewis had planned a council with the Indians for the following morning. I set up my easel near the site of the confab, on the east bank of the Missouri. Lewis harangued the entire tribe for above an hour, addressing them throughout as "children" and enjoining them to make peace with their Indian neighbors and with subsequent American traders. Next, he and Clark did a close-order drill with the men. After that they put on a shooting exhibition with their rifles, which only added to the Tetons' bewilderment when they discovered that not a single firelock was to be traded or bestowed upon them as a gift.

Their disappointment turned to anger when Lewis pronounced Black Buffalo "first chief of the Tetons." This so incensed Black Buffalo's two rivals that when Clark invited them to tour the keelboat, then attempted to send them ashore in the pirogue, they became obstreperous. Buffalo Medicine wrapped himself as tightly about the mast as bound Odysseus, and the Partisan seized the boat's tow-rope. Lewis, still aboard the boat, anchored a hundred yards away, lighted the long taper used to touch off the fuse to the cannon. High above on the bluff, several hundred Teton warriors strung their bows and nocked their arrows. Clark, very flushed in the face, exchanged sharp words with the Partisan, then drew his sword.

At the last possible moment, Black Buffalo intervened and persuaded the Sioux to allow the pirogue to rejoin the mother ship unmolested. But although a catastrophe, which almost certainly would have ended the American expedition altogether, had been narrowly averted, my uncle feared that the crisis had merely been delayed.

Two days later the captains departed. That night, True said, the Tetons planned to hold a council to determine what to do with "the meddling and warlike Martians," and we had best be present so we could alert Lewis to their latest machinations.

Buffalo Medicine spoke first. "These haughty fellows from Mars have forty guns, but they won't trade a single one. I say we must turn them back so that they don't arm our enemies up the river, the Mandans."

"Turning the Martians back is easily enough done," the Partisan replied, "but they may just return with more of their outlandish ilk. My thought is to lay an ambuscade in the narrows of the river north of our village and kill them for their guns and warship. Then we'll raid the Mandans and wipe them off the face of the earth once and for all."

The Partisan's speech was greeted with much acclaim. Black Buffalo, however, was prepared with a countering argument. As for seizing the Martians' guns and exterminating the Mandans, who then would their sons and grandsons fight? Which indeed they must do to prove who among them was bravest and most fit to be a chief. He conceded, however, that it had been most presumptuous for the Martians to designate him as first chief, since that was the business of the Tetons themselves; and, holding up the tricornered uniform hat Captain Lewis had

presented to him, he declared that he now and forevermore re-
nounced the title he had been given, and hurled the hat into
the fire.

There was a stunned pause, then a huge clamor, a swelling
roar that went on and on. But now my uncle stepped forward
with his long clay hemp-pipe, which he passed to each of the
three chiefs in turn. When they were sufficiently primed, he
distributed the one hundred hemp seeds he had earlier promised. After which he advised moderation in dealing with the
Martians, stating that if the Sioux harmed them, far more
would descend from the skies — more than the buffalo of the
plains, and fiercer, too. Adding that, among other depredations,
the Martians would no doubt confiscate all their hemp.

Faced with this prospect, the chiefs reluctantly agreed to allow the captains and their party to continue. But confiding to
me that the pacific effects of the hemp smoke were "as ephem-
eral as the sunny summer days that nurtured the plant to grow
tall and green," my uncle said we must leave to warn the captains that very night.

When Little Warrior and I retired to her father's tepee, I intended to tell her goodbye. In the event, coward that I was, I
could not muster the nerve, and instead asked her in my very
broken Sioux to tell my future, a skill that the Teton women especially prided themselves in. She indicated, by tapping her
head and shaking it, that only a very foolish person wished to
know his fate. To this I responded that I was interested in just
one aspect of it. Drawing a large circle in the dirt by the fire, to
represent the ocean, then making wavelike motions with my
hand and pointing to myself, I made her understand that I
wanted to know whether I would make it through to the
Pacific. This Little Warrior seemed willing enough to divine.
Fetching a small clay bowl of water, she looked several times

from the reflection of the firelight in my eyes to the liquid. Then she sorrowfully nodded yes, I would see the ocean. Which, she suggested by brushlike motions with her hand, I would also paint.

"Why so glum, then?" I asked, making teardrop tracks down her cheeks with my fingertips.

Little Warrior continued to regard me sadly. At last, by pointing first at me, then at the bowl, and nodding, then pointing to herself, then the water, and shaking her head no, she indicated that while she saw *me* at the Pacific, I was there alone, not with her. Then, holding her arms up at a forty-five-degree angle — the Sioux sign for the world — and pointing to herself and again shaking her head, she suggested that soon *she might not exist at all.*

Assuring her that such an unthinkable eventuality would make me the most miserable person alive, I snatched up the bowl of water and threw it outside, then took Little Warrior, now sobbing, into my arms and held her tight, saying the Sioux word for "no" over and over until at last her gasping breathing evened out and she fell asleep.

I waited only until I was sure I would not wake her. Then I rose, fetched my horse, and stole off into the night to join my uncle, who was waiting with his mule just upriver from the village. I told myself that we must leave immediately if we meant to leave at all, yet I knew in my heart that this was only part of the truth. The other part was that I was running away from my dear friend Little Warrior Woman, who would have followed me to the end of the earth.

25

With tears still in my eyes, I rode with my uncle some miles out into the western prairie before we turned north on a shaley ridge that would not hold tracks, figuring that we would cut back to the Missouri after we had shaken any pursuers. By midmorning, however, we could see a thick column of dust rising into the sky no more than ten miles downriver. "Aha," said the private. "Even as the Greeks pursued Paris after the rape of Helen, the Sioux pursue us, Ti. Launching not a thousand ships but a thousand armed riders. The race is on!"

"I'd almost rather have the Greeks and their ships after me, uncle."

"Aye. For that race would make us famous. This may get us scalped." My uncle chuckled and nodded and seemed to take considerable satisfaction in contemplating this terrifying notion.

We urged our mounts forward at a canter; but the tough little ponies of the Tetons could run all day without tiring, and by late morning the dust cloud was much closer. Short of a miracle, our pursuers would overtake us before nightfall.

What to do? While my uncle was even now preparing to take his customary noon observations, I feared that if we could not hit upon some immediate expediency we would be back in the hands of the Sioux within hours.

For his meridian calculations, True selected a level field not far from the river, which had at some time in the past year been under cultivation. Out came his Dutch clock and other instruments, and try though I might, I could not dissuade him from taking our position. While he occupied himself in this way, I passed the time by exploring the nearby prairie. Here and there dry brown cornstalks jutted up, with squash vines running between them. The plants were shorter than ours at home, no more than three feet high. The few ears I found were short as well, only four or five inches long, with dark purple kernels.

But if the corn was strange, just over a low knoll I discovered something stranger still — a completely abandoned city of earthen houses. Excitedly, I called for my uncle, now finished with his astronomical shoot, which placed us just east of Capetown. He wondered if his astrolabe had played him false and we had stumbled instead on the ruins of Old Carthage. With the Sioux bearing down upon us, I did not think we had much leisure to pursue this speculation, but he acted as if we were on an archaeological holiday. Leaving our mounts by a great cairn of colorful river stones, we walked through the streets between the silent houses. Inside many of these earth dwellings, of which there were at least three hundred, we found, to our horror, the remains of entire families. Their desiccated faces had been painted white — the universal custom, in Louisiana, when a tribe was ravaged by smallpox.

This dreadful discovery gave my uncle an idea. Our family having been among the first in Vermont to be inoculated against smallpox, which my uncle had feared we might otherwise contract on our many "voyages and expeditions," we were not concerned that we might fall prey to the plague ourselves. Therefore he declared that we would paint each other's faces and hands white and, securing our mounts inside one of the dwellings, hide up on the roof under a buffalo robe until the Sioux arrived. This we accordingly did, and none too soon, for we had no sooner concealed ourselves on the roof than the Indians appeared.

After going to the river to collect stones, the Tetons — of

whom there were at least four hundred — rode up to the memorial cairn at the edge of the village. Black Buffalo, Buffalo Medicine, and the Partisan leaped off their horses. Like their warriors, the three chiefs were painted in red and black stripes from their faces down over their necks and chests. When they were within a few paces of the cairn and ready to deposit their stones, my uncle sat up suddenly, whispering to me to do the same, and pointed a long white recriminating finger straight at the Indians. Who, to my amazement, fell back in dismay, with many shrieks and cries of lamentation.

The courageous Black Buffalo made a short rallying speech, the gist of which seemed to be that the war party should lay siege to the village from a safe distance and wait for us to come out, for we could not possibly be dead from the pox yet, and this must be some ruse. But as brave as these people were, so strong in their minds was the evil aura of the stricken village that they were already riding off in disarray. Finally, a man wearing a wolf mask and painted as black as night rode to the cairn and shook his lance at us. Lifting his head to the heavens, the blackened warrior let out a war cry more bloodthirsty than all the wolves of Louisiana could muster. He then began to ride around the abandoned village, shaking his lance and howling at the top of his lungs. Finally Black Buffalo and two other men returned and, though he resisted furiously, bore the black warrior off with them to the south.

My uncle and I remained in the village until we were certain that the Indians would not return, then struck out north toward the City of the Mandans. But I was unable to shake off the feeling that we had not seen the last of the Teton Sioux, and that our next encounter with them would not turn out so fortunately.

With the Mandans

26

I RATHER MISDOUBT, TI," said my uncle, "that either of us could have predicted that we would make our entrance into the Mandan City thusly."

"Why, no, sir. I think we could not have."

"In fact," he continued, "I think it very safe to say that not the grim patriarchs of old, not Prophet Elijah himself, nor even the prescient oracle at Delphi, could have forecast how we would come into the City of the Mandans."

Again I concurred, for we were being conveyed toward that city not on the shoulders of heralds, nor on an empurpled buffalo robe, but rather clapped up in a narrow cage of cottonwood poles. A Hidatsa raiding party had crept up to our campsite several nights before, swooped down upon us while we were asleep, and made us their prisoners.

The Hidatsas, who lived just west of the Mandans, at the place where the River of Flint Knives emptied into the Missouri, had been on a summer-long raid to the Rocky Mountains under the leadership of their great fighting chief, Blue Moon. In addition to us and our cage, which was being pulled along on a travois by Bucephalus and Ethan Allen, the raiding party was bringing back several dozen captured Shoshone and Arapaho slaves. Also, to exhibit at the great Mandan harvest fair, they had in cages a mountain lion with a long, switching tail, a wild sheep with massive curling horns, and a bearded wild goat — not to mention Blue Moon's two closest comrades, a full-grown grizzled bear he had raised from a cub and a war eagle with brilliant white and black plumage, which rode alternately on the shaggy back of the bear and on Blue Moon's shoulder.

Though my uncle had learned much of the Hidatsa language during the three days and nights that we had been kept captive in this strange circus caravan, he had not been able to discover what our captors intended to do with us. But as we approached the great Indian city on the bluffs above the Missouri, with the returning raiders shouting and singing, and people running out to see the spoils and wonders brought back from the mountains, he said, "Well, Ti, the little inconvenience of our temporary imprisonment notwithstanding, we have beaten Captain Lewis's party to the Mandans. Now, let us see who spies their city first. We will make a little game of it to pass the time, knowing that we have won the first half of the race with Lewis hands down."

"I offer you my greatest felicitations, sir," I said through rattling teeth. "But isn't our victory in the race rather like that of King Pyrrhus? Who, as you taught me when I was very young, defeated the Roman legions but suffered such heavy losses that his triumph was in name only?"

"Lewis will ransom us when he arrives, Ti. I have no doubt of that. It would look mean and low of him not to, you know, after losing the first half of the race to us. I acknowledge that being dragged into the city in a cottonwood-pole cage is not exactly the arrival I had in mind. But set your mind at rest. Even if we are not ransomed, I have a proposal to place before Blue Moon that will win our freedom and ensure the kindest reception for us with both the Hidatsas and Mandans for the entire winter. Aha! There's the city ahead. I spied it first. You must get up early in the morning to steal a day's march on me."

"Uncle, you seem to relish our situation."

"Say what you will, Ti, it is an interesting way to travel through the countryside."

The trade fair of the Mandans was held on a plain adjacent to the principal town of the metropolis. Here on the prairie overlooking the river, several thousand Indians had gathered for the annual fall market of the upper Missouri. As we were hauled into the center of the fairgrounds along with the catamount, the goat, the sheep, and the other captives, Indians from many tribes pointed and laughed at us. "Sit tight, Ti," my uncle said, as if I had a choice. "Soon we'll be as free as the birds of the air.

"Hail to Private True Teague Kinneson," he roared out at the top of his lungs. "The winner of the first half of the great race to the Pacific greets you."

The people, both the Mandans and their guests, crowded around the cage, and poked and prodded us in the most familiar manner. Some of the warriors fingered my long, light-colored hair and commented to each other in a very unsettling manner. Others seemed to be trying to purchase us.

"Blue Moon," cried my uncle in Hidatsa, or something approximating it. "This is a very shabby way to treat an American soldier who stood at the side of Ethan Allen at the fall of Fort Ticonderoga. I will fight fifty of your greatest warriors, including you and your bear, for our freedom."

"Do you know that with a single swipe this bear of mine can break the neck of a full-grown charging buffalo?" Blue Moon inquired.

"No doubt," said my uncle. "But without wounding you or the good bear or your fifty warriors with arrow, bullet, or blade and without doing lasting harm to any of you, I can rout you all from the field of battle."

At this bold declaration, Blue Moon laughed heartily. Then he spoke to his bear, which also appeared to laugh, as did his war eagle. Nonetheless, the Hidatsa chief could not turn down my uncle's challenge, which had been made very publicly; and the battle was scheduled to take place the following morning at sunrise on the Mandans' ball-playing field adjacent to the fairgrounds. In the meantime, my uncle asked that we be released from the cage on our word of honor that we would not try to escape. His request was granted, and he immediately began to prepare for the next day's engagement.

From a Mandan woman he bought a bison bladder as large as my mother's five-gallon beanpot and a square of buffalo hide with the hair still attached. Along the river he collected some tall bulrushes, and nearby he cut six cottonwood saplings two to three inches in diameter. From a Cheyenne trader he purchased a tanned antelope skin as tough as leather.

The Indians showed great interest in my uncle, with his gleaming copper head plate and chain mail and tall boots and courtly mannerisms. He bowed chivalrously to all the women and offered his hand in a forthright manly fashion to the warriors (who mimicked his gestures exactly, to much laughter), and entertained the children in a hundred little amusing ways, now quacking like a duck, now strutting like a tom-turkey in his belled stocking cap. Everyone was curious about his invention-in-progress, which looked like a featherless dead goose with several headless necks. When I inquired what it might be, he bade me wait and see — he believed I would be as surprised as the Indians by his ingenuity.

At dawn the next morning, at one end of the ball-playing field, my uncle positioned himself on Ethan Allen like a knight of yore preparing to enter the lists. Just at sunrise, with his invention in his arms, he commenced down the field at a slow and stately pace. At the opposite end, Blue Moon, on his warhorse, proceeded toward him at a walk, accompanied by fifty warriors on one flank and the grizzled bear on the other, with the eagle hovering about a hundred feet overhead, its white plumage sparkling in the sunrise. I attended on Bucephalus a few paces behind True, more terrified than I had ever been in my life, even during our encounters with the murderous Harpe brothers and the war party of the Teton Sioux.

Blue Moon nocked an arrow. "That good chokecherry shaft has my name on it, Ti," my uncle observed. "But never fear. We will live to use it as a toothpick. See the troops arrayed against us like the Persian cavalry facing Alexander!"

With this encouraging observation, he affixed the large end of his tin ear trumpet to his invention, raised the small end of the trumpet to his lips, and gave a long blast, at the same time compressing the buffalo bladder with a powerful squeeze and filling the prairie for miles around with the most hideous screeching squeal ever produced by the breath of mortal man. Rising in crescendo to an unbearable pitch, the screeling echoed and re-echoed off the sides of the slopes above the field, the waves of sound emanating outward met by the waves bouncing back, creating an unbearable field of pure horrible NOISE. Blue Moon and his men and all of the spectators dropped whatever they were holding and clasped their hands over their ears, so that the entire assemblage of Indians looked like my poor father, replicated a thousand times.

I had earlier, at my uncle's insistence, stuffed my own ears, and those of Bucephalus, with soft dried grass, after the fashion of Odysseus's men stopping their ears with wool so that only he would hear the Sirens' seductive strains. Even so, Bucephalus reared. The charging bear whirled twice, like a dog chasing its tail, and shot off toward the river. The eagle pulled out of its dive and veered away. But my uncle, on his deaf mule, continued into the very teeth of his enemies, blowing and squeezing and squeezing and blowing upon his homemade bagpipe for all he was worth.

To his credit, Blue Moon stood his ground — expecting, he later told us, to be swooped away at any moment by the thousand invisible shrieking banshees loosed by the pipes. But as the knight-errant drew near the stricken chief, in a gesture of magnanimity that he later said would no doubt be talked of on the upper Missouri for centuries to come, he left off his dreadful medley and, lifting over his head the rush strap by which the bagpipe hung from his neck, presented the instrument to his adversary. "Compliments of Private True Teague Kinneson, sir," he told the deafened chief. "Expeditionary, playwright, lexicographer, and piper through and through." The field was silent for a moment. Then, at this unprecedented act of graciousness, wave upon wave of roaring applause went up from the spectators, equally honoring the great Blue Moon and my uncle.

Later that day, the victorious piper instructed me to paint, in large red letters on a tanned buffalo hide, the message "Welcome to the Lewis and Clark Expedition from Private True Teague Kinneson, First to Reach the City of the Mandans, October 1804." But just as we finished hanging this rather boastful banner between the upper branches of two soaring cottonwoods on a bluff overlooking the Missouri, where the explorers would be sure to see it as they approached the community, an emissary from the Indian village came running with a most unexpected report. Blue Moon's war eagle, having apparently conceived a most violent romantic passion for the bagpipe, had swooped down upon his master and plucked the instrument out of his hands before the chief had any inkling of what was happening. The smitten bird of prey had carried it off to a tree-top, and he refused to let anyone, even the astonished Blue Moon, come near, lest his new inamorata be disturbed on her nest.

"Ah," said my uncle with his hand on his heart, "so great, Ti, is the power of love." And he liked the sound of this sentiment so much that, this time with a tear in his eyes, he said again, "So great is the power of love."

27

November 15, 1804
Charles and Helen Kinneson
Kingdom Common, Vermont, United States of America

Dear Father and Mother,
I write to you from the Mandan Indian villages some 1,800 miles, as the river winds, above St. Louis, to report that uncle and I are both in excellent health and progressing rapidly toward the Pacific Ocean. After an interval with the Teton Sioux, we forged ahead of the official expedition (with whom uncle supposes he is engaged in a race) and arrived here at the Mandans' well before them, in a manner I will describe to you in detail upon our return.

The Mandan and Hidatsa Indians, among whom we intend to spend the winter before resuming our journey in the spring, have been very little corrupted by outside influence, and their original society has remained almost perfectly intact. They dwell in a large metropolis — considerably larger than St. Louis or Washington — consisting of five villages strung out along the upper Missouri, each made up of several hundred circular earth lodges. The headman of one of these towns, Black Cat, has kindly invited uncle and me to stay with him and his family. Captain Lewis's expedition, when at last it arrived, built a fort upriver.

I miss you both very much, and also Vermont; yet each day here brings something new; and uncle says I am progressing as an artist by leaps and bounds and that "Louisiana is my Oxford and he my Scholia Aristotle." I hope to post this letter, of which I will keep a copy, in the spring when Corporal Warfington will return to St. Louis in the expedition's big keelboat. Captain Lewis and Captain Clark, with the main party, will continue to the Rocky Mountains in their pirogues and canoes, and uncle and I by horse- and mule-back.

Though the captains and their soldiers seem to be very fine men, uncle refuses to hold much commerce with them because of his belief that he, not Lewis, should have been selected to lead the official expedition. Nor, frankly, do they seem to know quite what to make of us. Perhaps we will become better acquainted over the

winter. I will try to write again before we leave, and
much look forward to that happy time in a year, two at
most, when you will once again see, in our beautiful
Green Mountains, your taller, browner, stronger, but
ever-faithful and loving son,

Ticonderoga

28

SINCE OUR ARRIVAL at the Mandans, I had painted many
of the principal men of the tribe, including their two main
chiefs, Big White and Black Cat. On the afternoon of Black
Cat's sitting, I noticed, loitering near the door of my lodge, a
tall, well-set-up, finely dressed young man, whose name in Indian sounded something like Fra-hank-a-line. I had seen Fra-
hank-a-line rouging his face and associating with the Mandan
womenfolk, and therefore supposed him to be one of the "exquisites" of the tribe — the Indians' designation for a species of
dandy-men, who dwelt together in a lodge designed for their
use alone, where they spent all day primping and preening and
fixing their ground-length hair. But I had also noticed that, unlike his painted brethren, this gentleman carried a war lance
and a bow four feet long and as white as ivory. Upon inquiring,
I learned that in addition to being a warrior of renown, Fra-
hank-a-line was also a famous Indian artist, whose stick figures
painted on tepee covers, depicting the exploits of various chiefs
and medicine men, were greatly in demand.

Finishing with the Cat, I invited Fra-hank-a-line into my painting room and began to sketch out his features. He stood for his portrait, the better to show off his hair, which was adorned with tufts of sweetgrass and bright feathers set at a swank angle, and so long that it swept the ground when he walked. I was quite delighted to have an opportunity to paint this tinseled fellow. He carried a fly-brush fashioned from a buffalo's tail, a fan of turkey feathers, and a medicine bag made of coyote skin, in which he kept all kinds of hoca-poca appurtenances — birds' feet, snakes' rattles, odd-shaped river stones, feathers, bear claws, and what have you — that the Indians believed protected them or gave them power.

Fra-hank-a-line, who was perhaps ten years my elder, had upon his painted face an expression of superior complacency and general satisfaction, as well as a knowing, amused gleam in his eyes, which were as blue as my own. He watched me paint for a while, then suddenly called out, in excellent English, "Come, sir. Have the goodness to swing your easel about and show me your efforts, that I may judge of their merits for myself."

I nearly dropped my brush and palette. When I showed Fra-hank-a-line the portrait, he tilted his head, closed one eye, and said in the assured manner of a seasoned man of the art world, "You could benefit from a few months with our great Indian painters, Ticonderoga. While I don't presume to detract from the energy of your work, it has no sense of telling a story or preserving history. Which, after all, is the *raison d'être* for all painting."

Again, I was speechless to hear an Indian, albeit a blue-eyed one, speak my native tongue so eloquently. Fra-hank-a-line proceeded to explain that he was the son of a Blackfoot chief's daughter and a North West Company factor. He and his younger sister had been orphaned as children when, visiting Fort Mackenzie, his parents had contracted diphtheria. The fur company had sent them to school at Sault Ste. Marie, where it became evident that he was something of a savant, and his sister as well. The girl had returned to their ancestral home in the Rocky Mountains several years earlier. Fra-hank-a-line was now on his way to visit her. He had gotten as far as the Mandan village this fall, and planned to proceed up the Missouri and then north to her village in the Land of the Glaciers, deep in the Rocky Mountains, in the spring.

As I painted, Franklin — for this was his name in English — continued to lecture me on my craft. I could scarcely wait to introduce him to my uncle, but just as I finished his portrait, a terrific din of whooping, yelping, and drum-beating broke out. I was certain that the Teton Sioux were attacking. As I seized my rifle, the clamor was augmented by such a bellowing and stamping that I supposed our enemies to be funneling a whole herd of buffalo through the village, with the design of trampling us to death.

Franklin, smiling at my panic, informed me that the annual dance to lure the bison had begun. He urged me to accompany him to the center of the village, where the entire population of men was gathered, as well as many women and children, well wrapped in buffalo robes against the piercing cold. In front of the great medicine lodge a dozen or so men painted with buffalo tallow mixed with soot and wearing masks made from skinned buffalo heads with the horns still attached were dancing in a tight circle. Nearby, with a pair of buffalo horns on his head, my uncle was supervising this quadrille, exhorting his pupils in the most amusing capers, parodying the feeding, watering, voiding, and mating of the buffalo. From time to time the old schoolmaster joined in the figure himself, in a kind of prancing shuffle, to demonstrate the proper execution of the steps. I was so distracted by True's ribald antics in the incarnation of a bison in rut that I could scarcely concentrate for laughing. Had there been any buffalo within fifty miles of us, they would certainly have heard this concert in their honor, though whether they would have ventured closer seemed doubtful. Franklin assured me, however, that the dance never failed to be effective. Explaining that perhaps this was because the ceremony always continued until a herd of these animals chanced by, whether this took two days, two weeks, two months, or until half the village died of starvation.

The savant then called my attention to some men standing on distant bluffs and eminences of the snow-covered prairie, whose task was to "throw their robes" — that is, to wave their blankets in the air to signal the arrival of any animals summoned by the dance. As I sketched on into the icy afternoon, the dancers wearied. When a man became too fatigued to continue, he would bend far forward, a signal for his fellows to shoot him with blunt arrows, at which he fell as if mortally wounded, instantly to be replaced by a fresh dancer. Onlookers brandishing knives then dragged the fallen man out of the circle by his heels and pretended, with a series of menacing cuts in the air, to butcher him as they would a buffalo.

This ritual continued uninterrupted for several days and nights, during which it was nearly impossible to sleep because of the din. By this time the village's meat supply was entirely exhausted. On the fifth morning, while I was sequestered in Black Cat's lodge at work on my painting of the dance, every woman in the village began to scream. I ran outside, brush in hand, to see them pointing at a parti-colored creature racing pell-mell on all fours toward the town from the west. When it stood up on its hind legs and looked around, as if scenting the air for danger, I saw that it was a man wearing horns and nothing else but the briefest clout about his loins. He was all striped in circular green, crimson, and saffron patterns, with dripping red fangs painted on his face. Franklin told me that the ladies were screaming that the Evil One, in the person of his provincial governor, Lord Phallus, was attacking the village, bent on perpetrating a rape upon them to people the region with more of his horned kind. Indeed, such seemed to be the case, for before him, as he rushed onward, Lord Phallus pushed a long blue stick with a flaming red ball at the end, resembling a grotesque, oversized buffalo member. Yet the women did not retreat from this monster. Instead, as he galloped into the village, they screeched with laughter and taunted and teased him with such unmistakable gesticulations that he soon attained a veritable frenzy of lust.

Now forth from the medicine lodge, to a huge roar, came the old Mandan conjuror Hawk Talons, bearing a long pipe, which he passed twice or thrice in front of the creature wheeling the phallus, putting him into a trance. Upon which the women, still laughing, seized the mobile organ, broke it into a dozen pieces, and threw it onto the fire; and the would-be ravisher was jeered out of the village in ignominy. But as he reached the outskirts of town he suddenly turned and whipped off his buffalo horns, revealing to the throng not the Devil but the good, honest visage of my uncle himself. To thunderous applause, the triumphant thespian was borne back into the center of the village on the shoulders of four young warriors, all the time donning and doffing his buffalo horns to the cheering onlookers, and calling out to Franklin and me that he had "violated none of Scholia Aristotle's unities, nay, not a one, in my little morality play."

But no sooner had Chief Black Cat conferred the title of

Great Conjuror upon our Vermont author-actor-lexicographer, investing him with a trailing bonnet decorated not with eagle feathers but with those of crows, vultures, and magpies, than the chanting dancers and drummers, who had kept up their work throughout the charade, were drowned out by a great cry of joy from the villagers. Everyone was pointing off to the north, where, on a swell in the prairie a mile away, a spotter was waving his robe over his head to signify the arrival of the buffalo.

The famine was over.

29

UNDER THE DIRECTION of Black Cat's son, the Otter, twenty of the village's best buffalo hunters went out to scout the location and size of the herd and to kill enough animals to relieve the villagers' immediate distress. I was invited to join this group, on Bucephalus. As we thundered past the excited spotter, still flapping his robe, he pointed toward a low ridge. On it we could make out half a dozen shaggy bison — the vanguard, everyone hoped, of a large migrating herd.

The best approach to these animals was through a narrow defile on a well-beaten trail used by northbound Mandan hunters for many years. But as we entered this gully, still about four hundred yards from the bison, they disappeared below the ridge top. The Otter reined in his pony and threw up his hand for us to stop. Herding buffalo were usually not so shy; moreover, we were coming at them from downwind. With a puzzled expression, he turned to Chief Big White's son, Turkey Man.

The Otter and Turkey Man seemed to be considering splitting our party or selecting another angle of approach. But after exchanging opinions, they merely shrugged and urged their ponies forward into the gully. I put my heels to Bucephalus, who was neck and neck with the Otter's spotted pony, there being just sufficient room between the walls of the ravine to admit two horses running side by side. Suddenly, at least forty yelling Sioux, bedaubed from head to toe in red and black war paint, all screaming like demons, broke out of a little side draw and galloped down upon us with their painted warhorses under full whip. At the same time, the grazing buffalo reappeared on top of the ridge, only to stand up on their hind legs, cast off their robes, and transform themselves into more armed Sioux, who began tossing a deadly volley of arrows down upon us. Masquerading as bison drawn by the buffalo dance, our enemies had lured us into a death trap.

Outnumbered two or three to one, we wheeled our horses and started back the way we'd come. From a gulch between us and the open prairie there burst forth yet another war party, cutting off escape. Arrows flew at us from all directions. I could hear them whizzing through the frigid air around my head and making a horrible ripping noise as they tore through the bodies of my companions and their horses, who were falling all around me.

It was my Mandan friends who saved my skin, though at a dreadful price to themselves. Wherever a man fell, several Sioux leaped off their horses to compete for his scalp, thereby allowing Bucephalus and me, by a stroke of sheer good fortune, to escape from the melee. I had nearly reached the mouth of the ravine when out from behind a swell in the prairie came a coal-black, wolf-masked warrior, whom I recognized as the rider who had circled the ghost village where my uncle and I had forted up earlier in the fall. Mounted on a pure black horse and carrying a black shield with a white wolf skull painted on it, he brandished a black lance decorated with red cranes' feathers. The black rider bore down on me as I galloped full tilt toward him. He drew back his lance arm. I raised my rifle and, at the exact moment that he released the lance, I fired. His weapon creased the left side of my head. But Black Wolf fell dead from his horse with a bullet through his heart.

To this day I do not know why I reined in Bucephalus and looked over my shoulder. Behind me the other Sioux were either rounding up the horses of my Mandan friends or working at their grisly task with their scalping knives, encrimsoning the new snow with the blood of their victims. As I beheld this slaughter, the Partisan's nephew, Blue Goose, ran up to the Otter, who was sprawled out with his legs trapped under his fallen pony. He lifted his victim's head by the hair and cut his throat, afterward taking his scalp in the same circular motion. Enraged, I leaped off Bucephalus, grasped the dead Black Wolf by his mask, ripped it off, and, pulling out my knife, served him the same. I was stunned by my own capacity for barbarism. I was more stunned still, upon looking down at the dead warrior's features, to discover that he was not a man at all. To my horror, I had shot, killed, and scalped Little Warrior Woman.

30

THE BISON APPEARED, of their own accord, a few days later. But for the rest of the winter of 1804–5, I didn't care whether I lived or died. I stayed in Black Cat's lodge day and night, but from the middle of December through February I did not paint a single picture. I spoke rarely and ate next to nothing. When my uncle tried to counsel me, I turned my face to the earthen wall of the lodge. I slept or lay in a stupor for eighteen or twenty hours out of every twenty-four. Later it was reported to me that for several days after the battle with the Sioux I refused to allow Little Warrior's body to be removed from my presence, hugging her close and speaking to her tenderly, until the natural processes made it necessary that she be taken away and placed on a burial scaffold on the edge of the village. After that I visited her frozen remains two or three times a day, standing in the fierce prairie wind until I nearly froze myself.

My uncle continued to exhort me not to give in to my grief, adducing a hundred instances from the classics in which despair had destroyed promising young men, from Hector to Hamlet. He allowed that he, too, had once experienced low spirits for a few minutes, when he first regained consciousness after striking his head at Fort Ti — but, recollecting that despair was a deadly and pernicious sin, he marshaled his will and proceeded with his life, though admittedly on a somewhat different plane.

Captain Lewis, learning of my misfortune, came down from Fort Mandan and tried to physic me with some all-purpose purgatives known as Rush's evacuation pills or "thunder-clappers" — bullet-sized boluses of calomel, chlorine, mercury, and jalap. But they did no more good for me than they had for poor Sergeant Floyd, who had died of a raging stomach colic the previous summer. Captain Clark, too, came by several times. He told me, with real feeling, that he was heartily sorry for the fate of Little Warrior, but that I must not blame myself, for I had no way to know her, all sooty and with a wolf's mask; and what sort of trick was it to try to murder a young blade for taking French leave when no lasting harm had been done? Clark told me a tale that I no doubt would have found most amusing under other circumstances. It seemed, he confided, that in the guise of an "exquisite" my elegant Blackfoot friend Franklin had been regularly visiting the Mandan ladies' societies to offer them his services not as a seamster or chef but rather a bedfellow, disporting himself with half a dozen different women each night. But even this revelation did not bring a smile to my face.

One February day Franklin himself appeared in my lodge in all his finery. "Ticonderoga," he announced, "there is a pretty sure cure for your sickness if you dare take it."

I turned away from him.

"Screw up your courage, lad," he declared. "The one remedy that our Mandan friends guarantee is the Okeepa. Get up on your hind legs and come along with me. You have my word: the Okeepa will cure you or kill you."

31

As I entered the village medicine lodge, to a roar of acclaim from the men, women, and children who had gathered in the public square to see the American undergo the Okeepa, I could not guess what awaited me. I had brought Little Warrior's wolf mask and, at Franklin's suggestion, my paintbrush and easel. The acrid odors of earth and peeled cottonwood poles filled the lodge.

When my eyes adjusted to the dimness, I saw Black Cat and Big White — both still grieving for their sons killed by the Sioux raiders — and eight or ten other headmen, sitting against willow back-rests on one side of the central fire. My uncle and Franklin seated themselves with the chiefs, while two men in bear masks conducted me to a cleared area in the center of the lodge, just opposite the dignitaries. Eight rawhide ropes dangled from a round hole in the ceiling twenty feet above me. My guides now placed me in the midst of these cords so that they brushed my shoulders and legs. Was I to be hoisted up and slowly roasted over the fire? Weakened from my prolonged fast and lack of exercise, I thought I might faint dead away on the spot.

Ranged in a rough semi-circle to my left were what I first mistook for four gigantic tortoises with eagle feathers attached to their shells. In fact, these were drums constructed from the tough neck skin of buffaloes — filled, I was later told, with "the first water created on earth." At each of these instruments sat a drummer. By my feet lay several splints of tough wood about six inches long and an inch in diameter. Beside them was a jagged flintstone knife.

My two conductors began to chant in unison, the words unintelligible to me and somewhat muffled behind their bear masks. Suddenly one of them bent over, seized the flint knife, and with three or four swift motions cut my buckskin clothing off my body. As I stood naked, holding my brush and easel in one hand and Little Warrior's wolf mask in the other, the conjuror proceeded to seize an inch or so of loose skin on each side of my chest just below the shoulder, and thrust first the jagged knife, then a wooden skewer, through my flesh in the most excruciating manner, while his associate affixed the ends of the dangling cords to these pieces of wood.

I was later told that the young Mandan braves who underwent this torture bore the knife and skewers with the utmost serenity, smiling at their tormentors and thanking them in the most gracious terms. Not Ticonderoga Kinneson. I howled like a lynx at bay, and would have bolted out of the lodge at the first haggling cut had not six assistants to the medicine men held me fast.

Now the surgeon wielding the knife began to hack into the skin at the backs of my thighs, calves, and upper arms and to ram through these apertures more splints. To these he attached, by short thongs, a buffalo skull, an elk antler, a freshly killed beaver, and two or three medicine bags crammed with sacred plants, stones, and amulets. Franklin, on our way into the medicine lodge, had assured me that the apprehension of the Okeepa was far worse than any actual pain I would experience. But as with so many fine-sounding sentiments, the exact opposite turned out to be true. Nothing I had ever experienced compared to the anguish of the butchery visited upon me by this quack and his accomplices.

I screamed bloody murder. But the professional percussionists at the tortoise-drums — all deaf from years of being subjected to their own music — beat their ancient instruments the louder, drowning out my wailing. This seemed to be the signal for several men on the roof to haul on the ropes attached to the splints through my shoulders and chest, raising me a foot or so off the floor. With the ponderous buffalo skull and other ceremonial paraphernalia dangling from the splints in my arms and legs, I was a bundle of pain.

Just when I supposed that the pangs of this dreadful crucifixion could grow no greater, two medicine men began to turn me with long poles — spinning me back and forth in ever-faster arcs. I could feel the flesh of my arms and legs tearing with the weight of the sacred objects. And all the time the drummers beat louder and louder.

Several times I lost consciousness and was dropped to the floor, revived with a dash of icy river water, and hauled up again. Once I supposed I was at home in Vermont, with my father inquiring how I could keep track of my uncle while depending from the smoky ceiling of a Mandan lodge like a fly in a web. In another hallucination, my uncle, dressed in a long flowing robe like Abraham about to slay poor Isaac, addressed the Mandans as follows. "My friends, I so love Louisiana and its people that I have given you my only begotten nephew, Ticonderoga Kinneson, to pierce with cottonwood splints, and hang up, and murder."

As the day wore on, I begged my Mandan sponsors for a little drinking water. But like Job's false encouragers, they said that if I could bear up under my extremity until sunset, they would take me down and pronounce me "Great Physician." Then I would go forth knowing that, having endured the Okeepa, I could survive any other torment, be it heat, cold, hunger, illness, mistreatment at the hand of man, or my own artistic inadequacies. When I began to pass out once again, my uncle jumped up and, with tears starting from his eyes, rushed forward, knife drawn, shouting, "Gentlemen, enough." But before he could cut me down, the six big hearties who had earlier held me fast for their physician's ministrations seized him and put him out of the lodge. A few minutes later the sun set, and, to another great roar from the villagers waiting outside, the medicine men severed the cords and withdrew the splints.

My torment was not yet over, though. As soon as I was able to stagger out of the lodge, with the buffalo skull and other weights still hanging from the torn and bleeding flesh of my arms and legs, the medicine men bound my wrists together with a rawhide strap and began to drag me all through the village, with the skull, amulet bags, elk antler, and dead beaver thumping along the frozen ground beside me. This sprint was called "the last race." Finally, one by one, the weights dropped off as the strips of skin to which they were attached tore free. When I shed the last of them I was simply left in the middle of the village, to recover or not, as the Great Spirit deemed best. But Franklin and my uncle carried me tenderly back to Black Cat's lodge and washed and bound my wounds, and said that I had come through my trial with flying colors. When I next awoke I found myself still clinging to my brush and easel, which I had never dropped throughout the entire travail, though Little Warrior's wolf mask had fallen from my hand just before I was lowered to the ground at sunset.

32

I HAD LAIN in a swoon for two days and nights, during which time a steady procession of Indians came to ogle the first American to undergo the Okeepa. My uncle was at my side the whole time, feeding me buffalo-marrow broth, tending my wounds, and encouraging me not to give up the ghost. But my first clear thought when I regained my senses was that Little Warrior was still dead.

Over the next month or so I engaged in a prolonged debauch — gambling with the Indians, swilling a highly intoxicating beverage concocted by the enterprising Field brothers the previous fall from dried chokecherries and buffalo berries, and consorting with a jolly, plump Mandan widow of about thirty who taught me many of the ways of her people and, not to put too fine a point on it, the ways of the world as well. Suffice it to say that she was very willing to be my mentor (and not in the way of Scholia Scholasticus!), and I her pupil.

My uncle finally had to take my paintings away to keep me from staking them in wagers. What I most regret about that time, however, is the missed opportunities to paint priceless scenes of the Mandans and to record, as well, the winter activities of Lewis's party. In February alone, the men worked nearly three weeks trying to cut the keelboat out of the river ice, where it had frozen solid; Captain Lewis assisted the trader Charbonneau's young Shoshone wife, Sacagawea, in a long hard labor with her first child, by crushing the rattles of a serpent into a powder, which he then administered to her in a potion to hasten the delivery; and blacksmith John Shields saved everyone from starvation by manufacturing battle-axes from the sheet metal of an old stove and trading these weapons to the Mandans for corn and beans.

At last I did a portrait of myself strung up in the medicine lodge, enduring the Okeepa. That was my first picture since the fall, and it seemed to bring me out of my downward spiral. Even Franklin agreed that this painting was a step in the right direction because, like his pictures, it told a story.

Throughout this time my uncle remained as busy as a honeybee in a Vermont hollyhock. He helped the men of the expedition, half of whom were illiterate, write letters to be sent home in the spring with Corporal Warfington. He set up a grammar school for the Mandans, teaching them simple English words and a bit of Latin and Greek "for their souls." In the evenings he gave fiery lectures on ancient history and the classics to anyone who would listen. He put on his comedy several times, and even took a touring troupe of Indian actors upriver to Blue Moon's village, where they performed *Ethan Allen* to an enthusiastic audience of Hidatsas.

Spring was coming on apace. The river was breaking up in

great plates and cakes of ice, and drowned buffalo carcasses by the hundreds clogged the open current. Willow buds were swelling. The prairie breezes smelled of thawing earth and fresh shoots of green grass.

With the arrival of warmer weather, the Mandans' official rainmaker put it into the gossip mill that a great and sudden flood was about to descend upon the land, drowning out all those who did not believe in his meteorological powers. But if his followers would clamber up onto the roofs of their earthen lodges, there to wait out the deluge, they would certainly be spared. On the morning of the predicted cataclysm — which dawned clear as a bell — Rainmaker and a handful of his fellow believers ascended to the tops of their houses, and the magician beat a large drum all day long in the bright sunshine, with no other result than to provoke the laughter of the villagers. About dark they were pelted down off their roofs with clods of dried buffalo dung. Much disappointed that the watery retribution had not been sent, Rainmaker put the best face on the matter by assuring the town that he had *fended off* the catastrophic flood by his mummery, for which service the people owed him a great debt of gratitude. The Mandans were about equally divided in their opinion of this miracle.

One afternoon a few days later a deranged-appearing Cheyenne staggered into the village. He said that while he was away from home hunting buffalo, he learned that his village had been burned and his family slaughtered by a great war party of whites and Indians. Although he had not seen these marauders himself, he believed they were under the direction of a Spaniard from Santa Fe and were now headed north to intercept and destroy another party of whites on their way to the great sea-ocean; furthermore, this Force of Terror, which numbered over three hundred, was annihilating all the Indian towns in its path.

After interviewing the Cheyenne through Black Cat, my uncle immediately conducted him to Fort Mandan, where, with the Cat assisting, he had him repeat his story to Captain Lewis (Clark being off with a contingent of carpenters hewing out cottonwood canoes to accompany the pirogues upriver). Lewis felt great pity for the Cheyenne, but in the end dismissed his tale as an extravagancy of grief and madness or, possibly, a rumor planted by the Spanish to stop the American expedition in its tracks. The next morning the Indian did away with himself by leaping off a high bluff into the swollen river.

On the afternoon of the Cheyenne's suicide, True said that he and I had some business to discuss. We rode out over the greening prairie together, stopping about a mile west of the Mandan village on an eminence from which we could see a great way up the winding river. "Ticonderoga," the private announced, "I must and will go on to become the first explorer to travel overland to the Pacific. I intend to discover or — ha ha — *rediscover* the Northwest Passage. Our little jaunt up the Missouri thus far has only whetted my appetite. Friend Franklin has agreed to accompany me. But you are nearly seventeen and man-grown. You must make your own decision."

Looking far up the river at the unknown land ahead, I hesitated. "Uncle, tell me. Is there any real reason to believe that we can reach the Pacific? Much less get there before Lewis and his expedition?"

"Reason, Ti? Why, yes. There is every reason in the world to believe so. But in the end, it is not reason that will see us through but our imaginations. Lookee, lad. What faculty was it that inspired Tom Jefferson and Lewis to launch their expedition in the first place? It was the imagination. They *imagined* what might be here in the West — the scientific wonders, the many splendid Indian nations, their 'practicable waterway' to the Pacific. The President *imagined* the benefit of this place called Louisiana to the United States, and Lewis *imagined* that, by dint of diligence and the ability to anticipate in advance the needs of his expedition, he could get through to the ocean. I imagined the same — and to get there first, and to fish in every fine river along the way to boot. Nay, Ti. The greatest achievements in the history of the world have all sprung from the imagination. Think of the adventures of Odysseus, Aeneas, and King Arthur, not to mention the great Don from La Mancha."

I still had my doubts, the more so since all the figures my uncle saw fit to cite were themselves creations of the imagination. But as the great knight-errant stood on the promontory, shading his brow with one hand and pointing west with the other, his eyes gleaming with anticipation of whatever great adventures lay ahead, I knew that I could never abandon him, nor did I wish to.

"Uncle, I'll give you my decision this instant. Where you and your wonderful imagination go, there go I. Here is my hand on it."

As the good man seized my hand, tears sprang to his eyes. "It is what I hoped you'd say, Ti. And believe me, the larks we have had thus far — although not altogether insignificant — will pale before those to come. Oh, nephew — the all-puissant Blackfeet, the impenetrable Rockies, the raging Columbia. Excelsior!"

On the day before the captains' expedition was scheduled to embark, Blue Moon planned to head out with a hunting party of twenty men for the Little Missouri River, which entered the Missouri proper about ninety miles above the Mandan and Hidatsa villages. His design was to press up the tributary to a bluff known as Buffalo Jump, and there, by setting the prairie on fire and creating a stampede, to drive the migrating bison over the brink of the cliff to their destruction on the rocky riverbank below. Their women, who would follow on the river with round little "bull boats" made from buffalo skins stretched over willow frames, would butcher the animals and take the meat back to their village. Our plan was to accompany Blue Moon's hunting party to Buffalo Jump, then strike out overland, reconnecting with the Missouri near the mouth of the River of Yellow Stones, which was the farthest west any white trader had ever penetrated up the river.

Accordingly, early in April, my uncle on his white mule, I on Bucephalus, and Franklin on his Indian pony rode out of the Knife River village with the Hidatsas, leaving behind the scene of the saddest season of my life, in a place I will always think of as the burial ground of my dear Little Warrior Woman.

The Force of Terror

33

LIKE NIGHTFALL and dawn, full spring on the prairie comes of a sudden, with a rush of warm wind, a drenching rain, emerald grass, and thawed potholes full of waterfowl. As our party of three headed west with Blue Moon, his bear and eagle, and the Hidatsa warriors, we encountered buffalo, elk, deer, and antelope everywhere. The songbirds were back, too — western larks and blackbirds, a bluebird closely resembling ours in New England, only with softer azure wings, and the bright cock robins that always precede the females of their tribe north, which made me lonesome for Vermont all over again. On our second day out I paused to do a miniature watercolor of a Canada goose nesting in a cottonwood — the only instance of a goose in a tree I had ever seen. I believe it used the former home of a fishing hawk.

Traveling with the Hidatsas, I was struck once again by how much more distance we could cover on horseback than the captains' party ever made paddling their cumbersome canoes against the Missouri's endless boiling current. The Indians pushed their ponies hard, and early in the morning of the third day, we swung up the valley of the Little Missouri.

Soon the river canyon narrowed and the air grew hazy, inspiring Franklin to name the place Portes d'Enfer. "Aye," said my uncle, bouncing along on his mule with his belled cap jingling and his arquebus cradled under his arm, "it makes me

long for the tree-cloaked hills of New England." A tear started
to his eye, whereupon he delivered himself of a violent attack
on sentimentality in literature; in conclusion, he flattered himself that his *Ethan Allen* was unblemished by such an abomina-
ble defect. He repeated this disquisition in Hidatsa for the
edification of Blue Moon and his warriors, defying them to tell
him differently. They nodded and said, "Ah — ah — ah," an
utterance conveying great approbation.

As we rode deeper into Franklin's Gates of Hell, the savant
pointed out that the rock walls of the canyon were seamed with
dark veins of bituminous lignite, some smoldering from fires
deep in the earth that had been burning since time out of mind.
The silent blue flames played over the escarpments like gypsy
lights, causing my uncle to declare that he would not care to
make this ride alone after dark.

We now found ourselves surrounded by the strangest geo-
logical configurations. On both sides of the river stood a forest
of soaring stone columns resembling great stalagmites. In color
they were yellow, red, copper, or brown, and they stood thirty to
fifty feet high and were two to four feet in diameter. Odd over-
lapping stones sat atop them, like the caps of meadow mush-
rooms. True examined several of these formations minutely,
then announced that they were made of weathered sandstone,
like the low sandstone cliffs overlooking parts of Loch Champlain at home, which had been worked into curious shapes by
the wind and water. But Blue Moon assured us that the columns were no more nor less than the petrified sex organs of an
extinct race of giants, adding that barren women from his nation sometimes came to this place, in the hope of being cured
of their affliction.

As we progressed up the canyon, the coal fires in the cliffs
burned brighter and the smoke thickened. At a place where the
murky river bent sharply, we came to a tall mound of white buf-

falo bones at the base of a precipice at least one hundred feet high. This was Buffalo Jump.

"Heyday!" exclaimed my uncle. On a shelf of rock above the opposite riverbank, he had discovered what he believed to be the ossified thigh bone of an ancient bison. To judge by its length, which was upward of eight feet, this animal must have been twice the size of a buffalo of today. Wielding the bone like a cricket bat, he said grimly, "Gentlemen, I will use this relic as a war club to do service against any and all who speak a word against Ethan Allen, or Vermont, or Scholia Aristotle's unities, or my play." At which Franklin said he thought it unlikely that we would meet in this hell-hole any such calumniators, or any living creatures at all. And indeed, all life here seemed to have been turned to rock, including the bison, the trees, and the fish.

"There were Gorgons in this land, Ti," said my uncle, as he limbered up his angling rod and tied a red and green fly that he called Kinneson's Pedagogicus onto his horsehair leader. "Behold the Medusa who cast the spell."

He pointed up at the exposed remains, in the eastern cliff, of a perfectly preserved winged lizard a good thirty feet across. I could hardly believe my eyes. But my uncle merely nodded, and Blue Moon, who had seen these marvels many times before, said that he would ride on up the river with his bear and eagle to a rock shaped like a bison, where he would say a prayer for luck in the buffalo drive to be held the next day.

As the afternoon waned, the wind began to howl through the canyon. The dark water gurgled and moaned, vanishing into subterranean passages, only to re-emerge darker yet. And though my uncle plied his rod diligently, dropping his Pedagogicus on the opaque surface of the Little Missouri with an aplomb that the great Walton himself might have envied, he could entice no fish to rise.

Around four or five o'clock, though Blue Moon had not yet

rejoined our party, we rode with the Hidatsas up a hidden winding path to the western bluff top and the open prairie. By now even the Indian warriors, who had taken an oath "to fear nothing and never turn back, be the danger however so great," were glad to be out of the canyon with its sulphurous fumes, blue fires, and stone monsters.

Here on the wide plain above the river, I was astounded by the multitudes of buffalo. By the thousands they were traveling north on a broad, beaten path about half a mile west of the brink of the cliff, accompanied by the usual gang of gray wolves on the lookout for a stray calf or sick old cow. Last year's prairie grass, still brown and dry, would burn well when the time came to set the fires.

While we waited for the arrival of Blue Moon, and the Hidatsa braves planned their strategy for the following day, I positioned myself on the edge of the bluff and began to sketch the stone menagerie preserved in the cliff opposite. Later I planned to paint a picture called *In the Chasm of the Little Missouri*. For the time being, I had entrusted most of my canvases to the care of the Shoshone woman Sacagawea, who with her husband and infant son had joined the captains' expedition, and whom I deemed the most reliable person to perform this service. She had promised to guard them faithfully.

By the time I finished my sketch, the buffalo had stopped for the day, to graze and to water at the prairie potholes. A silence broken only by the endless sweep of the wind had settled over the land. Franklin was plaiting some white swan feathers into his hair, and my uncle was frowning at the manuscript of his play, with an eye toward improving Ethan Allen's line "Surrender the fort in the name of the Great Jehovah and the First Continental Congress."

"How's this?" he said. "'Surrender the fort in the name of Yahweh' . . . no, damme. What is it I'm after here? This is maddening, Ti. Never take up the pen, except for your sketches. Writing will harry you to an early grave. I expect to be dead before I reach forty."

"Uncle!"

"Well, well. We all grow old in the end. But harkee" — cocking his head and reaching for his ear trumpet — "I trow a Punch and Judy show does wend our way. Hear the Merry Andrew's drum?"

All I heard was heat thunder, grumbling far off in the distance, and, nearer at hand, the buffalo lowing like barnyard kine waiting to be fed. But then I thought that I, too, could make out a muffled drumbeat vibrating down through the canyon walls below. The sound came from the south, accompanied by the eerie tinkle of little bells, as if a great caravan out of an antique storybook were approaching. The drumbeat became louder. And over it, and over the chiming bells, came a high, thin piping.

We moved our mounts back from the edge of the bluff. I fetched my spyglass from Bucephalus's saddlebags while Franklin whistled like a prairie curlew, motioning for the Hidatsas to approach the brink quickly, on foot and staying low. As I trained my glass upriver, around the furthermost bend came what appeared to be a brightly colored dragon.

34

BY DEGREES, the dragon resolved itself into a troop of horsemen painted over their entire bodies with moons, half-moons, stars, pentacles, and other arcane symbols. Their horses were painted as well, and the men sat them so easily that they might almost have been centaurs. Four horses pulled a cart conveying a drum ten feet high, which a gigantic drummer, wearing only a breechclout and with no hair on his head or body, beat at regular intervals with a stick as long as my uncle's old bison thigh. Behind the giant came more mounted men, also painted, all bristling with bows and arrows, muskets, and lances from which dangled many scalps. They carried shields bedizened with bits of glass that caught whatever rays of sun found their way into the gorge, magnifying the light a hundred times and hurling it glinting back into our eyes. As they came closer, I perceived tiny bells attached to their long hair and to the painted manes and bridles of their horses. Bringing up the rear of this devils' procession was a chief whose war bonnet was made entirely of fresh human scalps.

I handed the glass to my uncle, who studied the procession for a moment, then passed it to Franklin. "Anasazis," the savant said after a moment. "An ancient tribe of professional murderers and cannibals, whose remnants dwell in Mexico. I make fifty of them, with more coming."

He returned the glass to my uncle, who looked again, then said, "I see, gentlemen, that Hell hath let out for recess."

Attached to the painted leggings of these demons were more scalps, as well as shriveled human ears, sex organs, and fingers; and they sported bracelets and necklaces that appeared to be fashioned from human teeth. On they came, more and more, to the boom-boom-booming of the drum and the tinkling of the bells in their hair like the harness bells of a peddler's cart; some played unearthly melodies upon fifes and panpipes that seemed carved from human bones, while others shook castanets made from small human skulls.

They chose a campsite directly below us, just across the river from Buffalo Jump. As those in the vanguard began to mill about on the sandy shelf beside the river, more of their kind appeared from around the far bend. Some wore breastplates of such antiquity that they seemed to date to the time of the conquistadors and helmets of Moorish design from an earlier age still. Some of the painted riders appeared to be white renegades with cropped ears and brands like those of the murderous Harpe brothers.

Now came a moaning, like the sound the wind is said to make before a hurricane. Round a bend in the distance appeared wheeled cages transporting Indian captives. Other slaves, shackled and playing the part of beasts of burden, walked beside these rolling prisons with great packs on their backs. There could no longer be any doubt: this was the Spanish Force of Terror, advancing with the spring and annihilating everyone in their path, on their way to serve the captains' party the same, to prevent the Americans from laying claim to California and Mexico.

The horsemen who had first arrived in the canyon continued to ride round and round, trampling the ground in a tightening circle. When they had cleared a campsite at the base of the cliffs, they jumped down, hobbled their mounts, and began to gather up driftwood. The chained captives set up a louder wailing

A blast of bugles split the air as round the bend came two heralds with silver trumpets, followed by four milk-white horses bearing a tall palanquin, upon which sat a slender man with a pointed black beard and mild brown eyes, wearing a flowing white robe and a bishop's miter encrusted with jewels. On his knee perched a tiny child with alabaster skin, white hair, and pink eyes. She was plucking feathers from a large bird with an arrow through its neck, which I took to be a wild turkey, and strewing the feathers right and left with a kind of childish delight, squealing with pleasure when the wind caught one and whirled it away. Upon further scrutiny I could see that this creature was not a child at all but an albino woman, the smallest person, other than an infant, I had ever seen. Behind the palanquin came a wagon filled with costumed courtesans of both sexes, decked out in every imaginable mode of attire from short togas to animal skins.

Bringing up the rear of the caravan was a knot of still more outlandishly costumed riders — a tonsured "priest" in a cassock, a dancer in a red dress, one wearing a long funeral veil, another in a silk top hat, yet another in a crimson fez. In their midst was an Indian, also mounted, but neither he nor his horse was painted. His hands were bound together behind his back, and two of the Anasazis, one painted yellow, one red, led his horse by the bridle. As this trio came closer, I saw that the captive was the Hidatsa chief, Blue Moon. Behind him came six men bearing his dead bear on a long pole; and, turning the glass back on the white dwarf, I realized that the bird she was de-feathering with such glee was no turkey but Blue Moon's war eagle. It was all my uncle and Franklin could do to prevent the Hidatsas from attempting to rescue their chief on the spot, which attempt surely would have resulted in our own destruction.

Under the direction of the gigantic drummer and the chief in the war bonnet of scalps, the Anasazis began building up a pyre of driftwood. When the wood was as high as a man, the drummer lighted it and signaled for his fellows to bring him half a dozen slaves, whom, to my great horror, he summarily cracked on the head with his drumstick. The Anasazis then spitted the bodies of their victims on long poles and began to roast them over the bonfire. The hearts they cooked separately, then delivered on gold chargers to the bishop and his dwarf, who, enthroned on their palanquin, ate with silver cutlery. And all the while he feasted, the bishop watched these horrible proceedings with a benign expression in his gentle brown eyes.

Long before the roasting bodies were cooked, the giant seized one out of the flames and, with his drumstick, broke open the leg and arm bones to get at the marrow, which dripped down his chin onto his massive chest. After the banquet the musicians began again to play their bone fifes and shake their skull castanets; and the giant, now sated with marrow bones like Beanstalk Jack's ogre, beat on his drum — a steady, dolorous booming. All this the bishop watched approvingly while his tiny albino queen orchestrated the grisly revels with flitting motions of her little white hands.

Just at sunset, at the direction of the dwarf, the yellow-painted Anasazi and his red-painted fellow cannibal escorted Blue Moon, still bound to his horse, to a side ravine and thence to the prairie atop the bluff opposite our hiding place. There they gave a concerted whoop, jabbed his mount with their lances, and, riding abreast of him, drove him toward the brink of the precipice. I then witnessed the bravest act I had ever seen a man perform. When Blue Moon was less than fifty yards from the edge, he gave a piercing cry and clapped his heels into the sides of his horse as if, since he could not avoid his terrible fate, he would embrace it entirely. He continued to shout his war cry as he and his horse plunged over the edge, yelling all the way down until they were shattered to pieces at the foot of the cliff.

Again my uncle had to restrain the Hidatsas, outmanned as they were, from attacking the Force of Terror. He assured them that if they were patient a little longer, Blue Moon's death would be avenged. And he bade them listen carefully to his plan.

35

THE ANASAZI CHIEF and his outriders sat immobile in the twilight, watching my uncle and me ride slowly up the river valley as if in the final stages of exhaustion. We had left our weapons with Franklin and the Hidatsas, now hidden well back from the bluff behind the migrating buffalo. As we drew near, the Anasazis threw nooses around our necks, jerked us off our mounts, and hauled us stumbling into the camp. The mitered bishop watched us coming, with the alabaster dwarf on his knee and the giant at his side. As we drew near, the chief hurled his lance into the ground between us and the palanquin to indicate that we were to approach no closer. Then he spoke at length in a language unlike any I had ever heard. When he finished, the bishop turned to us.

"Good evening, sirs," he said in English. "I am Stephanos Nacogdoches, bishop of New Spain and the territory known as Louisiana. My war chief informs me that you rode out of the bowels of the earth on two chimeras spewing fire. He says he slew the dragons, then subdued you and led you here. Perhaps you have a less fanciful explanation of your presence?"

"We do, Don Stephanos," my uncle said. "My name is Private True Teague Kinneson. This is my nephew, Ticonderoga Kinneson. We have deserted from the party of Captain Meriwether Lewis and Captain William Clark, leaders of an American expedition of conquest. Your man found us half a mile north of here."

"Bishop Stephanos. Not Don — *Bishop*. My ancestor was the Moorish general El Ibrahim, who conquered Madrid not once but twice and crowned himself bishop both times. A title I have inherited. Whither bound, my friend?"

"Home."

"Home to old Spain? For I must say you much resemble another quaint old gentleman-soldier from that glorious empire."

"No, sir, though I appreciate the compliment. We are on our way home to the Great Republic of Vermont. But," he continued, "I've never yet heard that the Moors or the Spaniards either sacrificed human beings to pagan gods or practiced cannibalism."

The bishop nodded at the dwarf and the giant. "The Whore of Babylon and my grand vizier, whom I call Polyphemus, have refined a bit on the beliefs of my ancestors."

Meanwhile the dwarf leaned over and signaled to the giant, who drew his scimitar and whispered something to the bishop.

"Polyphemus wishes to cut off your head and feed your brains to the Whore," Nacogdoches said in the politest tones. "What think you of this proposal, Private True Teague Kinneson from the Great Republic of Vermont?"

"Polyphemus is giving you bad advice," my uncle said. "I think you need a new vizier."

So saying, he picked up the Anasazi chief's war lance and, to my utter astonishment, hurled it straight at the giant. Polyphemus dropped his scimitar, took several short steps backward with his hands clawing at the lance projecting from his throat, and toppled over backward onto the coals of the banquet fire. My uncle stepped forward and picked up the fallen scimitar.

"Your new vizier, at your service," he said, bowing to Nacogdoches. Then, turning to the onlookers and speaking loudly in Spanish, "Your bishop has a new vizier. Private True Teague Kinneson, Green Mountain Regiment of the First Continental Army under the command of Ethan Allen."

"What is my new vizier's advice?" the bishop asked, shaking

his head at the Anasazi chief, who most reluctantly unnocked the arrow he had strung.

With the point of the scimitar, my uncle slashed two lines in the sand at the foot of the palanquin. The longer line ran east and west; the shorter split the first at right angles. The bishop and the chief leaned forward. Even the Whore of Babylon craned her miniature white head out over the edge of the palanquin and fixed her watery eyes on the lines in the sand.

My uncle thrust the point of the scimitar into the ground partway up the short line. "You are camped here. The American incursionists are coming up the big Missouri in pursuit of us." He moved his pointer to the longer line. "Their company of thirty men will be in the gorge of the Little Missouri by tomorrow morning."

"They must wish to recapture you very badly, Señor Private True. But tell me. What is the exact purpose of your Captain Merry's trip?"

"Nothing more nor less than to link forces with an American army being sent round the Horn to the mouth of the Columbia River in five warships. From there they will march south to seize your precious metal mines in California, and thence to New Spain, coming at Santa Fe from the west and burning it to flinders. Finally to annex all of New Spain south to Mexico City."

The bishop lifted his eyebrows and tugged at his beard. Finally he inquired, "And as vizier to me, what would you do first?"

"I shall deliver Meriwether Lewis's entire expedition into your hands," my uncle replied. "I ask only that you let me serve Lewis the same as I did Polyphemus."

The bishop thought for a time, then smiled his benevolent smile. "Tell me this plan of yours, grand vizier."

36

THAT EVENING Nacogdoches told us more about his life. He had been born in Madrid, the son of a cardinal and a street whore, and at thirteen he had signed on as a professional mercenary, to fight under various Mediterranean beys and despots. He had come to North America in the employ of the Guild of Venetian Glass Bead Makers, who had engaged him to track down and assassinate several of their company who had defected to Mexico, where, in violation of their oath of secrecy, they shared the mysteries of their craft with others. While the Whore of Babylon nodded with delight, the bishop calmly catalogued how, by poison, garrote, arson, and a dozen other infernal devices he had eliminated the bead makers and their families as well. In Santa Fe he had entered the service of the Spanish governor, first as a spy, then as an Indian exterminator, ranging out as far as California and taking over a thousand scalps. But he quickly grew restless with this employment, and when the governor offered him the commission to stop Lewis's expedition by any means necessary, he recognized an opportunity to fulfill a long-held dream of establishing his own empire. Indeed, he had intended all along to turn this mission into a tour of annihilation and to declare himself Emperor of Louisiana.

Nacogdoches had begun, the past fall, by scouring New Spain for the worst dregs of humanity: banished Comanches, remnants of the Anasazis, parings and castings of mankind from the prisons of New Orleans and St. Petersburg, whence Polyphemus and the Whore of Babylon had come.

He and his crew had left Santa Fe on New Year's Day, escorted to the city's gates by a brass band and five hundred cheering citizens. On the second morning they had wiped out a Navajo village. From that day onward they had perpetrated wholesale murder, sacking the countryside and shooting, burning, or crucifying all the people in their path, keeping only enough prisoners to carry their gear and to serve as provender, for many of these monsters, including the bishop, had taken a vow to taste nothing but human flesh for the rest of their lives. As for Lewis's expedition, he cared not a whit for its success or failure. His sole objective was to possess himself of the Americans' guns.

As background for these ravings, the more chilling because of the bishop's mellifluous voice, measured phrases, liquid brown eyes, courteous demeanor, and benign countenance, the Anasazi musicians kept up a terrible symphony with their tinkling bells, rattling castanets, and bone flutes. While Nacogdoches spoke, I sketched his portrait. He praised the finished picture effusively, then crumpled it into a ball and tossed it onto the fire.

"Now, vizier," he said to my uncle. "Be so kind as to repeat to me your plan for the destruction of Captain Merry and his men."

"Gladly. His scouts and trackers know we're in this canyon. The entire party will be here tomorrow morning, and my nephew and I will lure them deeper into the chasm. Your chief and his men will station themselves on the bluff above. As the members of the expedition pass by below in single file, you can pick them off like ducks."

Nacogdoches said something in the ancient tongue to the chief, who nodded. They continued to confer for some minutes, after which the bishop told us that he and twenty of his men would remain in the canyon, hidden behind the oddly shaped stone columns, to cut off any chance of escape for Captain Merry. The rest of the company would wait with their bows and muskets on the cliff top, as my uncle had advised. After the massacre, the bishop would hold a great banquet and his men would feast upon their victims and smoke for jerky any leftover American flesh.

Meanwhile, the blue fires burned in the seams of coal, the death music played, and the slaves moaned. Finally all but my uncle and Nacogdoches, who claimed never to sleep, fell into a stupor.

37

BEFORE DAWN my uncle woke me to witness the bishop speaking confidentially to the Whore of Babylon, propped on his knee like a hideous white doll. A few minutes later we led the Anasazi chief and his men up the path to the top of the bluff. Leaving them there as the sun rose far off over the prairie, we rode north, guarded by the yellow-painted assassin on one side and the red devil on the other. The vast herd of migrating buffalo kept pace with us. I knew that somewhere beyond them, Franklin and the Hidatsas lay in wait. Soon we were out of sight of the main body of renegades. But how to rid ourselves of our escorts? As we rode, my uncle spoke to me briefly in English. A few minutes later he reined in his mule.

Pointing excitedly down the river valley, as if we saw the captains' expedition coming, we motioned for our guards to hide on the terrace above the river. Still pointing and now calling out, as though to the captains, we descended into a dip, putting a low rise in the prairie between us and the murderers. There we quickly dismounted, got out our flint and steel, and, beginning at the edge of the cliff and working our way rapidly back toward the line of migrating buffalo, began lighting the prairie grass on fire. The wind was in our favor, out of the northwest, and the grass took fire as quick as tinder. By the time Monsieurs Yellow and Red realized what was happening, it was too late for them to reach us. A high wall of flames, whipped on by the wind, was roaring toward them, driving them back toward the mob of assassins on the promontory.

As we approached the moving buffalo, still igniting the grass as we proceeded, we glimpsed rolling black smoke to the south and west. "Now for Act the Fifth, Ti," cried my uncle.

We reached the herd at a place where the path funneled between two steep hills, and lit the grass here as well. For a few moments we were surrounded by flames and bellowing buffalo. Then we were through the pass and riding hard along the western flank of the stampeding bison, toward Franklin and the Hidatsas, who were galloping our way from the south and firing the grass with long bulrush torches as they came. The prairie was now ablaze on all three sides of the projecting bluff.

Back and forth between the walls of leaping flames rushed the trapped crew of murderers, frantically trying to find some means of exit before the buffalo arrived. But the Hidatsas, led by Franklin and my uncle, were now in their element. Made reckless by their great rage and grief over the fate of Blue Moon, they rode through the fire and directly at the buffalo to drive them harder toward the cliff and the Anasazis.

As the bellowing animals bore down on the Force of Terror, followed closely by a wall of fire whipped on by a strong west wind, the assassins, in their Spanish mail and black Moorish helmets and remnants of their victims' clothing, made one last surge to break through the oncoming beasts, but to no avail. The bison were thundering toward them in a line five hundred yards long and at least twenty animals deep. Faced with certain death under the hoofs of the stampeding animals, the Anasazis turned and ran for the edge of the bluff. The man in the red dress was hooked up on the horns of a huge bull in the vanguard and carried over the precipice impaled. The Indian in the funeral veil was trampled beneath hundreds of hoofs. Their chief disdained to run. He lifted his arms high above his head, uttered a great curse, and disappeared under the rushing herd. Men and bison alike poured off the edge of the cliff and plummeted to the rocks far below.

It was now imperative to cut off the retreat of the assassins left in the canyon with the bishop. With the entire promontory ablaze, my uncle signaled to me and the Hidatsas to follow him back around the fire line to the hidden trail leading to the gorge below. Reaching the ravine, we rode as fast as we could down the path toward the canyon floor. There we met the remaining members of the Force of Terror.

"For the Great Republic of Vermont and Ethan Allen!" roared my uncle. Brandishing his prehistoric bison bone like another Samson, he rode into the mob of Anasazis and rene gades and drove them back down the canyon. Franklin felled a fleeing enemy with each shaft from his ivory bow. The remnants of the Force leaped into the Little Missouri, where they were easy prey for the Hidatsas.

In the midst of this melee, Bishop Stephanos Nacogdoches sat on his palanquin, still holding the albino dwarf on his knee and smiling benignly. With supreme impiety he lifted his hand and bestowed a benediction upon my uncle, who raised his ancient arquebus and shot him directly between his serene brown eyes, tumbling him and the dwarf into the river. The bishop promptly sank, and the Whore of Babylon was swept by the current around a bend and out of our sight forever.

Soon enough our enemies were all dead or being hunted down one by one, so Franklin and my uncle and I started back up the steep trail leading out of the canyon. Partway to the top, we paused briefly to regard the scene below. By now the Hidatsas had regrouped, and were beginning to look in a meaningful way toward the Anasazis' former captives — who wisely chose that moment to head south on the Force of Terror's horses, one man wearing on his head the bishop's miter, another the dancer's red dress. As the emancipated slaves proceeded up the Little Missouri to the reverberations of Polyphemus's great drum, I was very concerned for the welfare of any people they met on their way. For they seemed, all caparisoned in the bloody tattered raiment of their vanquished tormentors, to have taken up their mission as well.

"Look," Franklin said as we emerged from the gorge onto the scorched prairie. "The buffalo are moving north again. Nothing stops them."

He was right. But when I remarked to the savant that their numbers seemed inexhaustible, he shook his head and said he doubted not that within the span of one man's lifetime Louisiana would be all but empty of them, and of free Indians as well, and I had better paint both now while I could, for few others would ever have the chance. This I resolved to do, regardless of what else might befall us as we adventured our way west.

38

LATER THAT DAY, having left our Hidatsa friends behind to prepare the slaughtered buffalo, we began to encounter many bison with eyes swollen shut and most of the hair singed off their bodies. These were the sad survivors of the herd trapped by the fire, which had managed to burst through the wall of flames but were so badly burned that all they could do was stagger sightlessly over the prairie, bellowing in anguish, stumbling into gullies, and crashing into one another. This piteous scene brought tears to my uncle's eyes, but he insisted that I sketch it to show "the horrors of unfeeling and indifferent nature in the West, as well as her beauties." Then we spent several hours hunting down the burned buffalo and putting them out of their misery, after which he declared, "Oh, Ti. From this moment onward, I eat no more bison meat forever."

But that night, famished and with the savory fragrance of the buffalo back-steaks and tongues that Franklin was cooking wafting past his long nose, the private said that however it might be in other worlds, in this one every Jack and Jill, and every True Teague, too, must feed his body to preserve his soul. And he consumed his usual five or six pounds of meat with good relish, declaring afterward, over his half pipeful of hemp, "All's vanity in the end, Ti. What can we do in this short life but try to make our fellow creatures' paths as smooth and comfortable as possible, and leave the rest to Providence?"

This seemed like wise counsel. But later, as we sat by our campfire, I could not rid my mind of the hideous cruelties we had witnessed in the canyon on the Little Missouri. Finally I said, "Uncle, I believe there is much wickedness in Louisiana."

"Yes, Ti. And in the world at large as well."

"And yet Louisiana and the world at large were made by a good Creator, were they not?"

"They were, Ti. Very good indeed."

"And the evil in His creation is the handiwork of a certain Gentleman?"

"I have told you so many times. And told you true, Ti. And — ha ha — I am True as well. I have told you true and True I am."

"But here is the problem," I continued. "Do not some do evil in the name of doing good?"

"I fear they do, nephew."

"And others love evil for its own wicked sake? Like the Harpes and Bishop Stephanos Nacogdoches."

"Aye."

"Then how do we discern true good from evil?"

"Why, it's as simple as A Apple Pie. Our hearts tell us the difference."

"Is the heart never wrong, then?"

"No, never. Is it, Franklin?"

"No, sir, it is not," said the savant.

"But uncle," I exclaimed, "what must we do, then, with the evildoers?"

"Why," said he, with the greatest good will, inhaling the mild fumes of his cannabis, "we must chop off their heads!"

And with a wink at me and a tip of his stocking cap to Franklin, my uncle rang his bell, lay down, and fell soundly asleep. But I dreamed that night of devils in bishops' miters, and flaming buffaloes, and myself taking Little Warrior's scalp, and woke up wishing with all my heart that I was a small boy again and home in my own bed in Vermont.

The Great Falls

39

A FEW DAYS LATER we reached the place where the lovely River of Yellow Stones falls into the Missouri. At the junction of these two great waterways we stopped for a few days to rest. My uncle reworked his play and fished, I painted our battle with the Force of Terror, and Franklin rendered the same scene with bright-colored stick figures on a buffalo hide.

Franklin was delighted with my uncle's fly-casting, which he admired from the riverbank for hours on end. Expert angler though he was, the private had been unable to entice a single fish to rise to his lures since setting out from Fort Mandan. But fish or no fish, he said, angling with the fly was good for the soul, for it connected the angler through rod, line, and leader to rivers and the wonderful countryside they flowed through in an intimate way that no other endeavor did. He declared that fly-fishing was the most hopeful of all sports, and that hope, more than any other quality, was what distinguished us from the lower orders of life, such as fish themselves. Though he assured us that if he ever *caught* another fish, he would promptly release it, thereby giving it cause to hope that the next time it was hooked it might again be set free. And since hope was all he had to show for his angling thus far, he was more sanguine still, and he executed every cast — hundreds upon hundreds a day — as if he expected a hard strike momentarily and a great speckled beauty leaping at the end of his line. Franklin, in the meantime, had taken up the sport and had become as avid in its pursuit as my uncle.

One evening I offered to show the savant the art of perspective in painting. To my astonishment, he casually took up my brush and added to my picture of the battle a perfect representation of himself, bow at the ready, riding down on the Spanish force. The famous portraitist Ben West, I thought, could scarcely have done it better. "All great art is simple, Ti," Franklin told me with a superior gesture at his buffalo-hide painting. "But you must not suppose that we Indians do not understand perspective. Of course we do."

Heading west along the Missouri once more, we entered a land so vast, wild, and broken that it seemed to defy being painted from any perspective whatsoever. It was an incredibly harsh place of twisting draws leading nowhere, dry canyons, endless sweeping wind, no trees — Franklin said there was not enough rainfall here to support them — and barren red rock. Only the hardiest creatures survived in this hostile country. One evening I watched a pack of gray wolves decoy a yearling antelope away from the herd by flattening themselves out and creeping along on their bellies, then dashing off a few yards, then creeping again, until the antelope could not resist drifting away from the safety of the others to discover what these interesting animals might be. When they had cut it off from the rest, they chased it into the river, where they easily killed it by slitting its throat with their fangs, then dragged it onto a sandbar to devour. But before the wolves could begin to dine on their prey, a huge grizzled bear descended upon them and dispossessed them of their spoils without so much as a by-your-leave. So fierce was this monster that the magpies, which had already begun to feed on the lights of the antelope as the wolves disemboweled it, flew off in a panic at its first approach. I sketched the bear standing on its hind legs, looking east down the river as if guarding all upper Louisiana from interlopers. Franklin said that his Blackfoot relatives were as much fiercer than the grizzled bear as the bear was fiercer than the wolves and the wolves than the antelope. This I found very sobering. But as day succeeded day and week followed week, we saw no Blackfeet, and no other people in that desert of a landscape, which seemed as empty of humans and habitation as the moon.

Near the end of May we passed a vast palisade of white rock towering hundreds of feet above the river in the likeness of ancient ruins. Immediately my uncle claimed that we had discovered the lost city of Troy; and he showed us with great exactitude where the Greek army had camped, where the colossal wooden horse had been dragged into the city and poor Hector dragged around it by Achilles. I painted a quick impression of the hollow equine atop the gleaming white cliffs, with my uncle himself astride it in his knight-errant's gear, and both the horse and him eating one of my mother's cartwheel cookies.

One morning as we rode along the south bank of the river, we heard the distant roar of falling water. Around noon we came to a two-hundred-foot bluff over which spilled a thundering falls bigger and louder than any I had ever dreamed of. This was the Great Falls of the Missouri. We could feel its spray on our faces hundreds of feet away; my uncle calculated that it discharged upward of twice the volume of water of fabled Niagara, which we had "visited" several years earlier on a trip of exploration to celebrate my tenth birthday.

While making his hydraulic estimations, he was busy assembling his jointed fly-rod and tying a Pedagogicus fly onto his leader. On his first cast he hooked, played, and duly released a large, hard-fighting trout entirely new to us, with pinkish sides and orange slashes under its gills, which he named *Salmo secare jugulum*, or "cutthroat." This he did with great nonchalance, as though he had been landing and naming new fish by the dozen since St. Louis.

I set up my easel on a small island just below the falls and began to work on a picture that pleased me more than any I had done to date. Almost as if it had a will of its own, this painting seemed to solve a problem I had been wrestling mightily with of late, which was how to compress our journey, and Louisiana itself, into the finite space of my canvas. The solution was found in a technique that Franklin called the "tableau." Indeed, he told me that Indian artists had been using the method for centuries. With the falls as a centerpiece, I included many of the events and scenes of the past several weeks, since our battle with the Force of Terror, as follows. Far downriver I painted the River of Yellow Stones, merging with the Missouri from the southwest. Between the junction of the rivers and the Great Falls I inserted the soaring white cliffs my uncle believed to be the remains of ancient Troy. In the pool at the foot of the falls I painted my uncle a-fishing, and far off to the west, our next destination — the Rocky Mountains, white on top with everlasting snow.

This picture took me three days to complete. When it was finished, Franklin studied it from several angles. Then he made this pronouncement. "Ti, onto this sheet of canvas you have incorporated many miles and several weeks of experience. I congratulate you. Also, as we have progressed westward, your colors have become bolder and brighter, to match the hues of the landscape. They have more *value*, by which I mean they glow, as with an inner intensity. This rainbow thrown up by the spray of the falls is very fine, the colors blend from pink to peach to green. But here" — he took my brush — "you must catch some of the reflected light off those white cliffs, thusly, and for God's sake fill in your foreground. A prickly pear would do well here, here a sagebrush, there a bison skull — thus and thus and thus. Do you see?"

I did. But I feared that my uncle, with his devotion to Scholia Aristotle's unities, would scowl and hem and haw and wonder over my foreshortenings, not only of the perspective above and below the falls, but of time and action. To the contrary, he praised the picture highly. "I can see, Ti," he declared, "that for the whole of the painting, a strict faithfulness to what is real is not precisely what you aim for. Rather, you strive toward a realness imbued by the *imagination*. And is not this Louisiana an imaginative, mythical realm? Aye, even to the flying lizards and monsters that once dwelt here, and the ruins of antique cities. But — ha ha — is that old Odysseus I spy coming toward us? Sir" — he called out to the man he'd spotted across the river — "you are a long way from Ithaca yet."

In fact it was Captain Lewis, scouting out ahead of the rest of his party and quite astonished to find us here before him. But when my uncle said that we would bide with the expedition for a few days and help them ferry their belongings around the falls, the captain did not protest much, and even seemed glad to have a Blackfoot Indian with his party in this region. For all of the reports he had heard of that tribe indicated that they were the fiercest and most warlike people in Louisiana. And if the expedition could not avoid them altogether, at least it might have a helpful ally in Franklin — though the savant said he very much doubted that his presence would cut much ice with his relations, who would promptly kill us all if they caught us unawares. A warning which, you may be sure, we took very seriously indeed.

40

NEVER HAD I SEEN men toil so hard as the Corps of Discovery did during the portage around the Great Falls of the Missouri. As we had discovered soon after arriving there, the falls consisted of *five* separate waterfalls, and the shortest portage by them was an eighteen-mile route over the worst terrain since St. Louis. One day in early July the men set out in such a cloud of mosquitoes as caused my uncle to exclaim that the beplagued Egyptians never endured such a pestilence. He spent the rest of that morning inventing a nostrum against them, of which it may fairly be said that the remedy was worse than the malady. When at last he acknowledged to the explorers that the reeking unguent he had swabbed on their faces and hands consisted of one part elk's urine, one part grizzled bear's gall, and one part buffalo dung, they rushed coughing and gagging to the river and plunged into the water to scrub themselves clean. They were forced to interrupt these ablutions, however, when we began to be pelted with hailstones as large as winesap apples, causing us all to take refuge beneath the canoes and boats. I got a bruise on my head as large as a walnut and was very anxious for Bucephalus, Franklin's pony, and my uncle's white mule, which ran madly over the prairie in search of shelter. They turned up later, too lame and battered to be of use in drawing the boats and provisions on the great wheeled axles the men had cut from cottonwood trees, so the crew had to pull and push these rude carts themselves, with several grueling miles of the portage left to complete.

By midafternoon the temperature had risen to 109 degrees, and some of the men swooned dead away. The axles and tongues of the carts began to split in two, and the prickly pears grew so thick as to be unavoidable. One three-inch thorn lodged in that part of Silas Goodrich's anatomy where a man would least wish to entertain such a guest, causing an angry and painful infection. Joseph Field was struck on the ankle by a rattlesnake and required to be bled and have gunpowder applied to his wound, then painfully burned off. Two other men were driven into the river by an enormous sow bear with three cubs.

Every night the grizzled bears that were so prevalent in the region had tried to invade the camp and get at our food. They were prevented from doing so only by the tireless efforts of Lewis's big Newfoundland dog, Seaman, who patrolled the perimeter ceaselessly. Finally the captains decided to conduct a hunt to kill these troublesome animals. But my uncle said there was no need to slaughter such noble beasts; he would show us a much more humane way of dealing with them, at the same time that we celebrated our nation's upcoming birthday.

Accordingly, a few evenings before July Fourth, with the prowling bears out in force, Seaman barking, and the men keeping nervously close to the fire, my uncle produced his latest invention — Chinese sky rockets, made from a few canisters of gunpowder mixed with some vermilion-colored stones crushed into a crimson powder and packed into hollowed-out tubes of cottonwood about as big around as a man's wrist. Dressed in a sort of toga dyed red, white, and blue, and wearing Clark's best top hat, the private proclaimed himself Pro Patria Americanus — a figure I believe he made up on the spot. He then delivered an Independence Day speech in a thundering voice, to the effect that though Vermont had but recently joined the Union, we Vermonters still regarded our state as a sovereign republic *whose citizens must never be told what to do, what to think, where and whether to pray or to pledge their allegiance to any governmental power or potentate whose seat lay beyond the Green Mountains, except they did so of their own free will.*

At a signal from Pro Patria, the Field brothers and Sergeant Patrick Gass touched off the rockets, jointly intended to frighten away the bears and to celebrate the birthday of the nation whose prerogative to govern Vermont my uncle had just fiercely denied. But somehow the fireworks, in igniting, sped not heavenward but parallel to the ground, shrieking most hideously and exploding into a million red fragments about one and a half feet above the prairie. One missile, a little higher than the rest, tore through the hide coverings of the iron-frame boat Lewis was then constructing. Another killed a buffalo across the river. A third exploded near my uncle, setting his costume afire, upon which he plunged into the river to douse the flames, emerging a few moments later much chagrined. As for the bears, so far from being put to rout, they stood up on their powerful hind legs in a sort of semi-circle around the camp, with the great curiosity of their kind, and seemed very well pleased by the celebration. Which was immediately followed by a violent thunderstorm, during which my uncle was struck not once but twice by lightning, with no other ill effects than his being constrained to express himself for the next twenty-four hours in the tongue of ancient Assyria. During this interval, he composed a quatrain in that language, which he later rendered into English, called "Ode to Captain William Clark's Cottonwood Dugouts." It provides, I think, a very fair example of the Vermont playwright's epic style.

O noble tree with snowy seeds,
You have fulfilled our watery needs.

Dugout canoes, glorious boats,
That never sink but always float.

"The final line seemed lame to me at first, Ti," the poet
said, after Captain Lewis's iron-frame boat was repaired and
launched — and promptly started to take in water at the
seams. "But prophetic. The cottonwood dugouts, you see, *float*.
Lewis's boat does not. And now I believe that I will go a-
fishing, like old Walton's Piscator, and float some of my own
lovely feathered creations over the many *Salmo secare jugulum*
trout in this stretch of the river."

That evening, while casting his flies in the still water a mile
above the falls, he was so alarmed by a mysterious booming off
in the distance that he came posting back to camp with his galoshes flopping as if being pursued by twenty Blackfeet. Lewis,
who had heard the rumbling earlier in the day, maintained that
there was a wholly rational explanation for the noise. My uncle
replied that the explanation could only be witches. He then
coined an axiom, very amusing to the men, which was that
while he did not *absolutely believe* in witches, nonetheless he
could not rule out the possibility of their existence, and so
deemed it wise not to venture forth alone at night, or perhaps
even in the daytime, in regions said to be frequented by them.
The men led him on shamelessly, drawing him out into further
absurdities on the subject, then terrifying him by hooting and
moaning and flitting about after dark with torches and telling
tales designed to frighten children around the winter hearth,
every one of which my uncle credulously devoured.

41

H IS GREAT FEAR of witches notwithstanding, the next morning my uncle accompanied me to a plateau about ten miles from camp, where we promptly discovered the source of the mysterious rumbling. It was caused not by any supernatural agency but by the fighting of thousands of rutting bison, who crashed into each other with unspeakable fury in their annual ritual to determine which would mate with their females. Still, my uncle declared that the booming sound we had heard at camp was somewhat different from this unbroken bellowing — coming only at widely spaced intervals — and *that* sound he still believed to be the work of ghostly agents.

Wishing to learn as much as I could about bison, I observed the fighting animals through my glass for a long time. They appeared to be indestructible, continuing to batter away at one another long after I would have supposed their brains to be dashed to bits. Yet they never seemed to fight to the death. When at last one combatant had clearly prevailed, the vanquished bull limped off, leaving the nearest cow to the attentions of the victor.

Back at the camp, Franklin said he was surprised that the poor buffalo went to such lengths to accomplish what he was able to achieve with a few colored feathers in his hair and some face paint. The savant mentioned that bison were vulnerable to wildfires started by lightning. During thunderstorms he had witnessed bands of blue electricity racing along the horns of whole panicked herds, making them resemble so many spectral buffalo ghosting over the land — at which my uncle began to tremble violently.

Before leaving the subject of buffalo, I will add these curious observations. For drinking water they seemed to prefer the stagnant pools in their mud wallows to the clearest running streams. Sometimes at night it was impossible to sleep for their bellowing. In places their herds were so dense that we had to beat them out of our way with cottonwood branches. And I never did get their hump entirely right in my paintings.

Some of the most stimulating hours of our entire trip were those spent around the campfire conversing about the new animals and other wonders of the West. That evening, as we were telling the captains about our excursion to the buffalo mating grounds and I was working on a sketch of the fighting bison, Lewis happened to mention that on the river that afternoon he had seen a mallard duck, the first since last summer. He referred to it as a "duckinmallard," as Virginians were wont to do — giving rise to the subject of bird nomenclature.

"The mallard," announced my uncle, "is circumglobular, like its inveterate enemy the osprey, which sometimes, in the absence of fish to prey upon, will pluck up a waterfowl. It was given scientific status by Linnaeus in 1726. He saw fit to call it *Anas platyrhynchos,* from the Greek *platys,* broad or flat, and *rhynchos,* for beak. But as Ti will remember, when we visited Linnaeus in Sweden I disputed this name hotly."

"I did not know you had met the great botanist and zoologist in person, sir," Captain Lewis said.

"To be sure," my uncle continued, "'broad-beak' is not, strictly speaking, inaccurate. The mallard does have a wide enough beak, for it feeds mainly on aquatic plants, not fish, and therefore does not need a pointed bill for spearing purposes. But as I told Carl — I knew Linnaeus as Carl, did I not, Ti?"

"You did, sir."

"As I told Carl, why not something more suited to the mallard's majestic plumage? Why not *Gloriosus polychromatus*? Why, the blue-green sheen of the male's head alone is incomparable in nature. I defy you, Ticonderoga, to capture it in watercolors."

"I think I would need oils, sir."

"You would. For the bird's feathers themselves contain a natural oil that makes them gleam like precious gems. To return to Linnaeus, I was so exasperated with the fellow's poverty of imagination when it came to nomenclature that I took hold of his ruffled collar — this was after the king granted him a patent of nobility and he was styled Carl von Linné — I seized his ruffled collar — ha ha — and shook him by it, and his wig tumbled off." My uncle glanced at me for confirmation.

"It did, sir. You gave Carl von Linné a good old-fashioned shaking."

But thinking it likely that the captain, who was remarkably well informed about all things, knew very well that Linnaeus had died several years *before I was born,* I wished to vindicate True of any charge of deliberate untruthfulness. To that end, I approached Lewis later, as he walked away from the fire, and explained that when I was nine, my uncle and I had indeed made one of our frequent voyages *of the imagination,* in which, after crossing the Baltic Sea (my mother's stock pond) on my fishing raft, we had visited Linnaeus in Stockholm — our toolshed. For the occasion, my uncle placed my mother's cloth mop over his stocking cap for a wig in order to enact the role of the Swedish scientist — then pulled it off to question Carl in his own persona.

Lewis laughed. "Your uncle, Ti, is a remarkable man."

"Yes, sir. Citing the *Systema Naturae*, he fiercely disputed Linnaeus's entire system of classification. They — Linnaeus and my uncle — were engaged in such a furious argument over flower parts that I feared they would come to blows. Fortunately, my mother just then called us in for supper."

"Ti, did your uncle really think that you and he were visiting Linnaeus?"

"I asked my father that very question. He had a most excellent philosophical answer for me."

"What was it?"

"That he had no earthly idea *what* my uncle thought."

"A most excellent answer indeed, Ti," Lewis said, laughing again.

"But did you know, captain, that at home my uncle has his own folio, sixteen hundred pages long, and called *Systema Naturae Americanae*, in which, in defiance of Linnaeus, he has reclassified all the animals and plants known in the United States?"

"I did not. What is this wonderful system based on?"

"It is a sort of ascendancy of survival, based on which animal devours which other plant or animal. Man is at the top of the list."

"As he should be. But pray, Ti, which animal comes next in your uncle's system? The great African apes, I should imagine?"

"Why, no, sir. Hemp comes next."

"*Hemp?*"

"Indeed. Next to man, my uncle believes that hemp represents the highest order of life."

"Hemp is a *plant*, son. What can your uncle possibly be thinking?"

"His argument is that since man is the only being that much

benefits from hemp, save the wild birds of the air that eat its tiny seeds, it should rank second to man. Next to humankind, my uncle believes, hemp is the most sublime creation in the universe. I have heard him say so many times."

Lewis smacked his brow with his palm. "Your uncle believes *hemp* to be next to man in the order of creation? Well, well, well."

"I can't say myself, captain. I don't use it."

"Nor do I. But hemp is a sort of hobby-horse with your uncle, is it not? He rides it hard and hard. And yet he may have a point."

"He may at that, sir."

"Ti? I can never recall having seen your uncle in low spirits. Have you ever seen him down in the mouth?"

"Only in the presence of suffering. He cannot bear to see a man or an animal suffer. He thinks hemp would alleviate much needless suffering."

"As an herbal specific?"

"Why, yes, and as a preventive, as well. He believes that its mellowing effects would prevent us from getting ourselves into so much mischief. My uncle attributes all of our spiritual ills to our failure to use —"

"Hemp!" said the captain. Laughing and shaking his head, he walked off for one of his many nightly circumambulations of the camp, leaving me to contemplate what a very good man he was, and what a very good man my uncle was, and where *he* might be placed in his own system, or any system, of classification.

42

Iт ѕееметн, gentlemen," said my uncle one evening, "that the immediate problem for Captain Lewis is to get round these infernal waterfalls without succumbing to the bears, hail, heat, vipers, or thorns. I intend to use some good old-fashioned Vermont ingenuity to have him back on the river again in two days. Otherwise, our little race to the Pacific will be no challenge at all. A victory will mean nothing."

Just what, I inquired with some trepidation, did he have in mind? But he only chuckled, and said I would learn in good season. In the meantime, he would need Silas Goodrich, the expedition's best carpenter, and five other men at dawn the next day. And off he strode to harangue Captain Lewis about the matter, though it seemed to me that one thing Meriwether Lewis did *not* need at this time was another invention.

Early the next morning, clad in his chain mail, stocking cap, and galoshes, with Miss Flame Danielle Boone's little pink riding cushion stuffed inside his trousers for a codpiece, and besmeared with his stinking mosquito nostrum, my uncle rousted out the carpentry crew to search for the largest cottonwood in the area. Near the water above the third falls they located one with a girth of about three feet. This they hewed down, and from the bole sawed out four crude wheels. With the remaining timber they fashioned axles, a helm and deck, and three tall masts. Behold — a prairie ark was taking shape before our eyes. This wheeled schooner of the plains, which my uncle baptized the *Flying Dutchman,* was five full days a-building. When complete, it was a good twenty feet in length, with a capacity (declared the inventor) of ten tons. It was steered from the stern with a long cottonwood tiller reinforced with my uncle's prehistoric bison bone. To this land-frigate the admiral, as the men had begun to address him, stepped the masts, each with a full suit of sails stitched together from tenting material. He even added a jaunty little spritsail jutting off the front of the hulking machine.

Captain Clark had watched these proceedings with a very reserved expression. Now he inquired whether my uncle had ever sailed a ship before. At this the private drew himself up to his full height and said it would be very strange if he had not, having been raised just a stone's toss across the hills from Loch Champlain. Clark favored him with a thin smile and returned to his map-making. But George Drouillard inquired whether they should begin gathering up the animals of the plains, two by two, against the impending flood. My uncle, who was waiting only for a favorable wind to embark, said "Tooleree" and kissed his hand, and went a-fishing with Franklin to take advantage of a thick hatch of green drake flies on the water.

Sergeant Patrick Gass inquired how the good wheeled *Dutchman* might fare on such rough terrain, full of gullies, draws, ravines, and ledgy outcroppings. "She'll skim lightly o'er them all, like her namesake on the high seas, matey," my uncle assured him. Then he called up many nautical terms, such as weighing anchor, blue-water sailing, and the perils of a lee shore; he spoke of sails fore, aft, and mizzen, and ropes and pulleys and blocks, like a man who had been at sea his entire life. Finally he expressed a regret that the captains had sent the cannon back to St. Louis with the keelboat, for he would have loved to mount it on the *Dutchman*'s bow as a chaser.

Charbonneau was afraid of the ship. Sacagawea was amused.

Sergeant Ordway asked whether we might expect to sail it all the way to the Rocky Mountains, in which case two or three such vessels would save the party a world of paddling. My uncle took it all in good humor; smiling with great assurance, he said that we would see what we would see. He was habilitated for the maiden voyage with a pair of dark goggles fashioned from flakes of mica he had found on the Little Missouri and, over his stocking cap, Captain Lewis's best tricornered dress hat, which he had borrowed to give himself a proper naval air. Presently a breeze arose. The admiral was piped aboard by Pierre Cruzatte, sawing out "Yankee Doodle" on his fiddle, and assumed his position in the stern to the applause of the men. Seizing the bone tiller in both hands, he bade me — his only crew — to take my station in the bow; and in his stage voice gave the order to weigh anchor and "let her rip." Private Wiser cut the elk-rope thongs by which the ship was attached to stakes driven into the prairie. I unfurled the sails. *Snap!* As loud as a rifle report, the wind filled the canvas sheets towering overhead. The *Dutchman* gave a great lurching bound, and off we tore at a truly horrifying rate of speed.

Over prickly pear, over tufts of shortgrass, over sage and cactuses we bounced at a good twenty knots, while I clung to the foremast for dear life. Wrestling the tiller first to starboard, then to port, with all the strength of a latter-day Hercules, my uncle began to tack the *Dutchman* back and forth, as the ungreased wooden axles shrieked dreadfully. On our second sweep to the right I was certain that we would be driven into the river. Somehow my uncle got us back on course. But the gullies were so deep, the stone outcroppings so dense, the wind — fast rising to a gale — so strong, that at every moment the ark threatened to overset itself and murder us both.

We had now come nearly even with a mixed herd of buffalo,

elk, deer, and antelope, which began to run beside us. We easily outstripped them. But suddenly the *Dutchman* swung entirely around and we found ourselves headed back in the opposite direction, with the wind behind us. As we bore straight down upon the party's main camp, the men raced hither and yon for their lives. At the last moment we swerved away and headed straight for a deep draw at right angles to the river, which would certainly have put an end to our voyage altogether if, just before reaching the ravine, the ship had not actually taken flight. It sailed a good fifty feet through the air and came down on the far side of the gully with a jolt that pitched me out onto the prairie in a breathless heap. I picked myself up in time to see the ark, with my uncle still at the helm, making for the bluff above the river.

43

EUREKA!" cried the private, as the *Dutchman*, airborne again, hurtled over the edge of the precipice. He threw up one arm, evidently as a kind of farewell. As he did so, a sudden gust blew him clean off the deck and he plummeted to the river below, where Franklin, who was fishing with great unconcern, pulled him to safety. The prairie ark, for its part, wafted down onto the water with some of the grace of its spectral namesake ghosting through the night skies. Still under sail, it proceeded quite majestically with the current toward the thundering falls, over which it bobbed in stately fashion, then came to pieces on the rocks below.

When it was apparent that my uncle was unharmed — he was now standing with his hand over his wet goggles, in a sort of rapture — some of the men began to laugh. Sacagawea told her tiny son that he had witnessed a great thing such as he was never likely to see again. Lewis, having satisfied himself as to my uncle's safety, led a party to retrieve the *Dutchman*'s sails from the river below the falls.

That afternoon, however, Captain Clark took me aside. "Son," he said with a very grave expression, "a word with you. You and your uncle and your Indian friend had best ride out into the prairie or scout ahead up the river for a few days. For if I encounter Private True before I cool off, I'm afraid I'll have to shoot him. No, lad. Don't argue with me. Just do as I say. Do it now."

Though my uncle was much bruised, his pride was more so yet; for this reason, he was willing enough to absent himself from the expedition for a time. Endeavoring to cheer him as we rode out together that afternoon, Franklin said that the *Dutchman* was *in theory* a sound idea, but the terrain in the vicinity was not geared for such refined machines. As for the unexpected gale, Franklin reminded him that even King Aeolus had been unable to control the winds, and in his determination to go down with his ship, True had conducted himself with great honor. I promised to paint the scene, showing the *Dutchman* high over the river and my uncle still at the tiller, and to give him the painting to display in the elegant playhouses when he and his revised *Ethan Allen* took the great cities of the world by storm. He brightened up considerably, and said he believed he had acquitted himself manfully enough, and perhaps we would try the ark again, on smoother ground, on our way home from the Pacific, when the prevailing winds would be in our favor — though I fervently hoped that would not happen.

44

O N THE SECOND DAY of our banishment, while Bucephalus and I were hunting supper some miles apart from Franklin
and my uncle, we were overtaken by one of the terrific late afternoon thunderstorms that seemed to hammer those barren
fastnesses of Louisiana almost daily at that time of year. There
was no place to take shelter. All I could do was to continue riding miserably, fearing that if we remained stationary one of
those broad blue rivers of electricity, so much more terrifying
than any lightning I had ever seen in Vermont, would somehow
seek us out. Finally the storm passed, leaving the sky to the
west a deep green. Darkness soon fell, and I judged it best to
stop altogether until morning. When dawn arrived, neither
Bucephalus nor I had the faintest idea where we were.

All that day we continued to wander on the great trackless
steppe under thick, low clouds. If the sun had come out I
could have trended south toward the Missouri and sooner or
later rejoined Franklin and my uncle or the main expedition.
But with no sun and such dense weather, I did not know south
from last Wednesday. That night I was so exhausted that sleep
came hard; but around midnight, I dropped off and slept fitfully. In the hour before dawn I had a strange dream. Little
Warrior Woman appeared before me on her small Indian pony.
Not in her dark paint, disguised as Black Wolf, but as the pretty
young girl I had met on the prairie, wearing the same buckskin
apparel she had worn the day I discovered her with her arm
trapped in the badger den.

My dead friend said nothing. But she beckoned for me to rise and collect my belongings and follow her and her pony on Bucephalus. This I did, noting that as we rode we kept the North Star on our right shoulders. I was neither frightened nor saddened. In her steady eyes, sure movements, and dignified bearing, I sensed great purpose. I wanted to reach out and touch her, but feared that if I did she would vanish. A moment later I awoke, with the same sense of peace I had experienced in my dream.

It was still dark, but the sky was clear and the North Star as bright as I could ever recall. I saddled Bucephalus and began to ride, keeping Polaris on my right shoulder just as Little Warrior and I had done in my dream. Presently the sky behind me began to lighten and the stars in that quarter dimmed. A salmon-colored wash seeped out along the horizon, succeeded by a gold band blending into the soft blue canopy.

Just ahead, on a low rise, sat a figure facing away from me, toward the west. In the early light I perceived that it was a young woman, her hair sweeping down her back to the grass. As I approached, I called out my name and indicated that I was an American. I was quite astonished when she replied, in perfect English, "Hello, Ticonderoga. I see you're a dreamer, too."

The girl had a low, laughing voice, as though she found my name and everything else about me amusing, and as I drew closer I saw that she was about my age and strikingly beautiful.

"Kindly get off your horse, Ticonderoga," she said, "so that I can have a good look at you."

I dismounted, all the time unable to take my eyes off her. She wore a short antelope-skin dress, fringed with colored strips of buckskin and dyed quills. Over her shoulders was an ermine-skin tippet. She had a straight nose, full red lips, and a lithe figure, with lovely slender legs. Now she stood up and walked all around me, regarding me with interest. I was surprised to see how tall she was. Though still three or four inches below my height, she was at least five feet and eight inches. She was clearly an Indian, with skin the color of my uncle's copper crown, but her wide-set eyes were the deep purple of the sage at twilight. "Very well, Ticonderoga," she said. "Will you take my hand?"

She held out her right hand, which was shapely and long-fingered, the moons of her nails painted red, yellow, white, blue, and green. I started to shake hands with her. Instead she took my left hand in her right and led me to the edge of a nearby bluff overlooking a great curving stretch of the Missouri. So I had not, after all, been too far from the river when I'd stopped the day before with Bucephalus. As we stood hand in hand, looking down at the river, I could smell the crushed herbs and prairie flowers she had put in her hair, and the fainter, more delicate attar that seemed to hover over her, calling to mind the scent of sage.

"Once upon a time, a girl with eyes the color of the dark blue lupine flowers that blossom in the high meadows on Square-sided Chief Mountain, in the Land of the Glaciers, and with the natural scent of sage flowers, was born to a Blackfoot mother and a British father," she said in a conversational tone. "Therefore she was named Yellow Sage Flower. Since she had also, from a very young age, told fascinating stories about the animals of the plains and mountains, her name was soon lengthened to Yellow Sage Flower Who Tells Wise Stories. Sadly, the parents of Yellow Sage Flower Who Tells Wise Stories both died young. She was sent away to school. In time, she returned to her mother's people, and one Smoke, a young Blackfoot chief, was appointed her guardian. Now just as Yellow Sage Flower was renowned for being able to know what a mule deer or a panther was saying, Smoke was famous for his ability to shift shapes. In the blink of an eye he could turn himself into a badger, a grizzled bear, a buffalo, or what have you. But not content with being a wizard, Smoke wished for even more power. Therefore he became a great warrior. And a great warrior must constantly make war. So it should come as no surprise that when a band of Americans appeared in Blackfoot territory one summer, Smoke's first thought was to exterminate them."

At this a chill went up my back. But Yellow Sage Flower Who Tells Wise Stories shrugged and said, "Who could blame him? Fighting is what Smoke did to protect his people from being exterminated — by the Snake, the Crow, the Nez Perce, and a dozen other nations who would love to wipe every last Blackfoot from the face of the earth."

Yellow Sage Flower paused. Then she gave a sharp whistle. "Buffalo Runner!" she called out. A moment later a black pony with splashes of white on his sides appeared, with Bucephalus at his side. Yellow Sage took four or five running steps and vaulted over the pony's tail onto his back. Then together we rode west, along the top of the bluff, where who should we meet but my uncle, poking along on his mule and muttering some trial lines from a new poem or play he had in mind. He greeted us with the greatest nonchalance, as though we had never been separated by the storm and he'd known Yellow Sage Flower all her life. But when Franklin appeared a moment later, she put her hand to her mouth, burst into tears, and threw her white tippet over his head and her arms around his neck, weeping for joy and greeting him as brother. Though the savant was not quite so demonstrative, he seemed pleased to see his long-absent sister and patiently answered all her questions, explaining particularly that no, he had not turned exquisite, but had his own good reasons for adopting that guise. And after this most joyful reunion, all four of us rode on together toward the Blackfoot encampment.

Smoke's party was camped on the terrace above the river about a mile to the west. I estimated that nearly five hundred Indians were gathered here, including at least one hundred and fifty warriors armed with bows, lances, war clubs, and British muskets. I was frightened by these ferocious-looking people, who merely stared at us as we approached. But Sage led us directly to Smoke, a ruggedly made man in an unembellished deerskin suit, with eyes as black as the backing of a mirror. He observed us silently for a time, running his eyes first over my uncle, next looking at me, and finally at Franklin. Then, with Yellow Sage translating for us, he said to the savant, "My friend, I see that you, too, have learned how to shift shapes, and to shift loyalties as well. Congratulations, American, upon your new nationality."

Franklin did not condescend to reply, but merely smiled to himself. Smoke then angrily asked him to state one good reason why he should not, on the spot, destroy my uncle and me and then summarily kill every last man in the white party coming up the river. Before Franklin could reply, Yellow Sage Flower protested that a handful of Americans was no threat to the all-powerful Blackfeet, for they intended merely to pass on up the Missouri on their way to the great salt sea beyond the mountains. But nothing she said seemed to sway Smoke, who ordered that we not be allowed to leave the camp. Then he went to his lodge to put on his war paint.

45

THE BLACKFOOT war council was less elaborate than the ceremonies of the Sioux and Mandans. At twilight the men of the tribe gathered silently in a circle by the fire, and presently Smoke appeared covered in the skin and head of a grizzled bear. The claws dangled from his concealed hands and feet, and the bear's eyes and jaws were circled in red paint. Atop the animal's head was a set of buffalo horns.

In one paw Smoke shook a circular red and white rattle. In the other he carried a spear hung with scalps. As he began to perform a kind of slow, stalking dance, I sketched him, until finally he threw some powder into the ceremonial fire, creating a lemon-colored mist, into which he dissolved. Shortly afterward he reappeared in his own image, wearing only a red clout about his loins. When I showed him my sketch, he declared that now that he had duplicated himself, his people could see him in both his incarnations simultaneously, Smoke and Wa-tok-mic, the mystery bear who revealed the destiny of the tribe. "And that destiny," he said, with Franklin translating for us, "is to annihilate the Americans coming up the river."

As soon as the shape-shifter had finished laying out his plan to destroy the captains' party, Yellow Sage Flower walked to the council fire. "Pe-gap, pe-gap, pe-gap," chanted the people. Meaning, Franklin told me, "Tell us a story. Tell us a story."

"Once upon a time," she began, "there was a powerful Blackfoot magician named Smoke. He was also very bloodthirsty. And when a group of desperately ill Americans came into his land, he planned to destroy them."

"With what illness were these Americans afflicted, Yellow Sage Flower?" inquired a young man named Buffalo's Back Fat.

"Various incurable diseases of the brain and spirit," Sage replied. "But this did not matter to Smoke. In direct violation of the commandment of Napi, the Creator, never to harm the addlepated, Smoke and his misguided people killed them all. Napi was very angry and decided to punish them. The next morning when Smoke awoke and walked among his followers, he found them running about the camp on all fours. Some were barking like dogs, some grunting like bears, some howling like wolves, some digging in the ground with their nails like badgers. Many had cast off their clothes and were parading about in public. Others strolled here and there with clay cooking pots on their heads. And when Smoke tried to remonstrate with them, gibberish spewed out of his mouth. Dear people, here is what had happened. Great Napi had made the Blackfeet insane as punishment for killing the mad Americans. From then on, Smoke's people were no longer known as the Blackfeet, Lords of the Plains, but as the lunatic people."

At this juncture Smoke interrupted Sage's story. "What sort of nonsense is this?" he said. "My young ward is a fanciful storyteller, nothing more. Do you mean, Yellow Sage Flower, to suggest that the American incursionists coming up the river are actually insane?"

Yellow Sage Flower made a bow toward my uncle. Who sprang to his feet, approached the firelight, and, speaking slowly so that she could translate for him, announced that the Americans were indeed a company of madmen, beset by every extravagant caprice of a diseased mind, and that he was one of their number. "In the cruel custom of our country, we have been banished to the wilderness," he said. "Somehow we managed to forge our way well up the Missouri, but we'll surely die the most miserable death imaginable, of starvation and exposure, in the Rocky Mountains this winter. Unless, of course, Smoke kills us all first, in violation of Napi's strict injunction to the contrary." Then he said that in the morning, if the Blackfeet would conceal themselves on the bluffs overlooking the river, they would see for themselves exactly what he meant, as the members of the insane American party endured every manner of hardship by poling and hauling their cumbersome vessels up the river. For some days past, in a fit of hysteria, supposing their horses to be devils disguised as quadrupeds and bent on their masters' destruction, they had slaughtered them all.

"Go to the bluff tomorrow and watch the mad Americans," he concluded. "Judge for yourselves."

Early the following morning Smoke and his warriors waited in the tall grass on a cliff top above the Missouri as the captains and their party came toiling up the rapids into the narrow gorge that Lewis would later name the Gates of the Mountains. Some of the men were stumbling waist-deep in the icy water, hauling at ropes fastened to the bows of the canoes. Others were straining every muscle at the setting poles. Still others were paddling furiously. Yet the canoes and pirogues made next to no progress against the powerful current and were at least an hour covering a quarter of a mile.

The Indians watched for a short while, then retired to their camp greatly troubled that such mentally afflicted men should be cast out by their own people to die in the wilderness. Even Smoke was distressed to see such a piteous sight and to imagine the horrible fate of the expedition in the mountains ahead. Yet there was an outer limit to his sympathy. He declared that although he would not destroy the Americans at this time, in the autumn he would lead scouts to the mountains to cut their trail, and after they perished in the early snows his people could salvage their rifles.

At his order the Blackfeet then packed up their tepees to retreat toward the mountains. But before they left, Yellow Sage Flower drew me aside and said, "Now, Ti. Some four sleeps south of here, at a place called the Three Forks, three different rivers come together to form the Missouri. At my earliest opportunity, I plan to run away from Smoke and his warriors. I want you to meet me four dawns from today at the Three Forks and take me with you to the Pacific."

Then she spun around and sprinted toward Buffalo Runner, vaulted over his tail in her customary manner, and was off.

To the Mountains

46

Is NOT THIS JOURNEY of ours a fine frolic, Ti?" my uncle inquired the next morning as he and Franklin and I rode south toward the Three Forks.

"Sir," I replied, "we have just narrowly escaped being murdered again, this time by the Blackfeet. With the greatest respect, I do not know that I would have hit upon just that word — I mean 'frolic' — to characterize our perilous odyssey."

"Why no, nephew, you would not have. It would take a true lexicographer or — ha ha — the lexicographer Truc — to come up with so apt a description of our little journey. Either that or a man of singular ways and stays. I have noted something, Ti. You do not seem to have too many little ways and stays."

"No, sir. I fear I am most deficient when it comes to ways and stays, little or otherwise."

"It is not surprising. Your mother, for all her excellent qualities, is deficient in ways and stays. She was a Kittredge on her father's side and a Hubbell on her mother's. We Kinnesons, you know, are much stranger. My father was incomparable when it came to ways and stays. I thought of him just yesterday when we passed that colony of kingfisher-birds nesting in the clay banks above the river."

Franklin had been listening to my uncle very attentively.

Now he said, "This is most intriguing, True. In what way did the kingfisher-birds remind you of your father?"

"Because it is the very bird he adopted to be inscribed above the crossed pen and sword on the Clan Kinneson family escutcheon," my uncle said. "He believed that its blue topknot gave it an utterly unique appearance — and my father's physiognomy rather resembled that of the kingfisher. For Ti's grandfather was a locally renowned philosopher, and so busy with his books and philosophizing that he never brushed his back-hair in his life, and it stuck out behind like a kingfisher's crest."

It occurred to me to ask where my uncle had placed the kingfisher in his great *Systema Naturae Americanae.*

"Why, Ticonderoga," he said, "where else but between the turnip and the horned lizard? For like the turnip, which is neither potato nor beet, and like the horned lizard, which is neither toad nor reptile, the chattering kingfisher is neither fish nor fowl but partakes of the characteristics of both. The kingfisher-bird looks as though he went to sleep ten million years ago and just woke up and hath not yet bothered to comb his hair. He looks like a little mistake of Dame Nature that nonetheless worked out capitally in her great overall scheme. As our own mistakes often do, if we have but sense enough to turn them to our advantage."

We soon had an opportunity to test this new axiom when, at the Three Forks, we made the mistake of separating from one another. Franklin and my uncle and I parted very early on the morning of our arrival there, each of us to trace a branch of the three tributaries that conjoin to form the Missouri, with plans to meet back at the Forks that evening. Had we stayed together from the start, what I must now narrate almost certainly would not have happened.

The second serious error was mine alone. When, to my great joy, I came upon Sage a short way up the westernmost tributary,

I should have announced myself to her immediately and then ridden off with her to rejoin my uncle and Franklin. All I can say on my own behalf in this regard is that when I first spied her, preparing to bathe in a deep pool across the river, I was so transfixed that I could not bring myself to call out.

To be sure, the beautiful Yellow Sage Flower bathing in the river at sunrise was a glorious sight. I set up my easel in some young willows and prepared to paint her picture. To tell the truth, the fact that I was spying on her much enhanced my pleasure. After her dip she sat on a lizard-shaped rock by the water to dry off, rubbing some crushed sage on her arms and legs, repainting her fingernails, toenails, and scalp line, and touching up her cheeks with vermilion rouge. She donned her white antelope dress, and while she basked in the sunshine, I finished my picture. Never had my brush, or I, been so inspirited.

Then I made the third, and by far the greatest, blunder of the morning. Leaving Bucephalus and my rifle by the drying painting, I called out a greeting and began to splash my way across the river to her. There was a sudden yell, followed by a scream from Yellow Sage. Instead of returning to the horse for my weapon, I ran toward her — and toward four Indians on horse back, leading my uncle on Ethan Allen, with his hands bound behind him, his night-stocking askew, his face bruised, and his expression as dolorous as that of the Knight of the Woeful Countenance himself.

The Indians had surrounded Yellow Sage Flower and were shouting triumphantly. I half ran, half swam across the channel, only to be confronted by one of these warriors. Supposing them to be Blackfoot scouts who had come across True while in pursuit of Sage Flower, I shouted at them to mind their manners. But I was wrong on two counts. The horseman herding me up the bank toward the others had long hair that swept over his mount's tail and appeared much better dressed than the Blackfeet I had met a few days ago — indeed, he was the best-dressed Indian I had seen thus far, with the most elegant beadwork on his shirt and moccasins. I suddenly realized he was not a Blackfoot. More startling still, though as tall and well set up as any man, the rider was a woman. As were the other three.

By now two warriors had seized Yellow Sage, bound her wrists together, and carried her upstream to a little sand beach, where a third Indian was waiting with my uncle. Shoved along by my captor's horse, I stumbled on the slippery rocks. The horsewoman gave me a cutting lick across the back with her quirt. Infuriated, I seized her by the wrist with the object of yanking her off her mount. But while I was wrestling with her, one of the others came galloping down on me, and the last thing I saw was her stone war club descending toward my head.

Crows. Cawing black crows lined up on a limb. Four of them, with the Green Mountains of Vermont rising in the background. Then someone said, "Crows."

My head ached violently, but by degrees my vision returned and the four birds in the tree resolved into the four warrior women, looking down at me and laughing. My uncle, still on his mule, looked more sorrowful than ever. I tried to move, but my hands and feet were bound.

"These women are Crows, Ti," Yellow Sage said. "They belong to a society of female warriors, and they're on a self-proving mission, scouting for Blackfoot horses to steal. They know I'm a Blackfoot, but they can't figure out who or what you and your uncle are, and they don't know yet that your horse is across the river. Whatever you do, don't tell them."

"How, sir, do you find yourself in this fix?" I asked my uncle.

Who, for a rare moment in his career, seemed at a complete loss for a reply.

Then he said, "If you want the truth, Ti, I was taken whilst performing a private function in the bushes. What's more, these Louisiana Amazonians laughed quite uproariously at my predicament. I might have reached for my arquebus, which was near at hand, but modesty dictated that I first reach for my codpiece — I mean Flame's cushion — and hitch up my breeches. By then it was too late. This same Queen Hippolyta who rendered you senseless had me on the ground and trussed up like a Christmas goose; and damme, Ti, she was laughing the whole time. I shall never live this down."

My greater concern was that we might not live much longer at all. The women were now all talking at once, debating something, I thought. "Can you understand their lingo?" I asked Yellow Sage Flower.

"Scarcely anyone can, even them. It's a mishmash of clucks and clicks and gobbles. But we've had enough Crow captives around that I've gotten the drift of it."

"Just then I recognized the root word for 'fish,'" my uncle suddenly said. "It's quite universal among the Indians of America, suggesting a possible linkage dating back several thousand years to China. I wish my hands were free so I could get at my lexicon."

"Not to mention your weapons," I ventured to say, a bit vexed that he would be thinking of lexicography at such a moment.

"I gather," he continued, "that Hippolyta is rather sweet on me. We might purchase our freedom in exchange for my attentions."

In a high, utterly ridiculous voice, he called out, "O Hippolyta, Queen of the Amazons. Your admiring swain awaits you with all eagerness." He made big moon eyes at the giantess, accompanied by such contortions of his long face and lantern jaw, and such an attempt to bow in a courtly fashion while bound to his mule, that the four Crow women had to support each other to keep from falling on the ground with laughter.

"What do they propose to do with us?" I asked Yellow Sage Flower.

"That's what they've been arguing about," she said. "Tall Mare, whom your uncle calls Hippolyta, wants to tie us to cottonwood trees and use us for target practice. One of the others suggested that they skin us and stuff us with meadow grass like scarecrows. Another wants to roast us over a low fire."

"Dear Jehovah!" exclaimed my uncle. "We can't allow any of that. I have an idea they'll like better. It's called the Race for Life, and was often employed by the Persians with their Greek captives. An archer would shoot an arrow as far as his bow would throw it. That's how much of a head start they'd give the Greek. When he reached the arrow, the whole Persian army would tear out after him, and the Devil take the hindmost."

"How often did the captive get away?" Yellow Sage inquired.

"Why, so far as I know, never," my uncle said. "But there's always a first time. I'll wager that with these ladies after us, we could run like the wind. Go ahead and propose it, my dear. Not to put too fine a point on our predicament, I fear it's our only chance."

47

THE CROWS LISTENED to Yellow Sage's proposal, then nodded. It appeared that the Race for Life was on, though as Sage explained to us, she would not be required to participate in this contest, since our captors planned to make a present of her to Tall Mare's father, one Horse Stealer, who had recently lost his wife of many years. I scarcely knew whether to thank my uncle for his inspiration or curse him. But with the captains and their party still fifty or sixty miles away, battling their way foot by foot up the swift current of the Missouri, and Franklin off on the easternmost of the three tributaries, we had little hope of rescue. I had to agree that running for our lives would be better than being posted up for a target or skinned alive.

Tall Mare jerked me to my feet, cut the thongs binding my hands and feet, then freed my uncle. As she fetched her bow from her horse and nocked an arrow, an idea occurred to me.

"Quick," I said to Yellow Sage Flower, "try to talk her into shooting the arrow across the river. Dare her to do it. Say I challenge her to shoot across the river."

Yellow Sage Flower spoke fast, more clucks and gobbles. But Tall Mare laughed and shook her head. "Ha ha, Ti," chuckled my uncle. "Letting us cross the river is evidently more of an advantage than they care to give us. We'll have to come up with a different ruse."

"We'd better do so quickly," I said.

Sage Flower looked around, and her gaze alighted on the lizard-shaped boulder where she had been captured. She spoke in Crow again, and Tall Mare relayed her words to her three companions.

To us, in English, Yellow Sage Flower said, "I think I've persuaded her to shoot the arrow down near that big stone. I told them they should kill you where they found me, that it would make a grand story to tell. Now here's a story for you. I'll make it short. Long ago the Blackfeet trapped Sleek Otter out on the open prairie where he couldn't get away. Never having seen an otter before, they didn't know anything about his ways. So when he asked them to let him go down by the riverbank to say a last prayer to Creator Napi, they fell for it. Sleek Otter wad-dled down to the water, turned around, and instead of a prayer, shouted out a curse on the Blackfeet. Then he plunged into his natural element and disappeared forever."

As Tall Mare fired her arrow high into the blue sky, I said to Sage, "But we aren't otters."

"Think like one," she said. "It will help."

Tall Mare barked something at me as her arrow came to rest near the lizard rock.

"What did she say?"

"She said strip off your clothes, both of you, and hightail it," Sage said.

Now the Crow women were painting diagonal vermilion stripes on their faces. At the same time, I became aware of a large black cloud climbing up in the sky from the south.

"Ask her, with the greatest respect, if I may, for modesty's sake, leave on my tights and codpiece," said my uncle.

"Leave them on, by all means," Sage said, to my considerable relief, since I was no more eager than he to stand stark naked before her and the Amazonians. "Just go. And remember Sleek Otter."

"For Sleek Otter and for Scholia Aristotle!" cried my uncle, and broke into a lumbering sprint, which I thought to acceler-ate somewhat by taking his hand in mine and half-dragging him along beside me. I refused to look back, even when an ar-row whizzed just over our heads and another appeared quiver-ing in the ground by my bare foot.

"Run, run, as fast as you can," Private True called back over his shoulder to the Crows. "You can't catch me, I'm the —"

"Uncle, for God's sake, save your breath."

"Pick up the first arrow when you get to the lizard rock," Yel-low Sage Flower called out. "Use it for a weapon."

We continued to tear through the bankside willows. An arrow flew by so close that the feathers ticked my left ear. A moment later we reached the rock. My uncle stooped and picked up Tall Mare's arrow, then we leaped into the rapids below the rock.

Over the rushing water I heard yells. We quartered hard across the current that was sweeping us downstream toward a sharp bend. In midstream we seized a drift-log and got on the far side of it from the Crows, who were riding through the thick willows along the bank and loosing more arrows at us. Several passed inches above our heads, others thunked into the log. Then we were around the bend. As we passed near the opposite bank, my uncle began counting aloud in Greek so that our pursuers, if they were within earshot, would not know what he was saying. On three we made a surging dive, swam hard, and gained the bank.

From across the river I heard yelling as the Crows fought their way out around a thick copse of cottonwoods. Supposing us to be still in the rapids, they rode to cut us off below the bend. We dodged into the brush and started upstream. But we had contrived to get into a thicket of wild-rose briars, whose thorns tore cruelly at our bare feet and legs and arms. I gave the jay whistle I'd taught Bucephalus to come to. Ahead we heard something crashing through the thicket. I whistled again and we raced out of the briars — and narrowly escaped being trampled by Tall Mare riding toward us at full gallop. My uncle feinted one way, jumped the other, seized her by her trailing hair, and yanked her off her pony onto the ground. The force of the fall knocked out her wind. Leaping astride the Crow maiden, he raised the arrow he had picked up earlier high above his head with both hands. In Tall Mare's eyes there was only defiance. She neither asked for nor expected quarter.

"Uncle!" I cried.

But he had no intention of killing the Amazonian. With all his might he drove the arrow not into Tall Mare's windpipe but through her thick hair, pinning her head to the ground and rendering her temporarily helpless.

At just that moment Bucephalus galloped into the clearing. "Ha ha, Ti. The coy maid feigns indifference" — on the contrary, Tall Mare was struggling like a wildcat to free herself — "but I sense her ardent spirits rising. Ah, madam. If we had world enough and time . . . but for the nonce, forgive me."

With this, True struck the giantess full on the jaw with his fist, knocking her quite senseless. Then he leaped up behind me onto Bucephalus, and we posted hard for the ford upriver. We stopped only for my easel, with the painting of Yellow Sage Flower still attached, then galloped across the shallows, where I hurried into my clothes, slit the thongs binding Yellow Sage, cut the hobble-strings on the Crows' horses, and fired my rifle to drive them off. Sage jumped onto her black and white pony. I pointed south, toward the approaching rainstorm, to indicate that we should head in that direction. My uncle, however, still struggling into his chain mail, shook his head. "You and Sage strike out that way, Ti. I intend to ride overland, across the middle tributary I explored this morning, leaving just enough sign to lead Hippolyta on a merry chase while you escape. I'll find Franklin tomorrow or the next day, and we'll overtake you in the Land Where the River of Yellow Stones Rises. Don't try to dissuade me. For in our wrestling, the fair maiden stole from me that without which I cannot, in decency, proceed another mile in mixed company."

"And what, pray, can that be?"

"Flame's riding pillow," he replied. And, clapping his heels to his mule, the old knight-errant was off on what was, perhaps, the strangest mission in the history of chivalry.

48

LIGHTNING AND MORE LIGHTNING. Crackling rivers of electricity swept down the sky, and the rain came in such torrents that our tracks were wiped out almost before we laid them down. On and on we rode, half blinded by the deluge, which continued for several hours. At sunset it cleared, and over the mountains to the south the evening sky was the same deep green it had been on the evening before I met Yellow Sage Flower. Ahead, she told me, lay the Land Where the River of Yellow Stones Rises, a magical place where we would wait for my uncle and Franklin. For now, she suggested that we spend the night under a nearby ledge overhanging a little cul-de-sac, where we could light a fire and dry off without much fear of detection.

Here Sage offered to tell me her story. "As you know, Ticonderoga," she began, "not so very long ago or far away, a girl named Yellow Sage Flower Who Tells Wise Stories was orphaned by the deaths of both her dear mother and father, leaving her alone in the world except for her brother. However, her grandfather on her mother's side of the family happened to be none other than Old Napi — the Creator of the Blackfeet."

I could not help smiling. But Yellow Sage sprang up from the fire and said that if, in my great ignorance, I intended to make fun of her, there would be no more storytelling that night or any night. And she now wished she had let the Crows burn me at the stake to spare herself this mortification.

I offered up a thousand apologies, protesting that I would

never dream of laughing at her; but, having been raised in an altogether different place and manner, I needed a little time to adjust my thinking to the ways of the Blackfeet.

"You must say 'the ways of the Blackfeet, *Lords of the Plains,*'" she corrected me. "For that is who and what we are. Indeed, 'Blackfeet' is only our name in English. In fact, we are the Piegans, or Torn Robe People."

"The Blackfeet, Lords of the Plains, then. I am beginning to understand them much better already."

"Of course you are," she said, sitting down again. "Now then. I happen to be the apple of Napi's eye as well as his grand-daughter. But I shouldn't want you to suppose that my grandfa-ther and I always agree. Not by any means. For he arranged for me to marry Smoke when I turn eighteen. Which is why I de-cided to run away."

Although I had no notion what to make of this gorgeous creature and her stories, I assured her that I would do all in my power to help her escape from Smoke. We talked on together most companionably until at last we were both overcome by weariness, and so lay down on opposite sides of the fire and slept for the remaining hours of the night.

49

LATE THE FOLLOWING AFTERNOON, as Yellow Sage Flower and I rode south toward the Land Where the River of Yellow Stones Rises and our rendezvous with my uncle, we had our first quarrel. She wished to camp in the prairie by a little stream winding down out of the mountains. I thought it wiser to ride to a higher place that would offer us more protection from marauding Crows or Smoke's party. Finally Sage said she would tell me how Blackfoot couples settled disputes if I would get off my horse and sit down by the brook and devote my full attention to her. Sitting cross-legged facing me and about three feet away, she began.

"Soon after my grandfather created the world, Ticonderoga, he decided to make himself a wife — Old Woman. Being inexperienced in such undertakings, he sculpted his first spouse from one of the many glaciers in our homeland. But she was far too frosty for any of the purposes Napi had in mind, so he set her in the sun; and soon this unobliging woman was a small pool of meltwater, at which my grandfather laughed very heartily. Then he fashioned a more suitable helpmeet from Missouri River clay, into which he breathed life, and they were very happy together for some years. But disputes between a man and a woman being inevitable, Napi and Old Woman Two could not agree on how many children to have. So my grandfather decreed that he should have first say in this matter and in all matters. To his surprise, Old Woman Two immediately agreed — with the provision that second say be reserved for her. 'Fine,' Napi declared. 'I have first say. I say we will have one child. A son for me.' Old Woman Two smiled. 'And I, who have second say, say we will have two children. A son and a daughter for us.' At this, my grandfather was confounded. But he had to agree, and of course he never regretted it. Where do you want to camp tonight, Ti? Say your first say."

"Higher up, on the ridge."

"Are you sure?" She smiled, and I felt myself beginning to melt, like Napi's unfortunate first wife.

"Well," I said.

"I will now exercise my option as a Blackfoot woman with second say," Yellow Sage Flower told me. "And *I* say we camp here."

Which, needless to say, we did.

The next morning, as we ascended a great plateau, we ran across the tracks of four ponies headed in the same direction as we were. Sage assured me that this was the female Crow raiding party. What concerned me much more, however, was that intermingled with their hoofprints were those of my uncle's mule. So far from decoying the Amazonians away from us and recovering Flame's riding cushion, he had managed, it appeared, to be recaptured — or worse yet, killed, and his mule appropriated by his murderers.

For the rest of the morning we followed the tracks up through a handsome country of wooded dells, steep hillsides dotted with evergreens, wildflower meadows, and cold rushing streams. As we continued to climb, the soil became thin and rocky. I lost the Crows' trail entirely, but Sage had no trouble following it, and in the early afternoon she announced that we would surely overtake them by evening. Then she said she would show me a thing that I had never seen before, which I should be prepared to sketch for a most original painting. In a brush pile just below a hilltop she opened a sort of saddlebag, which she called a parfleche, and removed a leather string, with which she fashioned a snare. Then she scraped out a pit on top of the knoll and covered it with pine boughs. Soon we heard a squeal and saw a snowshoe rabbit struggling upside down by one of its big hind feet from the snare. Sage spoke to the rabbit in Blackfoot, quieting it immediately, then tied it by one leg on top of the cut pine boughs and secreted herself beneath them in the pit, bidding me hide with our horses in the nearby pine woods with my pencil at the ready.

For a time nothing out of the ordinary occurred. The tethered rabbit hopped about on the boughs. Except for a sifting breeze in the hot-scented pines, all was silent. Then a shadow glided over the hilltop. The rabbit froze. I looked up to see, black against the blue afternoon sky, a golden eagle plummeting earthward with its talons outstretched. Just before the bird struck the rabbit, Sage jerked it out of harm's way. The eagle screamed as it crashed into the boughs. Sage's hands shot out and grasped the bird by its legs. For the next several seconds everything was all beating wings and driving yellow talons and striking beak and determined girl. Then the eagle was standing on the ground beside Sage, and although blood streamed down both her arms, she was talking to it just as she had spoken to the rabbit. Presently it lifted into the air again, flying straight south in the direction the tracks had been heading. Yellow Sage signaled me to remain where I was while she bound her arms with some strips of blue cloth from her parfleche. After some minutes the eagle reappeared, landing beside her again. Through some private communication, it seemed to be reporting to her on what it had seen. When their conversation had ended, it flew away toward the west, and Sage returned to me with a delighted smile, though she refused to tell what she had learned.

We rode on, and in the early evening we came out onto a red-rock crag above a very large lake entirely hemmed in by mountains. This was the first lake I had seen since leaving St. Louis. I was amazed that it could lie so high. But Yellow Sage, who had been here before, was pointing at some people on the bank of a river meandering out of the lake's northwestern corner. "Let's ride down and take them unawares," she said.

As we galloped down the hillside, whom should I discern, standing by the lake, but my uncle. To my great relief, he was demonstrating the use of his fly-rod to Tall Mare, standing very close to him and watching with apparent admiration. He handed her the rod and, with his arm encircling her shoulder and his hand grasping her wrist, he helped her execute false casts, calling out instructions in his schoolmasterly way, as he had when he'd taught me to fly-fish on my mother's little stock pond. "Ten o'clock, twelve o'clock, two o'clock. Ten o'clock, twelve o'clock, two o'clock. Excellent, my young Hippolyta. You have a natural talent, my dear."

The fact that Tall Mare spoke not a single word of English did not seem to trouble either of them. To me he said, patting the bulge in his buckskin pantaloons, "Fear not, Ti. Not only have I made peace all around with our Crow friends, I have also recovered that which I earlier had lost." My uncle had indeed recovered Flame Danielle's pink cushion, though he appeared, by the same token, to have lost his heart.

But where was Franklin, whose tracks True had been following when the Crows apprehended him? Sage assured me that her resourceful brother would turn up when least expected.

Earlier that day, Yellow Sage Flower had told me that no people dwelt year-round in the Land Where the River of Yellow Stones Rises, which the nations of Louisiana considered a sacred place. But each year in late summer, the Crows convened for a trade rendezvous at the place where the river flowed out of the lake. To this celebration they invited all of the other Indians of the western plains and Rocky Mountains except, pointedly, their inveterate enemies from the far north, the Blackfeet.

That night we camped by the lake, a little apart from my uncle and the Crow women. Early the next morning I woke to discover Sage watching me. "Why don't you try to catch me, Ti?" she said. "I'm in the mood for a race." Before I could reply she leaped up and sped off down the slope toward the lake as fast as her feet could carry her, with me in close pursuit.

Sage was a fleet runner. But like my long-legged uncle in his day, I was able to outrun nearly anyone. She was quick, I quicker. I overtook her at the edge of the water, she tripped me, I sprang to my feet, and away we went again. With her long black hair flying, she shot me a mocking look over her shoulder, then stopped abruptly near a secluded bay — beside my uncle and Tall Mare, asleep in each other's arms and surrounded by a party of Crow warriors.

One of the men identified himself as Horse Stealer, the chief of the tribe and father of Tall Mare. Horse Stealer seemed very much amused by his daughter's attachment to my uncle, who, upon waking, turned as red as the sun coming up over the mountains to be discovered in such a situation. But he soon recovered himself and informed the chief, with Sage as translator, that he need not worry for his daughter's virtue, since he and Hippolyta were "just friends."

"Tib-Rep-Mic, you and your yellow-haired nephew, and even the Blackfoot girl, are welcome here in our sacred park," Horse Stealer replied. When Yellow Sage asked the meaning of my uncle's Crow name, the chief said, "Stranger Who Chose Not to Kill a Human Being" — meaning his daughter, when she had been at my uncle's mercy, pinned to the ground by her hair near the Three Forks.

Horse Stealer inquired where my uncle and I had come from. Sage explained that we were Americans, who lived far to the east. To this the chief responded that Americans would always be welcome in the Crow Nation, and he decreed on the spot that no Crow must ever kill or harm one, though he could not guarantee the security of American *horses*. For to ask a Crow not to steal horses would be asking the impossible. Smiling cordially, Horse Stealer invited my uncle to shake hands with him. He grasped my uncle's right hand in his, then with his left fist struck him a prodigious blow on the side of the head, knocking him clean off his feet, to repay him for striking his daughter.

Rising and rubbing his jaw, my uncle said that though no man had ever felled him before, nay, not in fisticuffs or cudgel play or any other wise, fair was fair and he took no umbrage. Then he and Tall Mare went off hand in hand to fish the River of Yellow Stones, which the private assured me was teeming with Kinnesonian cutthroats, offering the best sport he had ever known — though Yellow Sage and I were not entirely persuaded that fishing was the principal sport he had in mind.

50

OVER THE NEXT SEVERAL DAYS my uncle spent every waking — and sleeping — minute with his darling Hippolyta. In the meantime, while the Crows prepared for their annual fair, I began another tableau, with the lake as its centerpiece. Compacting my images, I combined images of several spectacular wonders I had seen nearby, including the outlet river and its falls, which cut through a deep canyon with gleaming yellow walls; a mountain of glassy black obsidian; a field of oozing muds colored blue, copper, green, and orange; and a mammoth hot spring of azure water. In the foreground I placed a geyser, which several times a day at regular intervals erupted into a gushing hundred-foot-high column of steam. The Crow Indians called this marvel the Weeping Maiden, and believed it to have once been a Shoshone girl from the mountains to the west who was jilted by her lover and still wept each day for him.

As I painted, Yellow Sage told me stories. Many involved the antics of her grandfather Napi, who, it seemed, had nearly as many little ways and stays as my uncle. Once, trying to pick the ripe purple berries off the *reflection* of a bullberry bush, Napi leaned over too far and tumbled head over heels into the river. To punish the bush he gave it thorns so that the only way people could pick its fruit was by whacking the branches with sticks. On another occasion, Napi accidentally set himself on fire while stealing a handsome pair of elk-skin leggings from the sun. Again he had to take to the river, this time to douse himself.

One night Sage told us a tale in which a young Picgan boy and girl fall into the clutches of a wicked witch. When she decides to cook the children alive, a mountain buffalo helps them escape, then drowns the evil witch in a river. "See how Tall Mare trembles," cried my shuddering uncle. "Do not worry, my dear Dulcinea. I will let no witches carry *you* away."

Though Sage had been educated at Sault Ste. Marie as carefully as her brother and spoke perfect English, as well as Blackfoot, Cree, Assiniboine, Crow, and Shoshone, she practiced all the ways of her Piegan mother. Her favorite dish was buffalo blood soup, which she whipped up from the fat and blood of a bison, sweetened with ripe huckleberries. Yet when my uncle fried up a mess of trout, she gagged at the sight of their orange flesh and said that even if they were starving, the Piegans never ate fish, which they reviled as unclean. Serpents and lizards, on the other hand, she held to be wise, healthy, and long-lived; from Horse Stealer, who was the tribal snake charmer as well as its chief and had brought to the rendezvous a box full of writhing vipers, she borrowed a lively bull snake five feet long, which she draped round her neck, then invited me to embrace her.

*   *   *

I was eager to do a painting of the Indians' trade rendezvous, but I was running low on colors and blank canvases and wished to husband what I had left for our journey to the Pacific. "Is that all the trouble?" Sage said after I explained my dilemma to her. "Go shoot us a buffalo."

I did as she bade me, and in the animal's gall bladder she collected about a gallon of rainwater from a pothole on a red mesa. This she boiled down to a thick, pasty substance, which she compounded with a little buffalo tallow to form a brilliant madder-red. From sage twigs boiled with the leaves attached she concocted a glowing yellow. She extracted a royal purple from the huckleberries that grew abundantly in the high natural parks of the nearby mountains, and a lovely azure blue from the dried dung of some teal who were raising a second brood beside the Lake Where the River of Yellow Stones Rises. White she procured from a snowy clay resembling our kaolin.

After scraping the hair from the hide of a mountain sheep, Sage tanned the underside with a mixture of buffalo brains and fat, smoked it over a fire-hole for a day, then set me to pounding it with a rock to make it soft and white. When I was finished, she stretched the hide over a frame of four willow sticks about the thickness of her little finger — thus making me a painting surface as smooth as canvas. To hold fast the colors, she showed me how to extract a more than passable sizing oil from wild sunflower seeds mixed with the glue from a boiled beaver tail and the hoofs of a buffalo. From the edge of a buffalo's scapula she cut a light, porous applicator that received paint well and applied it in an even flow; and for finer work she fashioned a true brush from a deer fibula tipped with the hairs of a bull elk's underbelly. Henceforward, while in the West, I would never be without the means to paint.

I finished *Indian Rendezvous at the Lake Where the River of*

Yellow Stones Rises on the last day of the fair. That evening the Crows put on a performance for the assembled tribes, which they called the Ballet of the Swimming Horses. Under Horse Stealer's direction, their ponies conducted an elaborate water-dance in the lagoon of the lake just above the outlet. It was very beautiful to see, and afterward, at the Crows' Tobacco Ceremony, my uncle presented the chief with a small sack of hemp seeds to plant in their home to the east. In exchange, the women of the tribe made him the first male member of Tall Mare's Amazonian society.

But no sooner had these ceremonies taken place than a hail of arrows and musket bullets announced the arrival of Smoke and a heavily armed party of Blackfoot warriors galloping up from the lagoon, bent upon capturing Sage and returning her to the Land of the Glaciers.

51

"WELL, UNCLE," I shouted over the roar of the river. "This is a very pretty situation."

"A very pretty situation indeed, Ti. The Blackfeet want Yellow Sage back and are determined to get her. The Crows are desperate to secure my services as commander of the Amazonian raiding party. The two nations have us surrounded. And if they don't wipe each other out first, I can't imagine what will happen. Two years ago we would hardly have dared hope for such an exciting —"

Exciting what, I never heard. "Adventure," I feared he might have said. But the word was drowned out by the thunder of falling water. My uncle, Sage, and I were ledged up with our mounts in a niche behind the first high cascade on the River of Yellow Stones, a few miles downstream from the lake. We had managed to flee into the woods during the skirmish the night before at the lagoon; but with dawn fast approaching, we would soon have to come out and deal with our pursuers, now arrayed on opposite sides of the river just below the falls.

"I beg your pardon, my dear?" my uncle shouted to Sage, who was attempting to say something to him over the terrific din. Out came his tin hearing trumpet, which he placed as close to her ear as possible. But the only words I could make out were "my grandfather."

"I hope this works," I said as Sage and I led the horses down the bank toward our Crow allies at sunrise. "It seems most improbable."

"Where Napi is concerned, the more improbable the plan the better," Sage called back. "What could be more improbable than making his first wife out of ice?"

I refrained from pointing out that it was exactly such experiments that caused me to be a bit skeptical of her grandfather's wisdom. But if my uncle could slip away undetected while Sage and I distracted the Indians, there was a chance — just a chance — that her idea might actually work.

The Crows and the Blackfeet were now hurling insults back and forth across the river at each other. Horse Stealer and his people blamed Smoke for breaking the time-honored truce of the fair. Smoke shouted back that the Crows had no right to detain Yellow Sage. Sage lost no time informing him that she was here in the Land Where the River of Yellow Stones Rises by her own choice, and would on no account rejoin them. But there was no doubt that the Blackfeet could cross the river, wipe out all of the fairgoers, carry off Sage, and kill me in the bargain if they wanted to.

"So I see you're ready to go against the wishes of my grandfather, Lord Napi," Yellow Sage called out over the rapids.

"I'm glad to learn that you alone know Napi's will," Smoke shouted back.

"As a matter of fact, I do. He spends his summers not far from here, and I've spoken to him very recently. I'll be glad to take you to him so that he can tell you himself."

"What kind of nonsense is this? Do you think I'd be so foolish as to let you lead me into a trap in some dark canyon?"

"My grandfather lives in no dark canyon but on a high, airy plain. Bring your soldiers if you're afraid to come alone."

Smoke agreed to accompany us, so long as the Crow force remained behind, which in fact they seemed very willing to do. But after Sage and I picked our way across the powerful river and we headed out with Smoke and his war party, the chief demanded again to know where we were leading him. Sage explained that Napi could be found in a nearby underground lodge, where he took a steam bath each morning to alleviate the ailments of advancing age. For, by her estimate, her grandfather was somewhat over ten thousand years old.

"Absurd," Smoke said. "Lord Napi is immortal and quite immune to human ailments."

"Be patient," she replied. "We shall see what we shall see."

Soon the terrain began to look familiar. Just ahead a little puff of steam went up from some rocks. Smoke gave a harsh laugh. "Is that great Napi's sweat lodge?"

"Yes," Yellow Sage Flower said. "Ride up and gather around the warm rocks in a circle if you wish to see him."

The disbelieving chief and his soldiers urged their mounts

close to the smoking rocks. Suddenly a voice thundered out in the Blackfoot language, "WHO DARES APPROACH MY SACRED STEAM BATH?"

At this all of the Indians but Smoke fell back in confusion. "Who speaks?" the chief said.

"I AM NAPI," roared the disembodied voice as the rocks began to send forth steamy exhalations. From deep in the ground came a muttering.

Smoke, to his credit, stood his ground and even pulled back his lance arm. But even as he did so, a hiss like ten thousand rattlesnakes emerged from the shaking ground, and up shot a huge jet of hot water and steam. Riders shouted as scalding droplets rained down on them. Smoke's pony whirled and galloped off, with the chief hanging on for his life and the rest of the horses thundering after him.

"Napi has spoken, my children," my uncle said, stepping out from behind a boulder with his tin trumpet in his hand. "Let us proceed to the mountains and the Ocean Pacific."

52

Two days later we were overjoyed to discover the tracks of Franklin's pony on an upper fork of the westernmost branch of the Three Forks. Nearby on a pole was a note from the savant saying that Lewis's party was laboring up the river some miles behind him, the shallows and rapids being very tedious to navigate in heavy canoes. Immediately my uncle forged ahead on his mule to meet Sage's brother. She and I stopped only long enough for me to sketch a hill in the shape of a swimming beaver, which occasioned the following conversation between us.

"Granted that the beaver is the most industrious animal," I said, "which, then, is the smartest?"

"Which do you think?" Sage said.

"The coyote? Or the gray prairie wolf?" I was remembering how the wolves had decoyed the young antelope away from the herd back on the Missouri, which seemed to me to require great ingenuity and perhaps even some power of forethought.

"Certainly not," Sage said. "Sister Raven is the smartest. For she can not only be taught to talk, she can always feed herself and her family, even in times of famine. Now, tell me, Ticonderoga. If Grandmother Beaver is the most diligent, and Sister Raven the smartest, which of our wild brethren is the most beneficial?"

"The horse?"

"Wrong again!" she cried out delightedly. "Brother Bison is the most beneficial because *he* provides us with both food and shelter."

Ahead a bobcat — a creature of great temerity, even in Vermont — sat on a cottonwood stump near the trail and watched us pass by not twenty paces away. "Why, if you know so much," said Sage, "does Bobcat have such a short little scut of a tail?"

When I admitted that I had no idea, she said, "About six thousand years ago, Bobcat stole a rabbit Napi was cooking for his supper. My grandfather tried to stop him, but all he got was the tail. Since then all bobcats have been born with short tails."

From her parfleche Sage produced a raw buffalo liver as large as my mother's doormat at home, and began to tear into it with her white teeth. After eating her fill of this delicacy she handed me what remained and insisted I try a bite; but I could not bring myself to swallow it. She laughed. And in this lighthearted way, we continued upstream toward the Land of the Shoshones.

The following afternoon we started up an Indian road to the west. There were fresh signs of many horses here, but we rode until nightfall without seeing another soul. The next morning we traced our way up a little rill until at last, near an icy spring encircled by lupines, we stood on what we judged to be the Great Divide separating the waters of the Atlantic and the Gulf of Mexico from those of the Pacific. Off to the west loomed range upon range of soaring, snowcapped peaks. Although I had expected to find more mountains between the Divide and the Columbia River, these were taller than any I had seen thus far, and blocked the way along the entire western horizon. Even Sage seemed daunted. Not only was there no discernible waterway through these peaks, there seemed to be no pass at all. It was as if a whole new continent stretched out between us and the Pacific, with the most difficult part of our trek yet to come before we reached the ocean.

"What's that?"

"It's Tree Feller, the great red-cockaded woodpecker. He's hammering at a dead trunk in a place that echoes," Yellow Sage said.

The ringing blows resounded through the woods as we worked our way down the western side of the Divide beside a stream through the willows until, at the bottom of the ridge, in a bowl surrounded by steep hills, we discovered not the estimable Tree Feller but my uncle and Franklin, putting the finishing touches on a large log platform. "Not another prairie ark?" I inquired, after a warm reunion. Whereupon Franklin assured me that this was no ship but something altogether new and wonderful, with which my uncle hoped to call forth the Shoshone, who had melted into the mountains at their approach, leaving only trampled meadows where their horses had grazed and smoldering cooking fires by the stream.

That evening at sunset, we built up a leaping bonfire behind the platform. My uncle then strutted out onto the logs and announced to the empty hillsides that he would now present a one-man performance of his comedy, *Ethan Allen*. Without further ado he began to charge up and down the stage, acting out all the parts of the play. Sure enough, as the drama progressed, Indians began to appear on the slopes above, first by ones and twos, then in small groups, then throngs. When the play finally ended, with the fall of Fort Ti and Ethan's great speech, the audience maintained complete silence for above a minute. Finally, a child tittered. Then another. Soon, all over the hills, Shoshone men, women, and children were roaring with laughter. Never had I heard people laugh so hard. The Indians poured down off the mountainsides and shook my uncle's hand over and over. And the next day, when he indicated that he would like to muster up a troupe for another performance, there was such a press of volunteers that only the highest-ranking braves could be selected to participate.

When I was growing up in Vermont, our neighboring farmers said that certain men were "land poor," meaning that though they owned hundreds of acres, they rarely had any ready cash. Our new Indian friends were "horse-poor." The Shoshone had been driven off the plains into these barren mountains by Yellow Sage's Blackfoot relations, who had British muskets. And although the Spanish in California refused to trade guns to the Shoshone, or to any other Indians in their sphere, our hosts had a great abundance of excellent Spanish horses. Their encampment of about three hundred people owned at least one thousand first-class mounts; and it seemed likely that their chief, a fine-looking older man named Cameahwait, would be willing to trade some of them to Lewis's party, who would certainly need horses to cross the Bitterroots, as the mountains to the west were called.

Since there were several possible routes that the expedition might take over the Divide, my uncle asked Cameahwait if he would send some of his men out to find the American party and bring them along, with a letter from us urging them to come forward with all expediency. For the Indians had warned us that with fall coming on, and winter close behind, we and our friends must waste no time in getting through the mountains. As the scouting party to locate the official expedition was being made up, however, a young Shoshone named Goat Horns, who had been away on a week-long vision quest, rode hard into camp. He reported that after six days, no vision had been vouchsafed to him. But that morning, as he was morosely riding back toward the camp, he had encountered three apparitions near the cove of a creek just across the Divide to the east. These demons had advanced toward him, calling out repeatedly, "Ta-ba-bone," which in the Shoshone language meant "stranger" or "enemy." The wraith in the middle had rolled up his sleeves, evidently to show his white arms. This further alarmed Goat Horns by confirming his fear that these creatures were not men but ghouls. Putting his heels to his horse, he galloped for camp to warn his people.

Despite all our reassurances that the expedition meant them no harm, the Shoshone were terribly alarmed. At last my uncle broke out his hemp in order to put them in a more tranquil state of mind — and he pointed out that on his Dutch clock the witching hour of midnight was now past, so they did not need to worry so much over the possibility of apparitions.

This comedy of misunderstandings ended happily enough. Cameahwait and his people ventured out to greet Captain Lewis and hugged him to a fare-thee-well, since by now they were all under the affectionate influence of my uncle's cannabis. Then we went together in a party to meet Clark and the main body of the expedition, which, though much delayed on the river, eventually came straggling along. In an unexpected twist, Cameahwait turned out to be Sacagawea's older brother. But no sooner were we reunited with the captains than a most tragical disaster befell our own little party, which I must now narrate.

Early that evening Franklin decided to go a-fishing on No Return River, as the Shoshone called the tumultuous waterway that ran in front of their camp. Now the No Return was said by the Indians to flow a hundred miles before joining a larger river that they called the Serpent. The Serpent, after another two hundred miles or so, debouched into a major tributary of the Columbia. This network of watercourses would certainly have been our first choice, and the captains', too, for proceeding to the Pacific, but for one difficulty. According to the Shoshone, the first sixty or seventy miles of the No Return passed through a canyon said to be utterly unnavigable.

Just at twilight, while angling from a borrowed canoe below two long fish weirs in the pool in front of the Indian camp, Franklin hooked an enormous salmon. "Fish on!" he cried, as the silvery giant raced up the length of the pool, stripping line off his reel. The savant held his rod high over his head for maximum leverage (and show) as a great crowd of Indians gathered on the bank to see the outcome of this epic battle. My uncle, in the meantime, was running along the shore calling out all kinds of advice, much of it contradictory. One moment he told Franklin to keep a tight line, the next to let the salmon run or he would certainly lose his trophy. The fish jumped once, twice, thrice. "Heyday!" cried Franklin. "I shall call this fish Izaac Walton."

Izaac Walton leapt yet again. But then, as hooked fish will sometimes do, he took it into his head to make a dash straight down the river toward the raging whitewater below. "Follow the fish, the rapids be damned!" called my uncle. Whether Franklin actually intended to do such a foolish thing, I do not know. But the current above the rapids ran deceivingly fast, and before the Blackfoot sportsman knew what was happening, his canoe had been swept past the fish weirs and was bobbing down the river on the crests of the whitecaps. Sooner than one would think possible, our dear friend had disappeared around the far bend between the sheer red walls of the No Return, leaving our entire party stunned and grief-stricken — all but Yellow Sage, who said that Napi would never let his grandson drown in that or any other river. I was not hopeful, however. For mile after mile below our encampment the No Return was said to be one unbroken thundering cascade between high walls of rock; even Captain Clark, the expedition's best waterman, was obliged to conclude that no canoe could survive for ten seconds in such water.

53

FALL HAD ARRIVED. The clear slanting light, the bull elks bugling in the mountains, the aspens turning yellow along the river — all were signs of the turning season. Cameahwait was now warning us every day of the severe September blizzards common in the Bitterroots. He explained that we would have to travel *north* for several sleeps just to strike the pass through the mountains and that the trail through the Bitterroots was faint and uncertain, and game very scarce.

Yellow Sage seemed no more anxious over the impending crossing than over the fate of Franklin whom I continued to mourn. She sewed for herself and my uncle and me large buffalo-skin parfleches to carry extra food and gear; made each of us several pairs of spare moccasins; and dried some elk and venison jerky to take with us. But while she was a capable planner, like my uncle she seemed not to worry much about what lay ahead, but rather to live for today.

Sage loved to play with Sacagawea's little son, Jean Baptiste, or Pomp, as the men of the expedition called him. At our encampment in the Land of the Shoshone she ran about with him in her arms by the hour, chasing the cottonwood fluff blowing in the air. "Look, Pomp, it's snowing," she cried. "Catch a snowflake!"

At first the Shoshone were suspicious of Sage, since they and the Blackfeet were ancient and bitter enemies. But soon enough they were won over. For their littlest girls she made birchen dolls, and for the boys she fashioned hobby-horses from crooked-trunk firs. She taught the older boys a Blackfoot game similar to snap-the whip and showed them a contest called walking arrow. She would shoot an arrow into a tree, then each of the boys would shoot at it, and the boy whose arrow came closest would claim all of the other arrows; then she would shoot at another tree, and the game would continue, sometimes for hours on end. She showed the older Shoshone girls how to play a Cree game in which they kept a fist-sized ball stuffed with elk hair and wrapped in tanned buffalo hide aloft with their fists for minutes at a time. In another game a short pole was thrown through a small rolling hoop segmented with rawhide spokes.

From willow sticks Sage made my uncle a handsome backrest, and from the gray shale abundant near the No Return River a new hemp-pipe. One morning she surprised a lumbering porcupine and tossed a deer hide over it, which it immediately filled with quills from its lashing tail. After releasing the indignant animal, she colored the quills red, green, and blue and made a beautiful star-shaped medallion for Sacagawea to wear on her best robe. Sage's method of dyeing the quills fascinated me. She wrapped them in dampened dye-plants, then placed the little packages under her sleeping robe for several nights until the weight of her body pressed colors into the quills.

"Oh, to be a package of quills," I teased her. Whereupon she made me a spoon from the horn of a mountain sheep "to eat buffalo brains with and get smart."

Before leaving for the Columbia, Captain Lewis wished to compile some notes on the customs and manners of the Shoshone. One evening over supper he remarked that Shoshone men, while honest and generous, had little respect for their women, of whom they were "sole proprietors." Also, he accused them of being lazy, stating that their horsemen refused to walk anyplace, even the shortest distance. And they frequently boasted of heroic deeds that they had never performed. Lewis glumly concluded that there was little hope of persuading them, or any of the other Indians we had encountered, of abandoning war for peace, since in their society no man could rise to become a chief without having first proved his bravery in war.

"Why, sir," my uncle objected, "but think. What is your crony the President, and every other slaveholding American, but 'sole proprietor' of all the women in their quarters, and the men and children as well? As for the Shoshone's preference for riding, when did you ever, at home in Virginia, see any gentleman planter walk so much as fifty paces out-of-doors afoot? So far as exaggerated boasting is concerned, have you listened lately to your men bragging around the campfire of their conquests among the Shoshone women? You would suppose yourself the captain of a party of satyrs. As for the Indians' custom of choosing their leaders from their best warriors, what say you to America's choice for first President? George Washington was hardly elected for his Quaker sentiments. Human nature is human nature, sir, in a Shoshone tepee or a Philadelphia drawing room."

Lewis kicked the fire; then, citing the long hard crossing of the Bitterroots, which we must begin as soon as we had obtained enough pack horses through trade with the Indians, he turned in for the night. I could see that my uncle had made no headway with him on the subject of the Shoshone. As Yellow Sage remarked afterward, while we walked on the edge of the camp and watched the moon rise, Lewis was as sure of the superiority of Virginians as she was of the Blackfeet's.

"I have a question for you, Sage. Your mother was a Piegan, your father British. Is that right?"

"Yes. I hope that's not the question."

"It's not. The question is, are you more Piegan or English?"

"Worse and worse. For I can't and don't believe that at the heart of the matter, there's a particle of difference between the two. When it comes to ways and stays, however" — this with a sidelong look at me — "I am sure that all the *interesting* parts of me are Piegan. If you want the truth, your wonderful uncle is the only really interesting person I've ever met who *wasn't* a Piegan."

"I suppose you think Smoke is interesting," I said.

"He is. And has a great many good points as well."

"Such as?"

"He's the most generous member of our nation. Piegans value generosity above any other trait."

I was about to ask her to prove her point by giving me a kiss. But just then we were startled by a crashing in the nearby woods. Out of the trees about one hundred paces away stepped a pure white elk with a massive set of antlers containing seven points on one side and eight on the other.

"Oh, Ti," Yellow Sage exclaimed. "The legendary White Elk of the Mountains!"

She whistled to him and he bugled back, then vanished into the evergreens. Sage told me excitedly that White Elk, who had been created by Napi ten thousand years ago, was as immortal as her grandfather. I was happy enough to have been vouchsafed a glimpse of this ancient gentleman, but I was quite annoyed with him for spoiling my chance at a kiss.

Each evening White Elk appeared for a few minutes just at twilight in the meadow on the mountainside above the Shoshone camp, though he never allowed anyone to approach him. On the fourth morning after we first sighted him, two days before the expedition was to leave for the Columbia, Sage learned from Sacagawea, who had heard it from her husband, Charbonneau, that the Shoshone were planning to slip away that night for their annual buffalo hunt, leaving the captains horseless and without a guide, since Cameahwait was angry that they would obtain no guns in the trade. When we alerted Captain Lewis, he was furious with Charbonneau for not telling him this disturbing news immediately, and with Cameahwait for planning to betray him.

My uncle then went to the captain and explained that many years ago when he was in Spain on summer holiday, retracing the epic journey of Don Quixote with his Oxford tutor and mentor, the great Scholia Scholasticus Aristotle, they had concluded their journey in the city of Seville. And there they had witnessed a wonderful event called a *rodear*, a competition to see which of the most famous Andalusian horsemen could stay on the wildest horses and bulls the longest. Recalling this competition, True said he had wagered with Cameahwait and some other Shoshone leaders that the captains' men could easily best theirs at this sport; and the Indians had agreed that if Lewis's men won, they would provide him with all the horses he desired.

"Oh, sir," I interjected, "just yesterday Sage and I saw a party of young Shoshone ride down two grown mule deer in a show of horsemanship unlike anything ever dreamed of in the United States. What can you be thinking?"

My uncle said he knew very well what he was thinking, and that by tonight, the captains would have their horses and a good guide into the bargain — not that the guide was so very necessary, since he and I had come through these same mountains just the year before. But I, remembering all too well the unfortunate outcome of the *Flying Dutchman* at the Great Falls on the Missouri, anticipated the *rodear* with considerable concern.

That afternoon everyone convened in the natural bowl where, a fortnight before, my uncle had held his play and drawn the Indians out of the forest. There, under his supervision, a corral of lodge poles, about two hundred feet on a side, had been erected, within which the *rodear* would take place.

As impoverished as these mountain Indians were, it was amazing to see how richly they decorated themselves when the occasion required, with colored beads, seashells, elk-tooth necklaces and bracelets, richly dyed quills along their leggings, mother-of-pearl earrings, and tippets of otter pelts embellished with ermine tails. Their moccasins were ornamented with skunk tails trailing from the heels. And though I had heard Captain Lewis disparage the Shoshone for being "diminutive, with crooked legs and flat feet," on horseback they were a nation of princes.

The *rodear* began with Cameahwait driving twenty young, unbroken horses into a chute adjacent to the corral, where they milled about, biting and kicking at each other and whinnying angrily. To ensure fairness, each of the ten Americans who had entered the contest was asked to pick a horse. A Shoshone brave would mount it, while my uncle and Cameahwait counted off the seconds the rider stayed aboard. The American contestant would then ride the same horse. The animals had been fitted with bridles and reins but no saddles, which the Shoshone disdained.

What can I say? The men of the expedition were fine riders, especially Drouillard, Labiche, and Shannon. But no one could compete with the Shoshone, who usually stayed mounted until the horses were entirely fatigued and stood with their tongues lolling out and their heads down — though they recovered quickly enough to dislodge most of our riders within six or seven seconds.

Captain Lewis rode last, galloping into the corral aboard a vicious little walleyed, hammer-headed stallion that had thrown its Shoshone rider after half a minute. Lewis spent more time in the air than on the pony, which spun, plunged, twisted, and reared. Well before fifteen seconds had elapsed, the wretch twisted its ugly head back upon the captain, savagely bit his calf, and unseated him.

It appeared that the *rodear* was over and the expedition still without its horses. But my uncle again spoke with Cameahwait — showing him his arquebus as if he would trade that — and then announced that we would reconvene at sundown for a winner-take-all finale.

When the sun was sitting on top of the mountains to the west, we assembled at the amphitheater once again. As the sun sank, bathing the entire wild scene in a luminous orange glow, the great White Elk stepped into the clearing on the mountainside.

"Now, Ti," my uncle said in a hushed voice, "the precise nature of the wager I've made is that a member of our party will rope, ride, and break that splendid animal this very evening. If I win, Cameahwait will supply us with all the horses we need."

"And if we lose?"

"We won't."

"But if we should happen to?"

"Well, if we should *happen to,* I was under the necessity of promising the Shoshone the party's guns."

"Uncle, for God's sake. For *Jehovah's* sake. The captains will never relinquish their rifles. What have you done?"

"Watch and see," said he, handing me his spyglass.

Through the telescope I watched the elk walk proudly into the center of the lofty clearing. As he surveyed us from on high, a figure emerged from the opposite side of the opening Lewis, dressed in his best coat, uniform trousers, and cocked hat.

The elk whistled and tossed his massive rack. The captain took several measured steps, angling away from the animal as if indifferent to its presence. He reached down and picked some wild grasses. Then he stood stock-still looking out over the valley. The elk began to pace nervously back and forth across the meadow, coming closer to the captain with each pass, the way the young Indian who stole Bucephalus had approached me at my easel on the lower Missouri River. Though they were too far away to hear, Lewis seemed to be talking to the animal. I handed the glass back to my uncle, who peered through it once, nodded, and lighted half a pipeful of hemp.

As the elk approached him, the captain held out the grasses, then withdrew them a little, then extended his hand again. The Shoshone in the amphitheater drew in their breath in unison; no man had ever been this close to White Elk before. The animal bent his head to take the grass and, so quickly I could scarcely follow his motions, the captain grasped his antlers and vaulted over his head onto his back.

"Ha ha!" cried my uncle. "Let the bobsled ride begin."

Now ensued an incredible performance on the part of beast and man. As Lewis cartwheeled over his antlers, White Elk was already in the air, shrieking his fighting cry. With the captain clinging to his horns, he spun completely around, arching his great muscled back. Then he rushed into the woods. We could hear his antlers splintering dead limbs off the trees like rifle shots. I was terrified that he would scrape the captain from his back, crushing him against a tree like a deer fly. But moments later, with Lewis still aboard, the elk reappeared in the clearing and came charging straight down the mountainside toward us, while the Shoshone and the men of the expedition cheered madly and my uncle puffed away complacently in a haze of blue-gray smoke. As they approached at a full gallop, the rider stood up and threw off first the brocade uniform coat, then the trousers, then the cocked hat. It was Yellow Sage Flower in her white antelope dress, with her raven hair streaming out behind her.

She rode up to us and jumped lightly off her mount, and I

ran to embrace her. Cameahwait spoke to Clark. "He says to pick your horses, sir," my uncle told the captain. "And he'll supply you with a good guide, though I think we will accompany you as well. This remarkable young woman has made it possible for us all to continue together. I only hope that our nation remembers Yellow Sage's good service and that of many other Indians who have helped us, in treating with these people in years to come."

Clark looked at my uncle for a long moment, then at Sage, then at the Indians already rounding up horses from which the captains would select their mounts. Finally he nodded and said soberly, "I do, too, Private Kinneson. I do, too."

Crossing the Bitterroots

54

W<small>ELL</small>, T<small>I</small>," said my uncle through chattering teeth, "Old Toby has seen fit to conduct us a-sightseeing."

"That is a very kind way to put it, uncle. An extremely generous construction."

In fact, our elderly Shoshone guide, whom the men called Toby, had blundered off the trail and led us into the worst sink of jack-straw deadfalls, chasms, precipices, and blind canyons that ever existed. Thanks to the good offices of this fellow — who continued to assure us with the greatest confidence that it would be very strange indeed if he were lost, having been over the same route *fifty years ago as a boy* — we now found ourselves beside an utterly unnavigable torrent of whitewater at the bottom of a terrible pitch. To enliven this detour we had thick snow, driving rain, and pelting hail. Nevertheless, my uncle immediately strung up his fly-rod and stood in the blizzard for the better part of an hour casting for salmon, though by then the snow was flying so fast that his fly and line were indistinguishable, and I doubted that there were any salmon in the river at that time of year anyway. Except for a few grouse, we had seen no game of any kind for a week.

For supper that night we regaled ourselves with candles and boiled moccasins. Afterward we huddled around the campfire, more tired, cold, wet, and hungry than at any other time on our trip. Sage had saved a little of the elk pemmican she had made back at the Shoshone camp, which she now gave to Sacagawea and Pomp. I told her I was very touched that she would give away the last of her food. She replied that so long as she had a single morsel, she would never let a dear sister and her child go without. Then she told me the tale of Playing Dead Beside the Buffalo, a selfish young Piegan who had pretended to be dead to avoid having to share a buffalo he had killed.

Noting how keenly the men of the expedition were listening to this story, my uncle dragged several large drift-logs onto the fire and, standing so close to the flames that we could see their dancing reflections on his chain mail, he called out in his booming theatrical voice, "Expeditionaries! When Hannibal crossed the snowy Alps with his army, and they were near starvation, he designated the worst nights of the crossing as 'Truth Nights,' on which his soldiers could ask him any question and receive a full and candid answer. This he did as a means of holding his men's interest in life and providing incentive — for there is no greater incentive than curiosity — to survive their journey. I have calculated with my astrolabe that it will take us three more days to get through these horrid Bitterroots. Therefore I will designate each of the next three nights, starting tonight, as Truth Night. In the tradition of Hannibal Africanus, I invite you to put the first question to me. Any question at all, gentlemen. I promise to answer it truthfully."

The men edged closer to the fire. After a short pause Captain Lewis said, "I have noticed, sir, that you husband your hemp tobacco very carefully. Half a pipeful is all you take of an evening."

"Moderation in all things save love and chivalry," my uncle replied.

"I have also remarked that your excellent nephew does not seem to smoke hemp at all," Lewis continued. "No doubt you deem him too young to use it?"

"Captain," said my uncle with a sigh, "I am sorry to report that my nephew will never use hemp. He will never know the mild salubrious effects of this most choice herb."

"Then my question is this, private. Whyever not?"

"Well, sir" — here my uncle lighted his pipe — "it has to do with the single ongoing point of contention between myself and my good brother. Ti's father, you must know, feared that the use — even the very restrained use — of hemp might lead the boy to try opium, laudanum, and even rum and broad-leaf Virginia tobacco."

"That would be very bad, private."

"Very bad indeed. I, however, took the opposite side of the question. I argued from my own experience that hemp, taken in moderation, promotes moderation in all things. Indeed, when Ti was five or six, unbeknownst to his father, I used to give him a puff on my clay pipe as a reward for learning his Greek letters. He never seemed to suffer from a draught or two. But after my brother and his dear wife, Helen of Troy, learned of this little incentive to the boy's learning, they said that they would prefer he smoke no more. Of course I honored their wishes. Also, my brother said that the use of hemp made me — you will scarcely believe this, gentlemen — a little silly. Can you imagine? A dour old Vermont schoolmaster, a private in the Green Mountain Regiment of the First Continental Army, who did such creditable service at the fall of Fort Ticonderoga that Ethan Allen wished to promote me to sergeant — acting silly?"

"Inconceivable," said Lewis. "But let me understand this, sir. You gave hemp to a five-year-old to smoke?"

"Certainly."

"I am astonished. What were its effects? Do you remember, Ti, how your uncle's herb affected you?"

"I do, sir. I very much liked it. In those days I was troubled by a catarrh in the spring, when the dandelions first bloomed over

the meadows. The little puff of hemp my uncle gave me allevi-
ated that condition. But then my parents forbade me to use it
further, and a year or two later the catarrh went away of its own
accord."

Captain Lewis said nothing more. But Clark, whose curiosity had been piqued by my uncle's reference to Fort Ticonderoga, said, "Correct me if I am mistaken, Private True. But
was not Ticonderoga — I mean the fort, not your nephew —
taken without a shot?"

"It was indeed. So no doubt you are wondering at the nature
of that most creditable service to which I referred, at the fall of
the fort. It was this. When Ethan demanded of the garrison,
'Surrender the fort in the name of the Great Jehovah and the
First Continental Congress,' I cried out, as a clarifying quali-
fier, 'To which, nevertheless, the Independent Republic of Vermont pays no fealty.' Of course I meant the Congress, not Jehovah. It was just afterward that I had my mishap, by which I
mean striking my head against the gate. And that is what led to
my little ways and stays."

"It seems to me, private," Clark said, "that you were perhaps
not without a *few* small ways and stays even *before* your mishap
at the fort."

My uncle nodded. "Aye, sir. Ethan prized me highly for
them. After I called out at the critical moment that we Vermont boys would pay no fealty to Congress, he roared with
laughter, which much perplexed the British commander. But to
cut the tale short, I passed up promotion, preferring to remain a
private."

"Might I ask, then, *why* you passed up the chance to be pro-
moted?" Lewis inquired.

"Certainly, sir. And I will tell you — tomorrow night."

*   *   *

The next day it snowed steadily from dawn to dusk, snow such as I had never seen, even in Vermont, where we were certainly familiar with blizzards. The trail was covered so deeply it was impossible to know whether we kept to it or not, except where, at long intervals, we came to the faint scar of an old slash mark on a tree blazed long ago by Nez Perce Indians. The men were in tatters, their beards hung with long icicles. Some had wrapped rags about their feet, causing my uncle, with freezing tears in his eyes, to say that Washington's men at Valley Forge had presented no more pitiable a spectacle. We set out without breakfast — there was nothing to eat — and between the wind howling in the treetops and the horrid constant roaring of the river in the gorge far below, I thought we might all run mad. These Bitterroots were the most dire mountains I had ever imagined, stretching endlessly before us as tall and trackless as on the day of Creation. But that night around the campfire my uncle reminded the men of the story he had left hanging the evening before, and inquired if they were still interested in learning why he had passed up promotion.

"Why did you, sir?" Lewis asked. "By all means, tell us."

"Why, captain, the answer is as plain as the face of a Vermont schoolmarm. Put it to yourself. What creature on earth is more independent than a Vermonter?"

"I can't imagine."

"A Vermont *private* is," my uncle rejoined. "Look you, gentlemen. A sergeant must think of his squadron; a captain, of his regiment; and a general, of his country, not to mention his reputation in the eyes of posterity. But a private — ah, sirs. A *private* stands squarely on his own two feet and thinks and speaks only for himself. Is the mess maggoty? The commander a donkey? The war too long and too bloody? A private may say so. A Vermont private *will* say so. Aye, friends. True Teague

Kinneson remains a private forever. Now we will steal a little march on tomorrow night. Ask your third question. Kinneson Africanus awaits your inquiry."

"I should like to inquire of Kinneson Africanus," said Sergeant Patrick Gass, "with no reflection on your manhood, sir, where on earth did you come by the pink cushion that you wear inside your britches?"

Having promised to answer any question, my uncle agreed to divulge the secret if the men would promise to keep his explanation to themselves. And, having teased them on so that they forgot all about their frostbitten feet and empty stomachs and their dread of what lay ahead, he told them all about his abbreviated assignation with Flame Danielle Boone in the Chouteaus' garden at St. Louis and his subsequent encounter with Miss Flame in the canebrake at Boone's Settlement, and of how he had heard the thundering hoofbeats of her marriage-minded kinsmen descending upon him, and how she had tossed him her little riding pillow as a pledge of troth. "And so, stuffing the cushion down my pantaloons, I rode away with Ti, having lost my original codpiece, without which a young knight-errant's reputation is as dross."

"But, sir," Lewis said, "you *still* have not told us why you wear such an antique article in the first place."

"The best answer I can give to that very good question, captain, apart from its obvious use for modesty's sake when an actor treads the boards, is to repeat my brother's excellent reply to a traveler who, somewhat puzzled by that prominent item of my attire, made the very same inquiry of me. We were having a dram at the village hotel when the traveling gentleman said, 'Meaning no discourtesy, sir, and please forgive me for being inquisitive, but why, in the name of God, do you wear that codpiece?' To which, before I could reply, Ti's father gave perhaps the most philosophical answer ever given in the history of the world, which was this: 'Indeed, sir — why not?'"

My uncle then told the men that if they would go along the next day like the good soldiers they were and do as the captains bid them, and if they didn't all freeze to death or starve, he would tell them the following night how he had bested the Devil and expelled him from the Green Mountains forever.

The next day was by far the worst of the crossing. Weakened from hunger, the men had all they could do to catch their horses, some of which had scattered widely during the night in search of grass. We did not get under way until nearly noon, and by dark had made less than ten miles. Again the party's hunters managed to shoot only a few grouse, so the captains were obliged to order that a colt be killed for food. But how many more horses could they slaughter and still pack their gear through these terrible peaks? Clark wrote in his journal that the lack of food and the difficulty of moving through the wilderness had much "dampened the spirits" of the men. Lewis, however, reminded my uncle that he had one more tale to tell — that of himself and the Devil. After lighting his pipe, the private began as follows.

"Now the Devil, gentlemen, is also known to us New Englanders as Ned, the Black Man, the Horned Devil, Lucifer, Satan, and Old Harry. But he is known *principally* as the Gentleman from Vermont because Vermont has the greatest number of individualistical, independent-minded, cussed free-thinkers in the Union, and therefore provides him — I mean my Gentleman friend — with the most clients.

"So when Ethan Allen, who was the *most* individualistical and cussed free-thinking Vermonter of all, came to his deathbed, with me at his side, the Gentleman in question manifested himself in Ethan's bedchamber with a great tow sack in which to lug him off, in the same manner that said Gentleman had conveyed all Vermont free-thinkers to Hell since Vermont had existed. Ethan had just denounced the 'pious, prattling religiosity' of a parson he'd bodily tossed out of his chambers when — poof! — in a cloud not of smoke but of maple-scented steam, the old boy appeared before us."

"What did he look like?" Sage asked.

"Why, dear madam, he looked like — like a Vermont schoolmaster! He was tall and lanky, with a bottle-green frock coat and a mortarboard and a pedagogical expression — and he was already opening the mouth of the sack. But do not suppose that I sat idly by. No. I had my arquebus at the ready, primed and loaded, and I shot him. After I shot him I stabbed him. And after I stabbed him I tried to grapple with him with my own two hands. But it was all in vain. It was like shooting and stabbing and grappling with a man-shaped wisp of steam from a maple-sugar house. 'Damn you, sir!' I cried.

"'Too late!'" says he. 'But I'll bargain you a bargain, Private True Teague Kinneson. For I know you well, and to tell the truth I have had my eye on you for a great long while. Here it is. I'll spare Ethan if you can answer a riddle.'

"'I can answer any riddle ever riddled,' I said. 'But what, on the off chance that I don't' — the Gentleman being a canny fellow — 'would you want from me?'

"'Oh, nothing very material. We'll arrange that trifling matter later.'

"'Riddle away, then,' said I. 'With the additional understanding that, if you lose, you'll never set foot in Vermont again.'

"'Done,' said he, with an oily smile.

"And 'Done,' said I, with no smile at all.

"At this, Ethan muttered something.

"'What?' I said.

"'Foot or *hoof*,' said he in a ghastly low voice. 'Never set foot or *hoof* in Vermont.'

"'Yes, that you'll never set foot or *hoof* in Vermont.'

"Well, sirs. The Gentleman did not like this addendum because it balked his scheme to crawdad out of his part of the bargain should he lose. But he was so confident I could not answer his riddle that he said, 'Here it is, then, Schoolmaster Private Playwright Kinneson. Which state has the prettier autumn prospects, Vermont or New Hampshire? And why?'

"Now, being the Gentleman from *Vermont*, the old boy might be expected to plump for the Green Mountain State. But, knowing his subtlety, I expected a trick. So did Ethan, who beckoned me close and whispered, 'New Hampshire. Tell him New Hampshire.' I drew in a breath and said, 'The answer to your riddle, sir, is New Hampshire.'

"The Gentleman frowned and smiled at the same time. 'Is that your final answer, schoolmaster?'

"'It is.'

"'Well,' said he, fiddling with the mouth of his sack, 'you say right. New Hampshire has the better views. But that's only half of it. It might save Ethan, but it won't save you.' He gave the sack a shake, and whatever was inside hissed.

"'So I'll put it to you once more. *Why* is it that New Hampshire has the finer prospects?'

"Again Ethan beckoned me close and whispered in my ear. And this time it was I who smiled. Drawing myself up tall and noting that I had a good half-inch of height on the Gentleman, I said, 'Because, sir, New Hampshire has many a fine, tall mountain from which a certain Gentleman may look out over the most beautiful place on the face of the earth — the great sovereign Republic of Vermont!'

"At which the Devil stamped his foot, and off came his slipper, revealing a hairy cloven hoof; he clapped his hand to his head, and off came his scholarly mortarboard, revealing two short scarlet horns; and he whirled around to leave, revealing, under his green frock coat, his pointy tail. But before he could be off, I wrested away the sack, trussed him up in it, and heaved it as far into Loch Champlain as I could. And since that time he has never set foot or hoof in Vermont."

"Did Ethan Allen recover?" Lewis asked.

"Why, yes," my uncle said. "Ethan did. But the next week he went to Town Meeting and drank his usual gill of rum afterward at a tavern. And during the telling of this very story, he died of a thundering apoplexy. But at least the Gentleman didn't get him, nor will that Gentleman ever enter Vermont again. Though when I hove him into the lake, he roared out of the sack that I had not seen the last of him, and the next time we met it would be on his terrain rather than mine, and I could expect a very different outcome. I believe that we may encounter him soon, for these hellish mountains they call the Bitterroots are exactly the sort of place I'd expect to find him."

Later that evening the captains made a bold decision. Early the next morning Clark, with six of the best hunters, would go on ahead of the main party, traveling as fast and light as possible, in the hopes of reaching, that day or the next, the Nez Perce Indians, who lived on the prairie to the west of the mountains. They would send back food to Lewis and the rest of the men coming along behind with the pack horses. My uncle volunteered our services to range out in front of Lewis's party and, with Yellow Sage's help, find and shoot an elk or a deer to fend off starvation.

Clark and his men departed at dawn, and Sage and my uncle and I shortly thereafter, taking with us an extra horse to carry back to Lewis any meat we found. Through a mix-up, the saddlebags of the horse we selected contained some of the expedition's medical supplies, which we discovered in midmorning when we stopped to drink at a little stream.

As we broke trail up the steep and heavily wooded side of yet another snowy mountain, we came across the tracks of a good-sized mule deer being stalked by a mountain lion. Sage thought we might be able to scare the cat away and overtake the deer ourselves in the deep snow. An hour later we reached a ridge-top saddle where the trail branched, with one fork going north and one west. From here we saw, about a quarter of a mile ahead, in a narrow place on the north path, a large mule deer hanging by its antlers from a tree branch. After a moment's reflection, my uncle opined that Clark and his advance party had left it there for us earlier that day, though why they would head *north* instead of staying on the main trail to the west, we could not guess. As we started toward the hanging deer, Sage suddenly reined in Buffalo Runner. In an urgent voice she said that in a dream some nights before, which she had forgotten until this very moment, Smoke, in the guise of a panther, had been waiting near a place just like this to recapture her. The deer was a trap, and on no account would she proceed.

I urged my uncle to turn back to warn Lewis immediately. But he continued up the trail, saying merely, "Let us then use this deer to prepare a special feast to set before the good Blackfeet. They must be as famished as we are."

"Uncle," I said, "I beg you. Smoke and his men won't rest until they capture Yellow Sage and have the party's guns in their possession to boot."

But nothing would do but he and I must ride on ahead to where the deer was hanging. While I skinned and butchered it — the hair on the back of my neck prickling the whole time —

my uncle built a great crackling fire and began to cook up, in our iron kettle, a most delicious-smelling venison stew, into which he incorporated some savory hemp leaves, ground very fine, and also some medicaments from the saddlebags on the spare horse. We left the big kettle of spiced venison simmering in its fragrant juices and headed back down the trail, giving the impression that we intended to bring up the rest of the party to partake of the luncheon.

After retracing our steps to the saddle, we drew our mounts off into the trees and lay on a flat rock on the ridge top to see what would happen. Presently Sage rejoined us. As we waited, the snow clouds began to lift for the first time in five days. Just as the sun broke through, forty or fifty warriors, covered with the skins of bears, buffaloes, and panthers, emerged from the forest. Led by Smoke, dressed in a catamount's skin, the Blackfeet began to share out the venison. In the meantime my uncle had spotted Lewis's party coming up the opposite side of the mountain, still two or three miles away but headed straight for us and the Indian party.

True chuckled. "Remember old Isaac, who in his dotage asked Esau to make a mess of savory pottage to regale his nostrils? No doubt you saw me add some condiments to the stew."

"Do you mean the hemp leaves?" I asked.

"Nay, Ti. The hemp was merely to make them calm. For this work we needed something more vigorous. Aye" — training the telescope — "see them? See them, Yellow Sage?"

He handed his spyglass to Sage, who began to laugh while trying not to make any noise. As the figures around the stew kettle scattered, she gave me the glass and put both her hands over her mouth to keep from laughing aloud. Through the eyepiece I saw the all-puissant Blackfeet rushing for cover. Some had their hands pressed tightly to their hinderquarters and some were hobbling with their buckskin trousers down around their ankles. This exodus was accompanied by reports, explosions, and detonations — not musket fire directed toward our party, but rather the effects of the handful of "Thunderclapper" purgatives with which my uncle had leavened the venison gravy. Every last Blackfoot, including Smoke, was staggering toward the trees with what, had our cows back in Vermont contracted the affliction, we would have called the scours. Sage and I could no longer hold in our laughter, nor did it matter. For we knew that the effects of just one of these powerful emetics, much less twenty or thirty, would put the Blackfeet out of commission for the rest of that day and well into the night.

In this way the Lewis and Clark expedition to the Pacific was saved by three tales told by a Vermont schoolmaster around a campfire and an old-fashioned dose of salts.

To cap our good fortune, the swirling clouds far to the west broke apart, revealing the glimmer of distant prairie. But before I could express my joy and relief, Yellow Sage astonished us by declaring that she must return home with Smoke or jeopardize our entire expedition and the captains' as well. Nothing I said would change her mind. All I could extract from her was a promise to meet me the following summer on our return trip from the Pacific, at Squaresided Chief Mountain in the Land of the Glaciers. And with that she hugged my uncle, kissed me on the cheek, leaped onto Buffalo Runner in her customary manner, and trotted up the north trail to join her people — vanishing into the wilderness as suddenly as she had appeared earlier that summer, and as much a mystery to me as ever.

55

I PAINTED *Crossing the Bitterroots* during the first week of October while the men of the expedition rested with the Nez Perce Indians, my uncle fished for a new kind of trout — a high-jumping salmonoid with a brilliant crimson stripe down its side — and Captain Clark burned out canoes from large pine logs for the last leg of our trip to the ocean. I began with a rough sketch and worked straight through that week, which was as sunny and bland as the preceding fortnight had been wintery.

The painting was another story tableau. If I had any one day in mind, I suppose it was the fifteenth or possibly the sixteenth of September, when we were lost in the mountains and trying to make our way up out of that terrible sink our guide had blundered his way into. In the background were range upon range of snow-clad peaks. In the foreground a precipitous mountain slope ended in a straight drop of several hundred feet to a river, which almost immediately lost its way in more mountains. Partway down the snowy mountain three pack horses were overset on their sides, legs splayed in the air. Around the forequarters of one, Sergeant Patrick Gass, looking gaunt and starved, was fastening an elk-hide rope, snubbed at the other end to a western cedar tree. Captain Lewis, hatless and in worn buckskins, stood beside the cedar. His left arm encircled the shoulders of Private Gibson, who, with Private Shannon and Private Willard, was hauling on the end of the rope to help raise the fallen horse and assist it up the slope. Just above them, around a campfire on the edge of the woods, sat the rest of the men, listening with rapt expressions, though otherwise in the last stages of fatigue, misery, and hunger, to my storytelling uncle. He stood up to the tops of his galoshes in snow, his stocking cap askew, part of his gleaming head plate exposed, his mail encrusted with frost. His whimsical yellow eyes glowed with humor and hope, and as he spoke, he faced west toward a narrow gap in the jumbled mountains, where a single patch of blue sky was visible and, far below, the slightest hint of prairie.

Down the Columbia

56

THE CAPTAINS leaned forward in the canoe. Drouillard, Lewis, Charbonneau, my uncle, and I all sat up straight. Sacagawea looked inquiringly downriver. Pomp, strapped to a board on his mother's back, had heard the sound, too. I could tell by his smile as, over the rapids, we heard it again; from around a bend just ahead came the clapping reverberations of gunfire.

"Paddle, boys," Lewis shouted. "Paddle for all you're worth. Someone's shooting at our men."

Having left our mounts with the Nez Perce for the winter, we were moving swiftly down the Clearwater River toward the Columbia in a loosely strung-out flotilla. Rounding the bend, we spotted the lead canoe drawn up on a sandy bar. Just beyond it the Serpent poured in from the south. On a tongue of land stretching out between the two rivers was a small palisaded fort, where half a dozen men stood firing off their rifles.

Suddenly Lewis began to laugh. The captain, who in his happiest moments was not much given to mirth, gasped, choked, and nearly fell out of the canoe with gales of laughter. He passed his glass to Captain Clark, who began to laugh uproariously himself. Clark handed the glass to me, and to my inexpressible delight who should I see but Franklin, being hoisted to the shoulders of the joyful advance party, discharging their guns not in anger but to celebrate this happy reunion with the savant, who had been given up for lost and now was found.

As we beached our canoe on the gravel shingle just below the fort, Franklin approached my uncle, drew himself up to his full height, saluted smartly, and declared, "Private True Teague Kinneson, I present you with this fort and the Territory of the Pacific Northwest, in the memory of Commander Ethan Allen of the Green Mountain Regiment of the First Continental Army."

Now came hugs, hand-shaking, and congratulations upon Franklin's miraculous deliverance. "How in the world did you arrive here safely, sir?" my uncle asked.

"Oh, the trip down the No Return was a pleasant outing, friend True. Izaac Walton towed me the entire way. Now if you'll just step into Fort Ti, you'll see such fortification work as will please you very much. I constructed it entirely with you in mind."

Franklin proudly led us through Fort Ti, where he pointed out its ramparts, garrisons, embrasures, rifle enfilades, parade grounds, and inner and outer walls, though in fact it was no more than a few sticks with the bark still attached thrust upright into the sand. In the center was a smoldering fire of green willow sticks.

"Welcome to the Land of the Columbia, gentlemen," he said. "Do you like your smoked salmon plain or on camas-bread toast?"

57

M Y UNCLE, FRANKLIN, AND I decided to canoe on to the
Columbia in advance of the main party, scouting to see which
sections of the big river were navigable and which not. For
though the Nez Perce Indians had assured us that the entire
way to the Pacific was readily manageable with a good craft, we
felt that, since the distance to the ocean was so short compared
to the distance from the headwaters of the Missouri to St.
Louis, and our altitude here still comparatively high, there
must of necessity be some terrible rapids and falls between ourselves and tidewater. My uncle said he heartily looked forward
to sluicing down them with such an accomplished waterman as
Franklin and thereby winning the Great Race to the Pacific —
though to keep it a contest he would advise Lewis from time to
time of the character of the water ahead.

We set out down the Serpent the next morning in Franklin's
Shoshone canoe. My two companions frequently plied their
angling-rods for salmon, of which there were huge numbers in
the river at that time, and all went very smoothly for several
days. In due course we came to the junction of the Serpent
with the Columbia, in a desert land of sage and black cliffs and
little else. Here my uncle left Lewis a note on a stick reading
"Smooth sailing. Excelsior!"

But three days later, we saw rising high above the river ahead
the smoky mist of a gigantic falls. Nearby a great throng of people had congregated for a fair even larger than the rendezvous
of the mountain people at the Lake Where the River of Yellow

Stones Rises. Later we learned that these were Wallawalla Indians, a name my uncle prized for its drollness. But when we
attempted to speak to them or communicate with sign language, the people took no notice of us. Though we spent the
whole morning walking among them, they appeared to look directly through us. This peculiar behavior alarmed the private,
who feared that we had come into a land of ghosts or, worse,
had been turned into apparitions ourselves, invisible to living
human beings.

The Wallawallas had congregated here to trade with several
other riverine nations for horses, fish, elk horn, Spanish goods
from California, and British goods from ships that had come
up into the mouth of the lower Columbia. Lining both banks
above the falls were house-sized stacks of salmon, which served
the people of the Northwest the way buffalo served the Indians
of the plains. They used fish for food, lamp oil, fuel, currency,
and sport. Among the hundreds of fairgoers were artists painting elk hides and tailors sewing elegant clothing. There were
dancers, medicine men, shamans dressed in bright costumes,
and even a party of exquisites, strolling here and there and
judging the wares with the nicest and most just distinctions.
Games of all kinds were going forward — horse races, foot
races, canoe races, bow and arrow contests. An old man from
the Chinook Nation was carving the upswept bow of a canoe
larger and more elegant than any we had seen into the shape of
a leaping salmon. Yet not one of these people acknowledged
our presence. Finally, Franklin suggested that we seek out an
interview with their chief.

Chief Dorsal Fin of the Red Salmon was a tall, stern Wallawalla in his fifties. As Franklin and my uncle told our story in
Nez Perce and sign language, he listened with an impassive
mien that I did not think boded well for us or the official expe-

dition to follow. When they were done, the chief frowned and said that the Columbia River people were only too aware of the enslavement of the California Indians by the Spanish, not to mention the degrading influence of the British and American traders upon the Clatsops and Chinooks at the mouth of the Columbia. At a council held two nights before, he and his people had resolved to harry all white incursionists out of their territory by whatever means necessary. Moreover, he had little doubt, from our having a Blackfoot guide, that we were in league with those traditional enemies of his nation. And although the truce obtaining at the fair prevented him from having us and the larger American party summarily executed, we should instantly return up the river and inform our confederates that by the time they arrived the period of general amnesty would be over. If they attempted to proceed, his warriors would spear them out of the river with their tridents like so many flopping salmon.

Both Franklin and I were of the opinion that we should instantly warn Lewis of this new difficulty, but my uncle had a different idea. To begin with, he acquired the Chinook canoe with the beautifully carved salmon in exchange for a quick painting that I did of it and its creator. Then he went to work on a new invention that he called an "im-pell-er." This device consisted of two paddles made of western fir, about six feet long and connected in the middle, which he attached to the stern of the canoe like the sails of a windmill, to be operated by an elastic belt made from a whale intestine he bought from an Indian who had come up from the ocean.

Franklin and I went to reconnoiter the falls and the rapids below. Though perhaps not so high as the Great Falls on the Missouri, or quite so loud as the thundering River of Yellow Stones, this Columbian cataract was more forbidding. The force of the falling water shook the ground under our feet, and in a smooth basin at its base was a swirling green vortex. Below the whirlpool was a roaring gut a quarter of a mile long and no wider than fifty feet, with several distinct terraces of dark rock rising on each side. An elderly Yakima River Indian named Butcher Boy was happy to inform us that these obstacles, though terrifying enough, were child's play compared to a narrows downriver, followed by yet another piece of broken water — four miles of cascades, falls, and rapids known as the Chute. Butcher Boy explained that the falls, the whirlpool, the gut, the narrows, and the Chute were called the Five Demons.

That evening we again sought an audience with Dorsal Fin of the Red Salmon, whom we found conferring with Butcher Boy about the best way to preserve our livers for trade to the coastal Tlingits. My uncle informed Dorsal Fin that if he dared accept, we would wager that we could beat him in a canoe race down the river through the Five Demons. To pique the chief's pride, the private warned him that he had invented a mechanism — his im-pell-er — that would add immeasurably to our speed.

"Yes, and I just returned from Washington, where Mr. Jefferson appointed me Emperor of the Columbia Territory," Dorsal Fin replied. And the jovial Butcher Boy, who was now measuring my uncle's head with a little colored string like a haberdasher's tape, gave his belled cap a playful little jingle.

My uncle said that though he knew Dorsal Fin and his watermen could not possibly be afraid to accept his challenge, it would be unfortunate to give even the impression of fear. He did not need to remind the chief how people *would* gossip of a long winter's day when there wasn't much fishing and time hung heavy on their hands. Nor how common it was for the impression of timidness to be mistaken for timidity itself, especially by willful subordinates or rivals consumed by jealousy.

Abruptly Dorsal Fin said, "Make yourself plain, old fellow. What are the stakes?"

"Our livers to do with as you choose" — with a nod at the beaming Butcher Boy — "against the safety of the oncoming American party. If you win you'll kill us and trade us for whale-bone bows to the Tlingits. If we win you'll grant us and the expedition to come safe passage to the Pacific and back."

The race was slated for the next morning. We would paddle to the portage path around the falls, take out our canoes there, put in again below the whirlpool, shoot as much of the gut and the narrows as possible, and continue down to the river's tidal line, below the Chute. There Butcher Boy and his associates would be awaiting our arrival, should we be fortunate enough to get through the rapids.

My uncle assured us that his im-pell-er blades would carry us through with flying colors. He continued work on his invention throughout the evening, while Franklin repaired to the women's private bathing pool, in a little secluded bay of the river, whence there issued many delighted shrieks.

I asked my uncle if he truly thought we could survive the rapids, much less win the race. He instanced many similar feats that had been thought utterly impossible until they were performed, including Hercules slaying the nine-headed Hydra, Odysseus blinding the Cyclops, and Beowolf destroying Grendel and his mother. When I pointed out that these heroes were mythical figures, not real men, he frowned and said myths were inspired by men and he hoped I was not suggesting that he was less than a man. He assured me that anyone who had ever taught a term in a Vermont schoolhouse, much less survived the slings and arrows of a literary career for thirty years, would not be daunted by a little broken water. Adding that no playwright worthy of the name, nor any painter, either, should ever shun an experience that might produce material for his work. Nonetheless, I slept very fitfully that night, waking a dozen times to the terrible roaring of the nearby falls.

At dawn Franklin appeared from the ladies' quarters, fresh as a daisy and bedizened with colored beads, an elk-skin coat, a new pair of moccasins, a shark's-tooth amulet on a hammered copper chain, and garlands of sweetgrass and late-blooming asters in his hair. My uncle, seeming unfatigued from his own night-long efforts, was delighted with his im-pell-er blades. Down-river the spray above the falls turned pink in the sunrise. To the beating of a dozen drums we prepared to launch our canoes.

Dorsal Fin had ten paddlers in his vessel, all of whom had greased themselves well with salmon oil against the icy river water. The chief explained that there were two portage paths around the falls, one on each side of the river, and offered us our choice. But as my uncle confidently wound up his blades, with the whale-gut throwing off droplets of dew as it tightened, he said that the Wallawallas should choose for themselves. The Fin replied that he would take the steep trail on the north bank, leaving the gentler path on the south for us, but that whatever else, we must not allow ourselves to be drawn into the slick above the falls. "It looks as innocent as a summer pond," he said, "but the current there is more inexorable than the fiercest rapids. Once a canoe is pulled in, there's no escape. Indeed, we send our condemned murderers and other great criminals down the slick on a raft with no paddle."

As we approached this Niagara of the West, my uncle continued to wind the wooden blades. Sure enough, before we knew it we were sucked into the deceiving slick and pulled at a terrible rate of speed toward the lip of the falls. True released the blades, and the canoe was flung forward, with the wooden paddles whirling round in a blur. We shot over the falls like a missile from a catapult, just clearing the boiling green whirlpool below. But we had no leisure to congratulate ourselves on our good fortune, as our canoe was instantly swept into the whitewater. A jagged black rock spanning most of the river loomed up ahead of us. Paddling frantically, we sped between it and the canyon wall. For several seconds I could get no air. Then we emerged from the maelstrom into a relatively quiescent stretch of water, though full of standing waves over more rocks. We were approaching the narrows — three miles of unbroken cascades compressed to a flume a hundred yards wide.

Here we had no choice but to leap out onto the ledges and, with elk-hide ropes, lower the canoe down several sets of plummeting rips. Upriver, Dorsal Fin and his oiled crew were shooting the gut below the whirlpool. Next came some miles of turbulent but navigable water, through which our canoe held the lead. But the im-pell-er blades took a terrible beating on the rocks, and the whale-gut was losing its elasticity, so each time my uncle rewound it, we covered less distance. Again I looked over my shoulder back up the river. Dorsal Fin had gained so much on us that a moment later we were neck and neck.

As we approached the Chute, with both canoes now aided by a strong tailwind, the battered and split blades of the im-pell-er fell off altogether. At nearly the same instant, the Fin and his crew took the lead for the first time. And it became evident that our opponents intended to run the Chute itself, which, we later learned, no canoe had hitherto survived. Instantly my uncle seized up his large black umbrella with the Kinneson emblem of the crossed sword and pen and opened it to the wind. While Franklin and I fended off rocks with our paddles, True contrived to steer us down the last stretch of the rapids so cunningly, turning the umbrella now one way and now another, that we overtook Dorsal Fin's canoe several rods before the finish line and calm water, winning the race by a full length.

Instead of the desert of the upper Columbia, here were huge evergreen trees, thick undergrowth, and a misty sky. I let my hand trail in the water, brought it cupped to my face to wash off the grime and sweat, and tasted salt. Having traveled some forty-five hundred miles from Vermont, we had reached the Pacific.

58

THE INDIANS who had gathered at the finish line were very much impressed with our performance — all but Butcher Boy, who was so disappointed by the outcome of the race that he threw his marrow-hammer and other tools into the river. But my uncle pulled the canoe of the dejected Dorsal Fin up onto the sand beside the tidal pool, shook his hand, and loudly thanked him for *most graciously allowing us to win the race as a demonstration of his great generosity and hospitality to strangers.* Then he gave the Fin his umbrella. At this the chief brightened considerably. He declared that we had acquitted ourselves in the rapids very well, and even if he and his men had not deliberately laid off their paddles in the home stretch, he was quite sure that, with the help of the magic wind-parasol, we would have come in a *close second.* And coming in second to the greatest rivermen in the universe was no mean feat and nothing to be ashamed of. But Butcher Boy, who had now thought better of relinquishing his hammer and, neck-deep in the tidal pool, was groping around for it, called out that although *we* survived the Five Demons, the larger party to come surely would perish in them, and he still would have livers enough to trade to the Tlingits for a dozen new canoes.

That afternoon I began a new picture. In the foreground Franklin and my uncle and I sat in our canoe, with the private in the bow, his umbrella cocked at a jaunty angle over his shoulder, his "Chart of the Interior of North America" on his lap as he bent over it drawing the Columbia River. The canoe was about to shoot the rapids below a high falls, which I showed looming behind my uncle and slightly to his right. But the map extended beyond the canoe, and by degrees the blue line on his chart representing the river unspooled into an actual cascade of whitewater between black rocks, with a few sparse sage and cactus bushes clinging to the steep banks. In the center of the tableau the chart became a full-fledged picture, though still with the curling upturned edges of a map. It showed, in rapid succession, the compressed narrows, the Chute, and the tidal basin surrounded by glossy green rhododendrons and the lush undergrowth of the Pacific rain forest. On True's face was an expression of utmost concentration and delight. Along both banks of the river were soaring stacks of dried fish, wooden lodges, people spearing salmon, and the bustle of a civilization "as teeming as that of old Memphis on the Nile," as my uncle said in praise of my picture, with the full confidence of a man who had visited old Memphis himself. Far off in the distance were the snowy peaks of the Cascades and a glint of the blue Pacific. This picture pleased me very much. I called it *Down the Columbia*.

Winter by the Pacific

59

Now CAPTAIN LEWIS, who was never thoroughly comfortable with any Indians, detested the Chinookan people around the mouth of the Columbia River in particular. More than once at the expedition's winter quarters at Fort Clatsop, several miles inland, he called them low sneaking thieves; and indeed, some few of them were just that. But as my uncle immediately pointed out, where had they learned to steal but from the white sailors who had come to the Columbia and were reported to be a thoroughly disreputable set of fellows? Of the Clatsops, who had encouraged us to bide that winter on the south side of the river, the captain thought slightly better.

My uncle confided to me that Lewis's difficulty with these Pacific Indians was that he couldn't seem to get it through his head that the Clatsops and the Chinooks were *important*. The Sioux were important because they threatened to prevent American traders from passing by their villages on the Missouri and because there were so many of them. The same with the Blackfeet, only more so. The Shoshone were important because we had desperately needed their horses, the Nez Perce because they were tending our mounts over the winter. But the Clatsops and Chinooks were neither especially dangerous to the expedition nor especially useful, so Lewis tended to ignore them and to make hasty judgments about them. Finally he gave them to understand that they were unwelcome around the fort and he did not wish to hold further commerce with them.

The Pacific Indians did not think much more of Lewis than he of them. Unlike the Shoshone, most of whom had never seen men with white skin, the Clatsops and Chinooks had for years been accustomed to white sailors and so saw nothing about the Americans to marvel at except for the odd fact that the party refused to trade seriously with them. In fact, the expedition was running out of trade goods. But the Clatsops and Chinooks could not understand why people would come all this way if not to barter. Like Sage's Blackfeet, all of the Indians we had met in Louisiana and beyond prided themselves on their generosity; when I tried to explain that the captains and their men were low on trade goods, my Chinook friend Doubting Seal only asked why the Americans didn't simply *give* his people some of their supplies.

Along with learning the Blackfoot language from Franklin during our winter at the Pacific, I painted hard. And when I ran out of colors and ran low on blank canvases, I fashioned paints from the minerals and plants of the area, as Yellow Sage had taught me, and substituted tanned elk and deer skins for canvas. As I continued to refine pictures from our journey, I found myself working more like Franklin, using bright colors and simple figures with the principal aim of telling a story and preserving a record of what had happened. *Crossing the Bitterroots* and *Down the Columbia* prefigured much of the work I did afterward.

During December and January I painted both a Clatsop and a Chinook village and many artifacts from the culture of each. My uncle, however, wished to fish and explore more of the region. So at the end of February, Doubting Seal invited us, and Franklin as well, to accompany him up the coast on a fishing and sightseeing expedition. Promising that he would show us many wonders we had never seen before, the Seal added that he would have been glad to take Lewis, too, but for his patronizing attitude toward the Chinookan people. And he seemed to derive considerable satisfaction in thinking that Lewis would *not* have the pleasure of seeing these things. My uncle was in a tizzy of curiosity, the more so because he hoped on this journey to meet the ferocious Tlingits, whom he believed to be the descendants of Norsemen. For indeed, every three or four years they swept down, in their ocean-going canoes, from their home in the far north to plunder the coastal villages of the Clatsops and Chinooks.

We set out in two sea canoes, the Seal, his father, the ancient Chief Tillamook, and I in one, Franklin and my uncle in the other, and six powerful Chinook paddlers in each craft. Behind us we towed a third, empty canoe, I supposed to carry back the spoils of our fishing and hunting. We made a gaily colored little procession in our painted canoes with high carved sterns and long shelf-like cutwaters. My uncle stood on one of these extensions to fly-fish. Like our paddlers, he wore a suit of arrow-proof moose-hide armor, and, over his stocking cap, a tall, brimless conical hat, woven of cedar bark and bear grass, cunningly designed to shed the rain, and brightly studded here and there with salmon flies.

"When in Rome," he called out in explanation of his costume, completed by his mail and galoshes. Adding that he was a "man of whatever country he traveled in." To complete the picture, he had bound a short fir plank to the back of his head, under his rain-hat, by a very tight leathern thong around his forehead, with the intention of flattening out his cranium as the Chinooks did. But this method was effective only with infants, and so uncomfortable besides that he soon abandoned the device, saying that if his Maker had wished him to have a flat head he would no doubt have been born with one, and he would have to be satisfied with his copper crown, which was probably enhancement enough anyway.

In this way we proceeded north along the coast for several days, seeing many curious rock formations, catching hundreds of salmon, killing two smallish whales for their blubber, and keeping a sharp eye out for any sign of the Tlingits.

On the fifth day of our trip, we came to the handsomest coastline imaginable and saw, lying on a sandy beach, the bleached white bones of a one-hundred-foot-long whale. Here I began my tableau *Wonders of the Pacific* by painting some jutting offshore rocks under a watery January sun such as emerged briefly from the sea-fog every three or four days. In a tidal pool in the center foreground, just off the beach, I added a score of animals and birds previously unknown to science, including Kinneson's purple sea urchin, the black-turbaned Kinnesonian snail, a bird my uncle called True's oyster-catcher, and another he named Teague's cormorant. The whale skeleton I revitalized in all its former glory and represented leaping through a huge hole in the middle of a bronze-colored boulder. When Franklin looked at the painting, he said it lacked only some human beings. He advised me to paint my uncle, fishing from the bow of our sea canoe, with his fly-rod bent in a springing arc, playing the leaping whale. This I did, with the sunshine reflecting off his chain mail and copper crown.

While I painted, Franklin fly-fished, taking four of the five new varieties of salmon we had discovered on the Pacific Coast. Nearby my uncle discovered a grove of maple trees, not as tall as our lofty sugar maples at home, and with slightly smoother bark and much broader leaves. As it was coming on spring here, and the sap was beginning to rise, he set about carving hollow spouts out of alder twigs an inch in diameter; notching the maples about three feet off the ground, he conducted the sweet drippings from the trees through these spouts into water-tight cooking baskets that the Chinooks had brought with them. Then, in a large kettle, he boiled down some very passable, if rather dark, maple syrup, which he refined into cakes of delectable sugar.

While my uncle was maple sugaring and I painting and Franklin fishing, the Chinooks built a cedar post-and-plank house, similar to their fine dwelling lodges, with the carved head and maw of a whale for a doorway. This edifice, about thirty feet long and ten feet wide, was situated on a promontory overlooking the sea where old Chief Tillamook had journeyed long ago, as a boy with his father, to kill his first whale. Inside the house they placed the spare canoe.

Doubting Seal now explained that his father's time to die was at hand — he had sensed it coming for several weeks — and he had asked to have his tomb constructed here. Accordingly, one evening Tillamook very cheerfully hobbled into the whale-house, climbed into the canoe with a paddle to help him on his great voyage, and lay down singing the sea-hunting song he and his father had sung long ago. Doubting Seal explained that we should not grieve, because by this time tomorrow his father would be embarked on a passage more wonderful even than our great journey across America.

My uncle thought for a moment, then said, "Ti, fetch me my hemp."

"Oh, sir," I said, "the chief will surely have no need for hemp where he's bound."

"Nonetheless, Ti, fetch it."

I brought my uncle his Dutch clock, from which he removed the seed-pouch — he had only a few ounces of hemp left —

and put it in his carpetbag. Then, with a long, fond look at the old Knight of the Woeful Countenance painted on the clock case, he said, "Well, friend, a marvelous new adventure now awaits you as well." As Tillamook settled himself comfortably in the heaven-canoe, my uncle handed him the clock and his sextant and astrolabe and told him that with these navigational implements he would at all times know exactly where he was in the universe *and* what time it was at Greenwich as well. Whereupon the chief thanked him very graciously and said that while he hunted whales with his father and other ancestors, he would certainly check the time on the clock and take his position. And if a lull ever fell over the conversation (which he thought unlikely, his father being a very garrulous, jolly old fellow with a hundred jokes for all occasions) he would not be surprised to see that it was *twenty after the hour.*

I was deeply touched by this scene, yet wondered what it might signify that my uncle was willing to give up the clock. I hoped he was not planning any such voyage as Chief Tillamook's very soon. He assured me that this was not the case and that, indeed, for the last several months he had felt little need to orient himself. And while he hoped that in other respects his ways and stays had not diminished, for he wished always to be "true to True," he felt "better in his head" than he had since his old accident. He would willingly have given Tillamook his belled cap as well, he said, but he wanted first to trade the cap to Smoke in exchange for safe passage past the Blackfeet on our return trip. I did not think Smoke would much desire the cap, but I said nothing.

The next morning old Chief Tillamook was dead. This somber event occasioned a philosophical discourse between Franklin and my uncle on the nature of heaven. Franklin said that each Indian nation had its own afterworld. The Blackfoot heaven, for instance, was located just north of a lovely land called the Sweetgrass, in the heart of the Land of the Glaciers. True, who was equally certain of a place of eternal reward, conceived of paradise as a sort of extension of Kingdom County, Vermont, only perhaps with slightly milder winters, like these here on the Pacific. And he said that all of its residents were about my age, for he could not imagine a more idyllic situation than to be a boy or girl forever in a place like Vermont. So, despite the departure from this world of the old Chinook chief, this interval of painting and fly-casting and maple sugaring and philosophizing beside the Pacific was another of those very happy times that seemed to make all of our ordeals worthwhile. At such times I understood perfectly why we had made such an arduous odyssey and I would not have traded the experience for anything. My uncle felt the same way and even coined another of his famous axioms: "To be human is to travel." Franklin said this was perhaps the most philosophical statement made since the days of Solomon and Socrates. Doubting Seal agreed, pointing out that when you turned the axiom around — "to travel is to be human" — it made every bit as much sense.

In the meantime I finished my tableau, painting the whalehouse burial vault of Chief Tillamook on the crag above the bay. Everyone said it was my best work. My uncle allowed that it brought to his ears the constant sharp cries of the seabirds, the crashing breakers, and the scrape of pebbles drawn back down the shingled scree by the retreating waves. He inclined his long tin ear trumpet to the picture to listen to the pebbles rattle along the beach and said aye, aye, he could surely hear them. As indeed he could, the actual beach and the breaking waves being about fifteen feet away. And he claimed to smell the briny tang of the ocean in the air around the painting as well.

* * *

Heading back toward Fort Clatsop, we encountered a cold and steady rain for three days, but Doubting Seal would not allow us to build a fire for fear of attracting a Tlingit raiding party. On the afternoon of the third day, the Seal and I were again in the lead canoe, two or three miles ahead of my uncle and Franklin, who had lagged behind to enjoy a few final hours of fishing.

As we started round the headland between us and the Columbia, I noticed a small cloud out at sea coming our way. Approaching quickly, it split into two clouds, then three. I trained my pocket glass on them, then sharply drew in my breath. In its lens was a three-masted sailing vessel.

"A trading ship!" I shouted, handing the glass to Doubting Seal.

But he shook his head and passed the telescope back to me, indicating that I should look again. What we had sighted was no trading vessel but a warship flying a coal-black flag!

As we continued around the breakers off the headland, the ship gave chase, and Doubting Seal chose this time to inform me that last fall, about a month before our arrival on the coast, the same vessel had put in at the mouth of the Columbia and sent a party ashore making inquiries for *an American expedition coming overland under the command of one Captain Lewis*. I demanded to know why the Seal hadn't told us about the ship sooner.

"Why, friend," said he, "did not Captain Lewis expressly say that he was not interested in anything we had to tell him or in holding further commerce with us? We would gladly have informed him of the ship, but we did not wish to seem forward or impertinent."

Ahead some hundred yards, a tall spout of water jetted up, as if a whale had breached. It was followed immediately by the clap of cannon fire. Another spray, fifty feet to our right, was accompanied by another report. A third ball, launched flatter, skimmed past our canoe, skipping several times on the surface of the ocean like a flat stone on a Vermont millpond. Whoever they were, these people meant business.

We were still a mile or more away from the big river when a thunderous, rolling explosion filled the air and water all around us with flying lead. The ship had fired a full broadside at us. Several stone formations just offshore were sheared off or entirely demolished by the volley; a massive cedar tree on the shore snapped completely in two, as if struck by lightning. When it fell into the water, a huge wave washed over our canoe, swamping it. All we could do was cling to the gunwales and await the next volley.

60

I HAD AN IMPRESSION of a boat swooping down on us full of red-coated soldiers and a club descending toward my head; of being hauled aboard a ship in a sort of net, of seeing Doubting Seal and his paddlers shoved belowdecks; and of passing out and coming to briefly, then passing out again.

As my vision cleared, I realized that I was aboard the warship. I was thirsty and had no idea how long I had been unconscious. When I called out in a croaking voice that I wished an interview with the ship's commander, a rather elderly, close-shaven man in a green frock coat stepped forward and identified himself as the ship's first mate. The mate, who seemed very friendly and spoke in what I believed to be a British accent, assisted me to my feet and ushered me into a large, well-lighted cabin at the stern of the ship, where an austere-looking gentleman in a black suit sat at a desk reading a Bible. "Captain John 'Mute Jack' Jamieson, at your service, young sir," said the mate.

The captain looked up, and I perceived that around his neck on a string hung a small slate much like that upon which I had learned my ABC's. The word "Speak" appeared on the slate seemingly of its own accord. As Mute Jack erased the word with a black cloth, his eyes, which were as black as the cover of his Bible, never left mine. He waited for my reply.

"Captain," I said, "my name is Ticonderoga Kinneson. I am a member of an expedition of discovery and exploration led by my uncle, Private True Teague Kinneson, from Vermont and the United States."

Jack Jamieson continued to regard me. Then the name "Meriwether Lewis?" appeared on the slate. I shrugged as if unfamiliar with the Lewis party, and repeated that I had come west with my uncle, and wished to be set ashore at Jack's earliest convenience.

The captain and mate then took me back out onto the deck, where the ship's marines were drilling, barefoot and soundless. Their discipline was impeccable, their silence terrifying. A wild thought of trying to lure the ship onto the breakers off the headland flashed across my mind. But by now my mouth was too dry to speak. At a nod from Mute Jack, the mate hurried to fetch me a drink. The beverage turned out to be seawater, and in a choking spasm I lost consciousness again.

It was now dusk, and I could see that we were anchored in the mouth of the Columbia. Under Mute Jack's gaze, the crew was practicing running the cannons in and out, working in deadly

silent fashion, the cannon wheels being muffled in cloth. Presently he assembled the ship's crew, and the mate told them that
he believed Lewis's party was encamped not far distant. Mute
Jack's plan was to remain with the ship while the marines proceeded upriver in the cutter to locate the Americans by their
campfires and report back. Just before dawn, the ship would sail
into the estuary and bombard the Americans, after which the
marines would mount an assault on the camp and finish off any
survivors in whatever manner they saw fit.

   As darkness fell, the captain dispatched the cutter and marines, with the elderly mate at the tiller. I could not think what
to do, short of leaping over the side, which would have been
pointless under the circumstances, the tide here being too powerful for any man to swim against. My head was beginning to
spin again when, from the dark water below, a seal barked.
Then another. Swarming up the side of the ship and over the
rail in the starlight came an army of demi-creatures, with the
arms, legs, and bodies of men and the heads of giant seals, walruses, white bears, sharks, and whales, each barking or roaring
or bellowing or braying after its kind. And each came bearing a
bow or a lance or a club, with which they immediately started
round the ship's deck, prosecuting their grisly business, while I
watched in horror. There were halibut-headed men and ray-
headed men, men with the heads of giant crabs and mollusks
and sea-denizens stranger still, beaked squid and octopi and,
most ferocious of all, a man with the head of a salmon, wielding
a great white club. At his side fought a warrior in a narwhal
mask, bearing a bundle of the sharpened tusks of his watery
namesake, which he hurled at the ship's crew with deadly accuracy. With one he skewered Mute Jack's arm to the wheel.

   The captain wrenched free, then flung himself back onto the
wheel, with the clear intent of spinning it entirely around and

broaching the ship. The narwhal-man pitched a tusk directly through his chest, driving him over the rail and into the sea, where milling sharks converged on him with all the swift ferocity of their kind.

In the meantime the mate's raiders in the cutter, hearing the death screams of their fellows, raced back to the ship. Under the salmon-warrior's direction, two of the forward cannons were charged with grapeshot. As the sloop passed below the ship's bow, the guns were trained directly down onto the marines and a double volley fired point-blank, clearing the deck of living men, all but the mate in the frock coat, who came running up the sheer side of the ship like an ape and leaped lightly onto the rail. His coat now glowed a bright green; two short red horns sprouted from his head, a flaming pointed beard from his chin, and two hairy cloven hoofs appeared where his feet had been. "I'll see you in Hell yet," he boomed out to the salmon-headed man in the voice of twenty demons. Spreading his cloak, he made a great leap upward toward the mast; but the salmon-man reached up as he passed overhead, caught him by one ankle and the tail of his frock coat, and, spinning entirely around, hurled him far out to sea, where he vanished like an extinguished meteor.

"Tooleroo," said my uncle's voice from inside the mask. "Hell is the place for him, Ti, and I think we won't pursue him there. But what a play it would make if we did!"

"Water," I managed to say. I remember drinking as though I would never stop, and after that I remember nothing else until morning.

61

WHEN FRANKLIN AND I saw the pirate ship," my uncle was telling me, "we headed for shore. Our intention was to carry our canoe over the headland, cross the Columbia, and return with the captains and their men to attack the ship by night and rescue you. But up a little creek we ran right into the Tlingits, who were on their way downstream in three war canoes. I confess, Ti, that for a few uneasy minutes it appeared as though all was over for us. I won them over by offering them maple sugar on wappato bread, toasted, which they declared the best dish they'd ever laid a lip over. As it turned out, the pirates had just attacked and burned several Tlingit villages north of Vancouver Bay, and the Tlingits were eager for a way to avenge these depredations. I spoke to them first in Norse, but discovered that they have unfortunately lost the language of their Viking ancestors. So I was obliged to address them in Russian, of which they have some rudiments. I asked if they were familiar with the old saw 'to kill two birds with one stone.' They were not, but had an equivalent saying, 'to catch two salmon on one hook.' Therefore, I inquired if they would like to catch two salmon on one hook by eliminating the crew of the warship which had destroyed their villages and then annihilating, in the bargain, the Russians at Fort Barrow, who have oppressed their people for nearly a century. The Tlingits said yes, they would very much like to do that; but they did not see how it was possible. I laid out my plan for a nocturnal attack on the ship, I to lead the assault in the mask of a king salmon, and

Franklin wearing the headpiece of a narwhal. Is that not a very pretty story?"

"It is, sir. But tell me, who were these pirates?"

"Why, Ti, according to papers in the captain's cabin, no more nor less than a gang of renegade Englishmen, sailing under a letter of marque, or private commission, with orders to capture or kill Meriwether Lewis to prevent America from establishing a claim on the Northwest Territory. We have saved the expedition's skin again, nephew. Though Franklin and I agree that it will be best not to mention this little episode to anyone, including the captains, lest it provoke another war between America and Great Britain."

I said, "I congratulate you, sir, on the success of your attack. And upon finally dispatching your Gentleman friend back to where he belongs. But I was very surprised that it was the first officer who turned out to be he and not the captain, who was a hideous mute, bloodthirsty fellow."

"It is not astonishing, Ti. My old friend, you see, is much more of an *abettor* than a doer. It's odd. I rather miss him already. I was not entirely in jest when I said that an expedition to his fiery purlieus would be matter for a great play. There is precedent, you know, in Virgil and Dante. But let that go for the nonce. Paint a picture of me in the salmon mask applying the Old Scotch Spin or, as it is also called, the Devil's Ceilidh, to my friend. He will trouble us no more, I think. It — I mean the Ceilidh — is guaranteed to keep him away."

While a crew of Tlingits acquainted themselves with the particularities of sailing the captured warship, my uncle introduced me to his new friends from the north. There were three divisions in the Tlingit raiding party, each consisting of fifty men. The names of their chiefs were Ice Bear, Walrus, and Tsar Nicholas, and under their escort we now repaired to the stream where they had surprised my uncle and Franklin. The creek was hemmed in on both sides by tall western cedars. A soft spring rain had begun to fall, and the raindrops slipping off the trees into the still water, the dense fog, and the silence of our paddlers all enhanced the mystery of this place. Soon we put in at a little sandy shore. The Tlingits then led us along a faint path up a knoll and down the other side into a twilit clearing. Silently, Chief Ice Bear pointed upward.

"O dear Jesu!" cried my uncle.

We were surrounded by gigantic sea and coastal beasts with human features, twenty or thirty feet tall, scowling down upon us in the dusk as if they meant to devour us. But Franklin bowed and called up to them, "How do you do, good sirs? Pray, tell me. Is the salmon angling lively in these parts?"

By degrees, I gathered my wits together and realized that the giant apparitions were, in fact, the trunks of trees, elaborately carved into the shapes of walruses, seals, whales, bears, and salmon. Several had multiple heads, with human-like faces and open maws painted blue, red, or yellow. In all I counted fifteen figures. Chief Walrus told my uncle that these relics were the handiwork of his people, who from time to time convened here in the cedar grove to carve new memorials to their own fierceness.

Tsar Nicholas, a renowned sculptor, now began carving into a fresh cedar the frowning visage of Private True Teague Kinneson himself, in commemoration of his signal action in dispatching the Devil back to Hell.

In the meantime, the Tlingits prepared for a victory celebration. First they built a large bonfire, into which, to my considerable surprise, each man threw his animal mask and one or two treasured personal items. Also, they lighted trench fires to roast elk, bear, salmon, and many delicious viands from the ship's pantry, not to mention the deceased crew members thereof. Which, the Tlingits complained, were quite fishy-tasting from having been at sea too long. They looked at my uncle and at me, felt the flesh on our arms and hams, and said jestingly (I trusted) that they preferred good lean landsmen to sailors any day of the week.

The following day came the division of the spoils. As guests of honor, Franklin, my uncle, and I were offered our pick. I selected a little china teapot with periwinkle-blue flowers for Yellow Sage Flower Who Tells Wise Stories. My uncle's eyes were larger. He wanted two hundred yards of pink silk, one hundred of yellow, and a large metal cooking brazier, along with a goodly supply of charcoal, from the stores of an Indiaman that the pirate ship had captured and burned off Peru. Finally it was Franklin's turn to choose. The chiefs told him that, as he had personally killed ten men, including the ship's captain, and fought with more deadly purpose than they had ever witnessed — though this was not to detract from my uncle's heroic work — he was to pick whatever his heart desired, even if he chose to strip the ship of all remaining plunder. He told them he would like to sleep on their most generous offer and make his selection on the morrow.

More than once during our long journey to the Pacific, my uncle had remarked to me that the one thing we could rely on was that each new day would bring something entirely different from the day before. The following morning was no exception to this precept, which he called "Kinneson's Axiom of Perpetual Surprises, Most of Them Bad but Some Good and Others Bad but Susceptible to Favorable Interpretations." Soon after dawn, Franklin closeted himself for several hours with Walrus, Ice Bear, and Tsar Nicolas in the cabin of the captured ship. When their tête-à-tête was completed, he came forth all smiles and addressed us as follows. "My dear friends, the great and only constant in life is change. Last night I went to sleep a

Blackfoot savant. This morning I was made a Tlingit chief. Yes, my companions. I have been invested as Chief Narwhal. And, in order not to draw out a sad fact, I must now take my leave of you. For my new people have chosen me to lead them in the all-out naval assault on their Russian oppressors at Fort Barrow, and I have chosen for my reward the ship itself. We weigh anchor within the hour. Part we must, I to fight the Russians, and you, Private True, to guide the captains home to safety. And Ticonderoga to make his reputation as the first artist of Louisiana. Work on developing strong story lines in your pictures, Ti. You may yet turn out to be the Michelangelo of the American West. Or" — this with great good cheer — "you may not."

Chief Narwhal turned back to my uncle, clasped him close, clapped him on the back several times, and declared that his *Comedy of Ethan Allen* was without doubt the finest thing of its sort in the history of the universe. And if he ever, in any port in the world, heard a critic hint that the play violated any of Scholia Aristotle's unities, that wretch would rue the day he had been born. Upon which, all gleaming in his white antelope suit and colored feathers and long, single-tusked whale mask, the new chief stepped to the quarterdeck of the *Tlingit*, as he had named his vessel, and issued the order to raise the anchor. My uncle and Doubting Seal and I watched from the Seal's canoe as the crew sprang to the rigging and unfurled the sails; then the *Tlingit* dipped its bow and skimmed lightly off to the northwest. A few miles off the coast it swung due north, putting on all sail possible, and fired off a cannon in farewell.

"Thither goes a great man, Ti," my uncle sighed. "I'd fight to the death the fellow who said otherwise. Heaven above knows that Franklin — I mean Chief Narwhal — may have his little ways and stays; but he is a noble fellow, and the best friend who ever walked God's green earth. He will make a splendid Viking chieftain. Oh! The salt spray gets in my eyes. I weep."

62

March 22, 1806

Charles and Helen of Troy Kinneson

Kingdom Common, Republic of Vermont, U.S.A.

Dear Father and Mother,

I write hurriedly to say that after a most productive
winter by the Pacific, uncle and I leave with Captain
Lewis tomorrow for our return trip up the Columbia
to the Rocky Mountains, thence down the Missouri to
St. Louis and so home. We are both in excellent health.
Our arrival may precede that of this letter, which I
have left with my friend Doubting Seal, to entrust to
the care of the first homeward-bound American
trading vessel to put in at the mouth of the Columbia.
But I must not omit to mention — in the bustle
of preparing for our departure I nearly forgot — that
we will be making a brief detour on our return trip,
to the Land of the Glaciers.

With haste but fondest regards from

Your loving son,

Ticonderoga

63

URING AN OTHERWISE uneventful trip from the Pacific back up the Columbia, Serpent, and Clearwater rivers to the Bitterroot Mountains, Captain Lewis had a serious misunderstanding with the Nez Perce Indians. As it turned out, these people were quarreling among themselves and at first refused to give back our horses. How the recrossing of the Bitterroots could be undertaken without mounts was a very anxious concern for everyone. But my uncle announced that he had yet another little trick up his sleeve, and the Indians would soon be so grateful to him that they would return all of our horses and be clamoring to give us a great many more besides. He assembled the entire American party, along with the chiefs and the most athletic young men of the Nez Perce Nation, and said that he intended to teach them a great and marvelous game, which he had invented in his former profession as a schoolmaster for his scholars to play at recess.

He divided the men into two thirty-man teams, with Lewis and the American expeditionaries on one side and us and twenty-eight Nez Perce on the other. He then arrayed the Indians on our team in strategic positions around a riverside meadow, in which he placed four square bags stuffed with fir needles and spaced about one hundred feet apart, making the shape of a diamond. Next he produced a fist-sized sphere he had fashioned from a kind of gutta-percha made of gulls' feathers bound together with pine resin and wrapped in elk hide.

Handing his prehistoric bison's thigh to Drouillard, the

party's hunter, my uncle strode out on the playing field and de-clared, "Gentlemen, I will hurl this ball — which I have named 'Punisher,' for reasons that will very soon become apparent — toward George Drouillard. He will strike it — *if he can* — then attempt to run to each of the sacks, which I call 'safe-sacks,' in turn before a member of my team can recover the ball and strike *him* with it. He may, however, tarry on any safe-sack he wishes, there to be secure from persecution, while the next striker on his team essays to solve my cunning serves. When ten explorers have been struck off a safe-sack by the Punisher, or have fruitlessly swung the bison's club five times without touching the ball, the two sides will reverse positions and my team will strike. The first team to send one hundred men safely round the circuit wins."

Then in his great stage voice he cried out, "Let the first game of Kinneson-ball begin."

Drouillard stepped up to the first safe-sack. My uncle smiled grimly, windmilled his throwing arm round his head several times, twisted his body into a dozen fantastical contortions, kicked his lean shank high, and blazed the Punisher by Drouil-lard — who, a full second after the missile had passed, made a feeble hacking motion with the bone.

"You must do better than that, frog-eater," cried my uncle. "Try this for size." Again he wound himself up like a top and hurled the Punisher at the expedition's hunter. But Drouillard, however skillful at bringing down game, had no notion what to do with his striker and actually fell to his knees trying to hit the ball. Five times my uncle threw. Five times Drouillard missed.

"Sit down now, varlet, hang thy head in shame; root up some truffles, swine," cried my uncle. And to John Shields, who batted next: "Hey, striker, hey, striker. What? Art blind? You missed by a furlong."

Hapless Shields had the same luck as Drouillard and was

subjected to even more abuse from my uncle, to the great amusement of our Indian teammates and several hundred Nez Perce spectators. The next two strikers, Privates Pryor and Bratton, met with an identical fate. Moreover, my uncle continued to make up new rules as the contest progressed. When Bratton elected not to swing at an offering that flew high over his head like a flushing grouse, it was counted as a miss for the batsman, on the grounds that the ball was strikable. As indeed it would have been, had the man stood ten feet tall.

Captain Lewis encouraged his men greatly; but my uncle's servings were all but impossible to strike, and after the first four batters had gone down, Lewis came forward and said he would now show how it should be done. My uncle laughed and cried, "Step up to the sack, captain, and wield the striker if you're able, not like a doddering old woman but like a man." So saying, he whirled his arm, twisted, kicked, called Lewis a crippled donkey, and hurled the Punisher straight for his head. As Lewis threw himself to the ground, the ball grazed his temple. "Hi, hi, five men down," shouted my uncle. "What say you to that, Captain Clark?"

Rushing up to Lewis, who was still sprawled on the ground, Clark cried, "What do I say? I say you've done for the captain, you madman."

My uncle replied that Kinneson-ball was no effete gentleman's pursuit, like cricket, but a rough-and-tumble *American* sport, in which anything was allowed if you could get away with it, and winning was the only objective, and to stop whining and drag Lewis off the field so that the contest could proceed.

In the event, Captain Lewis shakily stood up and, though still dazed, was told sharply to go sit down and reflect on how to acquit himself better when next he struck. Then, in a frenzy of false starts and leg-kicking, throwing sometimes over-handed, sometimes under, and sometimes from the side, my uncle proceeded to knock down, or stun, or cause to swing wildly in self-defense five more members of the American team. At which juncture they were very glad to take to the field and give us our turn to hit. In truth, the bison-bone club was too ponderous for all but the biggest and strongest men to swing. But when my uncle's turn came, he proved himself as able a striker as a hurler, dealing the gutta-percha missile thrown by Clark such a blow that it sailed entirely over the Clearwater River into some fir trees on the opposite bank. Whereupon he capered round the safe-sacks, kicking his legs out in front of him like a Prussian soldier, while Lewis sent his big Newfoundland dog, Seaman, to fetch the ball.

The game of Kinneson-ball proceeded until dusk, with our team eventually winning by a score of 100 to 2. The Indians were so delighted with this new entertainment that they gave back the expedition's horses that very evening and made my uncle an honorary shaman, calling him Too-lap-stran, which, loosely translated, meant "Noble Hurler and Striker in the Greatest Pastime Ever Invented."

64

BETWEEN THE MARATHON game of Kinneson-ball and our departure for the Bitterroots, I sketched and painted several new birds. One was a woodpecker with a crimson throat and black back feathers tinted with a green sheen, whose bright neck plumage my uncle found especially effective in tying flies for the huge numbers of crimson-sided trout then in the Clearwater. Next I painted a large, jay-like fellow, though rounder and fuller in the body than our blue eastern jays, with a longer beak. Also a lovely orange, red, yellow, and black bird, which some of the men called a parrot. My uncle reprimanded them, pointing out that in shape, song, and boldness of coloration it resembled a tanager. But when he saw one of these birds eating wasps, the way a small boy gobbles sugar-trifles, as they emerged from a thawing mud bank above the river he was so horrified that he refused to add it to his *Systema Naturae Americanae* and claimed it to be a stray blown up from the tropics of old Mexico.

We started out to cross the Bitterroots in mid-June and were driven back once by the high snow in the passes. But late that month we accomplished the crossing in a period of several days, after which Captain Lewis divulged the following plan, which would split the party into three divisions. Captain Clark would travel by way of the River of Yellow Stones through the heart of the Crow Nation, back to the Missouri. Sergeant Ordway was to accompany Clark to the headwaters of the Beaverhead and from there take a small party down to the Three Forks and on to the Great Falls. Captain Lewis, with Drouillard, the Field brothers, and my uncle and me, would explore north to the forty-ninth parallel and the southern boundary of British North America. Our party would then link with Ordway's at the falls on the Missouri, whence we would spin on down to the mouth of the River of Yellow Stones and rendezvous with Clark.

My uncle pointed out to Lewis that this plan was fraught with danger, especially Lewis's leg of the trip. For Smoke had vowed that no American would ever again pass through his territory alive; and the Blackfoot chief had the will, intelligence, and might to back up his threat. "Lookee, sir," said he, "this is as poor a scheme as a man of otherwise good judgment could devise. You know old Caesar's maxim, 'Divide and conquer.' You're dividing your own forces so that they can be conquered. The Crows won't kill Bill Clark and his party, but they'll surely steal their horses. If the Blackfeet spot Ordway's crew loitering on the Missouri, as their sentinels are certain to, they'll pick 'em off like flies. And you, captain, scouting around in the heart of their country, why, you'll call down the whole nation on us."

"Private True," Lewis replied, "experienced as you are in all military matters dating back to Caesar —"

"And before," said my uncle.

"As experienced as you are in all matters dating back to Caesar *and before,* Captain Clark and I have managed to get our party to the Pacific and back across the Bitterroots without consulting with you overfrequently. I will much appreciate your confining yourself to working on your play or refining your wonderful game of Kinneson-ball."

"What did you yourself recently call the Blackfeet, captain? 'Vicious, lawless, and abandoned,' as I recall. And there are several thousand of them. You're jeopardizing your entire expedition. Why?"

"Why, sir? To see if any of the tributaries to the Missouri rise north of the forty-ninth parallel, as Albert Gallatin advised the President to have me do, thereby extending the Louisiana Territory into British North America. Mr. Jefferson would be much pleased to learn that such is the case."

"Mr. Jefferson would be much better pleased by your safe return. I cite from learned Thucydides, in his *History of the Peloponnesian Wars,* in which Pericles, the great Athenian orator, urges war with Sparta yet cautions his countrymen against *overextending their forces by taking unnecessary risks.* Hearken to Pericles, the wisest of the wise. Draw in your horns, sir."

Clark looked grave, but it was Lewis who made the strategic

decisions for the expedition. Under no circumstances would Clark say a word to undercut his friend and fellow captain.

"The President specifically directed that you do nothing inconsistent with the party's safety," my uncle persisted. "Surely he would say —"

"Enough!" Lewis barked. "I'll hear no more of what you think the President would say, private."

At which my uncle drew himself up straight and tall and said, "Softly, my good man, when you try to silence a freethinking Vermonter. I don't belong to your sorry little ragtag party, to be ordered about like one of Tyrant Napoleon's footsoldiers. I am a veteran of Ethan Allen's regiment and as free as the north wind blowing off the Green Mountains."

But Lewis merely snapped that, being "free as the wind," my uncle had his blessing to leave immediately and let that same wind blow him back to Vermont. For he was weary unto death of providing protection and assistance to people who had been nothing but a thorn in his side since leaving St. Louis.

Enraged, my uncle said he was not surprised "that the final reward of one who had many times preserved the expedition from annihilation was to be banished from the company of the very men who owed their lives to his good offices, but that justice would prevail in the end." He bade me immediately collect my possibles and paintings, and thus we struck out overland on our own just as we had when we began the trip more than two years before.

This time, however, we had with us, besides Bucephalus and Ethan Allen, three Nez Perce pack horses carrying, in large cedar-bark baskets, the bolts of yellow and pink silk and the cooking brazier and charcoal my uncle had taken from Mute Jack's ship. And we were headed into the heart of the most powerful and belligerent Indian nation in North America.

Chief Mountain

65

T<small>I</small>," SAID MY UNCLE, "do you think I was unduly harsh with
Lewis?"

"You were very harsh, uncle," I said, "but quite rightly so.
Captain Lewis's venturing up here into Blackfoot territory is a
bad business. I fear that he may draw down the entire nation
upon us."

It was mid-July, and we were camped again near the Great
Falls, preparing to head north to the Land of the Glaciers in
the morning. Compared to the earlier legs of our journey, our
trip here from the Bitterroots had been somber. I knew that our
angry parting from Lewis had been weighing on my uncle's
mind, as it had on mine.

"I was hasty," my uncle agreed. "But let that go. I need now
to write to our friend the President; and I shall be more than
fair to Lewis in my epistle. Take a letter, Ti."

July 19, 1806
Thomas Jefferson, President
Monticello
Charlottesville, Virginia
United States of America

Dear Mr. President,
I write to you from near the Great Falls of the Missouri,

having beaten the captains and their "official"
expedition to the Pacific.

Sir, these western lands are more wondrous than even
you ever conceived. Let me be candid. Here there are
no great mammoths, no mountains of salt, no lost
wandering tribes of Israelites or Welshmen. But the real
wonders, the crashing of these Great Falls, the marvels
of the Land Where the River of Yellow Stones Rises, the
rugged beauties of the Pacific coast — all exceed
anything to be found in our tame, unimagining East.
The West is bountiful in furs, fish, grass for to graze
cattle, timber, fresh water, and noble prospects; and
there is more of it than any one man could view in fifty
lifetimes. I doubt not that it is equally rich in minerals,
both precious and practical. Yet its real treasures are its
wonderful people. Their customs of marriage, warfare,
burial, hunting, architecture — all are as diverse as
their languages. They possess every art we do — music,
painting, oratory, storytelling. In some cases they are
skillful agronomists, in others uncanny boat-builders,
in yet others superb horsemen. I beg you to honor their
political divisions, their histories, their persons, and
their dignity. They most assuredly are not "children."
They are endlessly intelligent and endlessly resourceful;
they love their families above all else in life; they are as
fond as you are of good conversation, good food, subtle
jokes, travel, art — in other words they are good
Americans.

Item: Please remember the soldiers of the expedition, for they are all good men and true. Let me begin with that fine officer, William Clark. Like Lewis, he sought, at your behest, the shortest practicable waterway to the Pacific. Finding that there was no such thing as a Northwest Passage, practicable or otherwise, he discovered instead, in himself, a great gift for map-making, for tactical decisions, for negotiating whitewater, and for negotiating with and understanding the nations of Louisiana and the Northwest. He was ever able, fair, truthful, quick to take the Indians' part, and sympathetic with the least of those people, as well as the greatest. In his steadfastness as Meriwether Lewis's friend, he enabled Captain Lewis to lead the party to the Pacific, an accomplishment perhaps unexcelled in the annals of exploration, on this continent or any continent, *though you will remember that I got there first.*

Sergeants Gass and Ordway, hunter Drouillard, fiddler Cruzatte, who brought the men music to keep up their spirits, the honest Field brothers, the deft fisherman Silas Goodrich, *et alia.* — though Irish, French, English, Welsh, Indian, or Scots, they are all Americans. Make no false distinctions between them when you consider how to reward their extraordinary courage and loyalty. Black York, Clark's slave, was much admired by the peoples we met as a prodigy of wit, strength, good nature, and good sense, and as much a help to the expedition as any other man.

Item: I only wish you could make the acquaintance
of my particular friend, the Blackfoot savant Franklin.
He chose to sail north in the ship _Tlingit_ with his new
friends of that nation. His hope is to destroy the Russian
fort at Barrow, Alaska, and to free the Tlingits from the
onerous yoke of those most brutal oppressors. On behalf of
Franklin, who likewise provided invaluable assistance
to Lewis's expedition, I ask that, should you decide to
annex Alaska, you treat with the Tlingits, not the
Russian usurpers. They are a fine, fierce, independent
nation of artists and rovers, and could put a million or
two in American currency to good use. I believe that
their living tree-carvings rival the great sculptures of
the Greeks.

Item: Captain Lewis. What more can I say about this
great and good man, other than that you chose well in
appointing him as the leader of the expedition? He and
I agreed on little; yet he is a gentleman of undaunted
courage, whose firmness and perseverance as a leader
and father of his men yielded to nothing but
impossibilities. I do not recommend him for any political
or government office; he needs to be active at all times.
Send him on another expedition. Send him to explore
— the planet Venus. I have a new invention in mind, a
sort of electrical rocket that will — but I will tell you
more of this later. To return to Lewis, wherever you send
him, make certain first that he finishes his journals
and transcribes his field notes into them, for they are the

record of a great man and a great venture, second only to that of

Your friend,

Private True Teague Kinneson

"Add a 'tooleree,' Ti," my uncle said when I read the letter back to him just before we turned in for the night.

"Pardon me, sir?"

"Add a 'tooleree' after my signature. It will indicate that I wish the President well, but, as a Vermonter, that I intend to pay fealty to no one and to take no man, and no merely human enterprise, too seriously."

66

A WEEK LATER we were camped at the conjunction of the Marias and Two Medicine rivers, just south of the Land of the Glaciers, with the soaring, snowy summit of Squaresided Chief Mountain in the foreground. While we had as yet encountered no Blackfeet, we had found signs of recent campfires and seen smoke in the distance. We suspected that they were aware of our presence, too, and might well be drawing us into a trap. That day we had also seen some signs that Lewis had come this way with his party of three men a few days earlier.

For the past several evenings my uncle had spent his time sewing together his wondrous lengths of pink and yellow silk cloth, as if fashioning a great tent or pavilion. Although I had inquired several times what he was making, he had been very coy and close-mouthed, saying only that it was his boldest invention to date.

"Is it something to trade with the Blackfeet?" I asked as we watched Chief Mountain and the peaks behind it fade into the twilight.

He smiled knowingly.

"A stage curtain? For a grand production of *Ethan Allen*?"

"Try again, Ti."

"Not, heaven forbid, sails for another *Dutchman*?"

"Not sails, lad. But let us leave the new invention and return one last time to my old friend, the Gentleman from Vermont. You may be surprised, Ti, to learn that I no longer hold him in much consequence."

"I am surprised, sir. He has certainly caused us — and mankind — enough trouble."

"He has. But recently I have concluded that the more important struggles in this world are not those between us mortals and the Devil, or even between Good and Evil. Rather, the more difficult conflicts are those between human beings, in which — confound this dull needle; that's the third time this week I've sewn my thumb to the cloth — do you attend?"

"I do, uncle. I am sorry about your thumb."

"Thank you. It is nothing. I was saying, the more difficult conflicts are those in which both parties believe themselves to be in the right."

I considered this proposition. "This seems a mighty paradox, sir."

"Exactly, Ti. Our lives are mighty paradoxes." And with this pronouncement, my uncle gave the bell on his cap a vigorous jingling, and continued sewing until it was too dark to see his needle.

67

As soon as it was light we started up the Two Medicine toward the Land of the Glaciers and Chief Mountain. We
continued about ten miles along the stream, which was very
low at this time of year. As we rode, I mused about what I
would say to Yellow Sage Flower when we were reunited and
what I would do with my life when and if we got safely back to
Vermont.

In the distance we could see a range of peaks higher than
any we had traveled through thus far, with Squaresided Chief
Mountain between us and them and a little apart from the rest.
But in the late morning we were led by the smoke of a campfire
to a most alarming sight. A black pool of what appeared to be
blood lay drying on the ground near the fire, with more blood
about three hundred yards away behind a large boulder. The remains of four Indian shields were smoldering on the fire. The
tracks of Lewis's Shoshone horses led due south. Five or six
other riders seemed to have fled west on smaller ponies.

My uncle said nothing until he ascertained these facts. Then,
in that businesslike, military manner which I had first witnessed back on the Natchez Trace in our encounter with the
Harpes, he said, "Ti, short of the captain's death or capture, this
is as bad a situation as we could imagine. Precisely what happened here I'm not certain. But it's clear that Lewis, Drouillard, and the Field brothers are riding hard for the Missouri
and their rendezvous with Sergeant Ordway. Some of them
may be wounded."

I had surmised as much myself, but now a terrifying idea occurred to me. "What is to prevent the Blackfeet from returning in great numbers and wiping out Lewis's entire expedition?"

My uncle looked off to the west in the direction the Indians had gone. "Us," he said.

He nodded, and his yellow eyes gleamed with purpose. "This will be our plan, lad. You cut directly for Chief Mountain and Yellow Sage Flower. I'll follow the Indians and persuade them and their cohorts that it isn't in their best interest to pursue Lewis. We'll meet on Chief tomorrow or the next day."

"But what if you *can't* persuade the Blackfeet —"

With my uncle, however, there was never a moment's doubt once he had made up his mind. "Excelsior!" he called out. And immediately posted west, waving his stocking cap over his head like a young squire off on his first quest.

On I rode, into the late afternoon. As I drew closer to the huge square mountain, I saw ahead on the prairie a tall dust cloud, which seemed to move neither toward nor away from me. From it came a doleful chanting, which rose and fell in an eerie rhythm unlike any singing I had ever heard. Presently I dismounted, and climbed a low rise about a mile from Chief Mountain. Through my pocket glass I saw, near the base of the mountain, at least a thousand horsemen with whitened faces, cantering in a gigantic circle around a scaffold upon which lay two figures wrapped in robes. As the Indians rode, they sang a strange hymn, now rising to a howl of anger, now falling to a dirge. This had to be a funeral ceremony for the men killed on the Two Medicine, whose blood my uncle and I had discovered. But who were they? Indians or Americans?

Scattered over the prairie near the scaffolds stood several tall western firs that had sprung up a little beyond the tree line at the foot of the mountain. Their trunks were dense with dead branches for the first fifty or sixty feet up from their base. Tied to several of them, in the tangle of dead limbs, were crude human effigies wrapped in red, white, and blue cloth. As I watched, one of the circling riders dismounted, ran to the base of a fir, and flung a lighted torch onto a pile of kindle at its base. Instantly the entire tree took fire, the flames whooshing up the trunk in a crackling roar and engulfing the cloth effigy, to a shout of triumph from the riders.

As I watched the burning fir tree through my glass, I felt something hard and cold on the back of my neck. Spinning around, I discovered Smoke's particular friend, Buffalo's Back Fat, staring straight down the barrel of his musket at me.

On our way across the prairie toward the circling warriors, Buffalo's Back Fat angrily told me that earlier in the day several young Blackfeet had ridden into Smoke's camp at the foot of the mountain with the corpses of two of their comrades. According to their account, the evening before, while scouting for bison on the Two Medicine, they had run into four Americans. The Indians and the white men had agreed to camp together. But when the Americans revealed that they planned to return to the Rocky Mountains soon and trade not only with the Blackfeet but with their ancestral enemies, including the Crow and the Shoshone, the youths had decided to steal their horses and rifles as a warning of what would follow if the whites tried to carry out their plan. At dawn there had been a skirmish. One of the Indians, a favorite cousin of Smoke's named Side Hill Calf, had been shot, and another had been knifed to death. The ceremony I had been watching was both a funeral and a war dance.

The riders were now wheeling about the scaffolds in several concentric circles. Some of the men were inflicting gashes on their legs with knives and jagged pieces of flint. A man wearing bison horns broke out of the outermost circle and galloped toward us. He rode around me once, then reined in his pony and stared at me with eyes as black as the Missouri on the darkest night of the year. "So," Smoke said to Buffalo's Back Fat, "you've caught one of them already. The young wizard who makes men with paints."

To me he said, "Where is the old man, your traveling companion?"

"I don't know," I said in the Blackfoot I had learned from Franklin over the winter.

Smoke studied me. "Tomorrow morning, wizard, when the funeral is over, we will pursue your American captain, lie in wait for him and the other murderers where the River of Yellow Stones flows into the Mother of Rivers, and wipe out the entire party as we should have done last summer when they first appeared. In the meantime we will see if evil wizards who duplicate people in paint can be burned."

He turned to Buffalo's Back Fat. "Lash him up in a fir tree," he said. "Maybe that will flush out the old man. Then we'll serve him the same."

There was a heaviness in Smoke's voice and eyes that made me think he took no pleasure in this business and no pleasure in contemplating Lewis's destruction. I realized that he believed he was in the right, just as the American party did. My uncle's wise words — "our lives are mighty paradoxes" — came back to me, and I knew better now what he had meant by them.

Like the effigies around me, I was bound to the trunk of a tree about thirty feet off the ground in the midst of dozens of tinder-dry dead limbs. Nearby, the pitchy trunk of the tree that had earlier been lighted afire continued to smolder. And although one might imagine that the Okeepa ritual I had undergone back at the Mandans would have prepared me for such an ordeal as this, I found that it had not.

"Smoke," I called down, "where is Yellow Sage?"

"Where you can't get at her with your wizardry."

The Blackfeet continued to ride in concentric circles, tightening in on me as the sun dipped toward the peaks to the west.

Buffalo's Back Fat and Smoke began piling brush around the base of my fir tree. I thought of Joan of Arc and other old sainted martyrs. But I was no saint, nor did I wish to become a martyr. I imagined my remains, a charred husk of a person on a blackened tree. The white faces of the riders glowed blood-red in the sinking sun, which was now a huge crimson orb, like the shining glass ornaments on our Yuletide tree at home. Thinking of Vermont and Christmas reminded me of my parents, sitting in our farmhouse kitchen, my father scanning last week's Boston paper to see what items he could glean for the *Kingdom County Monitor,* my mother rolling the fragrant, gingery dough for her cartwheel cookies and talking happily about our reunion.

Smoke remounted his pony and joined the innermost ring of riders. Someone had already handed him a lighted pine torch.

As the sun started to drop from sight, its upper half turned from red to pink, with bars of yellow across it. The sun actually seemed to be moving toward me through the sky. The Blackfeet looked up and seemed transfixed as on it came. Suddenly I realized that it was not the sun but a great ball moving through the sky. No, not a ball — a balloon! Drifting our way on the evening breeze came a vast balloon with a basket depending from it and, standing in the basket, the figure of a man. The Indians watched in perfect silence. Even Smoke seemed spellbound.

"The sun is about to swallow us up!" Buffalo's Back Fat exclaimed.

Smoke narrowed his eyes. When the air-craft drew almost overhead, its pilot reached into the bottom of the basket and produced his tin hearing trumpet. Lifting it to his ear, he roared, "In the name of the Great Jehovah and the First Continental Congress, surrender Ticonderoga!"

As my uncle fed more charcoal to the brazier affixed just below the mouth of the great pink and yellow silk bag, a second figure arose beside him, a woman with long dark hair, wearing a white dress. Yellow Sage Flower threw a rope over the side and descended hand over hand, as fast as a sailor. By the time she reached the ground the balloon was directly above our heads. Holding the rope like a tether, Sage called out, "Smoke. Private True Kinneson, on high in his great sky-barque, orders you to release your captive. Hurry! Cut him down before the private hurls brimstone at you or shoots you with his great gun with the belled muzzle."

But no sooner were the words out of her mouth than a sudden gust of wind caught the balloon and yanked the rope out of Sage's hand. In a twinkling the balloon and the basket, with my uncle inside, had lifted high into the firmament, sailing east faster and faster on the strong breeze. And though my uncle called out encouragingly to me and waved his jingling night-stocking as triumphantly as if my rescue had gone exactly as planned, soon the silk bag was just a speck in the heavens. Then it was gone.

With great presence of mind Sage said, "Piegans, Lords of the Plains, I come with a story. Hear my tale. There's a message for you inside it."

"No more tales, Yellow Sage," Smoke said. "These Americans are evil people. They must be destroyed."

"If you don't wish to hear it, put your hands over your ears like the wayward child you remind me of. But first you will cut the young painter down from the fir tree. He wasn't with the men who killed Side Hill Calf and Elk Ivory, and he hasn't harmed anyone."

"He is a dangerous liar," Smoke said. "With his paints he makes things that are not so appear so. Such a sorcerer must be burned."

"Hear my story before you determine his fate. What harm can there be in cutting him down?"

"We will leave him there," Smoke said. "Don't press your luck, Yellow Sage Flower. You have permission to tell your story. Be quick about it."

Sage gave Smoke a fierce look, but he merely gestured for her to begin.

"People," she said, "you all know that many of the original Piegans were animals. In those early days a catamount named Tawny Panther was born in the Piegan Nation. Tawny Panther was a great artist. On cured buffalo robes and tepee covers he depicted in paint the many accomplishments and victories of his people. He even painted Napi making the world and his first and second wives, Old Woman and Old Woman Two. But eventually Tawny Panther began to long for a wife himself. He went to my grandfather and said, 'Great Creator, I have painted you making the world and given you the completed picture and many other pictures as well. You have said that these pictures please you. Very well. Now I want you to create a panther wife for me.'

"But Napi, as you know, never liked to do for his children what they could do for themselves. He said, 'No, my large feline friend. I won't make you a wife. But you are an artist. Make your own wife with paints. If your picture pleases me, I'll breathe life into it.'

"So Tawny Panther painted a beautiful panther-woman. My

grandfather was delighted with the picture. As he had promised, he invested it with life, and named the panther-woman Mint and gave her the natural scent of the fragrant wild plant that grows near our beautiful streams. And Tawny Panther and Mint were joined together in matrimony. But I ask you, my lords, when in the course of human events, or animal affairs either, did matters ever run smoothly? Soon enough Napi, who as we all know has a wandering eye, began to lust after Mint himself. Knowing this, the brave Tawny Panther challenged the old trickster to single combat at dawn."

A murmur went up from the Blackfeet.

Sage looked at me. "Quickly, Ti," she said in English. "Challenge Smoke to fight you on Chief Mountain at dawn. Your lance against his."

Though my heart was beating fast, I called out, "Smoke! I challenge you to meet me on Chief Mountain at dawn. Your lance against mine."

The chief rode forward to the base of my tree. "Agreed," he said. "I will meet you in Red Paintbrush Meadow, on the lower southeast slope of Chief Mountain, at daybreak tomorrow."

Just then the moon lifted above the plains to the east, as orange as the field pumpkins my mother grew between her rows of corn at home in Vermont, causing the white clay on the faces of Smoke and the other Indians to shimmer and glow.

"But Sage," cried Buffalo's Back Fat, "you didn't finish your story. What about the combat between Napi and Tawny Panther? How did it end?"

"I will tell you how the story ended tomorrow evening, after the combat between Smoke and Ti."

"By tomorrow evening," Smoke said, "my men and I will be many miles from here, riding to annihilate the Americans. That is my first say."

"And my second say," Sage shot back, "is that the winner of your duel will determine the fate of the American party. Now you will cut the painter down from the tree and let him properly prepare himself for tomorrow's combat."

Later, as Sage and I sat a little apart from the beclayed riders, I scanned the moonlit side of Chief Mountain through my telescope for any sign of my uncle's balloon, but I could see no trace of it. As I set down the glass, Sage said, "Ticonderoga, your uncle is fine. Napi has many wonderful new adventures in store for him, I promise you. In the meantime, I must tell you that Smoke has promised *me* ten buffalo hides for tepee covers, and a new chokecherry bow, and two Crow servants to wait on me hand and foot if I marry him. What could you give me that could possibly match all that?"

"Only this," I said. Opening the metal tube containing my paintings, I extracted the picture I had done the year before, which I called *Yellow Sage Bathing at the Three Forks*. I unrolled it and handed it to her. "It's yours," I said, "however tomorrow turns out."

A delighted smile came over Yellow Sage's face; for a moment she looked more like a girl of thirteen or fourteen than a young woman of eighteen. But then she whipped the picture away from the firelight and said, "Who is this brazen hussy? I shan't have you looking at her. If you want the truth, I'm very jealous. I may have to burn her up. In the meantime, I'll finish the story of Napi and Tawny Panther. It is very true that my grandfather had a twelve-foot-long lance tipped with the feathers of a war eagle, which had never missed its mark. What's more, like Smoke, Napi can change himself into any animal, and even make himself invisible. But the artist Tawny Panther was more powerful still. For he could make what was invisible, except in his head, visible. Hear now how the wily Blackfoot panther used his lance to defeat my grandfather, then lived happily ever after with his fragrant wife, Mint, in the Sweetgrass beyond Chief Mountain, in the Land of the Glaciers . . ."

68

AT DAWN, SMOKE, wearing red and black war paint and carrying his feathered lance, and I, with my easel, paints, brushes, and the metal tube containing all my finished paintings, rode our horses toward Chief Mountain with an escort of twelve Blackfoot warriors. At the base of the mountain I gave my rifle and ammunition to Buffalo's Back Fat to hold for me, telling him that I would rely entirely on my "wizardry." Smoke assured the other riders that well before noon he would be back with my scalp, and he ordered them to be ready, along with his thousand warriors, to ride to the place where they would ambush the Americans. The other men rode off without looking back, and Smoke and I started up the first slope.

As we approached a stand of tall firs, he said to me, "There is a glade on the other side of these woods, American. I'll meet you there in the same time it has taken us to ride this far" — which was about an hour. Then he appeared to transform himself into a wisp of mountain fog and slipped out of sight into the woods.

I dismounted, removed my belongings from Bucephalus, and took off his saddle and bridle. "Now, sir," I said. "For two years and more you've served me better than I could ever have wished for. Regardless of what happens to me today, you're free." I whacked him on the flank, and he nickered once and headed back down the mountain.

I started into the woods and some minutes later reached the glade Smoke had mentioned. Here, surrounded by lupines and paintbrush flowers, I set up my easel and went quickly to work.

Smoke was approaching. I could not hear him, but I could smell the tang of charred wood as a man-shaped column of smoke drifted toward me across the opening. Abruptly, the Blackfoot chief appeared in his own shape, not far from where I was kneeling. So swiftly I could scarcely follow the motion, he brought back his lance and hurled it straight through my chest. With a war cry he sprang at me, flourishing his knife — only to discover that a painting of a man cannot be scalped. His shout of triumph turned to a scream of anger. But by then I was gone from my hiding place in the nearby forest, and he was left with nothing but a torn painting. The great Smoke had killed a picture.

Noon. The sun beat down through the stunted trees and glanced off the cliffs above me. I was faint from lack of food, but there was plenty of water on the mountain, and the breeze off the ice fields above the cliffs was cool. This time I was wedged into a fissure in a rock wall. Just as the sun reached the meridian, a white wolf trotted up the defile. He tested the air with his nose, howled, and transformed into Smoke, who instantly threw his lance through my second painting. When he realized his mistake, his cry of rage was not a man's but a wolf's. He changed back into the animal and, with a dodging motion, ran off howling.

So far, Tawny Panther's stratagem had worked perfectly. But I knew I would see Smoke once more before nightfall. And our third encounter would determine Lewis's fate as well as my own.

Sunset was less than an hour away. All afternoon I had eluded the shape-shifter, who had taken the form now of a wolf, now a bear, now a bighorn sheep. As we climbed higher on the mountain, up onto the steep snowfields, where I needed to use the metal tube holding my paintings as a walking staff, I grew weaker.

I found the ice cave exactly where Yellow Sage had said it would be. And just as she had told me, it seemed to go entirely through the side of the mountain, a natural tunnel with frozen blue walls. I hurried through the passageway, past flickering images in the ice of long-dead Blackfoot chiefs and medicine men. At the far end I removed my paintings from the tube and arranged them around the walls of the cavern so that the slanting sunlight shone in on them, illuminating my tableaux of the Great Falls, the Land Where the River of Yellow Stones Rises, the Bitterroots, the Columbia, and all the rest. Then, with the last of my strength, I set up my easel and rapidly began to paint what might very well be my final picture.

I stood in deep shadow and regarded what I had created — a portrait of myself at the easel, placed so that the low rays of the sun shone fully on it. Again I smelled smoke. My adversary appeared suddenly in the mouth of the cave, this time in his own form. He took two running steps and hurled the lance straight through the painting and the easel. Instantly I stepped forward and turned the torn picture around to show, on the reverse, the painted figure of Smoke himself. When the magician saw whom he had destroyed, he screamed. Before my eyes he transformed into a catamount, crouching to leap at me.

"Smoke!" I shouted. "Look around yourself. You know what powerful medicine my paintings hold. I will give them all to you in exchange for the safety of the American explorers. You and the Blackfoot Nation will have dominion over all the vast country they portray."

The cat's long tail twitched. Then he sprang. My head struck the wall of the cave and all was black.

I could not have been unconscious for more than a few moments, but when I opened my eyes, struggled to my feet, and stepped out of the cave, the only creature in sight was a war eagle with a gleaming white head, flying toward the sinking sun with the tube containing my paintings glinting in its talons. The bird gave a piercing cry, and as it screamed I caught on the evening air the scent of sage. The girl standing beside me pointed to the west, toward a land of rolling green hills, blue lakes, and quick rivers gleaming in the afterglow.

"Once upon a time an American painter named Ticonderoga fell in love with a Blackfoot girl of innumerable ways and stays named Yellow Sage Flower Who Tells Wise Stories," she said, and as she continued her story we headed down the mountainside together toward the Sweetgrass.

July 3, 2003

Dr. Stephan T. Black Elk, Curator
Museum of the American Plains Indians
Browning
Blackfoot Nation, Montana Territory

Dear Dr. Black Elk,

Thank you very much for your prompt confirmation of the safe arrival of the crates and your most welcome news that their contents were undamaged. I am also delighted, though of course in no way surprised, that your preliminary tests have confirmed the authenticity of the paper and ink of the manuscript. As you pointed out in your letter, the accuracy of my ancestor's narrative, or of parts of it, will no doubt remain a matter of debate, particularly among our good friends the Lewis and Clark scholars, for decades to come. But I am happier than I can say that you have already found "several good western university presses" interested in publishing it. Wouldn't it be ironic if the publisher turned out to be my dear, skeptical late husband's former place of employment, the University of Montana?

I am also happy to accept your most gracious invitation to deliver the keynote address at your upcoming Lewis and Clark bicentennial celebration, and to formally present the manuscript to the museum and unveil the contents of the crates in person. My husband loved to tease me about rattling on forever once I got started on Ti and True — until, as I have suggested to you, we had to table the subject to preserve harmonious relations. But I promise not to take more than ten minutes, or fifteen at most, to say what I have to say about my interesting ancestors.

In the meantime, you asked if I could provide a bit more of the history of True and Ti Kinneson for your press release. Gladly.

Over the several decades following the L and C expedition, Ticonderoga Kinneson established himself as the first American painter of Louisiana. Many of his contemporaries felt that he wanted only a small measure of additional technique to do for the West what Audubon and Wilson, say, did for the East. His large story tableaux recording the bison hunters, the Red River buffalo-cart brigades, and the annual summer rendezvous of mountain men the likes of Bridger and Carson are quite incomparable, as are his dozens of portraits of the Blackfeet, Crow, Assiniboine, etc. He painted the gold rush at Sutter's Mill in '48, the silver stampede in Nevada, the great covered wagon trains to Pikes Peak. He was there to see it all happen, and he recorded it faithfully. If Ti's purpose, as he hinted in his narrative, was to tell the story of Louisiana, and his life and times there, he did it well, taking a page from Franklin and other contemporary Indian artists.

Ti's beloved wife, my great-great-grandmother, Yellow Sage Flower Who Tells Wise Stories, died in the smallpox epidemic of 1838, leaving Ti, their daughter, Helen of Troy Kinneson, her husband, Crouching Panther (Smoke's son), and their daughter, Sacagawea Kinneson. Ti himself lived to the advanced age of ninety-one, and continued painting all his life.

As for True, he successfully made the balloon trip in the Dutchman Two *from Chief Mountain to St. Louis, swept the ravishing Miss Flame Danielle Boone off her feet with tales of his great adventure, and married her two days later. True's famous father-in-law, Daniel Boone, was reportedly so glad to see his spinster daughter settled that he presented his old adversary with a bearskin and a five-dollar gold piece and proudly gave away the bride. The happy couple then returned to Vermont to meet Ti's father and Helen of Troy, and soon afterward proceeded across the Atlantic, taking the stages of London and the Continent by storm with the private's great new epic,* The One True Account of the Lewis and Clark Expedition, *and its cast of more than two hundred American Indians.*

Now to the contents of the crates. I would suggest that the museum arrange them chronologically, beginning with Ti's pictures of the Natchez Trace and St. Louis, moving on to the firelight council of the Teton Sioux and the Okeepa ceremony of the Mandans, Buffalo Jump on the Little Missouri, and then the great tableaux, highlighted by Crossing the Bitterroots *and* Down the Columbia. *But exactly how you will present Ti's paintings in your new wing is, of course, up to you.*

You kindly asked if I had a favorite painting that I might like to keep. At eighty-three, I don't wish to keep any of them — or anything else, really, except perhaps my wits about me until Napi sees fit to call me to the Sweetgrass. But yes, I do have a favorite. Forgive a bit of vanity on the part of an old lady, Dr. Black Elk. It's Yellow Sage Bathing at the Three Forks, *and for the purely shameless reason that I rather fancy that my magical great-great-grandmother resembles me at that age. Then, too, I am terribly partial to Ti's portrait of True flying away in his great pink and yellow balloon, waving triumphantly, mail and head plate gleaming in the sunset.*

Finally, in response to your question, I would like to suggest an inscription for the plaque at the entrance to the new gallery. Why not let Ti have the last words? As in fact he did. When True died, in 1846, Flame and their children asked Ticonderoga to write his uncle's epitaph. It is engraved on his stone, next to Flame's, in a windy hilltop cemetery up in the far northern mountains of his beloved Vermont. I cite it overleaf.

> *Sincerely yours,*
> *Cora Soaring Eagle Kinneson*

PRIVATE TRUE TEAGUE KINNESON

1748–1846

The first American to visit the Pacific Ocean by
land; a playwright of note; the first and best lexicographer
of the languages of the Indians of Louisiana; an ingenious
inventor; a classicist and schoolmaster nonpareil;
a fervent Aristotelian; a loving brother, husband, father,
grandfather, and uncle, whose imagination was unfettered
by either convention or fact; whose hopefulness
and good nature yielded to no force, human or natural;
and whose ways and stays ranked second to none
in the history of the world.